HARLEY MERLIN AND THE MYSTERY TWINS

Harley Merlin 2

BELLA FORREST

ONE

Harley

A massive ball of fire came at me.

I dropped flat on the ground and felt the scorching heat of the blaze as it shot past, warming my back before it dissipated somewhere behind me. I jumped back to my feet and put my hands out. My palms felt hot as I summoned the flames within me, eager to pay it back in kind.

Panting and covered in a sheen of sweat, I managed to produce a flurry of small fireballs, which I shot toward Wade. *Poof! Poof! Poof!*

He ran across the training hall. My blazing balls missed him by inches every time. I cursed under my breath. Wade chuckled as he slowed down, then stopped.

"You'll have to get more precise with your shots, Merlin!" he said, breathing heavily.

He came back to the center of the hall, his tall figure reflected in the black marble floor and in the four walls surrounding us. I caught snippets of myself as well, and of Preceptor Nomura standing on the edge of the training space, which was marked with a thin line of white paint that glowed whenever one of us crossed it.

"Hey, I'm better than I was a month ago!" I retorted.

"Watch yourself, Crowley! You lose points if you leave the training space," Nomura interjected.

Wade gave him a quick glance, then shifted his focus back to me. Sometimes it was difficult to concentrate with Wade Crowley looking at me. His deep green eyes seemed to pierce through my very soul, and in combination with the large curls of his black hair and the way his dark blue pants and vest hugged his athletic figure... well, I had to put in additional effort to focus on his magical abilities so I didn't get plastered all over the floor.

"Come on, Merlin. Hit me. I just lost ten points dodging instead of blocking your fireballs," Wade said. "Attack me again so I can get them back."

I laughed mockingly, then put my hands out again. He took great pleasure in riling me up—I could feel it in my chest. There were definite perks to living with Empathy. When we trained, Wade focused more on the action and less on his emotions, which allowed me to read him accurately. Outside the training halls, he was guarded, aware of my ability to feel him. He'd been practicing emotional control over the past couple of weeks. I could feel that, too. He didn't like me knowing how he felt.

"I don't know about that, Crowley. I've got you running around like a monkey already. It's only a matter of time before I get you all hot and crispy!" I replied.

I produced over two dozen small fireballs this time and worked on perfecting my aim as I released them at Wade. Some he dodged with smooth and fluid moves. Others he swatted away with his hands. Without his ten Esprit rings lighting up orange to prevent his skin from burning upon contact with my fire, he had to use his raw Fire Elemental ability to protect himself.

"Well, for someone who, up until a month ago, didn't even know what a magical was," Wade said, "you can hold your ground. I'll give you that."

"I could do a lot more if *someone* would just let me use my Esprit!" I shot back, gritting my teeth.

This was a non-Esprit training session. Only our raw powers were allowed, and I hated it because even without his rings, Wade was a fearsome adversary.

He ran toward me, grinning like the devil.

Like the rookie that I still was, I froze.

He moved so fast that I didn't even have a second to react. He stopped about ten feet away from me and released another fireball at full strength. I gasped and crossed my forearms in front of my face. I summoned my own fire to protect me, but I moved one split second too slow.

Wade's fireball smacked right into me. The force of its impact threw me backward. I landed on my back with a painful thud, then slid past the training circle.

Thanks, physics!

Once I stopped, I stared at the black marble ceiling for a few moments. I heard Nomura click his teeth.

"Too slow," he said.

"Gee. You think?" I replied dryly.

Wade showed up in my field of vision, smirking as he looked down at me. He offered me a hand. I slapped it away, then shakily got myself back up and wiped the soot from my face. This wasn't the first time I was getting my ass handed to me, anyway.

"If it's any consolation, you're slightly better than last week," Wade said, trying to encourage me yet again. It didn't happen often, and I knew he meant it, so I gave him a soft nod in return before I frowned at Nomura.

"I'd be a lot better with my Esprit, you know," I said.

Nomura shrugged. "And I told you that the Esprit is useless if it's taken from you. Harley, you must be able to defend yourself and deliver strong attacks without it. The power is inside you already, and we're training you to master it without the aid of a trinket."

"There's not that much power in me to begin with," I murmured, then pointed two thumbs at myself. "Mediocre, remember?"

A month had passed since the gargoyle debacle, and the coven had yet to arrange a second Reading for me. It wasn't exactly a regular custom, and it had taken them a while to find a new physician willing to relocate to San Diego. Still, I was wiser and better trained than the first time I'd set foot inside the San Diego Coven. I knew a little bit more about myself, too, even though it broke my heart. Harley Merlin was my real name. It sounded better than Harley Smith, I had to admit, but it carried a dark and painful history.

Hiram and Hester Merlin were once two of America's most promising and powerful magicals. Until my father killed my mother. My aunt, Katherine Shipton, had his child before he married my mother, and it was a well-kept secret until I got here. *Katherine was and, unfortunately, still is a murderous psychopath.* The complexities of my family tree were still mind-boggling. She vanished years ago, but her son—my cousin *and* half-brother, Finch —managed to infiltrate the San Diego Coven.

A plan had been set in motion. The Bestiary was sabotaged. Gargoyles were let out. People died. I managed to catch Finch, who turned out to be a Shapeshifter—a rare ability among magicals, from what I was later told. It was a bloody mess.

The full scheme was still unraveling, though. Even with Finch in Purgatory, the magicals' central prison, Katherine was undeterred. Based on what she'd already accomplished through her son, along with her criminal record and the fact that she'd yet to get caught, we all knew she was going to do much worse, and it was only a matter of time before she'd strike again. Worst of all, she knew I was alive now, and that couldn't be good—not for me, anyway. Everyone had thought that I'd died with my mother when my father killed her, but I hadn't. I was born and in my father's care for about three years, before he surrendered, then got himself put on trial and executed.

I had a bone to pick with Katherine Shipton.

The gargoyles she'd helped sic on me had destroyed my car and my apartment, and they'd tried to eat me more than once. Her son, someone I'd come to actually tolerate despite his abrasive behavior, had also tried to kill me. Me, his own blood. The entire sequence of events made my stomach churn. Looking back, I'd had a more than turbulent first week in the San Diego Coven, but I survived it all.

Now, it was all about honing my magical abilities. I had a lot of catching up to do, especially when compared to other magicals my age. On top of that, I wanted to become stronger and better so I could be ready when Katherine Shipton emerged again. Of course, according to my first Reading, I'd been deemed a Mediocre—a magical with limited powers, despite my varied abilities. I was a Telekinetic, an Empath, *and* a full Elemental, with command over fire, earth, air, and water. And yet, I was held back and most likely unable to fully develop. Both Alton and Wade had been present at my Reading, and they knew Adley couldn't have fumbled or falsified it, despite her relationship to Finch. Besides, they'd already interrogated her with a charmed lie detector. We knew for a fact that her interpretation of my Reading had been sincere and accurate.

"Just because you were labeled a Mediocre doesn't mean you're incapable of getting better at your craft," Nomura said firmly. "You can still be effective and even deadly. Remember, I was branded a Mediocre for twenty years, until I found my Esprit, and I was already a preceptor when that happened. I took my so-called Mediocrity and I made something better of it. Technically speaking, you could do a Reading of me right now, and I'd still be a Mediocre, though my abilities and techniques are infinitely superior. Your blood shouldn't dictate what you can do as long as there's willpower."

Hiro Nomura had quite the story to tell as a warlock. He'd fought plenty of battles, the details of which I knew nothing about, but the slim scars on the side of his face said enough. I never saw him wearing anything other than his black silken tunic with broad sleeves and the two swords strapped to his back—together, they were his Esprit. The longer sword was the *katana*. The short one was the *wakizashi*. Together, they were the traditional duo of weapons sported by Japanese samurai, but for Nomura they served as his Esprit, objects capable of channeling his Chaos energy into more powerful spells and magical attacks. Had he not told me he was a Mediocre, I would never have guessed.

Nomura was one of the six preceptors of the San Diego Coven, in charge of educating the young magicals in the arts of Physical Magic. Dylan Blight and I were his eldest students—both of us nineteen and lost through the foster system from a young age, recently found and reintroduced to the magical society. Granted, Dylan's induction had been much smoother than mine and didn't involve multiple attempts on his life by flesh-eating monsters and psychopathic half-brothers he had no idea existed in the first place. No, that hot mess was mine and mine alone.

"I just feel stronger with my Esprit," I replied. "More confident, more focused. Now that I've found it, I have a hard time being without it. My Telekinesis and Fire, in particular, are insanely better when I'm wearing it!"

"It doesn't matter. It's still just a gadget for the time being. The better you are at controlling your natural abilities without your Esprit, the more powerful and precise you'll be *with* it," Nomura said, then sighed with frustration. "I'm not here to teach you how to cheat better, Merlin. If you want Esprit training, you can wait until I deem you ready, or you can ask O'Halloran for private lessons. At your own risk. Frankly, no amount of Esprit training will make your natural abilities better."

I seemed to have a knack for irritating Nomura. According to Wade, that required tremendous skill—and he didn't mean it as a compliment. I lowered my head slowly, once again disappointed that I couldn't train with my Esprit under his guidance.

Nomura noticed my childish disappointment, then groaned and rolled his eyes. "Crowley, put your Esprit on," he snapped.

Wade nodded, then took his ten sterling silver bands from his vest pocket and slipped them on his long fingers. He breathed deeply and smiled. I knew that feeling all too well now, of putting an Esprit on and experiencing the surge of power through every fiber of my body. It happened every time with my ring-bracelet.

"Now what?" Wade asked.

"Well, Merlin here doesn't think one can do much without an Esprit these days, so I'd like to prove her wrong. Fight me," Nomura replied, before removing his swords from his back and handing them over to me.

Wade stared at him, blinking rapidly as he tried to process the unexpected order. Nomura raised an eyebrow, then moved to the center of the training area. Each room of the San Diego Coven continued to amaze me. They were all different in design, size, and function, seamlessly wrapped within a giant interdimensional pocket right where Fleet Science Center stood. Like all the other covens, ours was wirelessly powered by the Bestiary, which had become our responsibility for the next hundred years, as demanded by tradition. The monsters inside the Bestiary were raw Chaos energy expelled by magicals during Purges. It was all a natural flow of Chaos, repurposed to fit our needs as witches and warlocks in a world that wasn't ready to learn of our existence.

Nomura's training hall was my favorite, mainly because of its design simplicity, and it was made entirely from Chaos energy converted into matter. It was a black marble box, with each surface polished and glazed to perfection. In the middle was the training circle. There was nothing else, and yet so much happened in this room on a daily basis.

"Excuse me, sir?" Wade asked, gawking at Nomura.

"I said fight me. With your Esprit," Nomura replied.

"But you don't have yours—"

"That's very observant of you." Nomura cut him off, sarcasm dripping from his voice. "Quit wasting my time. Come at me."

It took Wade another couple of seconds to assume an attack stance. Judging by the look on his face, he wasn't used to sparring with Nomura. There was fear in his heart, too. He was genuinely afraid of Nomura's abilities, and I worked hard to stifle a chuckle when I realized that.

"I'm going to show you how a magical can defeat his opponent, even without an Esprit," Nomura said, looking at me. He then motioned to Wade. "Come on, Crowley, I don't have all day!"

"I'm sorry, sir," Wade mumbled. His rings lit up bright orange. Flames gathered around his fists.

Nomura assumed a defense position, his arms slightly bent in a kung-fu-style pose. As soon as Wade released the first round of medium-sized fireballs, Nomura used his Telekinesis to swat them away like pesky flies.

"Crowley! Don't be such a wimp! Give me something serious to work with!" Nomura barked.

I held on to his swords, biting my lower lip to stop myself from laughing. There were very few people in this coven who chewed Wade's ass, and Nomura was one of the top three. Wade came from a legendary bloodline. His mother was the director of the Houston Coven, and his father was on the Texas Mage Council. How he'd ended up with a mild Irish accent I had no idea, but it had a way of making my skin tingle whenever he opened his damn mouth. His parents had to be first-generation Irish immigrants, I figured.

Wade exhaled, then launched a second attack. This time, as Nomura requested, he didn't hold back. His fireballs were perfectly round and highly concentrated, burning hot red as he hurled them at Nomura's head. The preceptor grinned and used his Telekinesis to slice each fireball in half.

My jaw dropped as Nomura advanced toward Wade, who continued his flaming attacks. Wade's speed and precision were no match for Nomura's agility, though, and the preceptor disabled each fireball with his Telekinetic whips. Before Wade could throw out another round, Nomura's invisible whip grabbed him by the throat.

With one flick of his wrist, Nomura threw Wade out of the circle.

"Oh, snap," I breathed, watching Wade hit the ground and roll like a potato across the marble floor. "Are you okay, Crowley?"

Wade groaned, then scowled at me. He managed to get back up and went after Nomura again. He was angry this time—and if there was one thing I'd learned the hard way during Physical Magic training, it was that anger served no one other than your opponent.

Nomura successfully deflected Wade's attacks, using only his Telekinesis. Of his three main abilities, it was the one he trusted most during combat. Sometimes he used his Earth Elemental skills to manipulate the shape and size of his Esprit swords, turning them into chillingly effective weapons. Nomura was also an Air Elemental, but he rarely used that power. Not that he wasn't good with it. On the contrary. It was extremely intense and not suited for training purposes, he'd once said.

Wade managed to slip through Nomura's defenses and delivered a fiery blow, using a flaming whip. He'd already figured out that fireballs weren't going to touch him. Nomura hissed when the whip cut through his silken tunic. Wade froze, terrified that he'd actually managed to injure Nomura, who grinned and turned his fear into an opening.

The preceptor dashed across the training circle and delivered a dizzying array of kicks and punches. It threw Wade for a loop. Nomura then used his Telekinesis to grab him by the throat again, this time his hand making the gripping gesture just inches away from Wade's skin.

"Now, you're mine," Nomura announced. "I can finish you off before you even think of a way out."

"Yield. I yield," Wade croaked.

Nomura chuckled as he released Wade and looked at me. "See, Merlin? Focus on how far you can push your raw power first, then worry about fine-tuning or amplifying it with your Esprit."

I nodded slowly, in awe of what I'd just witnessed. Wade's ego was bruised, but he, too, looked impressed by Nomura's fighting skills.

"You really think I can be as good as you?" I asked.

Nomura gave me a faint half-smile. "You're really hung up on that Mediocre label, aren't you, Merlin?"

"The Reading was clear, sir," Wade replied, giving me a sympathetic look. "Adley de la Barthe may have had her shortcomings, but she was a stellar physician. And our patented lie detector doesn't... lie."

Ah, yes. Adley. The unsuspecting accomplice. Adley had come to the San Diego Coven a couple of years back as the physician. She'd fallen for Finch, who'd played her into keeping his Shapeshifting ability a secret. She paid dearly for her mistake, and she was now serving time in one of the cells in our basement, awaiting a trial date. But Wade was right—despite her weakness for a friggin' psycho magical, Adley had built quite a reputation as a physician. And her Reading had been clear about me: I had all these abilities and, even though I was a full Elemental, which was ridiculously rare, I was also a Mediocre.

"Didn't Alton agree that Merlin should do a second Reading?" Nomura said, frowning. "I thought Adley had suggested the same, too."

"Yes, sir," I replied. "I guess the new physician will do that, though I haven't had the chance to talk to him much, lately."

"Of course you wouldn't." Nomura sighed. "Krieger took over all of Adley's projects. He's got his hands full for a while. Nevertheless, you should get tested again, if only for your peace of mind. I doubt you'll get different results, but Chaos can surprise us sometimes. Who knows?"

That statement somehow filled me with hope, despite Nomura's generally pragmatic approach. His teaching techniques had that "tough love" vibe, but most of his students honed their skills over the years. Hell, I'd already come a long way.

One month in this place, and I had much better control over my Telekinesis and Fire than before. Despite my complaints about not being able to use my Esprit during Nomura's training sessions, I had to admit I was making progress.

Deep down, the fear of one day facing Katherine Shipton pushed me to try harder, to do more, and to learn as much as I could about myself and my family in the meantime. When Finch was carted off to Purgatory, he had sneered at me and said that this was far from over.

The troubling part was that I believed him. So, if there was so much as a 10 percent chance that I wasn't a Mediocre after all, I wanted that second Reading. Katherine Shipton was most likely plotting something big and terrible, and I felt as though it was my responsibility to take her down. To prove that the Merlin name still stood for the goodness and greatness of this magical world, and not the murder and mayhem that my father had left behind.

TWO

Harley

I'd grown accustomed to life in the coven.

I liked it. A lot. I'd even learned to control my Empathy around crowds of people! And we were getting awfully close to a deadline, on my part. The probation month was coming to an end soon, and the San Diego Coven was quietly waiting for me to make a decision. *Should I stay, or should I go?*

I'd yet to decide, but I did appreciate how Alton didn't pressure me. In the meantime, I continued to enjoy my midcentury-style room in the coven, my pretend part-time job at the Science Center's Archives and Library, and, most importantly, the free meals.

Lunch was served in the banquet hall, with its pristine white marble walls and long dining tables. Some of the seats were empty —the coven had lost people during Finch's gargoyle attack. Over a dozen had died, and at least twenty were still in the infirmary, recovering from their wounds. There wasn't enough magic in this world to fix certain injuries. It was up to the magical's body to fight and heal itself, as best as it could.

I skipped past the knot in my stomach caused by the sight of empty seats and stopped by the buffet first. I loaded my plate with chunks of bread and a heap of cheesy grilled potatoes, which I then slathered in one of the chefs' signature gravies. My body demanded food, drained of the energy I'd burned during my training with Nomura and Wade, and my mind required nourishment after the early morning courses in Alchemy and Occult Chemistry. Needless to say, I was making progress on all magical fronts, but I was useless if left "hangry."

Looking around, I spotted my Rag Team at one of the long tables. A couple of seats away from them were Finch's old teammates, including Garrett Kyteler, who still carried that broken-hearted-boy look on his handsome face. I still had a bit of a soft spot for him, but I blamed it on my hormones—just my body responding to an attractive individual. Nothing more, nothing less.

No longer overwhelmed by crowds, thanks to my Empathic self-control, I kept my focus on my friends as I walked over to them. They'd saved me a seat.

Santana Catemaco, Tatyana Vasilisa, Raffe Levi, Astrid Hepler, Dylan Blight, and Wade Crowley. They weren't just my teammates anymore. We'd grown closer as a group. We'd learned to work together and to trust one another. Most importantly, they supported me in my quest to improve myself. I knew I would forever be in their debt for everything they'd taught me so far, knowingly or otherwise.

"There she is!" Santana exclaimed as I glided between the long tables to reach them. "Heard you had quite a fiery experience in Physical Magic earlier!" she added, chuckling.

They were all smiling, happy to see me again. It warmed me inside to feel that. The only one who was still guarded and weirdly nervous around me was Wade, but I decided not to rub his face in it after the ass-whooping he'd just gotten from Nomura.

I sat down at the table and proceeded to scarf down my lunch. As usual, I left little room for talking, washing my food down with a glass of sparkling water, which Raffe was courteous enough to pour for me.

"It was intense, yeah," I replied, then tackled another piece of potato. "This gravy, though…"

Astrid giggled. "I know, right? I've been trying to get my hands on the recipe, but the chefs hold on to it like it's a state secret."

"So, how are you coming along with everything?" Santana asked. "I haven't seen much of you this week."

I gave her a brief shrug. "Really busy. But I think I'm doing okay. I mean, it's definitely better than when I first got here."

"Still a long way to go, though," Wade interjected.

I narrowed my eyes at him. "Hello, Captain Obvious."

That was part of our routine. Banter and sarcasm were essential parts of my dialogue with Wade. I didn't quite understand what purpose it served him, but for me, it was a good way to keep my mind sharp. I enjoyed our back-and-forths. Well, I enjoyed delivering solid burns to Mr. High-and-Mighty-Crowley, anyway.

"It's true. You're nowhere near our proficiency levels," Wade replied, pushing a broccoli stalk around his plate with a fork.

"Oh, I know. Wait till I get there, though," I said. "I did manage to make you sweat this morning. I'll take that minor victory today."

The others instantly turned their heads to look at Wade.

"Did she kick your ass?" Dylan asked, grinning like the Cheshire cat.

"You wish," Wade muttered, pretending to focus on his almost-empty plate. "Nomura had us training without our Esprits again. Needless to say, Miss Merlin here still can't wrap her head around that."

"I'd just love to get more training with my Esprit, not only without it," I grumbled.

"You heard Nomura. First, you need to hone your raw abilities," Wade replied.

"Oh, Miss Whitehall is here," Tatyana said, watching the director's table. We all followed her gaze and found Alton having lunch with the preceptors, accompanied by Imogene Whitehall and Leonidas Levi, Raffe's estranged father. Raffe and Leonidas didn't get along and only really saw each other during these official visits.

Raffe didn't look happy. "Ugh. He didn't even say he was coming."

Imogene glanced around the banquet hall and smiled when she saw me. I gave her a polite nod in return, and she winked back. It felt as though we'd already had a full conversation. Imogene was one of the few people whose emotions I couldn't sense, but her gentle expression and bright blue eyes always put me in a good mood.

Out of all the stuck-up figures in the California Mage Council, the authority directly overseeing coven activities in the state, Imogene was the only one I was wholeheartedly fond of. Even before I found my Esprit, she'd advised and encouraged me. Once the whole issue with Finch and the Bestiary was resolved, she took the lead on the Council and defended us, ultimately awarding our coven with over a thousand points toward the end-of-year bonus. In my book, that made her super cool and a breath of fresh air, compared to the elitist snobs she had to work with. I'd bumped into her before, mostly in Waterfront Park during the occasional day out, and we caught up over tea now and again. She was, by far, one of the kindest magicals I'd ever come across—in complete contrast to the pompously stiff Leonidas Levi.

"I wonder what they're doing here," I said, chewing on my last piece of bread.

"It's probably about the gargoyle incident," Raffe replied. "They're most likely doing follow-up, making sure everything is okay."

"The cleanup operation was a success, though. It took us two weeks to wipe everybody who was in the area at the time, but we did it," Wade said. "Mage presence isn't really necessary at this point. We have it under control."

Astrid's AI, "Smartie," had done a stellar job of scrapping and manipulating CCTV and social media footage, as well. Tobe was back and had Preceptor Bellmore assisting him in further securing the Bestiary boxes. Everything seemed to be back on track, so I was inclined to agree with Wade.

Raffe sighed. "You don't know my father well enough, then. Once he sets his sights on a coven, he'll watch over it like a hawk and swoop in at the first mistake. Plus, he's not very fond of Alton."

"Surely, Imogene balances him out, right?" I asked. "Like she did at the hearing."

"Oh, you mean when my own father was ready to sink my coven, and Imogene intervened and set the record straight after you came in and testified? Yeah. You could say that," Raffe replied. "It doesn't matter if Imogene is here, though. They're both part of the California Mage Council, and it's not just the two of them. All seven of them are watching us now. After what happened with Finch, they're worried."

"Well, the concern does stem from the fact that they now know it was Katherine Shipton's doing. That she's still very much alive and kicking," Santana said. "They're quaking in their boots, man."

"She was really bad, huh?" I sighed, losing my appetite. Fortunately, I'd already gone through most of my plate, leaving a handful of crusts on the edge.

"Haven't you been reading up on the Shiptons?" Tatyana asked, raising an eyebrow.

"Alton promised he'd dig up all the information he has on them and the Merlins, if I focus on training and learning," I said. "He's yet to deliver, but, frankly, I can't say I'm looking forward to reading up on my family history. I've been studying about my abilities, mostly, and the Bestiary. It feels less... toxic."

"Not ready to deal with your past, huh?" Tatyana replied.

I exhaled. "Willing, sure. But no, not ready."

"Whatever you need, we're here. You know that, right?" Santana said, smiling softly. "My Orishas like you, by the way."

I chuckled. "Oh, yeah, after that ride they took me on with the gargoyles, I'm sure!" I replied, remembering the button in my throat, which the Orishas—powerful Santeria entities commanded by Santana—used to amplify my voice and draw the gargoyles back into Balboa Park and away from the city streets. The experience was impossible to forget, as it had left me with a small scar on my throat, where the button had burned through at the end.

"Well, yeah. They think you're a tough cookie. They like tough cookies," Santana said.

"That explains why they obey *you*," Raffe interjected. It surprised Santana, and it must have taken some effort on Raffe's part. My heart was pounding like a maniac—my Empath senses were picking up Raffe's feelings. He was nervous, yet brave enough to give Santana a compliment. He liked her. A lot. But there was a part of him I'd yet to wrap my head around. Raffe struck me as a dual character. Warm and friendly, shy and helpful on the outside, but with a dark and poisonous storm brewing on the inside. He didn't like talking about himself, which made it difficult for me to ask about the mixed emotions I sensed. I had a feeling I hadn't earned his full trust on that. And no one on our team spoke on his behalf.

It was kind of an unspoken rule: *Only Raffe talks about Raffe.*

"Thank you, Raffe," Santana replied, her lips stretching into a dazzling smile. It made my heart flutter—once again, that was all Raffe. I was swooning over her because of him.

"When is your second Reading?" Astrid cut in, looking at me.

Out of everyone in our circle, Astrid and Santana had been the most vocal about me doing a second Reading. Neither believed that I was really a Mediocre, and, as much as I tried to stop myself from experiencing potential disappointment in the future, I didn't believe it, either.

"I have no idea. I haven't talked to Krieger about it yet," I replied.

"Ah. Wolfgang Krieger!" Astrid replied, faking a German accent and making us all chuckle.

I glanced to my right and noticed Garrett watching me. Rowena Sparks, Poe Dexter, Lincoln Mont-Noir, and Niklas Jones were with him, talking and laughing about something. But Garrett wasn't listening. He was focused on me. I felt another pang, remembering that I'd never see Ruby Presley again. She'd died in the gargoyle attack, and even though we hadn't really gotten along, her passing was still a terrible tragedy.

"I heard some pretty creepy stuff about Krieger," Dylan said.

Garrett smiled at me, but there was a tinge of sadness in his blue eyes, which I was convinced had something to do with Finch. Out of everyone in his crew, Garrett had been the most affected, since he and Finch were best friends. I couldn't feel him as an Empath, either, but his face said plenty. He was still hurting.

He'd repeatedly apologized for his verbal attacks on me, too. After all, he'd been the one to tell the entire coven what I'd just learned at the time—that I was the daughter of a mass murderer. He knew that the sins of my father had nothing to do with me, but, according to Finch, Garrett was pretty upset about how close Wade and I were. That, in and of itself, was ridiculous, since there was nothing going on between Wade and me. The heart was a fickle thing, in Garrett's case. He was still one of the hottest guys in the coven, but I just couldn't look at him the way he looked at me. I didn't feel that spark, the proverbial *je ne sais quoi*.

Our only date had gone sideways after Wade showed up with Clara Fairmont, then got into an argument with Garrett. That episode still puzzled me, weeks later. What had Wade been thinking, when my purpose had been to get intel out of Garrett regarding their Bestiary investigation?

"Define creepy," Tatyana replied. "The man has quite the reputation as a physician. In fact, I'm told he's one of the best in his field, able to mix medical science and magic in ways never seen before."

"You're quoting out of his profile in the *San Diego Coven Gazette*, aren't you?" Astrid said, heavily amused.

"That's what it says!" Tatyana chuckled.

Garrett then moved his sights to Wade. Again, I noticed a tinge of sadness. He and Wade had once been close friends, and neither wanted to talk about what happened between them. Still, I was curious.

"Most of the rumors you've heard about Krieger are unfounded," Wade interjected. "He is kind of creepy-looking, though."

"Rumors, as in how he snatches young magicals from their beds, does horrible experiments on them, then wipes their memories and puts them back in their covens?" Astrid replied.

"Or how he did a whole Dr. Frankenstein thing a few years back and made a new magical from different body parts, before having to put the creature down after it blew up his laboratory?" Santana chimed in.

"What about that time he slipped powerful toxins into the Miami Coven's lunch, and they ended up going berserk for an entire afternoon?" Raffe joined the Spooky Krieger train, laughing.

"Miss Merlin!" A male voice made my head snap and instantly silenced everyone at the table. I recognized the German accent right away.

"Dr. Krieger," I murmured.

Wolfgang Krieger had the most silent footsteps in the San Diego Coven. No one ever heard him coming. Case in point, the entire Rag Team were frozen in their seats, their eyes wide with horror as they hoped he hadn't heard anything they'd just said. Their anguish was my anguish. *Damn Empathy!*

Krieger was a tall man in his mid-forties, with broad shoulders and short, slick blond hair. His eyes were a pale and clinical blue, devoid of emotion. He wore a white lab coat over his gray suit at all times, along with a pair of small, thin-rimmed glasses. For all intents and purposes, Wolfgang Krieger, originally from the Berlin Coven, seemed designed to instill fear in the hearts of his beholders.

"Dr. Krieger, we didn't see you there," Astrid managed, her voice uneven.

"You're not supposed to, Miss Hepler," Krieger replied flatly.

His emotions were clear to me—sheer amusement, with an undertone of insult. He felt offended by the rumors, which he'd obviously heard, but he seemed to take great pleasure in tormenting my crew. I wasn't one to get on the physician's bad side before my second Reading, so I kept that little nugget to myself and watched my teammates quiver before him. Even Wade seemed wary, and that made me smile.

"Anyway, Miss Merlin," Krieger continued. "I believe it's time we arrange a second Reading for you. It's been on my to-do list for a while now, but Miss de la Barthe's other projects have been keeping me quite busy. I do apologize for taking so long to find you."

Astrid's German impression hadn't been far off. Krieger's accent was strong, cutting through his English like a giant clumsy knife.

"Dr. Krieger, it's all right. I completely understand," I replied politely. "I suppose Adley's work was a lot to take in?"

I had no idea what I was talking about, since I didn't know anything about the previous physician's projects, but I was hoping that Krieger would tell us. He nodded.

"Yes, the magical detector is quite an ambitious project," he said. "Miss de la Barthe was exquisite in her field. I must give credit where it's due."

My eyebrows rose. "Magical detector? Someone's still working on that with Adley gone?"

Krieger stilled, his forehead smooth and his gaze cold. "You know about it? It's supposed to be top secret."

"I suppose it's not top secret, since you just told us about it," I replied with a smirk, secretly surprised that he'd actually played into my little scheme. "But don't worry, I haven't told people. I only overheard it myself from Alton and Tobe."

Krieger shook his head. "I'm either getting old, or you're very good at getting people to reveal things they normally wouldn't," he replied, then smiled briefly. "But you're right. It's not a secret. It's just that not many people here talk about it, mainly because Adley didn't tell anyone about what she was doing, except Alton and Tobe. And yes, I've taken over the work she's done so far."

"So, what's a magical detector, exactly? I never got the details," I said.

"We're trying to develop a detection technique, based on the Reading. Something simple that would allow us to identify magicals out in the human world, without their blood," Krieger explained. "The project is still in its incipient stages, but the theories behind it are sound and rather promising."

"You want to have a detector handy to identify new magicals," Wade concluded. "Without a fuss and without the humans noticing."

"Indeed, Mr. Crowley. Our purpose is to find the magicals before their powers manifest so the covens can bring them in and take care of them," Krieger replied.

That sounded like a very good idea, but at the same time, I couldn't help but worry about how easily such a tool could be used to hunt magicals instead of helping them. If this device fell into the wrong hands, like those of Katherine or some other evil bastard looking to do harm, or even the humans if they knew about us… I didn't even want to think about it.

"Anyway, Miss Merlin. I will make time in my schedule over the next couple of days for your second Reading," Krieger added. "Please make sure you're available."

"Yes, sir," I replied.

A knot formed in my throat. It was finally happening. The second Reading. The confirmation of my Mediocrity or the debunking of it. I was definitely nervous about it. I had my work cut out for me in both scenarios. With the certainty of Mediocrity, I had to work twice as hard to get to a level where I could feel confident enough against someone like Katherine Shipton. If, however, I wasn't a Mediocre after all, I still had to work and push myself to take on someone as deadly as my aunt. Not knowing for sure was the worst part, though.

"And don't worry, I've upgraded the Reading syringes," Krieger said, grinning.

"Oh. I'd forgotten about that part," I murmured, getting the chills as I remembered the size of that monstrous metallic syringe that Adley had used to draw my blood. "Glad to hear about that, I suppose."

"I've had trouble getting some of our new magicals to sit down for a Reading," Krieger replied. "And I'm not one to tie the young-sters down. That's just... barbaric! I figured it was better to redesign the tool itself and make it more child-friendly."

Looking at him now, Krieger wasn't creepy at all. He was actu-ally quite sweet, and his emotions were all positive as he spoke to us. There was no deception... nothing to ring any alarm bells. The rumors were definitely ridiculous.

"I'm sure the young magicals of the San Diego Coven are grateful for that," I said, smiling.

The Rag Team was still frozen, and Krieger didn't let that slide, either. "Now you can all go back to repeating folk tales about how I boil babies in cauldrons," he quipped, then gave me a playful wink. "And I'll be in touch, Miss Merlin, to schedule your Reading."

I snorted a laugh as he walked away, overwhelmed by the face-burning embarrassment inundating me. Santana, Astrid, Raffe, Tatyana, and Dylan were all red-cheeked. Wade, on the other hand, was stifling a smirk. Mr. I'm-Right-All-The-Time.

"So, he heard everything," Astrid whispered.

"He totally did," I replied, feeling my ears get close to melting temperature.

They needed a minute or two to recover from the shame, while I struggled to regain my composure, dealing with their sheepish emotions. Still, I was pleased we were still given assignments together as the now-notorious Rag Team, whenever delicate coven work was required. We'd done a good job during the gargoyle inci-dents, so why split us up?

Alton rose from his table, leaving Imogene with Leonidas and the preceptors, and made his way toward our table. He exchanged a nod with Krieger as the physician passed by him and headed for the exit.

"Morning, team!" Alton greeted us. "Meeting in my office in twenty minutes?"

"Morning, Alton," Wade replied, his brow furrowed. "Did something happen?"

Alton put on a flat smile. "We'll talk in twenty minutes," he said, before returning to his table.

That instantly put us all on edge, especially me. My nerves were already bending and stretching to new limits. I wondered if this was about Katherine Shipton.

Maybe it was time to settle that score. I certainly looked forward to it.

THREE

Harley

Alton's office was always a pleasure to be in. I would've loved to have such a sweet slice of the coven all to myself— provided I was ready to commit to being there for the rest of my life. I was already tempted to do it, but part of me still wasn't ready to let go of my independence.

Sure, the gargoyles had trashed my place, but I could just rent another apartment and remain a Neutral. Alton had already said he'd support my decision, if that were the case. But I wasn't fully into that, either. There were perks and drawbacks, no matter what I chose to do. I just had to weigh everything carefully first.

Santana, Wade, Raffe, Astrid, Tatyana, Dylan, and I waited patiently in front of Alton's desk as he dug through his drawers for a file. Santana and Tatyana took the armchair seats, while the rest of us stood quietly with our arms crossed.

A few minutes passed, and Alton cursed under his breath, seemingly unable to find what he was looking for, until he gasped. He shot back up and waved the manila folder around as if it were his most prized possession, beaming at us.

"Found it!" he exclaimed, then took a seat behind his massive walnut desk. "Now, before I start, how is everyone doing?"

We looked at each other, before Wade took the lead on that answer. "Fine, for the most part. Merlin here is studying and training. She's also doing a decent job in the Archives. The rest of us are monitoring reports from the human world, in case anything slipped through the cracks since the gargoyle incident. So far, it's been quiet."

Alton analyzed each of our expressions with a half-smile, then nodded slowly. "That's good. It means that Astrid's efforts came through."

Astrid blushed, her lips twirling into a sweet little smile, flanked by the cutest pair of dimples. I'd already learned not to let this adorable side of her fool me—Astrid was as fierce as they came, especially for a human. "My AI is automated now," she said. "Smartie detects anything related to the incident and automatically sends alerts to my computer. From there, I analyze every line and assign magicals to deal with any issue that might require our intervention."

"It's been a month, now." Santana sighed. "It shouldn't be a problem anymore."

Alton shook his head. "It's not. But it's better to monitor and double-check than find ourselves with our pants down, don't you think?"

He had a way with words. It was even funnier because of his Southern drawl. Despite his crisp suits and perfectly groomed appearance, Alton still had the spunk and humor of a bayou man, and it was one of my favorite things about him. He looked at me, his expression firm but his heart brimming with affection. Alton Waterhouse was extremely fond of me, for some reason. I figured this was as close as I would ever get to fatherly love in the coven, and I welcomed it.

"First, I know I promised you some information on your parents, Harley," he said, "but it took me a while to get to it. Part of me wasn't sure I should give you everything we have, since you might not like the whole truth. But I think you're tough enough to read through it all and make up your own mind. I trust your judgment."

"No problem about the delay, Alton. As you might've noticed, I haven't exactly insisted," I muttered.

"I understand why. I suppose you don't feel like you're ready for the whole truth, huh?"

I shrugged. "You could say that, yes."

"Well, it's time to get ready," he replied, then pushed the manila folder across the desk. "This is for you. All the information that I was able to gather regarding your parents and Katherine Shipton. The latter will be of particular interest to your entire team."

My brows furrowed and my stomach tied itself up in knots as I took the file and flipped through its pages. My heart swelled, then broke repeatedly, as I saw my mom and dad in different photos. In one of them, they were with Katherine Shipton—all three smiling like everything was right in the world. It struck me as odd, without reading the text documents enclosed in the folder.

The physical resemblance between Katherine and my mother, Hester, was striking. The same wild green eyes, the fiery red hair, the slim figures and sharp cheekbones...

"They were twins, Hester and Katherine Shipton," Alton said, noticing the photograph that had captured my attention.

My blood ran cold. "Whoa. Twins? I mean, I knew they were sisters, but *twins*?"

"Not identical," Alton replied. "But yes. Twins. You'll find more info in there."

"Do we have any news about Katherine?" Wade asked, and the question prompted me to reluctantly close the file. As much as I wanted to tear through it now, we still had a briefing, based on the second folder still present on Alton's desk. I would study it later.

"Not exactly, but she's part of the reason I wanted to speak with you this morning," Alton replied. "There have been rumors, though we haven't been able to verify any of them. Katherine Shipton is still in the wind, her location unknown. The one thing we are aware of is that she's planning something big, and that it involves the magicals here in San Diego. That's all we were able to understand from Finch's vague statements, anyway," he added, running a hand through his brown, wavy hair. "We're worried she might be targeting those we haven't pledged into the coven yet."

Shivers ran down my spine. "What makes you say that?" I asked.

"In here, I have a list of potential new magicals," Alton replied, then opened the second folder. He turned it around and pushed it forward so we could all see the names. "We were supposed to reach out to them, make sure they're magicals, and bring them into the coven. Two of them went missing early this week, and we can't find them anywhere. They're not showing up in the human databases either. It's like they simply vanished. Plus, there are rumors among the city's Neutrals and the rogues passing through. There's something brewing. Something dark."

"That's not good," I said, hearing my voice tremble.

Gloom settled over the room, weighing heavily on my shoulders. We were all worried—none as badly as Alton, though. He felt responsible. He'd been with the coven for over three years, since Wade managed to get Halifax fired for his incompetence. Alton had been working to improve SDC since, and this clearly set him back. Additionally, he cared about magicals in general, putting his heart and soul into his work to make sure they were all protected. Personally, I disagreed with the plethora of coven regulations that suffocated this effort.

That was just one of the reasons I was inclined to join the San Diego Coven—so I could help change some of their antiquated rules.

"It isn't good. Which is why I've decided to call the Rag Team back into action," Alton said, looking at each of us with a twinkle in his emerald eyes. "The coven needs your help."

We'd been called the Rag Team when we were first assigned to cleanup after the initial gargoyle attacks—wiping the memories of witnesses, removing any magical evidence from the scene, and altering or deleting CCTV and social media footage were the extent of our responsibilities at the time. We were the underdogs. Undervalued for the most part, we ended up leading the investigation into the Bestiary sabotage in the end.

But the name had stuck.

"Okay. What do you need us to do?" Wade asked, taking a deep breath.

"I've got one of O'Halloran's investigative crews of security magicals looking into the disappearances, but I need you and your team to check out these other potential magicals," Alton answered, nodding at the list. "Some of them are young, so caution and subtlety will be required. Some are closer to their teens, and thus can be more easily reasoned with. These are all individuals linked to strange phenomena, as described by human witnesses. Objects moving on their own. Fires starting out of nowhere. Water sprinklers going berserk, and so on."

"How do you know these kids are responsible?" I asked, checking the names on the list and their home addresses. Most of them were in the suburban areas, which I deemed preferable to mid-city magical outbursts. The residential neighborhoods were easier to manipulate, since there were fewer people whose memories required wiping or altering. I hated that part of that job, but I understood why we had to hide the existence of magicals.

"We've been monitoring them from afar, through magicals infiltrated in their schools and neighborhoods, as well as through CCTV," Alton explained. "We need you to confirm they are, indeed, magical, and talk to them about coming into the coven for protection and education."

"I'm pretty sure their parents can protect and educate them, if they're adequately informed," I replied.

Wade shook his head. "It's not feasible if the parents are foster humans. We have protocols for that. Under no circumstances can the humans be involved."

"That's... insane," I blurted out. "So, what, you want the parents, foster or natural, to willingly surrender their kids to the coven?"

There was one thing that I wasn't completely comfortable with. The way covens interacted with human foster parents. I knew that magicals could only be born from magical parents or at least half-human and half-magical couples. I also knew that some magicals were abandoned and slipped through the cracks of the human foster system—hence, me. But still, humans chose to take care of kids like me. To protect us from harm. To love and raise us. They deserved more than a spritz of amnesia magic.

"They won't remember anything," Dylan interjected, noticing my expression. His anguish burned through me. This was quite personal for him. "Once we get there, we convince the kids to come with us and we alter the parents' memories, until the kids are grown enough to control themselves. Then, they're reintroduced to their parents, if they want that."

"This protocol applies to magicals in the foster system with human parents, though," Alton added. "Magical parents usually don't think twice about bringing their children into the coven. Humans aren't emotionally or intellectually equipped to deal with such changes."

"Intellectually equipped? As in what, they're too dumb to get it?" I snapped. I shifted my focus to Dylan. "Is that what they did to your mom and dad? Wiped you out of their memories?"

"No. I was already eighteen when I was discovered," Dylan replied. "I had some wiggle room with what I told my foster parents. They weren't happy when I said I was sticking to a local community college, but they got over it. They don't know what I can do, what I am."

I breathed out, unable to process the concept. I scowled at Alton. "And you're okay with that? You're okay with taking foster kids out of their homes and tossing them in the coven? Do you have any idea what we go through before we find a decent family, to then have it taken away from us?"

"Harley, before you dismiss this, please go out there and watch how it's done," Alton said. "I can't say it's the best solution in every case, but it is in most. I'm sure you'll get a better understanding of it once you're out in the field."

"Just follow my lead and it'll be fine," Wade replied, giving me a reassuring nod. "The magicals are always safer in the coven."

"Especially now that we know Katherine Shipton is on the loose, right?" Raffe cut in, raising an eyebrow.

Alton nodded. "Precisely. No foster parent can protect a magical from a witch like Katherine. We need to get to those kids before she does."

"So, we're afraid Katherine will snatch them first," I mumbled.

"Yes, Harley. Two are already missing, and there are rumors flying around about her building an army. The purpose is yet unknown, but her record doesn't leave room for any positive assumptions, if you know what I mean," Alton said.

"It's probably linked to her wanting to become a Child of Chaos. She probably needs the magical muscle to get that kind of power," Tatyana suggested.

Boy, that must have been a lot of muscle, since the Children of Chaos were the very sources of our power, to which we were all deeply connected, one way or another. Chaos permeated everything, and so did the Children, extensions of raw energy like Darkness, Light, or the natural elements, among others. This was like a mere mortal looking to dethrone the ancient Ares, god of war, or Poseidon, god of the sea. Just bordering on crazy, yet somehow... seemingly doable?

"We should stop assuming and get some facts, before anything else, where her plan is concerned," Alton said. "Let's focus on these kids for now. They need us."

My aggravation began to subside. I figured I could help bring the magicals to safety—temporarily, at least, until we fixed our

Katherine Shipton problem. After that, I could push to have the kids placed back with their families if they wanted to return. They didn't have to be glued to the coven to benefit from its protections and education.

Wade ran a finger over the list, then looked at Tatyana. "Okay. Here's how we do this, to cover more ground. You, Dylan, and Astrid take the right half of the list. They're all in the east and southeast of the city. Santana, Raffe, and I will take the left. They're on the opposite side, north and northwest," he said, then nodded at me. "Harley, what'll it be? Left with Tatyana or right with us? Your choice."

I thought about it for a minute, until I noticed that one of the addresses was close to the Smiths' place. "I'll go with you, Santana, and Raffe," I said. "My foster parents are in the area. I'd like to pop by and check up on them while we're there."

"That won't be a problem," Wade replied. "Good. That being said, let's get on with this, and meet back in my office in the evening to draw up a preliminary report."

"Ugh, can't we meet somewhere bigger than a matchbox, please?" I retorted.

Wade narrowed his eyes at me. "At least I *have* an office."

"What good is it if you hit your elbows on the walls all the time, huh?" I replied with a devilish grin. His tiny office was one of the few aspects of life in the coven that he could never clap back on. Even he'd agreed, albeit not in public, that it was ridiculously small. I knew it was a gratuitous shot, but I just reveled in riling him up once in a while.

The others chuckled. Alton stifled a grin, then put his hands behind his back.

"I look forward to seeing some progress," he said. "If you need anything or if you run into any kind of trouble, call O'Halloran or Preceptor Nomura immediately. If all else fails, I'm here as well."

We all gave him a brief nod then left him in his office.

Once we were out, Wade filled me in on what I needed to

prepare for this mission, according to the coven's usual protocols. Then, we agreed to meet back by the magnolia trees in the living quarters in an hour, to give ourselves some time to suit up and plan our routes, based on the addresses in the file. We each snapped photos of the list before spreading out and returning to our rooms.

Suits were needed for this kind of mission, since we were meant to impersonate Social Services employees on a routine checkup of the foster kids. It was the most inconspicuous way in which we could insert ourselves into new magicals' lives without alarming the adoptive or foster parents. The coven issued some phenomenally well-crafted ID cards for this type of work.

Heck, we'd pulled off Homeland Security during our Bestiary investigation. Social Services was going to be a breeze.

FOUR

Harley

The one thing I'd forgotten to do in the morning was check the dreamcatcher. Tobe had been kind enough to give it to me on the off chance it might help me remember something about my life before the orphanage.

It was a charmed dreamcatcher, with black beads and red, peacock-like feathers. I hung it above my headboard at night and whispered an old Navajo word to activate it. Once I fell asleep, it captured all my dreams—and boy, was my head a pile of weird or what?

As I slipped into a dark gray pantsuit, matched with a simple white shirt and black leather flats, I thought I'd have a look at what I'd dreamed the night before. I was pleased to see that the nightmares had subsided, ever so slightly, no longer dominating my sleep with gruesome gargoyles tearing the flesh from my bones.

I'd had plenty of those during the first two weeks after the incident. I'd dreamed of Adley and Finch kissing, then laughing at me as they tossed me into Quetzi's glass box in the Bestiary. That ancient Aztec snake had eaten me alive more times than I could count.

Sometimes, I dreamed of Ryann and the Smiths, and a future vacation in Maui. Even there, the gargoyles found me.

In the midst of all this, however, there were barely any earlier memories resurfacing. I kept dreaming the same scene with my dad holding me and his sister, Isadora, telling him to get away before they caught him. By "they," I assumed she meant the covens. After all, my dad was a wanted man for killing my mom and other magicals at the time.

I had to admit, I was a little frustrated with the dreamcatcher, though I only had my brain to blame for not digging deeper into my subconscious. Then, as I experienced the full audio-visual of my last dream for the previous night, my breath hitched.

"Holy crap," I murmured, suddenly finding myself sitting in a small living room with cream walls and white curtains.

The sun inundated the room, casting a golden glow on everything, including the satiny fabric of my teeny-tiny straw-yellow dress. My little hands and bare feet made me realize that I was still a toddler, sitting in... my father's lap, in one of the armchairs. The image around me was incredibly crisp, better than what I'd seen before through the dreamcatcher.

"Look at that," my dad said, showing me a photo of him and my mom.

I teared up, recognizing the ballroom photograph I'd found in my mom's trinket box, along with my Esprit and the deck of cards. I heard myself coo and gurgle, reaching out with my chubby little fingers to touch the photo.

"That's Mommy and Daddy, Harley. Before all the hurt happened."

My dad's voice was broken and shaky. I looked up at him. The toddler version of me saw him as the familiar face, the savior and caregiver. The grownup me, however, saw a handsome and tormented man, with teary blue eyes like mine and thick, black hair. I was so conflicted at that moment. It hurt worse than when Finch slammed me into the banquet hall ceiling shortly before he let all the gargoyles out.

"We were happy then, sweetie," he added, smiling. "You weren't even in the plan yet, but, boy, were we happy to learn you'd join us in this world!"

Tears streamed down my cheeks as I gripped the dreamcatcher's leathery edges and prayed to all the possible gods that this dream wouldn't end abruptly, like the others. This was as close as I would ever get to my dad. Yes, he was a murderer, by all accounts, but... he was still my father, and he seemed so sweet and kind. So different from the homicidal maniac he'd been described as before.

"You know, if I could go back, I would do it all again," my dad whispered. It felt so strange, as if he were actually standing next to me, his lips just an inch away from my ear. "I would fall in love with Hester again... I'd marry her. I'd watch you grow in her womb. Hold you in my arms on your first day. Kiss you goodnight and do my damned best to make this world a better place for you. I'd do it again, baby girl..."

"Isn't there something you'd change, though?" A female voice made my father raise his head.

I instantly recognized her. Isadora Merlin, his sister. The blue eyes, the long black hair, the ivory skin. Yes, I'd seen her before. Even as a toddler, I seemed to remember her. I was happy to see her, too.

My father sighed, before giving her a weak smile. "I think we both know what I would change," he replied.

"But you can't, Hiram," Isadora replied, looking equally heartbroken.

Were they talking about Mom? Katherine?

"I can't dwell on it, either," he said. "But I can still take care of my little girl and make sure she's safe until I find a way to stop all this."

"You're a danger to her, Hiram. You know that."

"I can handle it!" my dad snapped, then lowered his voice when he noticed my anxiousness. "I've made it this far, haven't I?"

"Barely, but…"

Isadora's voice faded away.

"No. No! No!" I croaked, gripping the dreamcatcher's edges even tighter. My palms were sweating and my heart was thumping, struggling against my ribcage. "No. Please, don't stop! I need to know!"

I couldn't control the flow of my dream, though. It had already gone, dissipated into darkness prior to me waking up. That was definitely a memory I'd just seen. Not a nightmare or a Salvador Dali-type dream. It was an HD memory, better than the one I'd fished out before, from the murky depths of my subconscious.

It left me with a ton of questions. My watch beeped twice.

"Time to go. Dammit," I muttered, then put the dreamcatcher under the bed, grabbed my phone and keys, and walked out to meet the rest of my team.

I looked forward to the evening already, knowing I'd have a chance to sit down and read through my parents' file. Maybe there was something there that would answer the new questions I had. What did my father think that he could "handle"? What was it that he would've gone back in time to change, if given the opportunity?

Was it what he'd done to my mother? His affair with Katherine Shipton?

I wiped my tears and glided down the stairs, focusing on the present. The past wasn't going anywhere. The answers were there, waiting for me to find them. In the meantime, however, there were magicals who needed my help and the coven's protection.

My parents were gone. But Katherine Shipton was still around and eager to wreak more havoc.

FIVE

Harley

W ade drove us in his black Jeep.

I missed my Daisy, but after the gargoyle incidents, my beloved Mustang had been reduced to a pile of junk metal. I owed Murray the gargoyle for that, and I planned to repay him in kind. He was back in the Bestiary, super secured in his charmed glass box, but that didn't stop me from plotting my revenge. To be honest, the one responsible was Finch, who'd let Murray out in the first place, and he was pretty much taken care of already. But there was a hole left in my heart, and I figured that pranking the hell out of the monster that had destroyed my car might help fill it, even if just temporarily.

We were headed toward Sunset Cliffs, one of the finer areas of San Diego, composed mostly of one- or two-story houses and direct access to the ocean. It was beautiful and sunny in these parts, with short palm trees sprawling out of front yards and music blasting from some of the backyards—it was a Saturday, and the weather was perfect for a barbecue. I could even smell the charcoal burning through the open windows.

"We're about ten minutes away," he said, keeping his eyes on the road.

"What do we know about these people?" Santana asked from the backseat.

I'd been sly enough to call shotgun as soon as we'd gotten to the Jeep. For that, I'd also been trusted with a copy of the file. I flipped through its pages and read some of the information out loud, for both Raffe and Santana to hear. Knowing Wade, he'd already memorized it all, word for word, since he was the poster child of the overachiever.

"Micah Cranston, aged five," I said. "Has been in the foster system since he was two. Bounced around for a while, until he turned three and was adopted by Susan and Larry Cranston. He's been with them since. Mom's a teacher. Dad's a construction fore-man. It says here they both have fertility issues, which is why they chose to adopt. They've each got a 401(k), and they're already saving up for his college fund. They sound like good people."

I was already getting sucked into my humane side, the one that didn't want to separate a child from his parents. Even though I was aware of the threat surrounding his life here, I couldn't bring myself to even think of taking Micah away. There had to be another way.

Of course, I was annoyed with myself. I'd thought I'd already made a concession over this, but my heart, the fickle and treach-erous little organ that it was, had decided to sabotage my reasoning.

"What incidents led the coven to believe he's a magical?" Raffe asked.

"Oh. Um, wow," I said, raising both eyebrows as I scanned a witness account. "Objects levitating and swirling around him. This happened more than once. His parents moved him to a new kinder-garten after three repeat incidents."

"That's all?" Wade replied.

"What? That's not enough? Do you want him to pull the San Andreas Fault and reorganize California's landscape before he's deemed a magical?" I chuckled.

"No, Miss Snappy, I just thought he might have been manifesting other abilities, too," Wade said.

I turned the page on Micah's file. "Nope. That's all we have. A Reading would give us more."

"Do we know anything about his biological parents?" Wade replied.

I shook my head. "Left at an orphanage by a stranger. No birth certificate, nothing."

"Okay, that's a little odd," Santana chimed in. "Has anyone checked the hospital records for any missing babies? I assumed they have an estimated birthday for the boy."

I glanced over my shoulder at Santana. "No one checked anything. He just popped up on the grid when he was one year old."

"Someone must've taken care of him until then," Wade mused, scratching his chin. The sunlight made his sterling silver rings twinkle for a moment. It reminded me of something, but I wasn't sure what, exactly. It was just one of the many eerie and impossible to describe flashbacks I'd been having lately while fully conscious. "We should definitely look into this," he added.

"Let me guess, I get the research gig?" I scoffed, turning another page on Micah's file.

Wade smirked. "You're the rookie, so of course."

"Hey, remember what Alton said!" Santana jokingly warned him, though I wasn't sure what she was talking about.

"Zip it, Santana," Wade groaned, rolling his eyes.

"What?" I asked, slightly amused.

"Santana, I'm serious. Shush," Wade insisted, ignoring my question.

I looked at her again and found her grinning. She waited for a few seconds, occasionally checking Wade's expression in the rearview mirror, then dragged the cat out of the bag. "Alton told Wade to be super extra nice to you so you're more inclined to stay with the coven. I was just reminding him that giving you the grunt work doesn't exactly qualify as 'being nice.'"

Wade let out a long, frustrated sigh, briefly scowling at Santana through the rearview mirror.

"She needs to go through all the hoops we went through, Santana. That includes some paperwork," he replied firmly. "Just because Alton really wants her to stay doesn't mean she shouldn't learn some things the hard way like the rest of us."

My heart swelled a little. "Aww. Alton wants me to stay."

"Duh! We all do!" Santana retorted. "Even Mr. I'm-Too-Cool-To-Express-My-Feelings over here," she added, nodding at Wade.

That I could sort of agree with. Something had changed between Wade and me since Finch had been apprehended. I couldn't put my finger on it, but our dynamic felt somewhat different—in a good, yet troubling, way. At times, there was an intensity between us that was hard to figure out. It made my heart flutter in ways I'd never experienced before. Most of the time, however, we just seemed to really get along, between layers of sharp jokes and sarcastic remarks.

"Yeah, I can see that," I murmured, then pressed my lips into a thin line to stop a smile from splitting my face.

All of a sudden, I felt nervous. That wasn't me. That was Wade's heart pounding and echoing into mine. He cleared his throat, his knuckles white as he gripped the wheel and pulled over.

"We're here," he announced.

As soon as we got out of his Jeep and saw the lovely house and lush front yard, with two SUVs parked outside, I knew that little Micah had hit quite the jackpot with the Cranstons. He was looking at a prosperous and healthy childhood. His bike was on its side, covered in stickers and settled between two hydrangea bushes.

Better than some southside orphanage, if you ask me.

"I'll take the lead," Wade added. "You watch, you listen, and you learn. Got it?"

I sighed deeply. "Mm-hm."

"Is that a yes?" he asked.

"Oh, go already!" Santana grumbled, motioning for him to go ahead.

My throat was already dry, and I was pretty sure I was sweating, but I could easily blame it on the weather. It was nice and hot, definitely not pantsuit temperature. Judging by the looks on Santana's and Raffe's faces, they weren't too comfortable. The jackets were going to come off soon.

I handed the file over to Wade. "There you go. Take the lead," I said.

He didn't hesitate as he went up the pathway and knocked on the door. We gathered behind him, wearing our friendliest faces. We had to give the Cranstons the right impression. Their minds were easier to manipulate with false memories if they weren't under distress—or so I'd learned from Preceptor Sloane Bellmore, who taught Charms and Hexes.

As soon as the door opened, we were greeted by Susan, Micah's adoptive mother. She seemed kind and soft by nature, from what I could pick up as an Empath. It certainly matched her petite figure, auburn hair, and mom jeans.

"Can I help you?" she asked, standing in the doorway.

"Hi, Mrs. Cranston. I'm Wade Munson. These are my colleagues, Santana Gomez, Raphael Smith, and Harley… Smith," he replied, giving some fake last names and flashing his equally fake ID. "No relation," he added. "We're from Social Services."

In an instant, I was gripped by concern, mirrored by Susan's furrowed brows. "Is something wrong?"

"No, no, not at all!" Wade replied, in a bid to reassure her. He sucked at this, though. The dude couldn't bring himself to smile if his life depended on it. "We're just here on a random visit, to check on Micah, make sure you have everything you need. You know, the usual."

Susan eyed us carefully, wary of letting strangers in her house. I gave her a warm smile and a friendly nod, then showed her my also-fake ID. "We do this once every couple years. It's not meant to reflect poorly on you in any way, Mrs. Cranston. We're simply making sure you're all happy as a family, and we're here to offer advice and counseling if you need it."

She nodded slowly, then opened the door for us.

"Come in," she said. "We just made lemonade."

"Fantastic! I hope you have ice!" Raffe replied, delighted.

We followed her into the living room, and I took a moment to analyze the place. The house was clean and neatly decorated. There wasn't a particular style present, but rather a mish-mash of designs and cultural infusions. The walnut furniture was loaded with secondhand books and fancy-looking first editions. The wall art had an Andy Warhol vibe, though the wallpaper itself was cream and simple. Vases of different shapes and sizes adorned the side tables, and the centerpiece rug reminded me of Peruvian weaving, rich in color, with geometric patterns. They'd done this place up piece by piece, as well as they could afford it at the time—but they did invest in quality.

I was becoming more and more convinced that Micah was in good hands here.

There were pictures of him all over the walls, along with some of his kindergarten drawings. Those actually kind of matched the decorative Warhol-esque paintings they'd been hung next to. It tore me apart to think we'd now have to take him away. It was cruel.

Pots clanged in the kitchen, followed by a round of boyish giggles and Larry Cranston's muffled voice. By the sounds of it, they were having a lot of fun in there. Susan chuckled, then motioned for us to sit down. Wade took over one of the armchairs while Santana and Raffe settled on the couch. I preferred to stand, feeling far too nervous to sit still for more than a second.

I browsed the bookshelves that covered half of the eastern wall. There was an entire shelf dedicated to parenting books. The Cranstons had obviously done their homework on the topic. They were also huge fans of true crime and psychological thrillers, from what I could tell. One of them had a thing for soapy romance novels

—my money was on Susan for that particular guilty pleasure. It made me smile.

"Larry! Micah! Come in here with that lemonade, and bring some glasses, too!" Susan shouted toward the kitchen at the end of the hallway. "We've got visitors!"

"How many glasses?" Larry called back.

"Seven, honey!"

"Whoa, lots of people!" little Micah exclaimed.

We all smiled at the sound of his voice as Susan sat in another armchair and cleared the coffee table, making room for the lemonade. Soon enough, Micah's footsteps echoed through the hallway, along with the clinking of glasses. He was the first to enter the living room and stop and stare at us, a curious glimmer settling in his brown eyes.

Larry emerged second, carrying a large tray with glasses and a massive pitcher of ice-cold lemonade. I instinctively licked my lips. Micah seemed to be wondering why we were here, and there was a hint of concern hidden beneath his curiosity. I had a feeling he was aware that our presence was related to his Telekinetic abilities.

"Hi, Micah," Wade said. "I'm Wade, and these are my friends. We're just passing through."

"Well, our door is always open!" Susan replied, smiling. Micah mirrored her expression, his tiny teeth making me melt on the inside. He was the sweetest little thing, with his blond hair cut short and fuzzy.

"How are you all doing?" Wade asked, looking at Susan and Larry.

Larry frowned, giving his wife a questioning glance. "They're from Social Services, honey. Just a routine visit. Nothing to worry about," she briefly explained.

"Oh! Um… we're doing well, I guess," Larry replied. "The neighborhood is quiet. We've got a lot of community activities. Barbecues on Sunday with some of our neighbors. The private school down the road is great for Micah. We're adjusting."

Wade nodded, then flipped open the file, giving Micah the occasional glance. "I understand you moved him to this kindergarten halfway through the year," he replied. "Was he having trouble in Point Loma?"

Susan and Larry looked at each other again. This time, they were both nervous. Humans were slightly easier to read than magicals from what I'd noticed so far. Their emotions were a tad looser. Children, in particular, were quite intense. Micah was flaring with panic. He kept a pretty good poker face for someone so young, but his eyes betrayed him.

"It was too far from here," Susan said, then took a deep breath to calm herself.

Oh, they were hiding something, for sure.

I'll take "Our Child is a Telekinetic" for $1,000, Alex.

"You teach at Point Loma High School, don't you? Wasn't it more convenient to drop him off and pick him up from next door?" Wade asked, raising an eyebrow.

"Not really. Kindergarten schedules differ from my high school, and Larry is the one who usually handles Micah's school rides," Susan explained, then proceeded to pour lemonade in all the glasses. Her hands were shaking, and Wade didn't let that go unnoticed.

"Are you nervous, Mrs. Cranston?"

Susan laughed, the pitch uncomfortably higher than usual. "No! I mean, not really. I'm just sort of uneasy, I guess."

"Why would you be uneasy?" I asked, prompting Wade to give me a stern sideways glance. He was slightly irritated, but I didn't care. He was way too serious for this family, making what we were about to do much, much worse.

"I thought we were okay with Micah," Susan replied, her voice shaky. "He's healthy and growing well, he loves us, and we love him back—so much. We're... We're happy, and I'm worried whenever Social Services is in the room."

"We haven't heard from you since Micah was three," Larry

added, crossing his arms. "I figured something must've happened for Social Services to come around now. I don't know, maybe his biological parents showed up or something."

"Are you sure you want to discuss that with him present?" Wade asked, watching as Micah climbed into his mother's lap and sipped from his plastic cup, which was also filled with lemonade.

"Oh yeah, Micah knows everything about our family," Susan said, smiling at her little boy with so much love, I almost teared up.

"Well, I don't want you to worry," Wade replied. "We're just making sure that everything is as you expected—that your family life is healthy and not impacted by any sudden changes. Like I said, the basics."

From what I was feeling, however, that wasn't enough to soothe the Cranstons. They still worried, and for good reason. We were about to take their child away from them, and Wade was leading them on with these pretty little lies, just so they wouldn't be too distraught and their minds would be more malleable for the memory wiping. It pissed me off.

Something took over in that instant—a part of me that had lain dormant since my faceoff with Finch. Energy burst through me, bright and furious, making me stand straight and walk over to Micah, who watched me quietly as I approached him and his mom. Wade didn't say anything, but he, too, watched me with intense eyes. Santana and Raffe were quiet and confused. This wasn't part of the plan.

I crouched before Susan and Micah. "Micah, why don't you tell us about the accidents that got your mom and dad to move you to this new kindergarten?"

As expected, both Susan and Larry were shocked and mortified, their jaws dropping. To my right, Wade was fuming, Santana was slightly amused, and Raffe was... well, I couldn't always tell with him. I got both concern and glee, in a mixture that made my blood chill.

Micah, on the other hand, felt relieved.

"What are you talking about?!" Susan blurted, tightening her arms around her son.

I gave her a sympathetic smile. "I think you know, Mrs. Cranston," I replied, then looked at Larry. "You're both aware that your boy is... special, right?"

"Who are you people?" Larry gasped.

"We're here to help," I said, getting back up slowly so as not to startle anyone.

"You're crazy!" Susan replied, getting aggravated.

I'd seen this coming, but I had a lot of faith in them, especially in Micah, who couldn't take his eyes off me. Wade pinched the bridge of his nose, no longer hiding his frustration.

"All you had to do was shut up and let me do my job," he muttered.

"Tough luck. Change of plans, Wade. We're doing this my way," I replied dryly.

"You don't get to decide what—"

I cut him off. "No! *You* don't get to decide what happens to Micah. Micah and his parents get to decide what happens to Micah, because that's the humane thing to do!"

The Cranstons were petrified—understandably, since they didn't have the full story as to why we were here. Heck, they didn't even know what a magical was. It was too late to go back now, so I returned my focus to them, while Santana whispered something in Wade's ear. Whatever she told him, it seemed to stop him from getting angrier. I could feel the blaze subsiding within me.

"Mrs. Cranston, your son is extraordinary, and I mean it in the best way possible," I said to her. "Have you ever heard of Telekinesis?"

She blinked several times, then looked at Larry and Micah before nodding. "We figured it was something like that... The internet wasn't too helpful, though," she murmured.

"I would imagine so," I replied. "Your son is what we call a 'magical,' Mrs. Cranston. And chances are that moving objects around with his mind isn't the only thing he can do."

"How do you know all this? Who the hell are you people?" she croaked, tearing up.

"We're like him," I said, then smiled at Micah. "We're just like you, Micah. Look."

Without further ado, I focused my Telekinetic lasso on the lemonade glass I'd yet to pick up from the table and gently lifted it in the air. I moved it around the room as a perplexed family of three watched it glide with no one touching it, then I settled it back on the coffee table.

"I'm losing my mind, aren't I?" Susan breathed. "Larry, did you put something in the lemonade?"

"Mom, no. She's like me," Micah interjected, then got down from her lap and came closer, looking up at me. "You're like me."

I nodded. "I am, Micah, and, unlike you, I never had anyone come tell me what I am or what I can do," I replied, then gave Susan a warm smile. "Trust me, Mrs. Cranston. Micah is rare and precious, and if the government or any of the regular humans find out what he is, he'll be in a lot of trouble. I suppose you know that, since you've been keeping his ability a secret, moving him from one school to another."

Susan took a minute to answer. This was a strangely reassuring experience for both her and Larry. They were worried, still, but there was some kind of comfort found in knowing that their son wasn't the only one. Had they not seen what he could do with their own eyes, they probably couldn't have processed this situation without falling into hysteria.

"What's a magical?" Micah asked.

"A witch—or a warlock, if it's a boy. A magical has abilities that humans have only written about in fantasy books. That could be anything from manipulating the natural elements to incredible strength or the ability to talk to the dead, among other things.

They're also able to cast spells. Actual spells," I said to him. "But you're one of the good guys, trust me."

He sighed, as if a great weight had been removed from his shoulders. Anguish quickly followed it. "Is that why I'm an orphan?"

"You're not an orphan anymore, Micah. You've got Mr. and Mrs. Cranston now. You have parents, buddy," Santana chimed in, following my lead.

Wade and Raffe were both baffled, watching the exchange with wide eyes.

"Yeah, but my real parents... are they magical, too?" Micah replied.

"Most likely, yes. At least one of them is. Magicals are never made, they're always born. And there has to be a magical in the family for that to happen. Witch or warlock, or both," I explained, then looked at Susan again. She was the matriarch of the family; I could tell from the way in which Larry quietly sought her gaze for comfort and approval before he spoke. "Mrs. Cranston, there are others like Micah, like us. We're all part of the San Diego Coven. We stick together. We scour the city for young witches and warlocks who might've slipped through the cracks. Magicals like me and Micah. I was a foster kid, too. But I only recently found the coven, and it has changed my life."

"So, what, you can teach him to control his powers?" Susan asked, genuinely curious.

"That and so much more. The coven trains and educates its magicals, as part of its pledge to protect and give them a purpose. We have safe facilities, with comfortable living spaces. They feed us, they teach us, they find us jobs and help us develop ourselves and our careers, no matter what we choose to do with our lives. They've helped me so much already, which is why I'm here talking to you," I said.

"What's the catch?" Larry cut in, eyeing us suspiciously. "There's always a catch."

"There is, Mr. and Mrs. Cranston," Wade interrupted, standing up. "Micah needs to come with us for his own safety."

"What? No!" Susan said.

"No way in hell!" Larry added.

"Maybe there's another way," I murmured, giving him a pleading look.

"What other way, Harley? Micah is in danger on his own, living among the humans like this! He can't control his powers now, and it'll be a while till he can," Wade retorted. "Until then, do you really expect him to go to school and whatever? Seriously?"

"You're not taking my son away from me!" Susan snapped, her lip quivering.

Micah was getting anxious, to the point where the glasses and pitcher started shaking on the table. This wasn't an earthquake. This was little Micah losing control over his Telekinesis.

Dammit. I should've seen this coming.

"I don't want to leave my mommy and daddy," Micah moaned, his eyes filled with heartbreaking tears.

Wade's rings lit up blue as he shook his head in disappointment. He was about to do something cruel and extreme because of the coven's stupid regulations, but I wasn't ready to give up just yet.

"Hold on!" I said, slipping between Micah and Wade. "Wade, listen to me! There has to be another way."

Raffe sighed. "We have to keep the boy safe, and you know why."

"What if he stays with his parents here but they transfer him to the coven's school, huh?" I offered, mentally congratulating myself for this last-minute spark. "They'll bring him to the coven every morning and pick him up once they finish work. That way, they spend evenings and weekends together, and Micah is monitored and educated properly, as per magical standards. You save up on your memory-deleting spells, and there will be one kid who won't hate you with the fire of a thousand suns for tearing him away from his family!"

Silence settled over the living room. The glasses and pitcher stilled.

Susan, Larry, and Micah stared at us, then at each other for a while.

Wade was livid, and that annoyed the hell out of me. But I was getting different vibes from Raffe and Santana.

Raffe took a deep breath and crossed his arms. "You know, that doesn't sound too crazy," he whispered.

"Have you lost your mind, too?" Wade retorted, then raised an eyebrow at Larry. "You did put something in the lemonade, didn't you?"

Raffe chuckled nervously, looking at Larry, who was utterly baffled. "He's kidding. He's just kidding."

"He doesn't look like he's kidding," Larry replied.

"Yeah, well, Wade doesn't do basic social cues," I cut in.

"Wade, Harley is on to something here," Santana intervened, thankfully in my favor. "Micah doesn't have to be in the coven 24/7 at this point. I could easily set something up here to alert us if anything goes wrong."

"What could go wrong?" Susan asked.

"Like we said, Micah is young and not in full control of his powers," I replied, just as Wade opened his mouth to reply. I gave him a wink. "Come on, dude. Work with me. Don't be a jerk. Kids need to be with their families."

"The coven is their family," Wade answered.

"Screw you, Crowley!" I blurted. "It's easy for you to say that. You grew up with parents! Kids like Micah and me aren't always that lucky!"

The minute that followed was the quietest and most intense in my life. Technically speaking, I'd just screwed the pooch on coven regulations. The worst-case scenario saw Wade not giving a damn about my plea and wiping the Cranstons' memories, then picking Micah up and hauling him back to the coven.

I didn't want to bring Katherine Shipton's name into the

conversation. There was a less rational part of me that desperately wanted Micah to be happy and stay with his family. We could watch over them. Plus, we didn't really know for sure that she was involved in any of this—not 100 percent yet, anyway. Stirring any kind of panic based on our hunches would've been unproductive, to say the least.

If we got any later confirmation that Katherine had her skeevy fingers dipped in this pie, I'd be the first one to show up here again and take Micah away. But, until then, the kid had every right to enjoy his family. At least for a little while longer.

Wade's shoulders dropped in what felt like defeat.

"Santana, can you have eyes on the boy at all times?" he asked her. It took a surprising amount of effort to stop myself from jumping around with sheer, unadulterated joy. At the same time, I felt guilty. I'd just screwed up his entire operation—I had a history in this field.

"Yeah, I can fuse one of the Orishas to Micah's energy signature," Santana replied. "I'll set some traps for potential magical intruders. It'll at least keep them busy till the Cranstons get out or until coven security gets here."

Wade exhaled as he looked at the Cranstons. "For the time being, Micah can stay with you," he conceded, prompting the little boy to cheer and run into his mother's arms. Susan picked him up, showering him with kisses. "But should there come a time that we require Micah to move into the coven, even if just temporarily, you both need to be okay with that. If that happens, it will be only for his personal safety. Believe it or not, we're not too crazy about separating children from their families."

Susan nodded enthusiastically. "Thank you!" she said, her eyes sparkling with relief.

"He will need to be at the Fleet Science Center, every day, from eight a.m. until six p.m.," Wade continued, his tone flat and firm. "Under no circumstances will you attempt to flee. We will know, and we will find you. Is that clear?"

This time, all three Cranstons nodded vehemently, making me smile.

"We'll be careful," Larry said.

"Needless to say, you will keep the existence of magicals a secret," Wade replied. "It's bad enough I've got a nightmare of explaining over Micah to do now. The last thing we want is human attention."

"We will have eyes and ears on you, wherever you go," Raffe said, adding his share of grave warnings. I'd softened the Cranstons up too much and too fast. He and Wade were both trying to make up for that. "We will know if you tell anyone. Should you break this arrangement in any way, you will never see Micah again."

"Jeez, dude," I grumbled. They weren't going to have eyes and ears on them wherever they went; that was just tough talk meant to intimidate. The magical alarms in the house were enough.

"Shush!" Wade said. "You're done talking for now."

I gave him that much. After all, he'd agreed to break coven rules and go against Alton on this due to my persistence. He deserved to "put me back in my place."

We left the Cranstons with instructions and details about Micah's new life and expectations as a magical. Santana carried out her Santeria magic around the house, while we waited by the Jeep.

Wade didn't even look at me. The silence was painfully awkward, but I was willing to put up with it. I'd walked out of that house with a major victory under my belt. Maybe I could bring about some positive changes to the San Diego Coven, after all. Micah felt like a good first step.

SIX

Harley

I sat in the passenger seat, outside Micah's house, watching the occasional car go by—families headed for the beach. Santana was inside, planting charms and traps for potential magical hostiles. Wade was outside leaning against the hood and gazing at the ocean as it rippled in the distance, while Raffe was in the back, behind me, playing games on his smartphone.

"You have to talk to me at some point, Crowley," I said, craning my neck out the car window.

"I don't have much to say right now. Pardon me if I'm more focused on how I'll explain this to Alton," Wade replied, then slid off the hood and got behind the wheel.

"I would say I'm sorry, but I'm not," I mumbled.

"Of course you're not sorry. You just messed up centuries' worth of policies because you let your emotions get the better of you," Wade fired back.

"And you went along with it!"

"She has a point," Raffe interjected, still playing. "We could've just taken Micah and wiped Susan and Larry's memories."

"Yeah, and then we would've had to alter the boy's memories, too, so he wouldn't be traumatized or distressed. Then *we* would be the monsters," Wade said. "This was supposed to go smooth and easy. Go in, tell the parents what's going on with their kid, get the kid to understand that he's better off with us, then wipe the parents' minds and take the kid. *Easy.*"

"You make it *sound* easy," I replied.

"I've done it before. It's smoother when you ease the kid into it. Like I said, there are protocols in place. All you had to do was follow my lead," Wade said, a muscle ticking in his jaw.

"Hey, if it doesn't work out, I will be the first to admit my mistake, I promise." I sighed.

"Good. Because if something happens to him, I'll be looking at you," Wade muttered, giving me a stone-cold sideways scowl.

That made me mad. "Nah, you don't get to back out of it. We're in this together. The four of us. We'll all be ready if something happens. But Santana's putting charms and stuff in the house, isn't she? If Katherine or one of her buddies comes around, we'll know. Won't that help our mission to catch her?"

Wade stared at me for a half-minute, then smirked. "You're okay with using the kid as bait?"

The realization hit me so hard, I was seconds away from changing my mind and charging in there to get Micah, whether he wanted to leave or not. But that conflict didn't last long. I had to be pragmatic about this. Katherine Shipton was a threat, not only to Micah but to every other magical out there. If this could be used as a way to draw her out, might as well.

I wasn't comfortable with the idea, but I wasn't fine with telling Micah and his parents that we'd changed our minds, either. There had to be a limit to our monstrosity, as members of a coven. I knew better than most what it was like to grow up without parents. In the end, that mattered more than almost anything. Micah had a better shot at a healthy and happy childhood with Susan and Larry around. Even with mind-wiping and other magical tricks, the trauma of separation could still leave marks on a child's subconscious. I didn't want that for Micah.

The front door opened. Santana came out and dropped a small leather pouch in the flower planter next to her, then came to the car.

"We got a problem," she said as she got in. "Found this in a trinket bowl in the lobby."

She handed Wade a small business card. There was a symbol on its back—an eye in the middle of a triangle, framed by a circle, embossed in black. Wade turned it over and read the front.

"The Ryder twins," he said. "From the San Diego Coven?"

"Yeah, the weirdest thing happened in there," Santana explained. "I put charms and traps in place to alert us if anything happens and summoned an Orisha to keep an eye on Micah at all times. All that was fine, until I found this card. I asked Susan about it, but she had no idea. Neither did Larry. Or Micah. No one knew how it had gotten there. They don't remember anyone else from the coven coming to visit. They only employ a babysitter once in a while, and occasionally the neighbors visit for a barbecue. That's it."

"Okay, that's weird," Raffe said, then took the card from Wade and sniffed it. I stilled as his eyes glimmered red for a split second.

"There are no Ryder twins in the San Diego Coven," Wade replied.

"There's no trace of anything or anyone on this," Raffe concluded. "Normally, there would be the scent of a person's touch, at least. But there's nothing. Which is even weirder."

I didn't have time to wonder about Raffe's ability to track scents like a friggin' wolf at that point. We had a bigger concern: who'd left the card? "Why don't the Cranstons remember? Do you think their memories were wiped?" I asked.

Santana shook her head. "I had my Orishas scan them. There was no memory tampering."

"So, someone snuck in and left it there?" I replied, even more confused.

Wade turned the key in the ignition. The engine roared to life, and he looked at us. "Or someone they know isn't who they think," he offered. "We'll need to look into them. And we need to tell Tatyana and the others about it. Astrid can check our systems for the Ryder twins."

"Have you ever heard of them?" Santana asked, checking the card again.

"No. But there's got to be a reason why that card was left there," Wade replied.

A thought crossed my mind, raising the hairs on my back. "Do you think it was left there for us to find?"

"Maybe. Thing is, it says 'The Ryder Twins of the San Diego Coven' on it, but that's not our insignia. It's different." Wade said, then looked at Santana. "Call Astrid, send her a photo of the card, and ask her to check that phone number, too. Maybe she can trace it."

"Should we call? See who's on the other line?" I asked.

Wade drove us out onto the main road. "Not yet. Let's see what Astrid comes up with first."

In hindsight, leaving Micah seemed even more risky than before. At the same time, laying alarms in his house could help us, if those Ryder twins came by again. All of Santana's charms were designed against magicals, so if any of them came in, even posing as friendly neighbors or whatever, we'd be notified.

SEVEN

Tatyana

From the moment Harley walked into the coven, I knew we had our hands full—and not really in a bad way, though the girl was a magnet for trouble. I liked the team she'd unwittingly helped form. We were all misfits in our way, but together we were stronger than most magicals in San Diego. I'd been looking forward to another mission with Harley on board. It was never boring.

Case in point, Santana called me to share some updates, sooner than I'd expected.

"We found a business card from the San Diego Coven—" Santana began.

"Was it from the Ryder twins?" I asked, turning over the card I had spotted in the Travis family's seashell trinket holder.

I'd been going over things with Linda and Evan, Mina's magical parents. Of course, we'd had no idea they were magical—they were new to San Diego, having moved here less than a year ago, and they'd yet to reach out to the San Diego Coven.

"You found one, too?" Santana asked. She sounded as uneasy as I felt.

"Yeah. Not good, huh?" I replied.

"It's a little fishy, but we can't exactly connect it to Katherine Shipton right now. It's cause for concern, though. Are you still at the Travis house?"

"Mm-hm. Going over the details with Mina's parents. How's it going over there?" I muttered, occasionally glancing at Linda.

Santana chuckled. "Harley got Wade to leave the kid with his parents and make him attend coven classes like it's a normal school. Granted, we had orders, but you know Harley. He should've seen this coming," she added in a lower voice, as if not to be heard by the others in her crew.

I had to admit, it didn't come as a surprise. It was one of the things I liked most about Harley, actually. Rules weren't her forte, but she had a way of putting her foot down—and Wade conceded, which was quite a wonder to behold.

"He'll get used to her eventually," I said. "I'll let you know how the Travis situation pans out once we're done."

"Good luck!" Santana replied, then hung up.

Astrid was already checking the database for the Ryder twins, using her Smartie tablet to connect and comb through the system.

The Travis couple were sitting on the sofa, pale and worried for their six-year-old daughter, while Dylan checked every corner of the living room and the rest of the house for any foreign charms or spells.

"Why didn't you contact the coven when you first got here?" I asked Linda.

Mina was a special little girl, with Telekinesis, Water, and Air Elemental abilities. She'd begun manifesting all three from the age of four, making it difficult for her parents to keep her safe in an all-human elementary school. They should've entered their local coven, as per the magical laws.

Linda sighed, rubbing her face in frustration, as Evan decided to keep little Mina busy with a children's book about a super-friendly dinosaur. In comparison, my childhood had been the stuff of nightmares. The Russian sorcerers, known as Kolduny, didn't take their kids to the aquarium on the weekend, nor did they read us stories from colorful fairytale books. No, they took us to the graveyard to talk to dead people and made us read obituaries in the evening, to "understand the scale and permanence of death."

I would've loved to have a dad like Mina's. Evan seemed so kind and sweet, looking at her as if she were the very reason he was alive and breathing. But I had to make do with what I had, and, despite the distance and cultural differences, I did miss my mom and dad a little.

"We were Neutrals back in Baltimore," Linda replied. "We were taking our time here, thinking that a new home and a new school would help keep Mina's abilities under the radar for a little while longer."

"You have to understand, we grew up in covens," Evan added. "It was cold and impersonal, and, even though we were surrounded by magicals, we were lonely. There was no specific attention or affection given to magical children. There usually isn't, and we fought hard to change that, but the Baltimore coven wouldn't budge. We were allowed to leave and buy a house in the city, and we acquired our Neutral status without much of a fuss."

"But then, Mina was born. We'd had fertility issues," Linda said. "We didn't think we could even have children. She was our little miracle." She sighed, lovingly watching her daughter as she turned a page of her storybook.

I showed them the Ryders Twins' card. "This was in the lobby with your keys. Who gave it to you?"

Linda reached out to take it. She turned it over, then frowned slightly. "They introduced themselves as Emily and Emmett Ryder. They came over a couple of days ago and said they were from the San Diego Coven. They were in the neighborhood and thought they'd stop by to say hello."

"What else did they say?" I asked.

"Well, what every other coven magical says. They wanted us to come with them or to at least have Mina attend their magical training classes," Linda said. "Which is why I was a little surprised to see you guys here, today. I found the coven's persistence to be rather... odd."

Astrid shook her head, her gaze fixed on the tablet. "The Ryder twins don't work for the San Diego Coven. They're not affiliated with us in any way."

"Even the logo on the card... it's wrong. It's not ours, though it does claim to be ours. Maybe it's done on purpose, to mess with us? I don't know," I added, then looked at Linda again. "You should bring Mina in. You know it's time. Had it not been for the kindergarten incidents, we would've never been alerted in the first place."

Evan let out a breath. "Maybe it is time, honey."

"We're not going to live in the coven!" Linda snapped. "I spent years trying to break free so I could have a simple life. We both did, Evan. We want something different—better—for our little girl."

"I completely understand that, Mrs. Travis, but these are special circumstances," Dylan replied, as he came back into the living room, then gave me a brief nod. "The house is clear. What did Santana say about the card?"

"There was one at the Cranstons' place, too, but they had no idea who put it there. They checked the parents' memories," I said. "There was no tampering. Whoever left the card, they did it inconspicuously, either by sneaking in or pretending to be someone else."

"But the Cranston kid is okay," Astrid chimed in. "They laid charms and traps around the house and left him to be with his parents. Alton's going to blow a fuse over this." She chuckled.

"Yeah, we don't usually let magical kids stay with their parents," I muttered, then retrieved the card from Linda to examine it again.

"Do you remember what the Ryder twins looked like?" Astrid asked.

"A lot like each other, for starters. The only difference, apart from the fact that one was a woman and the other a man, was the hair," Linda recalled. "Emily had short black hair, and Emmett's was long, down to his shoulders. Both pale-skinned, with brown eyes...

Nothing that stood out, really. They looked young, in their early twenties."

"They were nice and friendly," Evan replied. "They weren't pushy or persistent. But they did say it would be safer for Mina if she went to live in the coven. Of course, we said no, not without us, and they said we could go with them, too."

Dylan groaned, looking out the window. "What is their endgame? I don't get it."

My phone beeped. It was a text from Wade, which puzzled me. I read it over and over, five times, then decided to do what he asked. "Dylan, I've got a bag of charms in the trunk. Would you mind bringing it in, please? We need to rig the house," I said.

He seemed confused. "I thought we were taking them all back to the coven with us."

"Wade spoke to Alton about this. Turns out our director wasn't all that miffed about Wade leaving a magical child in his human parents' care after all. He said we should do the same with all the families on our list. Talk to them, verify the magical abilities, instruct them on emergency scenarios, and charm the hell out of their houses and cars," I replied.

Astrid smirked. "Laying traps, basically."

"And using our kids as bait?!" Linda asked, suddenly alarmed.

"Well, you two are here, and you can hold your own, right?" I retorted, raising an eyebrow. I lacked Dylan and Santana's sympathetic and warm nature. I had my own way of dealing with my role as a protector of the coven and its magicals. I focused on the strategy, with less concern for people's feelings. That probably made me seem coldhearted, but it also allowed me to get tactical in every situation. It just worked for me. "We don't know what the Ryder twins' intentions are, but once we set the charms, we'll know the instant they come back."

"Did the Ryder twins seem aggressive or displeased with your decision to keep Mina here?" Astrid asked.

Dylan left and came back with my charm bag, plopping it on the coffee table. The sound of the zipper coming undone drew Mina's attention for a moment, before she shifted her focus back to the friendly dinosaur story.

"No. They smiled and said they understood," Linda replied. "They also said they'd talk to the director and make a case for us. We thanked them, then they took off. They left the card in case we changed our minds. That was it."

Astrid sighed. "I can't find them in the regional database. There's another place I can try, but I'll need Alton's clearance," she said, then texted him.

I took several small leather pouches from the bag and handed some to Dylan. "Do the top floor. I'll do the ground floor. Find corners, nooks, and holes to stick them in, one per room," I said.

He nodded before vanishing up the stairs. Linda left Evan and Mina in the living room with Astrid, following me around the house as I looked for the right spots to hide my little alarm charms. They were rigged to react to foreign magicals, as I'd prepared two separate batches of charms for this type of situation—one for non-magical households, and one for magical families. The latter, which I was using, were more potent and aimed at magical strangers.

"So, you think we should stay here, then," Linda said as we stopped in the kitchen.

I opened the counter door beneath the sink and stuffed one of the bags in the corner, behind the garbage bin. I crinkled my nose at the smell, then got up and washed my hands. Technically speaking, I was a bit of a germaphobe.

"For the time being, yes," I replied, and gave her one of my cards. "This is my personal number. If anything feels even remotely strange, call me. Otherwise, carry on with your lives, but please, for Mina's sake, bring her to the coven, even if it's just for school hours. She needs a magical environment to properly develop and to under-stand the secrecy required to protect herself and her loved ones."

Linda nodded slowly, tearing up. "I will… I will. I just… I wanted her to have a normal life, even if only for a couple of years."

"That's delusional, and you know it. Mina will never have a normal life," I replied, then felt a little bad when Linda seemed to get even sadder, close to weeping. "And that's not a bad thing at all," I added, giving her a half-smile. "A magical environment will nurture her more than a human school. She'll come out stronger from it. It's time you accept that, Mrs. Travis."

"I have no choice," she said, shrugging.

"Go be with your husband and daughter, Mrs. Travis. Astrid will instruct you on emergency scenarios, while Dylan and I finish warding your house. And thank you for your cooperation."

She smiled faintly and returned to the living room.

I had a couple of minutes to myself in there, enough to notice the small symbols etched into the corners of the glass windows. Linda was doing her part in keeping little Mina safe, but those were lightweight charms, the kind that kept poltergeists and other angry spirits out. They kept potential monsters away, too, in a similar fashion to ultrasound repellent devices that the humans used to fend off rats. Not always 100 percent successful. Still, had to give Linda props for trying.

They weren't a stellar magical family, from what I could tell, and from what I'd picked up from Alton's list and notes this morning. Well, except Mina. Linda and Evan Travis were both Mediocre, according to the info we had on them, which was probably why the Baltimore coven hadn't been all that strict about them keeping their pledge and had allowed them to go Neutral.

Movement in the backyard caught my eye.

I went outside and found a little boy sitting in the small white gazebo. He was probably around eight years old and... dead. His figure was translucent, as if he were just a mirage, a wisp of a being that had once walked this earth. I couldn't help but feel sorry for him, to have died so young, but I wasn't surprised to see him there.

As a Koldunya, I could see dead people everywhere. Most passed on, though I didn't know where. The ones who stayed behind had trouble letting go. They became ghosts, like this little boy. In rare instances and with some rare magical paraphernalia, I could summon the dead who had already moved on, but they never knew where they came from or what sort of place they were going back to. They were all spirits, echoes of the living. My ability was also tied to geography—I could only see and summon the ghosts of those who had died in my location. I was also able to use their abilities if they were magicals, but only if I let them enter my body, which was, more often than not, rather risky, especially since I wasn't yet an expert in the field.

The little boy watched me as I approached him, and frowned when he realized I could see him.

"Who are you?" he asked.

I glanced around. This was a typical backyard. Short grass, a plethora of flower bushes, a kiddy pool and small patio with a brick barbecue. Mina's toys were scattered all over: plastic flamingoes, rubber ducklings, and a pair of underwater goggles, for her little "exploratory" missions. I understood why Linda and Evan wanted Mina to hold on to her humanity—she could do more of this and experience the unadulterated joy of just being a kid. I got that.

"I'm Tatyana," I said to the little boy.

Judging by his clothes and haircut, he'd been an altar boy at some point. He'd died in the white robe. I could almost envision him during Sunday mass, his mom and dad present and proud of their little boy. I swallowed back tears, then sat in the gazebo next to him.

Unlike my family, I never had an easy time with dead people. Death was tragic, and I couldn't get over the sadness it instilled in me. My parents, my brothers, and everyone else in my family got used to it. Despite my pragmatism and cold nature, death was the one thing I failed to immunize myself against.

"You can see me," the boy replied.

"Yeah, I'm a little different. I'm a magical." I sighed.

"Like Mina."

"That's right. And her parents," I said.

"Yeah. But Mina's the strong one." The little boy chuckled. "She scares her mom and dad all the time with her tricks. They can't do what she does."

"No, they can't. So, you know about magicals, then?" I asked, and he nodded. "Were you a magical, too?"

He shook his head. "I was just a boy."

"How come you're still here?" I asked.

He shrugged. "I like it here. This used to be my house. I lived here with my mom and three sisters."

"Oh, wow, three sisters?" I exclaimed, smiling. He mirrored my expression, showing off a small gap between his front teeth. He was the sweetest little thing. "What's your name?"

"Will."

"What happened to you, Will? Do you remember?" I asked, my voice unsteady. This was always a difficult question to ask. Some spirits didn't remember, but most did, and it was never a good experience. They were mostly calm and resigned to their fate, in a way, even though ghosts were still stuck in this realm—but when they remembered their deaths, most became irritable, even angry and erratic. Some were so traumatized by what had happened to them that all they did was replay their death, over and over, on a heartbreaking loop. Those were death specters, and it took a lot of time spent as a ghost to degenerate into one.

Looking at Will, I wished I could say or do something to help him move on, before he, too, got lost in such a loop. There was no cure for ghosts. No way to make them disappear. They had to move on, or they got stuck in limbo. I used to ask the spirits that had passed on for advice—trying to find a way to help ghosts move on, too. But all I ever got was "let go." That didn't really help.

"Someone hurt me," he replied. "Someone like Mina. Powerful, but mean and evil."

My blood ran cold. A magical had killed him. "Do you remember when, Will?"

He shook his head once more. "It was too long ago. I lost track of time."

I would've loved to have more time to spend with him, but the dead weren't going anywhere. I, on the other hand, had other places to be and more magicals to protect. I put my hand out, smiling at him.

"Touch me," I said to him.

Will sighed, sadness settling in his round blue eyes. "I can't. It goes right through. I tried touching Mina and her parents and everybody else I came across, but I can't feel anything."

"Try it," I replied.

He frowned, then put his little hand over mine. I could feel him, cold and almost liquid. He gasped when he realized he could feel me, too. "Whoa. How are you doing that?"

"I'm a special kind of magical." I chuckled. "The dead can feel me. It's weird, I know, but many actually find it comforting."

"Yeah," he murmured, gently caressing my hand.

A magical had killed this beautiful little boy. The worst part was that Will had died here, or somewhere in the area. Without a time-frame, however, I couldn't make much of his circumstances.

"I need your help, Will," I said. He raised his eyebrows at me, genuinely curious. He seemed willing to help, most likely impressed by the fact that he could touch me. I always employed this little trick to gain a ghost's cooperation. It worked, most of the time. "Now that you've felt me, you can find me anywhere. Just think of me and call out my name, and I will hear you."

"Okay..."

"I need you to keep an eye on Mina for me," I added. "She may or may not be in danger. We don't know anything for sure yet. But I've charmed the house, and I was hoping you'd stick around and watch over her. If she's in trouble, just reach out to me."

He thought about it for a moment, then nodded. "It's because of the twins, huh?"

"You heard that?"

"Yeah. I saw and heard everything," he replied. "I always do, even through walls."

"Were you here when they came?"

"I was. But I couldn't really see them," Will said, his shoulders dropping in disappointment. "There was something about their faces... I can't describe it. Mina and her parents couldn't see it, or they would've screamed or gotten scared or something. But I'll tell you, their faces were made of... black smoke. And I couldn't hear what they were saying, either. It was all warbled, like a bad radio!"

This was an interesting account, to say the least. I already knew that ghosts could sometimes see what our eyes couldn't. That they could hear what we couldn't. Will's recollection made me think that the Ryder twins were more than just imposter magicals *maybe* working for Katherine Shipton. It didn't feel like such a leap, in my opinion, with what we'd recently been through, particularly since we knew that Finch wasn't her only "minion." No self-respecting evil-doer would work alone.

There was something about them—something that a ghost had registered. Digging through my memories, I remembered reading about charms that could conceal someone from spirits. Maybe the twins had used something similar. I would have to ask my mom about that, and such a phone call was never easy to make. Well, my mom didn't make it easy. Ever.

I didn't yet have the ability to see through a spirit's eyes. That was a rare and difficult power to attain, and it came with years of practice and all kinds of unsavory herbal cocktails. My mother kept pressuring me to go back to Moscow, so she could initiate me in the process, but I loved San Diego too much. I was just beginning to make friends, to build a life here. I didn't want to go back.

The Vasilis clan and I didn't exactly see eye-to-eye.

"Sorry I can't help you more," Will added, breaking my train of thought.

"Thank you," I replied gently. "It's okay. Take care of yourself, Will."

He smiled, watching me as I went back inside the house. Astrid had just finished briefing Linda and Evan, with Mina curiously listening. Dylan came downstairs, giving me a wink and a smile when he reached the ground floor. My heart skipped a beat. There was something about that boy. I felt... different around him, in the best way possible. I wasn't a Vasilis daughter or a Kolduny when I was around him. I was just Tatyana, and it was such a relief.

Of course, I didn't let him know that. I didn't want him to be aware of the effect he had on me. That was my little secret.

"House is double-checked and warded," he announced.

"Good, we should go," I replied as we went back inside the living room. "We still have families to visit. Oh, and by the way, I just had a brief chat with a kid who died here. Killed by a magical, but I'll fill you in on the details later... And I think it's best not to mention it to the parents at all. I might just end up scaring them over something that could turn out to be really old news. They have enough on their plate." I didn't yet know when Will had died, but I was going to find out—provided, of course, that his death had made it into some news or records.

Dylan nodded. "All right."

Whoever or whatever the Ryder twins were, I wanted to make sure we could catch them. Whatever their intentions, I was dead set on finding out. If they were after Mina and the other magical kids, they'd have to deal with us.

Most importantly, if they were in any way involved with Katherine Shipton, they were in a lot of trouble with me, personally. That witch had already ruined so many lives, especially Harley's. Magic was Chaos and wonder, light and darkness, fire and ice, laughter and tears—a mixture of everything, but always in a splendid balance. What Katherine was doing, through Finch and his gargoyles, through the strings of murders and plotting against our community... it was filthy and obscene.

And I wasn't going to have any of it.

EIGHT

Harley

Contrary to what I'd expected, Alton wasn't all that furious about my intervention. I didn't hear the entire conversation he'd had with Wade over the phone, but I didn't hear any shouting. That, in my book, was a good sign.

According to Wade, Alton had protested the idea at first, then stopped and rethought the whole thing, in light of these Ryder twins. He'd agreed to let the magical children stay with their families, human or otherwise, so long as we placed charms and traps to notify us of any magical occurrences. These families were our best bet to catch the Ryder twins, and he doubted they'd come after them inside the coven. Alton didn't say if he knew who the Ryder twins were, but he was going to give Astrid the clearance she needed to do a nationwide search for them.

Personally, I was still worried about my decision. Maybe it would've been better if we took the kids with us, after all. Angry at myself over my own inconsistency, I didn't say much during our next visit. I let Wade take the lead as he told the parents what was going on with their child, since they were humans and had no idea what a magical was.

After a barrage of questions and voiced concerns, we managed to get them to send their son to the coven on a daily basis, while Santana left charms and traps, as per the new protocol. The Orisha she'd left with Micah was more for Santana's peace of mind, as she'd quickly become fond of the boy. She couldn't leave one at every house, since there were only so many with her to begin with.

What we were doing wasn't exactly ethical, since the parents didn't know about any rumors regarding Katherine Shipton, or that anyone else might be coming for their kids—yet this family had been secretly visited by the Ryder twins, too.

We found the card in their hallway, stuck in the mirror frame. Just like with the Cranstons, the Ledermeyers had no recollection of such a visit taking place. Only then did we manage to establish a pattern, based on intel from Tatyana, Dylan, and Astrid's second family visit, where the parents were magicals, like the Travises.

"The Ryder twins engage the magical parents and try to get them to hand their kids over, politely, and not in a persistent or disturbing manner," Wade said as we drove through a familiar neighborhood. "They leave the card, their names. They're seen and remembered. Whereas, with the human parents, they don't interact. My guess is that they sneak in and leave the card."

"As a message to us?" Santana asked from behind.

"I guess so, since they claim to be from the San Diego Coven," Wade replied, looking at the twins' business card. "We were apparently supposed to find the cards. I think they must have some kind of magical pull. Otherwise, what guarantee would there be that we'd even notice them in the houses during a visit? They're not placed in the most obvious of spots, yet here we are, finding them."

"Who could these people be?" Raffe asked, still playing games on his phone. He seemed sullen and distracted, not his usual calm and friendly self. I'd seen him like this before, but I never knew why he experienced these sudden mood changes. My instinct told me to leave him alone, though, so I did.

"Impostors. But definitely magicals. My money's on Katherine

Shipton. It coincides with the rumors we've heard, don't you think?" Santana replied with a shrug.

"Which makes me all the more uneasy to leave the kids in their homes," Wade said, giving me a sideways glance.

I had nothing to say to that. He was right, and I felt bad about it, but, at the same time, I knew and understood the importance of capturing Katherine Shipton before she did more harm to the magical community. She'd almost killed us all with Finch's help. It was safe to assume that she would try the same or worse the second time around.

Ugh, my life was already complicated enough, before I opened my damn mouth.

I looked out and noticed St. Clair's Café just half a block down the road. My face lit up, remembering the second reason I'd chosen to come with Wade, Santana, and Raffe to this side of town. The Smiths lived nearby, and I hadn't seen them in a while—before my induction into the coven and its cornucopia of weird and potentially deadly, to be precise.

Ryann was away at UCLA, so I figured they'd welcome a visit from their foster daughter instead.

"Can we stop at the café for a break? There's someone I need to see nearby," I said, pointing at St. Clair's.

Wade frowned. "Who do you need to see?"

"My foster parents. I just want to drop by and check in on them, that's all. Fifteen minutes, tops. I promise!" I replied, putting on my most innocent puppy face.

"I could use a break and a bagel," Santana chimed in.

"I need coffee," Raffe added, his voice low and gruff. It was a tad weird, as if it wasn't really Raffe talking. I'd heard it before over the past few weeks, but never for long enough to make me worry. Santana and Wade didn't show any signs of concern. I was definitely intrigued, making a mental note to find the courage and a good moment to ask him about his abilities as a warlock. Those glimmering red eyes I'd seen earlier were definitely involved.

"Fine. You've got twenty minutes, Merlin," Wade commanded, pulling over just outside the café.

"Make it thirty. There's always a line for the bakery," I pleaded, as we got out of the car. "I can't go to the Smiths empty-handed."

Wade rolled his eyes and motioned for me to go ahead. He didn't say anything, so I took his gesture as a "Whatever." Worked for me.

I left him, Raffe, and Santana at one of the tables outside, while I went in and grabbed three lattes and a small pastry basket, complete with scones and banana walnut bread—Mrs. Smith's favorites, and always a good bribe whenever I needed a favor. They also worked as a peace offering, and I'd had to get her plenty of those for my somewhat turbulent two years in prep school.

This time, however, they were just a heartfelt gift, something I knew would put a smile on Mrs. Smith's face and would save Mr. Smith the trouble of brewing more coffee before lunch.

When Mrs. Smith opened the door and saw me, she let out a gasp, then beamed like a nuclear reactor.

"Harley!" she croaked, a broad smile stretching her lips. "What a joy! What brings you here, honey? It's been a while!"

That was her way of saying, *"I've missed you, and where the heck have you been, child?!"*

I laughed as she leaned forward and kissed my cheeks. She then relieved me of the pastry basket, her eyes twinkling with delight.

"I know, and I'm sorry!" I replied. "I've been insanely busy lately, but I was in the area with work, so I thought I'd pop by and say hello."

I followed her inside the house as she led the way into the open-plan kitchen and dining room. This was still one of the best and most decent houses I'd lived in. It was simple and tastefully decorated in a pale blue and beige palette, with hardwood flooring and Art Nouveau lighting. The furniture was all sturdy and functional, and every surface had a little statuette or trinket box or anything that could serve as a decorative object. There was a reason why Ryann and I had gone to such a design-oriented prep school. Mrs. Smith had also been a student there.

Mr. Smith was in the kitchen, wiping his hands with a dry cloth. Over by the counter island stood a teenage boy in cream cargo pants and a pale blue polo shirt—the preppy uniform belonging to the same school. Ryann and I had worn cream skirts, which we'd both hated with the fire of a thousand suns. Looking back now, I understood why Ryann had been so quick to change to pantsuits in college.

"Well, it's a pleasure to have you here!" Mrs. Smith replied as she put the basket on the counter island, right in front of the boy. He seemed equally dazzled by banana walnut bread, from what I could tell and feel in my tummy. Either that, or he was just hungry. Mrs. Smith took the coffees away, helping herself to one and handing the second over to the boy.

She pointed at the third. "Harley, you're getting that one. Dad here needs to cut down on the caffeine!"

I chuckled, just as Mr. Smith hugged me, equally thrilled to see me. "Oh, Harley, glad to have you back! We've missed you!"

"I know... I'm sorry. I promise I'll visit more often," I said, relishing the feel of his fatherly embrace. With everything I'd learned over the past month, I needed this. So much.

As soon as I stepped back, however, I noticed the slight awkwardness in the room. There was always love in this place, and happy thoughts lingered from these people, but this time, it was a little different. The young man was excited and nervous—mostly because of me. We looked at each other for a little while as Mr. and Mrs. Smith exchanged glances.

"Harley, I want you to meet Jacob," Mrs. Smith said.

I shook the boy's hand and found myself instantly flooded by a mixture of adolescent emotions— hormonal angst, curiosity and concern. The latter was a feeling I hadn't felt since I'd first set foot in the Smiths' house. He was afraid he'd get carted off to another family. Jacob was a foster kid, like me. I could feel it in my bones.

"You're fostering again," I murmured, giving Jacob a warm smile. "I'm Harley. Also a black garbage bag kid."

"Oh," Jacob replied, genuinely surprised. "You... You're *the* Harley."

I laughed as Mr. Smith took out some plates from the cupboard and proceeded to serve up the scones and banana walnut bread slices. "*The* Harley? I take it I'm still famous in this household?"

"Of course!" Mrs. Smith exclaimed. "We always gush about you!"

"Harley, by the way, I ran into Malcolm at the grocery store the other day," Mr. Smith interjected. "He said you're working with Homeland Security now? Did I hear that right, sweetie?"

"I forgot y'all know each other," I said, wearing a nervous smile. Surprisingly, I wasn't the one on edge in that room. Jacob was close to screaming and running away, from what I was feeling.

Jeez, kid. What's gotten you so shaken up?

"Yeah, he was sorry to see you leave the casino job. I was surprised, actually," Mr. Smith replied. "I thought you loved that place! I mean, for your gap year, anyway."

"Speaking of which, have you decided on any colleges yet, honey?" Mrs. Smith asked. "Remember, our offer to help you with your tuition still stands. I know you want your financial independence and whatnot, but we do have a little set aside. Don't fall into some student loan trap, okay?"

I smiled. How could I not love these people when they were so kind and generous, and had always treated me as their own?

"I'm okay for now," I said. "I haven't decided on a school yet, but my worst-case scenario is another gap year until I make up my mind. I'm homing in on a career choice, though, and this Homeland Security gig has definitely opened up some new horizons for me."

"That's so good to hear, sweetie!" Mrs. Smith replied. "I guess this new job will definitely look good on any college application, right?"

"Oh, absolutely," I murmured. I felt bad for lying to them, but they deserved to be ignorant of everything magical. The whole secrecy thing was beginning to make a lot more sense to me, especially after my struggles with Finch and the gargoyles. There were creatures out there that these wonderful people didn't need to know about.

I looked at Jacob, irked by his stretched nerves. "You don't have to worry about me, dude, I'm not a narc or anything," I said to him, grinning. "I'm just an agent in training. We deal with domestic and foreign terrorists, not unruly teenagers."

Mr. and Mrs. Smith both laughed. Jacob only gave me a weak smile.

"So, when did you decide to foster again?" I asked Mrs. Smith.

"Oh, a few weeks ago," she replied, putting a slender arm around Jacob. The Smiths were beautiful people in their late forties, much like those stylish couples in American fashion catalogs—the handsome, mid-forties couples who wore cardigans and played tennis on Sunday.

In an eerie but sweet contrast, Jacob was remarkably different. The Smiths were both blond-haired and brown-eyed, tall and slim and perfectly tanned. Jacob was slightly shorter than me, stocky but toned, with long black hair and hazel-green eyes. His cheekbones and caramel skin tone had some serious Native American influences, but there was also Latino blood in this boy.

"Jacob is sixteen, and he just enrolled at your school," Mr. Smith said, giving Jacob a warm smile. "He's been with us for two weeks now."

Jacob nodded slowly. "Yeah."

"Well, tell you what, Jake—mind if I call you Jake?" I asked. He smiled. That was my okay to chop his name up for my verbal comfort. "Tell you what, Jake, you're the luckiest boy in the San Diego foster system. The Smiths are amazing."

Jacob chuckled. He was so shy but so eager to fit in, to settle, and to be loved. Everything he felt, I'd felt, too. He needed patience and encouragement, understanding and nurturing, and the Smiths were definitely the right people to do that.

"I know. They've been so great," he said.

"Aw, honey, you deserve it and more!" Mrs. Smith replied, dropping a kiss on his temple.

"Do you know anything about your biological parents?" I asked him, nagged by his underlying feeling of guilt and fear. Jacob was worried about something, and, judging by how bright and jovial the Smiths were, he hadn't spoken to them about whatever it was.

Jacob shook his head. "Never met them. Don't know their names," he said, his voice lower than usual. I sensed deception, but I didn't want to make a scene.

I was planning to dig into his past later, anyway. For now, I settled on getting to know him better and reading his emotions. I hadn't seen the Smiths in months. The last thing I wanted was to start an unpleasant conversation based on my Empathy, which they had no idea about, anyway. I, too, was lying to them, after all.

"Well, you're in good hands now, young man," Mr. Smith replied before motioning for the door. "Now, grab your bag and let's go. Your coach will kill us if we're late again!"

Jacob gave him an enthusiastic smile, then picked up his lacrosse stick and training bag off the floor. Mr. Smith hugged me again and kissed the top of my head.

"It's Jacob's third practice with Coach Mueller," he explained. "You know how tardiness gets his pants in a twist!"

I laughed. "Hah, the old tortoise is still kicking, huh?"

"Harley!" Mrs. Smith gasped, in a delicate attempt to reprimand me.

I gave her a shrug, noticing Jacob's amusement. He knew what I was talking about. "What? He does look like a tortoise."

Mr. Smith chuckled, grabbed one of the pastry plates, waved us goodbye, and walked out, followed by Jacob, who gave me a brief glance over the shoulder. A few seconds later, the front door closed behind them. Jacob was definitely worried about something, but I wasn't sure what. I was going to find out, though. Covertly. Behind the Smiths' backs. Like the sneaky little devil that I'd become...

Mrs. Smith kept smiling at me, and her affection filled me with warmth. Ryann had inherited more than her good looks; kindness ran in the family.

"What?" I asked, blushing.

"You are getting even more beautiful, honey," she replied, before taking a bite out of a scone and moaning with sheer pleasure. "My God, these are amazing. St. Clair's, huh?"

"Just around the corner," I said with a grin. "And thank you."

"How've you been, Harley? Something's different about you."

Leave it to Mrs. Smith to read me like an open book!

I couldn't tell her everything, but I could at least share one important update with her. "I found my biological parents," I said.

She stilled, her eyes wide with shock. "Oh, wow... Who are they?"

"Were. They're both dead," I replied, my voice trembling slightly. "Hester and Hiram Merlin. They were from New York. I'm not sure how I ended up in San Diego, but... at least I know where I come from."

"Honey. I'm so sorry." Mrs. Smith sighed, putting the scone down and taking my hands in hers. I welcomed the instant flow of affection. There wasn't pity there, but rather sadness. She would've wanted me to find my parents alive and well, without worrying about competition. She knew she'd been an amazing mom for the two years that she and her husband had me. They'd always own a huge piece of my heart.

"It's okay. I got closure, I guess," I said, giving her a weak smile. "So, tell me about Jacob! What's he like?"

Mrs. Smith instantly deflated. Mild sadness poured through me like a cold shower.

"He's a wonderful kid, you know?" she replied. "He's quiet, doesn't get into any trouble. Smart as a whip! But... I think he went through something. I think he had some bad experiences before, Harley. Like, really bad."

"What makes you say that?"

"He's got crippling night terrors. He wakes up screaming and sweating," Mrs. Smith explained. "I tried to talk to him about it. I spoke to Social Services, too, but they couldn't tell me anything. They said his last foster mom died, which was why he went back into the system, but that he'd been treated well, and that he was always on his best behavior. I don't know, maybe Social Services wasn't aware or something. You know how abusers can be, hiding in plain sight and deceiving everyone."

I nodded. "Yeah. All too well. How did his previous foster mom die, though?"

"I think it was a heart attack or a stroke. One of the two. It was sudden. No one saw what happened."

"Maybe Jacob is still recovering from that. It can be traumatic to lose a good foster parent, you know," I muttered, glancing around the kitchen. I smiled at the sight of souvenir fridge magnets. Half of those Ryann had collected during her European trips. I recognized Mrs. Smith's handwriting on a shopping list, caught under one of the magnets. I had so many good memories of this place, and I found myself wanting the same for Jacob.

"I get that, but I think there's more to it than that. I don't know, call it a mother's intuition," Mrs. Smith replied, then put on a pleading puppy dog face. I knew I'd learned that from someone... "Harley, can you help me?"

I blinked several times. Hope blossomed in my chest. That was all hers. "If I can, sure."

"Come by more often. Spend some time with Jacob whenever you can," she said, squeezing my hands. "You still have the house keys. You don't even have to announce that you're coming. Just pop by once in a while, play a video game with him. Take him out for ice cream or something. I think he'll be more likely to open up to you as a foster kid than me, the oblivious suburban mom," she added, laughing lightly. "I'm thinking he'll at least feel better if he talks about it. I don't need to know what happened, if I'm being honest. I just want him to forget the past and look into the future. I want Jacob to sleep well at night and live a better life here with us."

Her request kind of floored me. It also made me feel incredibly important and responsible, all of a sudden. Deep down, I liked it. I would've loved a little brother while growing up. Most of the kids I got attached to never stayed in my life for too long. Maybe Jacob was different.

The fear and guilt I'd caught from him did warrant my curiosity and concern. Assuming these emotions were linked to his night terrors, I figured I could at least try to help the boy. I owed it to the Smiths for having been such good parents, and I owed it to Jacob, too, in a way. Mrs. Smith was right. He deserved a good shot at life.

Getting rid of whatever skeletons were in his closet sounded like the right way to get started.

"Okay. I'll do it," I replied.

In less than a millisecond, Mrs. Smith had her arms wrapped around me. "Thank you, sweetie. Thank you so much. You are a great sister to Ryann, and I know you'll be an even better sister to Jacob."

I melted in her embrace, overwhelmed by the pure love and positivity oozing out of this woman. She could be really intense sometimes, but she was a beam of sunshine in my life. So, yeah, stopping by to talk to the kid once in a while wasn't an issue for me. After everything the Smiths had given me, it was the least I could do.

NINE

Tatyana

There was something odd about the Hellers' house. I could tell from the moment we got out of Dylan's silver Prius, for which we never ceased to torment him.

The house itself was nice and in the local suburban style, with two levels, a few palm trees framing the stony pathway, and flowers bursting through the front yard. Nothing out of the ordinary. But there was a vibe that just didn't sit well with me, as if the air was thick and eager to suffocate me.

Astrid and Dylan didn't seem affected. I brushed the feeling away for the time being, blaming the uneasiness on my previous encounter with the ghost of little Will—whose death was beginning to nag me. On the way here, I'd used my smartphone to briefly check for any news about a kid's murder at Mina's house, but I'd found nothing. Astrid had also put a search through Smartie, but no results had come up yet.

"Maria and Damian Heller," Dylan said, reading out loud from the file. "They're fostering Kenneth Willow, aged seventeen. His parents died in a car crash when he was twelve, and he had no immediate family, so he wound up in the system."

"If I'm not mistaken, there were reports of objects flying around in his presence, right?" I asked, while Astrid continued to work on her Smartie tablet. She was trying different keywords through the local database, while waiting for Alton to send her the clearance codes for the national database.

Dylan nodded. "Yeah. Plus some violent incidents at school, but most were attributed to a couple of kids with mental problems."

I knocked once and waited patiently with Dylan and Astrid by my side.

"Do you think they're home?" Astrid asked, her eyes glued to the screen.

"Their car is here," I said, pointing at the Chrysler in the small driveway. I knocked a second time, this time loudly enough to startle some birds in a nearby bush. "They're home."

It took a third knock to hear footsteps in the hallway.

The door opened, and we were greeted by Maria Heller. She was a Latina woman, a buxom beauty wearing a white shirt and casual jeans, with her long black hair caught in a tight bun. Her wide brown eyes fixed on me for a moment, but her expression was firm and… blank.

"Can I help you?" she asked, her tone clipped.

"Hi, Mrs. Heller?" I replied. She nodded and crossed her arms. I noticed her hands shaking. A little red light went on in my head. "I'm Tatyana Jones, and these are my colleagues, Dylan and Astrid," I said, following the fake last name protocol as I flashed my ID card. "We're from Social Services. We're doing our monthly visit, and we thought we'd stop by to see how you were doing."

She frowned. That was never a good sign. "We had Social Services come in on Wednesday. You guys getting confused now, or what?"

"This is a follow-up visit," I replied calmly, watching her expression. "Mind if we come in?"

Maria thought about it for a second, then sighed and motioned for us to follow her inside.

"Kenneth! Social Services is here!" she called out as she advanced through the hallway. She stopped and looked to her left. Her nostrils flared before she put on a faint smile. "There you are, sweeties."

She went into the living room. As soon as we joined her, I got that nagging feeling in my chest again—this time threatening to gnaw at my stomach. The living room area was decorated in a hacienda style. I recognized the arches and walnut furniture. I'd seen a similar arrangement back in my parents' summer house, on the outskirts of Mexico City.

In the middle, stiffly seated in a leather armchair, was Damian Heller, wearing a white polo shirt and what I lovingly referred to as "dad jeans." On the sofa, casually leaning on its left arm, was Kenneth Willow. Kenneth caught my eye—his outfit was crisp and neat, with starched cream pants, a white shirt, and beige vest, complete with a dark red bowtie. His reddish hair was combed back and loaded with styling gel, and his bright green eyes darted from me to Dylan and Astrid, then back to me.

He put on a broad smile as Maria stood with her arms crossed.

"Hi, I'm Kenneth!" the seventeen-year-old magical said.

I knew he was a magical for sure because of the small gem mounted on his bowtie. It was bright red, but it had a strange white glimmer. I'd learned to spot an Esprit before anyone else. This wasn't an inexperienced warlock. This one had found his Esprit.

"I'm Tatyana, and these are Dylan and Astrid. It's a pleasure to meet you," I replied, mirroring his friendly expression.

"What brings you here?" he asked. He looked at his mother and nodded at the spare seat next to him. Maria sat down next to him, keeping her slightly shaking hands in her lap and her eyes fixed on a random spot on the coffee table in front of them. "Social Services was already here. We're doing fine."

"I know, Kenneth. We're just here to follow up, that's all. We take great care to make sure that the children we place in foster homes are well looked after," I said. "Mind if I ask who visited you from Social Services on Wednesday?"

Damian was quiet as a tomb, beads of sweat trickling down his temples. He stared at me with what looked like crippling fear, despite his faint smile. Something was definitely wrong with this picture, and I didn't want to start trouble without knowing *what* was wrong.

Kenneth seemed strangely relaxed and cold compared to his foster parents.

"They asked the usual questions. You know, am I being treated well? Am I happy? How is my school life? What's it like at home? How many meals a day? Yadda, yadda, yadda." He chuckled. "Everything is okay here. My new mom and dad take great care of me and I, in return, look after them."

I caught a glimpse of Maria as she gave Kenneth a sideways glance. All of a sudden, I regretted not bringing Harley with us. She could always read a room better than anyone. *The perks of being an Empath.*

"Mind if my colleagues sit down?" I asked, pointing at the spare two-seater on the other side of the coffee table.

"Oh, by all means, please do," Kenneth replied, wearing that annoying plastic smile.

I'd met enough people in my life to know when someone was trying to lead me on. Kenneth was still younger than me. He'd yet to fully master the art of deception, but he was definitely well versed in it.

Dylan and Astrid occupied the two-seater, while I remained standing. I moved farther to my left, where the fireplace was. The mantelpiece was loaded with family photos and various trinkets collected mostly from Mexico—I recognized the colorful patterns and designs. The Hellers were eager Mexico vacationers, from what I could tell. They'd taken Kenneth with them, too, judging by the photos, but their postures and smiles were strained in those particular snapshots.

"Can you tell me the names of the Social Services employees who visited you?" I asked, my eyes fixed on a small marble bowl. There was a card there. The symbol was all too familiar. I picked it up between two fingers, then handed it to Dylan.

"Jane and John. But I forget their last names," Kenneth said. "Nice people, though. Really nice. They gave me a voucher for Wendy's."

I nodded slowly, watching Dylan's expression change as he reached the same conclusion—the Ryders had been here. He showed the Hellers the card. "Cheapskates. Have you spoken to these people?"

Damian frowned and shook his head.

"No," Maria replied.

"But they were here," I said.

Maria shrugged. "No, they weren't. I don't know where that came from. It doesn't look familiar to me."

"Kenneth, have you spoken to anyone named Emily and Emmett Ryder, by any chance? Did they give you this card?" I asked, shifting my focus back to the young magical.

His eyebrows arched upward. "No. That's strange. I wonder who left that there..."

Maria shot to her feet, suddenly switching into a friendly-house-wife-mode. "Would anyone like some horchata? I've just made a fresh, whole pitcher."

"I'd love some, thank you," I said, smiling.

She nearly flew out of the living room, while I kept my eyes on Kenneth and Damian. Damian couldn't even look at his foster son. I would've given anything to have Harley with us, at that point.

"So, Kenneth, what school are you enrolled in?" I asked.

"Gompers Prep," he replied. "I love it there. Everyone is nice. I'm on the debate team and on the baseball team! There's also a girl I like. I'm happy here."

Ugh, I wasn't buying it. It was as if he was trying a little too hard to convince me that everything was okay. My stomach was churning, and Dylan didn't seem convinced, either.

"Have you thought about college yet?" Dylan asked him.

"I'm sorry to interrupt, and sorry to ask," I interjected, "but is it okay if I use your bathroom?" I giggled, employing the bubblegum-blonde demeanor. That was always a good distraction. "I've had too much coffee."

Kenneth chuckled, then pointed at the hallway. "Sure! It's right next to the kitchen."

"Thank you!" I replied, then left the living room behind me and headed straight for the kitchen. I heard muffled voices behind me—Kenneth speaking to Dylan, and Astrid asking something, followed by Kenneth's answer.

I slipped through the kitchen door and found Maria there, struggling with an horchata pitcher. She was shaking like a leaf.

"Hi," I whispered. Even so, she was startled and nearly dropped the whole thing. I rushed over to her side and gently removed the pitcher from her trembling hands. "Sorry, I didn't mean to scare you. I was just—"

"You have to help us!" Maria breathed, her face pale and eyes filled with horror. "Kenneth... There's something horribly wrong with him."

"Whoa," I managed, then put the pitcher down altogether. "What's wrong?"

"He... He's lost his mind. I... I don't know how to explain it. He's been with us for a year now. And we knew he was... well, different. I have no better word for that. He scared us sometimes, but we managed to get along."

"What do you mean by 'different'?" I asked, trying to get her to tell me herself, though I was already suspecting what she was going to say.

"Oh, God, you're going to think I'm crazy! Listen, there's something wrong with this boy, and we've tried. We really tried, but... we can't anymore, and we can't get him out of our lives, either. He's holding us captive here. You have to help us. Call the police, the National Guard, the Army—whoever can help us, please!"

"Mrs. Heller, take a deep breath," I replied, keeping my voice low. I could still hear them talking in the living room, which gave me the window I needed to move things along. "Your son is special, isn't he? As in… not all that human."

She froze. She knew exactly what I was talking about.

"You've seen what he can do?" she croaked.

"Move objects with his mind?" I replied, aiming for the ballpark on this one.

"Listen to me… Listen very carefully. We are not bad people," she said. "We saw what he could do, and we kept it a secret. We wanted to keep him, to raise him as our son. He could be difficult sometimes, but we managed. It's true, he scared Damian now and then, but we talked about it. We fixed it. Then, two days ago, those people you asked about came by."

"The Ryder twins?"

She shook her head. "Jane and John… something. They said they were from Social Services, and that they wanted to talk to Kenneth, so… we gave them some privacy." Tears streamed down her cheeks. She was close to unraveling completely.

"Then what happened?" I asked, needing to keep her focused while I tried to start devising an action plan. This had the Ryder twins written all over it, despite the fake names.

"I don't know, but it's like they flipped a switch in him!" Maria murmured. My heart broke to see her in such a state. It reminded me why it was so important for us to have secrecy and rules, as magicals. There was no better example than this, really. "He went full psycho. We haven't been able to leave the house in two days. He put something in our food or our drinks… I don't know what, but when he goes out, we're paralyzed. We can't even speak! And when he's back, he torments us. He curses and beats us," she added, pulling up her sleeves.

My blood curdled at the sight of her cuts and bruises. Kenneth was downright savage.

"Oh, boy," I mumbled, feeling the rage course through my veins. "Did he say anything? As to why he's acting like this?"

She scoffed. "He says there's a new era coming. That he's going to be so powerful with *Chaos* in his favor, that he doesn't have to try so hard to be nice, that he can do whatever the hell he wants, and that nobody can stop him. He... He says the craziest things. He talks about witches and warlocks, and about how he'll kill all of them if they don't get in line, that—"

"That's quite a loose tongue you have on you, Ma." Kenneth's voice cut through the room.

My joints and muscles stiffened, and I realized the worst-case scenario I'd thought of was already happening. Maria yelped as an invisible force threw her backward and over the counter. She slammed into the dinner table, rolled over it, and landed on the marble floor, accompanied by broken glasses and a vase that she'd inadvertently taken with her.

Kenneth stood in the kitchen doorway, his index and middle finger pointed in our direction. The grin on his face sent chills down my spine. The gem on his bowtie sparkled red now. I took a deep breath, trying to get a feel for any spirits that could be hovering nearby. With no one around, I still had my Telekinesis to use against his.

"So, you lied to us," I remarked, my tone flat.

Kenneth rolled his eyes at me. "Obviously. The Ryders told me you'd be coming soon," he replied. "I made quite a mess in school, so you were bound to be notified."

"You know who we are, then."

He sneered. "Yeah, and I gotta say, not impressed."

I raised my hand to deliver a mental attack, but he was much faster than I'd expected for a seventeen-year-old. With one flick of his wrist, he had me up against the wall, an invisible force choking the life out of me.

"Son of a—" I grunted, struggling to release myself. *"Dukhi, vykhodyat! Dukhi, ty mne nuzhen!"* I managed to call out in my native Russian, summoning whatever spirits were in the area. One of them had to hear me. Otherwise I was screwed.

I heard Maria moaning on the other side of the kitchen counter island. I couldn't see her, but from the sound of crackling glass scratching the floor, I knew she was trying to move.

Kenneth tightened his Telekinetic grip on me, then tossed me across the room and smacked me into another wall. The impact knocked the air out of my lungs. For a second, everything went white.

"Dukhi, vykhodyat!" I cried out. *"Dukhi—"*

Dylan roared as he tackled Kenneth. Suddenly, I was free. I fell on my knees, coughing and wheezing and relishing each deep breath that I was still able to take. Dylan fought Kenneth like the athlete that he was, pounding him with his fists until blood sprayed out of Kenneth's nose.

Kenneth wasn't done, though. He kicked Dylan in the groin and pressed his palm against Dylan's forehead. My arms were weak. I could barely move.

"Magicis, ecce ego bestia tua!" Kenneth chanted.

"Oh, no," I murmured.

Latin spells in the hands of a psycho like Kenneth Willow were never good.

Dylan's eyes lit up yellow as he stilled. His strange gaze found mine, and I knew, at that moment, that I was officially and royally screwed. That was some old school hexing that Kenneth had whipped out. The kind that we'd learned was forbidden for being lethal.

Kenneth snickered and nudged Dylan to the side. Fear crippled me as I realized what was going on. Dylan growled like an animal, baring his teeth at me. His yellow eyes seemed slightly bigger, red veins popping around the eyelids.

"Yeah, so. I'll let this mutt take care of you," Kenneth said. "Enjoy the remaining thirty seconds of your life, witch!"

"Kenneth, don't do this!" I snapped. "Whatever the Ryders told you, it's not true."

I managed to slowly get up as Dylan moved closer. He wasn't himself anymore. He'd been turned into a mindless beast, and he was about to pounce and tear me apart.

"I'll be late for my appointment if I waste another minute here and, well, serving a future Child of Chaos does require some punctuality. Don't want to make a bad impression."

"Kenneth, don't!" I shouted after him, but he was already on the run, dashing toward the kitchen back door that led into the yard.

I launched a mental lasso at him, catching his ankle, and snapped him back. He fell flat on his face, groaning from the pain, and I managed to drag him back several feet before Dylan came at me. I had no choice. I had to let Kenneth go.

I focused my Telekinetic ability on Dylan instead. I pushed a barrier out, forcing him back as he grunted and snarled, clawing at the invisible shield.

Kenneth chuckled as he slipped out the back door.

I was so angry and distraught, I couldn't even focus properly. Seeing Dylan like that filled me with dread, mainly because I had no idea how to subdue him. He was insanely strong already as a magical, but this hexed-beast-mode made him even worse.

He broke through my mental barrier and lunged at me. I dodged and jumped to the side, just as Dylan crashed into the kitchen counter.

"Dammit, Dylan!" I called out to him, the real him, stuck somewhere inside his cursed head. "Dylan, I know you can hear me! You have to fight it!"

Dylan pulled himself away from the broken counter and came at me again. I tried to push him away with my Telekinesis, but he was too fast.

Before I could do anything else, he had me up against the wall, his hand gripping my throat and crushing my trachea.

"You've got to be kidding me," I croaked, struggling to breathe again. There was definitely a pattern in this scene, and it involved me getting choked to death.

I would've been the biggest embarrassment of the Vasilis clan if I let myself go down like that. My parents weren't even going to bother with a tombstone for my sorry ass.

The worst part was that I couldn't bring myself to kill Dylan. I could reach out and perform the worst act that a Kolduny could do. I could rip the spirit from his body—but that would not only take a dark toll on my own soul, it would also remove Dylan from this world.

A voice in my head begged me not to do it, and I couldn't understand why. In any other circumstance, I would've resorted to *udaleniye dukkha*, or "spirit removal," but I just... *I can't.*

"Dylan... Please," I tried again, my eyes rolling back. I was about to pass out. "Don't make me do this... Please, fight it!"

He tightened his grip on my throat. Everything went white again.

I summoned the last droplet of energy I had left, to do the unthinkable. My survival instinct had kicked in, and I could no longer ignore it, at the same time hating myself for having to do this.

Then I heard a loud clang.

A second later, I was on the floor, slumped on my side, coughing and wheezing once more. I blinked rapidly until I could see clearly again, holding my bruised throat. My skin burned where Dylan had gripped me.

Dylan was unconscious, lying on his back just a couple of feet away. Maria stood in front of us, panting, with a bleeding gash on her forehead. She firmly held a large frying pan in her hands. She'd smacked Dylan over the head with it.

Astrid rushed into the kitchen. She'd been assaulted, too, from the looks of her. Her lip was split and bleeding, and there were several small cuts on the side of her face.

"Oh, God, are you okay, Taty?!" She dropped to her knees next to me.

I nodded. "I... Yeah, for the most part. What the hell happened to you?"

"Mr. Heller happened," she managed, then looked up at Maria. "I'm sorry, Mrs. Heller, I had to knock him out. Kenneth did something to him."

Maria was shell-shocked, holding the pan and simply paralyzed.

"Did it involve a Latin chant?" I asked, regaining my breath.

"Yes! Where did Kenneth go?" Astrid replied, fearfully looking around.

"He's gone. He ran off," I said, and pointed at Dylan. "He did the same to Dylan. We need to tie them both down. I'm not sure conking them on the head stopped the hex."

Astrid fumbled through my jacket pockets and fished my phone out. "Mine got broken, sorry," she murmured, then dialed a coven emergency number that she'd already memorized by now. This wasn't her first rodeo.

"Maria, are you okay?" I raised my voice. It was enough to pull her back to reality.

She looked down at me. "No. But I'll live." She sighed and put the pan down.

"Okay. Good. Now, listen to me," I said firmly. "Do you have any cable ties in the house? Or really strong tape or rope? Or all of the above?"

She nodded.

"Hi, Astrid here. I need a cleanup crew and a containment unit at 14 Groveland Drive," Astrid said to whoever picked up on the other end of the line. "Yeah, we've got a magical spill. A rogue warlock on the loose, too. Kenneth Willow, seventeen. Yes. One of our own and one of the parents were hexed. Okay, we'll wait."

"Yeah, in the garage," Maria said, answering my question.

"Okay, Maria, I need you to get all of them in here," I replied.

"All of them?" she asked.

Astrid put the phone down, then grabbed a kitchen towel and came back to my side to wipe the blood from my face. I could feel it trickling down the top of my head. I'd gotten thrown around like a rag doll, after all.

"Yes, Maria. We need to tie your husband and my friend down before they come to." I sighed.

"Well, this is a mess," Astrid quipped.

"Yeah, I didn't think fostering would be so difficult," Maria mumbled as she walked out of the kitchen.

I felt sorry for her. But I was much more concerned about Dylan at this point. Whatever that hex was, it wasn't going to go away with plain head trauma. My stomach churned and my heart hurt. What would it take to get our Dylan back?

Most importantly, I knew for a fact that we were dealing with a whole new kind of trouble here. Those Ryder twins weren't just impersonating Social Services or coven staff. They were flat out recruiting young magicals and trying to take them away from us.

Their tactics made me wonder, though. There was a methodical approach here, and it differed from one family to another. If they were drawing magicals to the dark side, they were employing some very personalized strategies.

In Kenneth Willow's case, their approach had worked.

TEN

Harley

W e all met back at the coven inside the Bestiary.
After we heard what happened to Dylan and Damian
Heller, we were told to return from our field assignments. A
cleanup team was already handling their house and Mrs. Heller.
The other half of our Rag Team was transporting Dylan and
Damian, who were temporarily contained and in need of urgent
cure. They were too unstable to be kept in the infirmary, so Tobe
was waiting for us in the Bestiary, next to two large glass boxes with
brass edges and charmed locks, similar to those he used to restrain
the monsters.

The Bestiary was still a thing of wonder for me, despite the
horrors it housed. It was a giant egg-shaped hall with thousands of
glass boxes in various sizes, positioned on different levels, which
were connected by narrow sets of stairs. A central stem occupied
the middle of the Bestiary, a metallic structure with a myriad of
cables, linked to each of the boxes. That was how the Bestiary drew
its energy from the monsters, before redistributing it wirelessly to
all the covens around the world.

Wade, Santana, Raffe, and I were the first ones to arrive,

rushing past the glass boxes as we made our way to Tobe. I always had to tilt my head back to look at Tobe—the Beast Master, the only monster with a conscience. Despite coming out of a witch's Purge, his kind nature made him quite an asset, and he was subsequently put in charge of the Bestiary. Also, he was tall. As in, ridiculously tall. His lion head was adorned with a rich and luscious amber mane, his arms were feathered, and he had talons for feet. Other than that, he was as nice and normal as the rest of us. Sort of.

"Tatyana and some security magicals are coming in now with Dylan and Damian Heller," Tobe said as we reached him.

Adrenaline was already rushing through me, making my heart pound like a very angry drum. None of us had seen it coming. No one had expected to find a magical kid with an Esprit, corrupted by strangers and full-on psycho. The coven had had trouble bringing magicals in before, but nothing like this—not magicals who already knew ancient Latin curses. That was new.

The boxes that Tobe had prepared were big enough to hold two adults, with about forty square feet of floorspace.

"I take it we're treating them like monsters?" I asked, raising an eyebrow.

"We don't know exactly what curse was used on them, and they're acting like beasts," Wade replied and gave Tobe a polite nod. "Thanks for this, Tobe."

"They won't turn into black smoke, if that's what you're worried about," Tobe said to me, smiling. Or at least it looked as though he was smiling. That lion face wasn't always easy to read.

The doors opened in the distance, followed by a rush of footsteps and growls.

"What happened, exactly?" Tobe asked.

Wade exhaled deeply. "We're not sure. Tatyana, Dylan, and Astrid were visiting the Hellers, making sure their foster kid, Kenneth Willow, was indeed a magical."

"Turns out he's definitely a magical, and then some!" I added.

"He attacked Tatyana and his foster mom first. Dylan intervened and—" Wade tried to explain, until Tatyana cut him off.

"He put a curse on Dylan," she said, panting as she dragged Dylan in by one of the ropes used to secure him.

I held my breath at the sight of him. Something was definitely wrong—his eyes were glowing a bright yellow, and tiny red veins had burst around them, spreading across his cheeks, temples, and forehead. His hands were tied behind his back with tape, rope, and cable ties, and so were his legs. He was growling and squirming, baring his teeth at Tatyana as she maintained her firm grip. Her strength was impressive, though adrenaline probably played a part.

Tobe then took over and threw him in the glass box. Dylan immediately tried to dive out, but Tobe slammed the glass door in his face and put the charmed lock on.

"There. He's secured," he said.

Astrid came in next, accompanied by two security magicals who brought Damian Heller in. Kenneth's dad was in a similar state, with yellow eyes and red veins, snarling and growling and desperate to free himself. They put him in the second box, and Tobe closed it up with another charmed lock.

One quick look at Tatyana and Astrid, and I knew they'd put up quite the fight. They had cuts and bruises on their faces, and Tatyana was holding her side, grimacing from the pain. They were both scared and angry. I could feel it so intensely, it made my blood boil.

"Are you two okay?" I asked them.

They both nodded. "Yeah, just a little sore," Astrid replied, and continued flipping through her Smartie tablet. "I just got clearance from Alton for the nationwide database. I'm looking for the Ryder twins there."

"Tatyana, you don't look so good. You should go see Krieger," Tobe suggested, his concern weighing on my heart

"I'll be fine. I'll go after we fix them," she said, nodding at Damian and Dylan.

They were stuck in those glass boxes, roaring and ramming their shoulders into the walls, trying to get out. Of course, all their efforts were futile. These were Bestiary boxes, designed to keep actual monsters in. A couple of hexed people didn't stand a chance.

The security magicals left, while Tobe produced a pack of medical wipes from his feathers. The guy had lots of useful things stashed in his winged arms, including the Bestiary keys. I'd always wondered what else he kept in there...

"At least clean yourselves up a little before you get to Krieger. We can't risk infections," he said.

He gave a handful of wipes to Tatyana, and I took a few from the pack and proceeded to gently dab some of the cuts on Astrid's face.

"Thank you," she murmured, smiling softly, then resumed her database search while I kept cleaning her wounds.

"Okay, run us through what happened," Wade said, looking at Tatyana, who, in turn, had trouble taking her eyes off Dylan. There was so much heartache beneath that calm façade, it hurt me deeply.

Tatyana explained their arrival at the Hellers' place, followed by her conversation with Maria in the kitchen, until Kenneth appeared and attacked her and Maria.

"So, his behavioral change has to do with the Ryder twins, according to his mom," Wade concluded, frowning.

"I'm not so sure. I think he was always difficult and prone to trouble—at least that's what I got from Maria. But they said something to him, about a new world, about serving the future Child of Chaos, that kind of stuff. They turned him against the coven. Kenneth was never going to come in willingly. Whatever the twins and Katherine Shipton are planning, he's definitely involved," Tatyana replied. "They just got to him before we did. The parents didn't know anything about us or the coven, though. They only talked to Kenneth, in private. It was right after their meeting that Kenneth went full psycho on the parents."

"They're using different strategies on these families," I said, my voice trembling. "With the kids it's more complicated. But a teenager like Kenneth… It was probably easier to draw him into whatever they're scheming."

"Oh, absolutely." Tatyana sighed, running a hand through her blonde hair. "I'm still not getting this whole Children of Chaos thing, though. How does Katherine plan to do that? And what does she need magical kids for?"

Astrid shrugged. "I gave Smartie a search using the 'Child of Chaos' term, but there's nothing consistent coming through. I'll keep looking, but so far there's nothing on how to become one."

"As for the young magicals, Katherine probably needs some muscle for her own private army, who knows?" I said, trying to measure my breathing.

"What happened with Dylan? And Damian?" Wade asked.

Tatyana hesitated, and her grief hit me right in the solar plexus. Despite that, she continued to explain everything in detail.

"What curse did Kenneth use?" Tobe replied, keeping his eyes on Dylan.

Damian was getting tired, but Dylan was still squirming in his restraints while slamming his shoulder into the glass box. It felt horrible to see them like this, and the helplessness we all felt was quite difficult for me to handle. I hadn't experienced such grief and frustration since the gargoyle incident.

"*Magicis, ecce ego bestia tua,*" Tatyana repeated the hex words.

"That's forbidden magic!" Tobe gasped. "Good grief, how did that boy get his hands on such a spell? It's illegal!"

"I know," Tatyana replied. "It's a very ugly mystery."

Alton arrived, concern etched into his expression. "Maybe the Ryder twins gave it to him."

I was relieved to see Alton. There was something about his presence that seemed to have a calming effect on my senses, sometimes. It had to do with his tranquil nature. He never caved in, always searching for the solution, rather than allowing himself to be consumed by the problem.

I sensed his sorrow as he looked at Dylan, then Damian.

"Oh, it's definitely related to the Ryder twins," Astrid interjected, her eyes wide as she stared at the screen. She'd found something. "Emily and Emmett Ryder, born May 1, 1988, in Rio Grande, Texas. No records of their parents, but they were in the foster system for a while, before they were picked up by the Houston Coven."

"Wait, your mom's the director there, isn't she?" I asked Wade.

He nodded. "Yes. I'll call her later and find out if she knows anything. Not every archive in the covens was transferred into the magical population's electronic database. There'll be hard copies somewhere."

The magical population's electronic database was different from our library archives, which had been secured in their hard copy formats after a hacking incident, according to Wade. The electronic database contained all our information, much like the US government's records—only ours came with the results of our Readings and various tailored reports, depending on whether there were suspicious or criminal activities involved. Astrid could even put the equivalent of a BOLO out for the Ryders, and I knew it was literally the next item on her to-do list. All the US covens had access to the electronic database, and, sometimes, information from there was shared with non-US covens, if needed.

"What else can you tell us about them?" Alton replied, looking at Astrid.

She swiped across the tablet screen, her brow furrowed as she skimmed the information. "They weren't in the Houston Coven for long. They were kicked out for antisocial behavior. They'd been warned repeatedly. They were both transferred to the Phoenix Coven, but they just caused more trouble there, and some humans got hurt in the process. Someone in the Phoenix Coven took pity on them, from what I can see, because they had them moved to the Albuquerque Coven, instead of penalizing them. But they were just as bad there. They kept stirring up trouble between the magicals, mostly, pitting them against one another."

"That doesn't speak in their favor," Alton muttered, crossing his arms. "I'll reach out to Phoenix and Albuquerque for more records, then."

"It doesn't end well," Astrid replied. "They were kicked out of Albuquerque, too, but they were separated. Emmett was supposed to go to Miami, and Emily was transferred to Seattle."

"Opposite sides of the country," I said. "They probably figured they wouldn't cause as much trouble if they were kept apart."

"And they didn't want to jail them, either," Alton concluded. "I suppose there were only misdemeanors."

"Humans getting hurt is a misdemeanor?" I asked, clearly skeptical.

Alton nodded. "They mostly got only scratches. We consider it a misdemeanor if there's no proof of intent to harm humans. They were most likely accidental collateral damage, and I presume their memories were wiped."

"There was a lot of circumstantial evidence, too," Astrid explained. "As per coven regulations, they were entitled to a defense attorney, and the ones they had in each situation were well paid and very good at their jobs. In some cases, they made it out to be the other magicals' fault, portraying the Ryders as the real victims, being bullied and whatnot."

That, to me, smelled extremely fishy. "Hold on. Foster system magicals got their hands on good legal defense? That costs money. Right?"

Alton nodded. "Yes. It's one of the best-paid jobs in our world, actually. Our legal system is similar to that of the humans, and we litigate pretty much everything on the criminal spectrum. I think the covens will have all the court transcripts for each case. I'll check with them, maybe find out who their solicitors were."

"Either way, they never made it to Miami or Seattle," Astrid said. "They vanished. Fell off the radar completely. They just... slipped through the cracks, I think. Look, these are their most recent photos," she added, showing us the tablet screen.

I committed their faces to memory. They were attractive and

young, in their mid-twenties at the time. The similarities were there —the black hair and brown, almond-shaped eyes, oval faces and slim noses. Emily had the long hair, though, while Emmett's was short. It didn't make sense to me, since Linda had given us a different description.

There was mischief twinkling in their eyes, but nothing that screamed "sociopath" or "criminal." They smiled at the camera, as if they knew what was going to happen next. As if they knew they were never going to make it to Seattle or Miami.

"The Travis couple described them as in their early twenties, though," Tatyana said. "They're in their late twenties, according to their files."

"They probably still look very young for their age. It's not uncommon," Alton replied.

"Oh, yeah, with a good skin routine and proper moisturizer, you can cheat time for a few decades," Astrid said.

My heart was filled with affection—all bright and warm and fuzzy. It took me a few seconds to identify it as Alton's, as he fondly watched Astrid swipe through her files. She'd been with the coven for three years now, almost the same as Alton. Bonds were bound to happen, and I, like the others on my Rag Team, didn't know much about Alton's personal life, other than the fact that he was married to Isabel Monroe—whom I'd recently found out about. She was a magical, too, though she didn't do much work for them. She was on the Fleet Science Center's board of directors and collaborated with some local charities. I also knew that she and Alton didn't have kids. Maybe *we* were the kids.

"I'll refine my system search with this new info and the images as parameters," Astrid added. "I'll check every CCTV and social media post from the San Diego area. They're bound to pop up somewhere, at some point. Smartie's facial recognition software is sharp."

"In the meantime, we've got a little bit of work cut out for us," Alton said, glancing at Dylan and Damian again. "I know this curse.

It's called the Curse of the Magical Beast. It brings out the most feral side of us, witches and warlocks in particular. It works on humans, too, but, as you can see, Damian is already worn out. Dylan, on the other hand…"

As if knowing we were talking about him, Dylan growled and rammed into the glass again. He was simply unrecognizable, and it tore Tatyana apart.

"How do we fix him?" she asked.

"There's a cure," Alton replied. "This is rare and ancient magic. I actually know the curse; it's written in one of the Grimoires in our coven. I'll need to check the Grimoires in the Forbidden Section for the cure. But I know it'll need to be administered orally. One of us needs to go in there and do it."

Tobe nodded. "I've had my share of monster wrestling. I can take him."

Looking at Dylan, I couldn't help but wonder what had driven a kid like Kenneth to go dark-side like that, and how the Ryder twins had gotten their hands on such powerful spell work. This was ancient, heavy-duty, evil stuff, and most, if not all of it, was kept under magical lock and key in the covens. How easy would it be for someone to just walk into one of the Forbidden Sections and snatch such hexes?

They must've had inside help.

ELEVEN

Tatyana

E ver since Dylan came to the San Diego Coven, I'd had a bit of
a soft spot for him. He was so… different from the others. He
didn't look like he belonged here, with his short brown hair, cleft
chin, and varsity jacket. He was the typical jock, lover of sports and
weekends at the beach. His warm brown eyes spoke of summer
barbecues and athletic scholarships at some Ivy League school, not
of Chaos and magic and covens.

He always seemed out of his element, too. He didn't socialize
much, and he was the first to rush out at the end of the week to see
his mom and hang out with his college buddies. The coven, to him,
was more like a job. He spent most of the afternoons and nights
here, with magical training and whatever missions he was assigned
to. The mornings were always for college. He valued his academic
education, that much was obvious, and was still regretting his decision to stay here, instead of going to Yale. He'd had a full ride for
that, but the local coven was still catching some serious heat for bad
magical behavior, and Dylan had yet to fully control his abilities.

Most of his Chaos energy worked to amplify his physical
strength and speed, which was why he was *so good* at sports. His

Water and Telekinesis abilities came second and third, and he was still learning to develop and master them.

I liked him as a person because I knew that, deep down, despite the frat boy allure, Dylan was sweet, caring, and sensitive. Our little Rag Team was growing on him, and he'd started spending more time with us, dedicating some of his weekends to additional coven work, just so we'd all be together. He was loyal and noble by nature. His adoptive parents had raised him to be a fine young man.

But none of that mattered at this point. The Dylan I knew was gone, and we needed to get him back. Most importantly, I felt guilty. This had happened under my watch. I should've known that Kenneth was trouble. I should've followed my gut and neutralized the kid before he even came into the kitchen, protocols be damned.

I didn't, though. I thought I could handle it. I didn't think there was all that darkness and toxic rot beneath the preppy boy façade that Kenneth had been wearing. *My mistake.* And Dylan was paying the price. I had to fix this.

When Alton came back with the cure from one of the Grimoires, Tobe and Wade immediately sprang into action and helped him gather all the ingredients in a copper bowl with ancient Chinese markings etched into the lip.

"Xiao Fei, former director of the Beijing Coven, came up with a cure back in the nineteenth century," Alton explained as he laid out all the ingredients on a piece of cloth on the floor, kneeling before them and the bowl. "Before that, people afflicted by this particular hex were locked up for life. In some cases, they had to be killed. You see, the hex doesn't stop at what you see now."

Dylan had tremendous amounts of energy left in him, and he continued to wrestle against his restraints and roar furiously with each failure to free himself.

"Are you telling me it'll get worse?" I asked, and couldn't stop myself from giving Wade, Santana, Harley, Raffe, and Astrid a concerned frown. Part of me was trying to reach out to them for emotional support. I was genuinely overwhelmed, though it wasn't in my nature to ask for help.

Out of them all, Harley was the first to give me a warm smile. She could feel me. She knew exactly what I was going through, and, at that moment, I couldn't describe how nice it was to know that she was around.

"Much worse, I'm afraid," Alton replied. He then proceeded to measure and add the spell ingredients into the copper bowl, one by one. Fig leaves, twigs of Oliver Plum's Yew, angelica blossoms and cinnamon sticks, powdered green jade and salt from the Dead Sea, one ounce of Paris Green elixir—not the insecticide, but a magical substance made from extremely rare crystals—and a gallon of sweet water from TuoTuo, Yangtze's headstream. Sloane Bellmore and Marianne Gracelyn had an impressive reserve of spell ingredients in their repositories. "His body will become insufficient for his rage. Unless he is permanently tied down, he'll start hurting himself. All he knows now is to kill everything that moves. To wreck. To destroy."

Tobe stood by Dylan's box, with his feathered arms crossed, watching as he kept banging his shoulders into the glass. "Yes. I can see that."

Something snapped. Dylan's arms came out, finally free of their restraints. I held my breath, realizing he'd just managed to break through cable ties, industrial tape, and ropes. He punched and clawed at the box, until his legs were loose, too. His strength had finally overcome his physical limitations.

I took a deep breath and closed my eyes, making myself available to the spirit world. As a Kolduny, I could turn my spiritual ability on and off—otherwise I would've spent my entire life in extremely crowded places, even when I should've been alone. The coven was filled with ghosts, so there were plenty of people for me to talk to.

The darkness before me was gradually replaced by movement, wisps of bluish light, moving around us. All of them were spirits, lonely wanderers who couldn't let go after they'd died in the coven.

Sometimes, when I didn't want anyone else to know and hear what I was doing, I reached out to the spirits without using my body. My mind just opened up and they picked up on my brainwaves. They could read my thoughts, if I let them.

It took just a few seconds out there, in the real world, but in the veil, where I'd just entered, time flowed differently.

"I need help!" I called out to the spirits walking around me. "I need your strength!"

Of all the wisps that seemed to be ignoring me, one stopped. I'd gotten its attention. That was usually the first step, asking for help and getting one of the dead to answer. The spirit moved toward me and gradually regained its humanoid shape.

It was a man in his late twenties, with rich, curly black hair and wild green eyes. He'd broken a few hearts in his day, for sure. He wore jeans and a hockey jersey, stained with blood—most likely his. He'd died a violent death, yet his expression was one of curiosity, even slight amusement, as he stopped a couple of feet away from me. He was translucent, just like Will, the boy ghost I'd met back at the Travis house, but he seemed slightly more consistent. As if his spirit was more... condensed.

"I'm a Kolduny," I said to him.

"I know you, Tatyana," he replied with a smirk.

That made me shiver, but, then again, it shouldn't have come as a surprise. I'd been here for a few months now, and I'd called out to the spirits before.

"You do, huh?" I murmured.

"You're the only spirit-talker in this place. Among the living, anyway," the ghost said. "You're quite a celebrity around here."

"And who are you?" I asked.

He raised his chin with great pride. "I'm Oberon Marx," he declared. "Star athlete of the San Diego Coven!"

I was tempted to roll my eyes at him, but, instead, I gave him a polite smile. "I've heard about you," I replied. "You were a promising sportsman, right?"

He nodded enthusiastically. "Football, hockey, baseball, wrestling, swimming, mixed martial arts, and fencing. There wasn't anything I didn't excel at. Glad to hear I've left a legacy."

"You most certainly have," I said, remembering an article I'd read about him in one of the coven's updated history books.

"You called for help. I'm here. What do you need?" he asked.

Even through the darkness, we could both see the silhouettes of the material world around us. I pointed at Dylan's glass box. "He's been hexed," I said. "I need your strength to make him swallow the cure before he dies."

Oberon grinned, enthusiasm glimmering in his eyes. "Well, I made the right call to stop then, didn't I? That guy's a Herculean, if I'm not mistaken."

"Yes, he is," I replied.

"Herculean" was the title given to magicals with enhanced strength and speed, the "athletes" of Chaos, whose magical energy fueled their physical features. They were infinitely stronger, faster, more flexible, and more resilient than most humans. In many cases, they could really stand out if they wanted to. They were, essentially, superhumans. They weren't exactly rare, but their numbers weren't high, either. On average, there were between fifty and seventy per coven, with varying degrees of athletic prowess.

According to the lore, Hercules himself had been real, a hero of ancient Greece and a magical who... stood out, as well. They'd made up legends about him, so the title sort of stuck.

"You're in luck, Tatyana," Oberon said. "I'm a Herculean, too. One of the best in my generation, in fact!"

That made all the sense in the world, given his athletic career and fame among the magicals. He'd died sometime about twenty years ago, but the circumstances of his death were unknown to me. I couldn't remember much, but I could always look up articles about him in the archives. Either way, the day he passed away was a sad day for all the covens. That much I remembered.

"Tobe wants to go in there and give him the antidote, but it's my fault Dylan is in this state to begin with. I need to fix this," I murmured.

"Don't be like that. You didn't hex him." Oberon chuckled, then stilled and turned serious all of a sudden. "Or did you?"

"No, it was someone else. But I wasn't fast enough. I should've done more to stop it."

"Okay, if we're gonna do this, I need you to let go of that guilt. It ruins my vibe," Oberon groaned, rolling his eyes. "I'll help you. Tobe may be strong and whatnot, but he's underestimating us Herculeans. I dropped him on his ass more than once during my living days. I had a three-month training season in New York, at one point. He was one of my favorite sparring partners."

Back then, the Bestiary had been the New York Coven's responsibility. The timeline matched.

"You know how a Kolduny functions, right?" I asked, mentally preparing myself for the next step. He nodded. "I will let you in, and I'll lend you my body, but my mind is mine. You do as I say, okay?"

"Relax, Tatyana. You're not the first Kolduny I've ridden," Oberon said, grinning. That made me wonder who else he'd possessed among my kind, but there was no time for background checks. I had to help Dylan, and, as per Oberon's statement, Tobe wasn't enough to subdue him. "Open wide…"

That had come out wrong, and he knew it. "Ugh. Dude."

"Sorry. You know what I mean," Oberon replied, stifling a laugh.

I breathed deeply and opened my very being for occupation. Oberon stepped forward and into me, temporarily fusing with my flesh and bones. I felt cold, thousands of tiny electrical currents zapping through me at lightspeed. Oberon had taken over my body, but I'd retained my consciousness. It was rare for a Kolduny of my caliber to be overrun by a ghost. When it did happen, however, Santana and Dylan were always there to pull me back, so I could eject the wily spirit.

I opened my eyes, returning to reality, to the natural flow of time, just as Alton finished preparing the hex cure. It had turned into a thick, dark green liquid, which he poured into a glass bottle. Tobe reached out to get it, but I stepped in and snatched it from Alton's hand.

That took him by surprise. "Tatyana, what are you doing?"

"I've got this," I said, energized as though I'd just swallowed the sun.

It didn't take long for him and Tobe to figure it out. "You let a spirit in," Alton replied.

I nodded. "Dylan is a Herculean, and, no offense, Tobe, but you don't have the chops for him no matter how many monsters you've tackled before."

"Now, that's not exactly—" Tobe tried to object, but I cut him off.

"Oberon Marx," I said.

That was enough to make him back down. "You have Oberon Marx in there?"

"Who's that?" Harley asked.

"Oh. Big-time Herculean, star athlete of SDC about twenty years ago. Died a gruesome death in the late nineties, though the circumstances were unclear, from what I remember," Alton briefly explained. Judging by the look on his face, he was quite impressed.

"You're a fan of his?" I chuckled. I'd felt Oberon wanting to ask that question, and I could feel the pride swelling in my chest. The guy had lived to be adored.

"Most valuable player of the twentieth century, basically," Alton replied. "Well, he could've been. His untimely departure deprived us of a legend, but... I'm glad to see he's helping you."

I gave him a weak smile and looked at Tobe. "Don't get me wrong, I have all the faith in you, Tobe, but I feel responsible, and I can do this," I said.

Tobe nodded and got ready to open Dylan's box. Dylan had gone quiet, eyeing me like a very hungry wolf. "You have to move fast, Tatyana. And don't let him bite you," Tobe instructed. "The hex is transferable."

"Now he tells me," I grumbled, holding the bottle tight in one hand as I stepped in front of the box. "I'm ready. Let me in."

"Be careful, Taty!" Santana called behind me.

I knew they were all worried, but this was part of the gig. Chaos and magic were never rainbows and sprinkles. There was darkness and pain, danger and poison. Sure, there was wonder and healing, the accomplishment of extraordinary feats and a fusion with nature otherwise impossible to achieve. But most of the time, there were risks of all kinds to be factored into the life of a magical.

This was one of them.

Tobe opened the box, and I slipped inside at lightning speed. He locked me in there as Dylan stepped back. He was momentarily confused.

"Dylan, I know you're in there," I whispered.

He lunged at me, snarling like a vicious animal. I let Oberon take over my limbs. We tackled Dylan. He pushed me against one of the glass walls, but my legs jerked upward and I kneed him in the gut. He groaned from the pain but didn't let that stop him.

Oberon was phenomenally strong. I'd carried a tied-up Dylan into the coven mostly due to adrenaline, but this... this was something else entirely. I felt as though I were made of rock and steel. He punched me several times, but I hit back with my left fist, while my right hand was busy protecting the bottle holding the cure.

"Dylan, listen to me!" I panted. "I *know* you're in there! I need you to focus! I need you to stop this and drink the cure!"

He didn't seem to care. He was too busy trying to take a bite out of me. Oberon's reflexes were mine now, though, so Dylan didn't get that chance. I kicked him, then hurled him over my shoulder. He hit his head against the glass, temporarily dazed.

I popped the cap off the bottle and gripped Dylan by the throat.

"You're the only one I've ever felt a connection to, Dylan!" I said, my voice uneven and my eyes stinging from the tears threatening to come out. "Never mind that we're all worried about you. I'm the one in here, now, asking you... Dylan, please! Help me out here!"

I tightened my grip on his throat, enough to constrict his wind-pipe. He was struggling to breathe.

"I know you're different from other magicals," I added. "I know you can beat this. Let me cure this hex you're under, because this isn't you, Dylan. I want *my* Dylan back! We all do!"

He stilled all of a sudden, breathing heavily, his hands still clutching my forearm in an attempt to push me back. I couldn't help but thank the stars for Oberon in that moment.

He blinked. I'd managed to strike a chord in there, beneath the madness. For one moment, despite the yellow eyes, I felt as though I was looking at the real Dylan. *My* Dylan. I raised the cure bottle for him to see it.

"This will make you feel better," I breathed. "Let me make you feel better."

He didn't say anything, but he exhaled sharply. His muscles were twitching angrily. Every fiber in his body was probably telling him to attack, but he held back. This was my chance. I put the bottle's lip against his. He slowly opened his mouth, and I tilted the bottle but didn't ease my grip on him. I couldn't risk it.

He drank it all and snarled at me again.

Then, he froze, staring at me with wide eyes. The yellow faded, and the warm caramel-brown I'd grown to be so fond of came back in gentle ripples. The red veins withdrew.

"Dylan?" I croaked.

He blinked again, then dropped to his knees and retched all over my shoes. My stomach churned, mostly at the sight of what was pouring out of Dylan—it was a thick, black substance, riddled with tiny worms, and certainly not the liquid cure I'd just given him.

Tobe opened the box again and helped me out, while Wade and Raffe carried Dylan. He'd passed out, but he looked a lot better than the savage fiend I'd struggled with earlier.

"It's done," Alton said. "Good job, Tatyana."

I gave him a faint nod, then let out a long sigh.

"Thanks, Oberon," I whispered.

"You're welcome, darling," he replied, his voice echoing in my head.

"Time to let go," I reminded him.

I heard him groan, and sighed again when I felt his energy drain out of me. I experienced relief, thankful that I didn't have much trouble with letting a spirit go. I was getting better at commanding the ghosts, from what I could tell.

My arms and legs felt weak all of a sudden, and I was aching all over. All the strength I'd gotten from Oberon was gone. In its wake was a tired, jelly-like Tatyana. I was just grateful I didn't pass out, as I'd done in the past after a possession. I had learned a few breathing tricks, and perhaps I was making progress.

Dylan was on the floor, lying on his back while Wade checked his vitals. "He's okay," he said. "Quite stable, but we need to take him to the infirmary."

"Krieger should take a look, for sure," Alton replied. "Dylan will be out for a couple of days, though. And so will Damian," he added, handing a second cure bottle to Tobe. "You can handle an angry human, right?"

Tobe scoffed. "Now you're just insulting me."

Alton chuckled. Santana put an arm around my shoulders as we watched Tobe go into Damian's glass box and force him to take the cure. A beastly hexed human was much easier to handle than a Herculean, that much was obvious. The spell did give Damian ridiculous strength, but it wasn't above Tobe's level.

Wade and Raffe carried Dylan to the infirmary. I quietly watched them go, nagged by a dull pain in my chest.

I made it my mission to get my hands on Kenneth Willow. That little brat was in for a serious butt-kicking after what he'd done. Right after the Ryder twins. I had a bigger bone to pick with those two.

TWELVE

Harley

After Dylan was taken to the infirmary, Alton called in a cleanup crew to take care of Damian. He was given medical attention, then had his memory wiped—just like they'd done with Maria, his wife. The Hellers didn't need to remember this nightmare.

Wade, Santana, Tatyana, Raffe, Astrid, and I followed Alton into his office, where we briefed him on our progress so far. Each of our teams had visited two of the twelve families on the list he'd given us, before the Kenneth Willow incident.

"I know we still have more to run through, but the attack and Dylan's condition took precedence," Wade concluded his reporting.

I was restless, not just because of my own emotions, but also because of everyone else's. They were all worried and fearful, mentally bracing themselves for another potential disaster. We were still reeling from what had happened with Finch and Katherine Shipton, after all, and the rumors of her emergence were still buzzing in the background of everything we said and did.

"No, that was a good call," Alton replied. "However, we'll need to check on the other families on our list as soon as possible. I need you all on this, first thing in the morning. Until then, however, I'll send the Ryders' photos out to the security team and have them keep an eye on each of the remaining houses."

"Yeah, that'll work until we get there and debrief the families," Wade agreed.

"I'll prepare more charms in the meantime," Santana said. "I used up most of my supply for every room of the two houses we checked. I didn't think we'd need so many."

A few seconds passed in silence. I felt as though there was a big elephant in the room with my name on it. After all, I'd broken protocol with the Cranstons, and Alton had yet to say anything to me directly about it. That wasn't in his nature.

"About the Cranstons—" I tried to speak, but Alton was quick to cut me off.

"I know why you did what you did," he said. "You had good intentions. I get that. But it was against coven regulations. However, lucky for you, it proved to be a more viable strategy in the long run."

"What, using the kids as bait?" I snapped.

Alton raised an eyebrow. "I'm confused, Harley. I thought you wanted them to stay with their parents, magical or otherwise."

"Yeah, but… now we're using them as literal bait for the Ryders," I murmured.

"And? Do you think I'm happy with that decision?" Alton replied. "Far from it. I'm quite annoyed, actually. But you need to learn a lesson here, and we have no better alternative to try and capture two clearly hostile and dangerous rogue magicals. I would've loved to have the children back here, under our protection, but I've decided your way was… well, not better, but more productive."

I crossed my arms, not liking the guilt that was gnawing at my stomach. Deep down, I knew Alton was right. I'd had a few hours to think about my intervention. It was like picking the lesser of two evils, and I'd gone with the worst, thinking I was doing the right thing.

"So, you're doing this to teach me a lesson? You're leaving these young magicals out there for the Ryders to grab or influence or whatever, just to show me I'm wrong?" I asked, even more annoyed. I knew the answers. I just didn't like what all this had escalated to.

Alton shook his head. "No. I'm doing this because the Ryders became dangerous in a rather short timeframe. If it had been just the Cranstons, I would've been more adamant about bringing little Micah in. But it's not just them anymore. The fact that I get to teach you a lesson about why coven rules are so important is just an upside to this entire debacle."

That irritated me, but I couldn't do much to change it. I could focus on protecting the kids, instead, and finding ways to stop and capture the Ryder twins.

"Based on what we've seen so far, the Ryders have an agenda," I said, changing the subject. "And different approaches, depending on the magicals' ages and whether their parents are magicals. For example, Micah is only five, and his parents are human, so the Ryders left their card but didn't interact with any of them. Mina is six, but her parents are magical. The Ryders talked to them, pretending to be from our coven."

"And the Ledermeyers were human, while their kid, Samson, is a three-year-old magical," Tatyana said. "They had no recollection of the Ryders, either. Whereas with Kenneth Willow and the Hellers, it was clearly different."

"That's right. Kenneth is a young adult, and his foster parents are human," Alton replied. "They were aware that he was different, but they didn't send him back. They stuck by him. And when the Ryders came in, they only spoke to Kenneth, leaving the humans out of the conversation. From what I can tell, Kenneth was the first they successfully coerced to their side."

"They could've taken the kids, too, but they didn't." Wade sighed, scratching the back of his head. He was confused, and for good reason.

"They tried to get Mina's parents to send her to the coven," I said. "I mean, that's probably why they posed as coven members and why they left their card behind. Maybe the Ryders didn't want to test the parents' magical abilities. Maybe it was easier to just get Mina out of her parents' reach for them to kidnap her. Wouldn't it then be safe to assume that, had the Travises agreed, the Ryders would've intercepted and snatched her?"

Alton shrugged. "I'm not sure. It could be. A magical incident involving adults could've drawn too much of our attention, too soon. Without knowing how powerful the parents were, the Ryders could be trying to play it safe. But we don't have enough information. Nor do we know their intentions, or who they're working with, if they're working with anyone."

"Do you think Katherine Shipton is involved?" Tatyana asked.

My blood ran cold just from hearing her name. "If she is, we're in for a doozy," I muttered.

"The most important thing for us to do right now is to speak to the other families on that list," Wade replied. "Once we're there, we'll most likely find out more about what the Ryders have been doing or saying. We also need to make sure we're ready if the Ryders visit any of them again. I'm willing to bet they've already been to see the families we'll be seeing tomorrow."

"Did you find out anything from your mom back in Houston?" I asked.

Wade shook his head. "She's had her assistants dig through the files, but there's nothing. Either they were never recorded, or their files were wiped on purpose."

"The cards bug me, though." Santana sighed, pinching the bridge of her nose. "Why would they leave them with families they didn't even speak to? Do you really think they did it for us, Alton? Because that's the theory we were floating earlier."

We all looked at Alton, who seemed equally befuddled.

"That would mean they knew you were coming," he said. "And that makes me feel uneasy, because I gathered the intel from different magical reports from the field. Either the Ryders are following our coven operatives around, or we have a spy in our ranks."

"So, if they really are sending us a message, what *is* the message? That they're spying on us? That they're looking to drive magicals away from the coven? Both?" I asked.

"I think you'll have a clearer picture tomorrow, if there's a repeat of today's pattern," Alton replied. "What's crucial here is that you are all prepared. Kenneth Willow might *not* be the only kid they've subverted. Be on your guard at all times."

That made sense. From what I remembered reading in the file, there were at least two other potential teenage magicals that the Ryders might've gotten to. The last thing we wanted was a repeat of the Dylan debacle. The poor guy was looking at days in the infirmary under Krieger's care.

I worried about little Micah now. I'd been so eager to make sure he stayed with his family, only to later realize that maybe that wasn't such a good idea. It haunted me, but I had to keep pushing.

Santana gave me a gentle shoulder squeeze, prompting me to look at her. I found her smiling at me. "Don't worry, Harley, the charms are on point," she said, as if having read my mind. "We'll know the moment there's a threat."

"Thank you," I mumbled.

Looking back, I didn't miss the old days. I liked having people like Santana, Raffe, Tatyana, Astrid, Dylan, and even Wade around. They were reliable and protected one another. There was a bond among us that was hard to describe, and possibly just as hard to break, now.

They weren't just fellow magicals. They were my friends.

And I knew that I would need them by my side for what came next. Whether it was confirmed or not, it didn't matter to me—this whole thing reeked of Katherine Shipton. My instincts rarely failed me.

THIRTEEN

Harley

Dinner was rather gloomy. We didn't talk much, each of us worried about Dylan, the Ryder twins, and the fact that Kenneth Willow was at large. The coven had put out its equivalent of an APB on Kenneth and the twins, notifying all magicals in the California area of their presence. Alton was liaising with the California Mage Council on this as well. We were bound to get an earful from Leonidas Levi. He didn't like our coven much, mostly because of how we'd emerged from the gargoyle incident.

After dinner, I went back to my room to read my parents' file. Alton had been kind enough to prepare it for me, and it was time for me to delve a little deeper into my family history.

From what the timeline suggested, my parents got together shortly after Dad hooked up with Katherine Shipton. That mustn't have sat well with her, but love had this nasty way about it. Hester and Hiram Merlin tied the knot one year after they became an item, while Katherine stayed mostly out of the public eye.

Because of the legacy of both the Merlin and Shipton names in the magical community, my parents' wedding was a big deal, with coverage in all the coven newspapers across the States. Heck, I even found a clipping from the British papers mentioning their union. There were, of course, gossip columns dedicated to rumors about Katherine being quite upset about their relationship, but no one suspected that, years later, it would all go sideways so badly.

Based on what I'd learned from Finch, he'd already been born when my parents married. Katherine had sent him off to be raised by Agnes Anker, who gave him her last name. Apparently, there was still some stigma regarding magical children out of wedlock at the time.

My parents made an amazing magical team, it seemed. Both were powerful Telekinetics. My mom was an Empath, like me. My dad was a full Elemental. I'd gotten the best of both worlds, much like salted caramel. The Merlins were the pride and joy of the New York Coven, and my dad became the youngest magical to become a director. He was only twenty-five at the time.

"Wow," I murmured as I flipped through the file pages. "So, Alton isn't the youngest, per se. My dad was. Way to go, Merlin..."

During that time, my parents began working on a Grimoire together. That was extremely rare, from what I'd learned during Lasher Ickes's Magic History classes. The Grimoire was a book of spells, which not all magicals endeavored to create. It acted as a part journal, part instruction manual for new or modified spells. It was loaded with the magical's memories and energies. Alton had appended a note regarding the Grimoire.

A Grimoire is the most honest manifestation of a magical's connection to Chaos. Because we, as witches and warlocks, adhere to either Light or Darkness, so will the Grimoire be influenced by our Chaotic inclination. It is a book that can influence and even change minds, and it's a wonderful tool to have if one is on the side of Light. Where Darkness is involved, however, the Grimoire can become more like poison, rather than a cure, killing its reader slowly, but surely.

The fascinating part about Hester and Hiram's Grimoire was that it involved both Light and Darkness. After all, Hiram was Light, and Hester, as wonderful and kind and noble as she was, belonged to the Darkness. Therefore, their Grimoire attained an incredible and never-before-seen balance of both.

I'd learned from Preceptor Ickes and Alton a few things about the Children of Chaos and how we were connected to them. I, for one, understood that I was directly connected to Gaia, as an Elemental. Light and Darkness, however, had a different role to play in a magical's life, from what I remembered. Those with Darkness were drawn to the danger and death side of Chaos (though not necessarily to inflict it, per se). Light was more attuned to nurturing and growth. Gaia was, in her way, connected to Light, for example, which was why an Elemental was, most of the time, drawn to Light. I had to do a little more digging as to what Light and Darkness did to our magic, though. The details were rather fuzzy in my mind.

Moving on to complete the file, I found myself saddened by its conclusion. I read out loud this time, just to fill the silence that had begun weighing heavily on my shoulders.

"The Grimoire was never completed. With approximately 75 percent of its pages filled with wondrous new charms, spells, hexes and cures, thoughts, impressions and memories, it would be one of the greatest literary and technical creations of contemporary magic... had it been finished. An incomplete Grimoire will not have the same power and influence as a full one. The spells can still be used, but they wouldn't be 100 percent efficient. Once a spell is recorded into a Grimoire, Chaos somehow makes it official and universally applicable. It's a process we've never fully understood, but rather went with..."

Now, I was officially curious. Extremely curious.

The Grimoire was never completed because of what happened to my father—he went berserk, murdering several magicals and... my mom. Shortly before that, according to Finch, my dad had gone back to Katherine Shipton. And it was after they got together that he went all mass-murdery, and everything changed.

The one thing that everyone got wrong was me. They'd thought

I was still in my mother's womb when she died, and they weren't able to do an autopsy because my mother had been turned into ashes.

Tears streamed down my cheeks, but I kept reading. I couldn't stop now. I once again raised my voice, aggravated by the silence around me.

"Hiram Merlin disappeared for three years after killing Hester. The entire magical community mourned. The covens were in an uproar. A manhunt followed, but Hiram eluded them each time. Meanwhile, Katherine Shipton had gone on her own killing spree, killing dozens of high society magicals for reasons still unknown. The motives behind all the murders committed by both Hiram and Katherine were never discovered, nor could we verify that they were still together during those three years. Once Hiram surrendered, he claimed he was innocent. His alibis, however, didn't support his statement. The evidence was against him. The judicial authorities were never able to establish any other connection between Katherine and Hiram either, beyond their affair. It was considered an amorous triangle gone horribly wrong and treated as such. Hiram was tried and... executed..."

My voice faded.

I exhaled, put the file on my bed, and got up. I'd had enough of that epilogue. I knew what happened afterward, more or less. There were too many gaps in this known timeline for me to ignore them, though. Plus, the few memories I'd recovered of my father, along with the pre-murder stories about him and Mom, spoke in his favor. I had a hard time imagining him as an enraged or cold-blooded killer.

The one thing I needed to know more about, in the meantime, was the Grimoire.

Since it was also used as a journal to record important moments in a magical's life, I was certain I'd learn more about my parents, if I could get my hands on it. It was supposedly back in New York, but I knew where I could find more information about it. As part of a lead investigative team, and especially after my contributions to Finch's apprehension, I had unrestricted access to the most sensitive parts of the coven, including the Forbidden Section and the Secret Archives.

I also wanted to get a better look at a Grimoire, just so I could understand what it looked and felt like. It had been bugging me since I'd first laid eyes on them. The little devil on my shoulder insisted that I should do it, and I didn't even think to object.

It was past midnight when I left my room and quietly made my way to the Forbidden Section. The hallways were mostly dark and quiet. Everyone was probably already asleep—like I should've been, since I had to get up early to continue the family visits.

"*Tribus. Quattuor. Septem. Aperi Portium,*" I whispered the customized spell for this particular room. I touched the doorknob and heard the lock click.

I slipped inside and, just as I was about to close the door behind me, a foot came through, blocking it. It wore a black shoe. My first thought was Wade for some reason, but as I pulled the door back and looked up, I found myself surprised.

"Garrett," I murmured.

He stood in the doorway, wearing a sheepish smile. He had his usual cream pants, crisp white shirt, and loose, dark red tie, his dark hair freshly buzz-cut on the sides. His eyes were the color of a midnight sky in that light.

"Sorry, I just saw you in the hallway," he replied. "I was curious why you'd still be up at this hour."

I felt like a kid caught with a poopy paper bag, ready to drop it on the neighbor's porch and set it on fire. My face burned. I still had my guard up, especially around Garrett, even though I had full access to the place. I figured the old habit of sneaking into forbidden places died hard.

"Um. I was just… researching," I said.

Garrett raised an eyebrow. "In the Forbidden Section?"

"Yeah. I'm looking into Grimoires."

"Why? I doubt Preceptor Ickes would let you study one up close, unattended," he replied.

Ugh. I'd forgotten how seasoned Garrett was in coven matters. We hadn't talked much since the Finch incident. We'd exchanged a few words in the hallway now and then, but nothing that could be considered an actual, meaningful conversation. He'd already apologized about his nasty words regarding my Merlin origins, so there wasn't really bad blood between us, but, still, I'd been wary of attempting any form of friendship with him again.

My foster experiences had taught me to be on my guard at all times, especially after someone did me wrong. I applied it in full in the coven, too.

This time, however, a thought crossed my mind: maybe Garrett could help. Maybe it wouldn't hurt to be nicer to him.

I sighed. There was no point in lying to him. "I want to know what a Grimoire looks and feels like," I said. "And I want to find out where my parents' Grimoire is."

He blinked several times, then nodded slowly.

"Well, I don't think you should look at a Grimoire by yourself," he replied. "I'd be more than happy to show you one or two, for you to get an idea. They can be quite… intense."

"Okay. Thanks," I whispered, and stepped aside.

Garrett entered and closed the door behind him. The Forbidden Section was an enormous room with shelves covering the walls from top to bottom. There were hundreds of boxes in all shapes and sizes, scrolls and notebooks, along with an entire portion encased in charmed glass, where they kept the Grimoires. They'd had to put a spell on them and treat them as Bestiary creatures, given that they practically oozed energy and influenced magicals. In the middle, there were reading tables with chairs and empty notebooks.

My favorite thing about the notebooks was that they were magically rigged to prevent people from stealing spells from the Grimoires. Even if a witch or a warlock had access to a Grimoire for research and, instead of simply taking notes, they copied the entire spell or the chant required to cast it, the text vanished as soon as they set foot outside the room.

The coven sure knew how to protect its assets, though there was always a bit of wiggle room for failure. Case in point—Kenneth. He'd gotten that curse somehow, and we didn't know how the Ryders had gotten it.

"The Grimoires are high-level clearance only," Garrett said, stopping in front of the glass section. "You wouldn't be able to get through this without the proper spell. I doubt Alton would give you access before your Pledge."

That seemed reasonable, making my impulsive visit to the Forbidden Section sound downright ridiculous. "I didn't know that."

"That's cool. I'm here and happy to help," he replied, giving me a half-smile before he placed his fingers on the glass and whispered a spell. Wisps of light shot across the glass surface, lighting up the many symbols that were normally hidden. He opened the glass door and took one of the leather-bound journals out. "Let's see what this one's about," he added.

"How are you allowed to open that?" I asked.

"Alton put me in charge of curating the Grimoires for the next couple of months," he explained. "The task is given in rotation to avoid any of us being influenced in a negative way. Like I said, these babies can be pretty intense."

He walked over to one of the tables, then placed the Grimoire on top. It was a big and heavy-looking thing, with a solid black leather cover and a multitude of strange etchings on its spine. I didn't recognize any of the symbols.

We sat down in front of it, and Garrett untied the leather strings holding its cover and pages together. It looked rather old, with yellowed paper and a multitude of scribbles on the edges. The first page drew my attention. The writing was an attempt at elegant cursive, with curves and swirls, but sharp and scratchy throughout. To me, that denoted a feminine nature with a dark, rough side. Someone who tried to fall into a certain category, but could not quite rid herself of the demons within.

The second most interesting aspect was that it was written in French, and I could understand every single word. Garrett noticed my confused frown.

"It's written in French," he said.

"I know," I replied.

"Then what's wrong? You look troubled."

"I don't speak French. I never learned it. Yet I understand every word. How does that work?" I asked.

He chuckled. "It's magic. Grimoires are written in different languages to throw humans off, if they ever come across one. But a magical will always understand the tongue of Chaos," he explained. "It's in our DNA, I suppose."

The words on the first page sent shivers down my spine.

The Grimoire of Crimson Kite. Poison can be drunk slowly and feel incredible.

"That is so dark," I muttered, nodding at the text.

Garrett shrugged. "This is one of the forbidden ones. Technically speaking, we're not supposed to even look at it, but hell... You only live once, right?"

"Do you know who Crimson Kite was? That has got to be an alias or a pen name or something."

"I don't," Garrett replied. "But I'm assuming it's a woman, judging by the handwriting."

"Yeah, a slightly unstable woman," I said. "Look at the erratic shake in each word. It's like she was struggling to write like that."

"Mm-hm. Agreed," Garrett mumbled. He narrowed his eyes and turned several pages. "It's at least a decade or two old. Never handled this particular Grimoire myself."

"So, how do you curate them?" I asked.

"Well, I make sure the pages are intact. I wipe the dust and any residue off with special cleaning instruments and dry cloths. Where the ink begins to fade, I apply a rejuvenation solution that brings it back. Then I spray every page with a preservation serum. All brewed in-house by Preceptors Gracelyn and Parks," Garrett replied. "It's tedious. I've done six of them so far, with about a hundred left, but I won't get to do them all. Someone else will pick up where I leave off."

I nodded, and craned my neck to get a better look at the text on one page. It looked like a poem, with short lines and generous spacing in between, and red, green, and black drawings on the edge —a demon, a dragon, a swirl of strange-looking flowers, and several snakes, all displayed around the actual text. The title sounded interesting.

"The Curse of the Dragon's Kiss," I breathed.

Garrett said something, but I missed it. The text seemed to vibrate and jump out of the page. Every word made sense, and I could hear someone whispering in my ear.

There, in the Darkness, where evil and poison live...

My blood ran cold. My skin prickled, as if I'd just been dunked in a vat of ice water.

The Dragon sleeps...

Oh, Monster of Leviathan, Son of Chaos, Eater of Hearts...

I bid you, come hither...

I give you my heart, if you give me your Kiss—

"Harley!" Garrett's alarmed voice cut through. The slam of a book snapped me out of whatever the hell it was I'd just experienced.

I stared at him, the world around us suddenly back into focus. "What?" I replied.

"What the hell just happened?" Garrett croaked, his eyes wide with fear.

"What are you talking about?" I asked, then rubbed my face.

Needles were jabbed into my eyes—or, at least, that was how I felt. I needed several deep breaths to regain my full composure.

"We need to keep you away from this. You're too susceptible," he declared, and tied the strings back around the Grimoire. That was the slam I'd heard a few seconds earlier—Garrett closing the Grimoire. He put it back behind the glass casing, before whispering the locking spell and returning to the table.

The strange symbols lit up for a moment, then faded back into the glass.

"I don't get it," I said. "What happened? I was just reading that spell."

"Harley, you weren't reading anything. You were reciting. Your voice changed, your eyes rolled white into your head, and the table started shaking," Garrett replied. "Don't you remember any of that?"

I shook my head, shock clutching my heart. "What the..."

"Yeah, my thoughts exactly! I tried calling out your name a couple of times. It took a few tries to snap you out of it. That Grimoire had quite an influence on you."

I had no idea. "The letters were vibrating on the page. I heard whispers in my head, but from what Wade told me, that's pretty normal when looking at an open Grimoire. I didn't know I'd gone that deep down the rabbit hole. Sorry..."

"There's nothing to be sorry about. Just be careful," Garrett said, giving me a sympathetic smile. "Also, your parents' Grimoire won't be here."

"Oh, I know that."

"You won't find anything in the archives, either," he added. "Trust me, I've looked. Shortly after I heard you and Alton and I found out who your parents were, I checked all our records. They're keeping that Grimoire very hush-hush, in the New York Coven's Forbidden Section. They've removed all other references to it from all the other covens. Everything you need to know will be in New York."

I was surprised by how helpful Garrett was. His demeanor had certainly changed since the Finch incident, but this was still unexpected. It just didn't fit his otherwise abrasive, arrogant, and sarcastic nature.

"Thank you, Garrett," I said. "That's good to know."

"Now, come on, let's go before you hear another Grimoire call out to you." He chuckled and headed for the door. I was right behind him when he stopped and turned around, cocking his head to the side. "By the way, you have a very powerful connection with the Darkness, just so you know. I don't think anyone noticed—or told you, if they did."

"What do you mean?"

"Ah. I see they haven't taught you about that," he replied, the corner of his mouth twitching. "Kind of makes sense. Anyway, it's not my place to teach you that. You should ask Alton or Preceptor Ickes about Light and Darkness."

"Oh, yeah, I read... something about that, but I don't know much. Scratch that, I don't know anything," I replied.

He gently squeezed my shoulder. "It's cool. You should bring it up with Krieger, too, for your next Reading. You're due for another one, right?" he asked. I nodded. "Yeah, so check that out when you do it, then. But it's obvious from the way you reacted to Crimson Kite's Grimoire. You've got a strong link to Darkness."

"Is that bad?"

He laughed. "No. Not necessarily. Granted, most magicals with Darkness connections tend to be on the wrong side of magical laws, but there were and still are enough exceptions to not make it a rule."

Somehow, that didn't make me feel much better. Nevertheless, Garrett clearly wasn't the guy to ask. He'd specifically told me to get informed via Alton, Ickes, or Krieger. The one thing I knew for sure was that this whole affiliation with Light or Darkness wasn't exactly readily available information. One had to ask the questions, in order to get the answers.

I was exhausted. My eyelids were practically drooping.

Garrett turned around and opened the door, motioning for me

to go out first. As soon as I set foot in the hallway, I felt as though I could breathe again. The air inside the Forbidden Section seemed heavy, once I was out. That wasn't the strangest thing to have happened to me today, but it was certainly near the top. Garrett was right. That Grimoire had had quite an impact on me.

FOURTEEN

Harley

"What are you two doing here?"

Wade's voice ripped me from my inner thoughts with the grace of a drunk rhinoceros.

Both Garrett and I froze in front of the Forbidden Section's closed doors, and slowly turned our heads to find Wade a couple of yards away, glowering like a grumpy old caretaker. He hadn't gone to bed either, still wearing his pretend-Social-Services attire.

"Wade. Fancy running into you here," Garrett said.

There was something abruptly different about him, in Wade's presence. He switched to a dark and on-edge version of himself. There was so much tension between them, I could easily get blown up if I wasn't careful.

"What were you two doing in the Forbidden Section?" Wade asked, his tone clipped and his arms crossed.

"None of your business, Crowley. Don't you have some boots to lick or something?" Garrett shot back.

"Whoa. Chill. Both of you," I snapped. "I was just checking out the Grimoires, that's all. I do have clearance, if you remember."

"At this hour?" Wade retorted.

He was angry, and I couldn't for the life of me understand why.

"What are you, my guardian?" I scoffed.

"You should be resting, Harley. We have a long day ahead of us tomorrow," Wade said, his voice lower.

"Then why are you lurking around the hallways at this time of night, huh?" Garrett cut in. "It's not your business what she does and who she hangs out with when she's off the clock. So butt out, Crowley."

A muscle ticked in Wade's jaw. "I don't get why you're hanging around her like a little puppy. Or do you think any of us forgot what a jerk you were when you found out her last name was Merlin?"

"In Garrett's defense, he did apologize," I said, and put my hands out to stop Garrett from retorting with more hostility. "Listen, you two need to take a deep breath. First of all, I don't have to answer to anyone for my actions. I'm a big girl, and I know the coven rules. Second, Wade, Garrett, there's some history between you. I get that. So, for the sake of a more peaceful coven where I don't have to worry about breaking up a fistfight every time we meet, how about we all grab dinner somewhere nice, and just talk and hash it out? Huh?"

Garrett's eyebrows went up. Wade's furrowed into a confused frown.

"I can act as the mediator. We'll sit you both down, get you some nice drinks and a spaghetti or something—somewhere public and human, so neither of you is tempted to resort to magic in order to make some dumb, macho point—and sort this out. What do you think?" I added.

They looked at each other, then at me, and I suddenly felt vulnerable. There was something in Wade's gaze and flow of emotions that had the power to disarm me. In contrast, I couldn't feel Garrett, but his expression said everything: he was surprised and intrigued.

"I won't say no to that, provided that Crowley here leaves his ego at the door," Garrett said.

Wade exhaled. "If you're willing, then I'm willing."

That sounded like incredible progress. Before patting myself on the back, though, I had to make sure I had a commitment from them both.

"Okay. Good. We're on to something here. Carluccio's, eight p.m. on Wednesday?" I asked, figuring that was enough time for me to do a little bit of digging into both Garrett's and Wade's pasts. I had a feeling Alton could help me fill in some of those blanks.

They both nodded.

"Fantastic!" I exclaimed, before giving Garrett a friendly nod. "I'll see you tomorrow, and thanks for the assistance tonight."

Garrett smiled, and I instantly felt my blood simmer. That wasn't me. That was Wade. "No problem. Don't forget to talk to Krieger," Garrett said.

"Will do," I replied, then headed back to the living quarters.

I would've expected Garrett to come with Wade and me, but he stayed behind and went back inside the Forbidden Section instead. The first minute that followed was awkwardly quiet as Wade and I made our way down the hallway.

"Since when are you friendly with Garrett?" he asked.

"Since we're part of the same coven, and we should play nice?" I replied. "Besides, if I decide to stay here, I figure it's in my best interests for us all to get along."

My heart skipped a beat.

"You want to join the coven, then?" he murmured.

"I haven't decided yet. But that doesn't mean I can't help fix a couple of things while I'm here. This damaged relationship that you and Garrett have is a fine example of what I could help make right, if you're both interested."

"Clearly, we are, since we agreed to dinner. I didn't think he'd say yes, though," Wade muttered.

"Well, people can still surprise you, then." I chuckled.

"What were you doing in the Forbidden Section, though?"

I thought about whether I should give Wade all the details, but I decided I'd rather address my Grimoire experience with Krieger or Alton first. "I was looking for some information about my parents' Grimoire," I explained. "But Garrett said I wouldn't find anything here."

"Yeah, it'll be in the New York Coven," Wade replied.

I nodded and turned the corner, the living quarters area opening out before us with its large dome and pink magnolias in the middle.

"Listen, I don't trust Garrett," he added.

That statement brought me to a halt. I turned to face him. "Why do you say that?"

Concern gnawed at my stomach, and I wasn't sure whether that was me or Wade. I still had a long way to go with honing my Empathy readings.

"I'm not sure," he replied. "I'm thinking that if Katherine Shipton really is involved with the Ryder twins, then we can't trust anyone outside our little circle. Besides, you can't read Garrett's emotions, and you couldn't read Finch's, either. Garrett was best friends with Finch, who turned out to be Katherine Shipton's son. I may have been friends with Garrett in the past, but he's not the guy I used to know. I just don't trust him." He let out a tired sigh. "Is any of this making sense to you? Because, in my head, it does."

I thought about it for a moment. He made a couple of fair points, but the situation wasn't all that simple. "I specifically remember the stunned look on Garrett's face when Finch was revealed as the Bestiary's saboteur. It looked genuine. Also, let's not classify everyone whose emotions I can't feel as evil. I doubt my Empathy works like that. If we're to follow that reasoning, then Tobe is partially evil, because I can't feel most of him. Preceptor Sloane Bellmore would be evil, too. Imogene Whitehall..."

The mere mention of her name made Wade straighten his back and lit green fires in his eyes. I couldn't help but giggle, though there was an underlying nagging feeling that I couldn't quite shake on this topic.

"Good Lord, you have such a crush on her," I added, laughing lightly. Deep down, I wasn't really laughing.

"Yeah, you might be right about the Empathy part," he replied, ignoring the crush remark. "You said you don't feel a bunch of other magicals in the coven, either."

"Exactly. As far as Garrett is concerned, I'm not saying he's 100 percent innocent, nor that he has anything to do with this. Nothing is certain at this point. But nothing stops you from talking to him and at least airing out the closets, getting rid of the skeletons... You know, what reasonable adults do when there's conflict."

He seemed to relax as I said that. It was as if he'd been hoping I'd debunk this whole Garrett suspicion. Wade had once cared about Garrett, deeply, but their friendship had fallen apart. I didn't expect to fix it and make it right, but they could at least talk about it.

Speaking of getting unpleasant stuff out of the way, I'd been thinking about something lately, involving Katherine Shipton and Finch, and decided to share it with Wade as we reached the magnolia trees in the middle of the dome.

"Listen, I want to go down into the dungeons and talk to Adley," I said.

Wade didn't seem surprised. He smirked, instead. "We don't have dungeons, Harley. We have a basement. This isn't a medieval castle, with dark towers, dungeons, and alligator-ridden moats."

"You and your technicalities," I grumbled. "But yeah. Adley. I want to talk to her about everything that happened. It's been long enough. She's had time to stew, and I've had time to clear my cluttered head. If Katherine Shipton *is* planning a comeback with the Ryder twins or something, I think it's now more important than ever that I gather as much intel on that witch as possible. That includes talking to Adley de la Dartha. Maybe even Finch."

"I doubt Alton would let you go to Purgatory to talk to Finch, but I don't see a problem with speaking to Adley," Wade replied.

"But you'll have to be careful, Harley. She's a seasoned witch. She could've been faking some of her emotions, knowing you're an Empath. She could've known all about Finch's plans from the very beginning, then lied about it to avoid Purgatory. The only reason she's here is because we couldn't get her to confess to that. We managed to sentence her to a year in the basement for failing to meet regulations, since she didn't register Finch as a Shapeshifter after his Reading. Had we been able to take her down for conspiracy to commit murder through the gargoyles, she would've been tossed into Purgatory without so much as an appeal."

He made a fair point. I, too, had been aware of the possibility. But I also had confidence in my ability to read people with my Empathy. It was a link to one's soul, in a way.

"I get that. Still, I think I got a clear picture of her. I do think I need to talk to her," I replied.

Wade sighed and shook his head. There was something about him that I couldn't quite understand. Even with my Empathy, some of his feelings escaped me, particularly at that moment, as we stood under the magnolia tree and looked at each other. I sensed concern and curiosity, but there was something else—a thread I couldn't quite follow.

Remembering that physical contact amplified my power, I took hold of his wrist, feeling his skin against my fingertips. Wade stilled, his expression firm as he stared at me.

I, on the other hand, felt my knees weaken. My limbs were jelly. A wave of sweet and spicy warmth washed over me, filling me up. The sensation was incredible, like nothing I'd ever experienced before. It was as if Wade's subconscious was trying to reach out to me, to tell me a secret.

It felt like a high of sorts, impossible to forget, as time stood still around us. I glanced at my Esprit and noticed the white pearl glowing—it was definitely amplifying this physical touch for me.

I was glazed in liquid sunshine, until he politely pulled his hand back and looked away.

"Sorry," I murmured. "Sometimes I get a better feel for people when I touch them."

His eyes found me again. He was nervous. "And? What did you... feel?"

Heat burst through my cheeks. I didn't know what to say. Not only because I wasn't sure what I'd felt, but also because he didn't seem like he really wanted to know. Whether it was my Esprit amplifying my Empathy or not, I'd gotten a glimpse of a secret Wade, a side of him he'd been working hard to keep hidden. I kind of felt bad at the thought of him knowing I'd seen it. Sometimes, concessions were okay.

"Concern," I replied. "I know. You're worried. I appreciate it."

"I just don't want you to get hurt or fooled by anyone even remotely connected to Katherine Shipton," Wade said, his gaze softening on my face.

Just then, my phone beeped. I'd gotten a text. "At this hour?" I croaked, then pulled my phone out to check it. "Oh... It's from Krieger."

My heart was thudding. That was all me.

"What does it say?" Wade asked.

"He... He wants me to do the Reading tomorrow. Well, it's after midnight already, so today. At six a.m. What kind of monster is he?" I groaned. But, at the same time, I was excited.

"The early-bird type, clearly," Wade replied with a smirk. "Go hit the sack, Merlin. I'll see you tomorrow."

He didn't wait for me to respond. He glided up one of the staircases and vanished into his room. I exhaled deeply, reading Krieger's message again. With everything that was already going on, I had to admit, this was something I was really looking forward to.

The moment of truth.

FIFTEEN

Harley

I was barely able to sleep. Despite the fact that I was tired, I was wound up by what had happened the previous day. The anticipation of my second Reading played a substantial part, too.

At six in the morning, I knocked on the infirmary door. My hands were shaking, so I balled them into fists and kept them behind my back.

When Krieger opened the door and greeted me with a bright smile, I found myself at a loss for words.

"Good morning, Doctor," I said, my voice barely audible.

"Ah. Miss Merlin! Punctuality is something I value in people! Come in," he replied, stepping aside.

I walked into the infirmary. The white neon lights glowed overhead. Combined with the pristine walls and metallic details, it generated a brightness to which my eyes needed a few seconds to properly adjust.

In the middle of the room was the infamous Reading chair, complete with its leather straps. I couldn't ignore the flashbacks—my first time in this room with Adley de la Barthe, Alton, and Wade, and that big-ass syringe that could easily be used to stab and kill a medium-sized mammal.

As if sensing my raw nerves, Krieger shut the door and chuckled. "Relax, Miss Merlin. I promised I would make the process less painful for you. I intend to keep my word."

"I take it you, too, experienced the monstrous jab, huh?" I replied, stopping in front of the chair.

"Absolutely. It scars you for life," Krieger muttered. He walked over to one of the tables on the right. It was loaded with a variety of weird-looking instruments, copper bowls, and glass bottles filled with herbs and crystals. Next to them was a large, open notebook and a long-necked desk light. By the looks of it, that was Krieger's workspace.

"How is your magical detector work coming along?" I asked, nowhere near ready to sit in the chair. I was equal parts excited and terrified—not of the needle this time, but of the result. This was it. My one chance to find out whether I was really a Mediocre or not. Assuming, of course, that the first Reading had been wrong or incomplete.

"Quite well, actually. As I said before, Adley had done most of the research work. I'm simply following up on all her theories, putting each into practice. I've managed to identify a magical's energy signature, and I can scan it with a device I built, based on Adley's notes," Krieger replied, pointing at a remote-control-looking gadget on the table, alongside the notebook. The device was wide open, its cables and circuits spilled out under a magnifying glass. "I've managed to compare the energy reading to blood samples from the same magicals, and I've identified the markers to follow for a proper Reading."

"Oh, wow," I said. "That's quite some progress."

Krieger beamed with pride. "Yes, it is. However, I've yet to figure out a way to customize the device and make it function like the Reading bowl. This is where magic and science truly intertwine, and it's a massive headache."

"I'm sure you'll crack it."

"Right. I don't give up easily. There are some passages in Adley's book that I don't quite understand, but our libraries can surely shed some light. The magical detector won't happen tomorrow, though." He sighed.

"Well, you strike me as a pretty sharp tack, Doctor. You'll figure it out soon enough," I murmured.

He stared back at me, the corner of his mouth twitching. A minute passed in awkward silence before he spoke again. "So, are you going to stand there like a deer in headlights, or will you sit down and let me do the Reading?"

I laughed nervously and gathered the courage to sit in the chair. I kept my hands in my lap, eyeing the leather restraints. Krieger took out the copper bowl with its hieroglyph etchings, along with a square tin box and a... hypodermic syringe. I breathed a sigh of relief at the sight of it.

"That looks much better," I said.

Its stem was made of stainless steel, with runes engraved on one side, but the needle was short and extremely thin. It was nothing compared to its predecessor, the elephant tranquilizer. He placed them all on a small table, which he wheeled over to my side, and proceeded to mix the Reading ingredients in the bowl. From what I could tell, this was slightly different from my previous Reading.

Krieger combined a variety of powdered crystals and crushed herbs in the middle of the bowl, then picked up the syringe and smiled at me. "This won't hurt a bit," he said. "I had this made to order in a Washington craft shop."

"Yeah, I get that... What's up with all the paraphernalia, though? Adley didn't use that before."

"Ah. These are all amplifiers," he said, pointing at the bowl's contents. "They're meant to... let's say, zoom in on your blood. There would be no point in doing a similar Reading again. We'd get the same results. We're digging deeper this time."

Thankful that this didn't require any leather straps, I put my forearm out, allowing Krieger to draw my blood through that slim, nifty-looking syringe. I barely felt the pinch, and it was over before I could say "Abracadabra."He released the blood into the bowl and mixed it with a sterling silver spoon, whispering a spell. Within seconds, the dark crimson liquid flashed white, then swirled out across the hieroglyphs, drawing an intricate mandala pattern in the process.

I had no idea what I was watching, but Krieger was dazzled by the entire display. The flash faded away, leaving behind the dried blood swirls and lines. The final result made him grunt, while I held my breath, on the edge of my seat.

"What… Um, what does it say?" I asked.

He cackled, as if he'd just uncovered the secrets of the universe. "I knew it!"

"What? What did you know?"

"It makes sense now. Why it slipped past the first Reading…" he muttered, scratching his beard and virtually ignoring me. "No one would've looked twice, had they not known who your parents were, at the time. After all, Mediocrity births Mediocrity, but excellence would never—"

He stopped himself, then raised his head to look at me.

"What?" I snapped, close to breaking into a cold sweat.

"Miss Merlin, have you ever heard of a Dempsey Suppressor?" he asked, his tone eerily calm. I shook my head. "It was invented by Richard Dempsey, one of America's finest preceptors of Charms and Hexes back in the 1800s. It's a tiny little thing, a charm of sorts, able to suppress a magical's energy and completely distort a Reading. Dempsey crafted it as an experiment with the intention of using it against dangerous magicals."

"Okay. I'm guessing it has something to do with me?" I asked, rather rhetorically.

Krieger sighed, then put a hand on his hip and gave me a pitiful half-smile. "Miss Merlin, you have a Dempsey Suppressor in you."

"Seriously?"

Chills trickled through my veins as I tried to wrap my head around this revelation.

"The Dempsey Suppressor is a hidden, dirty little secret of the upper echelons in our magical society. They're not crafted by just anyone. The knowledge behind them is reserved only for certain individuals. Given the conditions of your birth and your noble bloodline, I can only draw one conclusion from this. Your father, Hiram Merlin, former director of the New York Coven, implanted a Dempsey Suppressor in you shortly after you were born."

That assessment felt like a punch in the gut. I took several deep breaths, trying to imagine how that would've come to happen. I decided to voice my thoughts, hoping that Krieger might be able to assist me in formulating a complete reasoning.

"I was in my father's care until the age of three, after which I was dropped off at an orphanage here, in San Diego…"

Krieger nodded once. "Yes. I think your father wanted you to be as normal as possible, despite your magical heritage. I suppose he wanted to keep you off the radar and out of the coven's sight," he explained. "The Dempsey Suppressor is certainly doing its job, Miss Merlin. There is power inside you, more than one usually finds in a witch, I should add. But it's toned down. Muffled. Which is why you were initially labeled a Mediocre."

"My father used a… Dempsey Suppressor to hide me from the covens… Adley de la Barthe said that, given my limited abilities and Chaos, I'd maybe get to do one Purge in this lifetime," I murmured, remembering my first Reading. "Since she'd thought I was a Mediocre. I guess she was wrong. I'm not a Mediocre after all."

"Oh, you are anything *but*! Miss Merlin, you are one of the most powerful magicals I've come across in my lifetime, and, trust me, I've done a lot of Readings before you. If we could find a way to remove the Suppressor, we would unleash your full potential."

"Wait. *If?*" I asked. "What do you mean, *if?*"

Krieger shrugged. "The Dempsey Suppressor, in addition to

being a highly complex and rarely approved charm, is also meant to be permanent."

My stomach dropped. I slumped in the chair, as if the burden of ages had suddenly been released on my shoulders. Nevertheless, I wasn't ready to resign myself to living a limited existence. My very soul was on fire, eager to discover the full extent of my power. I needed it now, more than ever, with Katherine Shipton lurking around.

"You said you use it on dangerous magicals. I suppose you're referring to those imprisoned in Purgatory," I said. "But didn't Dempsey think of a way to undo it if, say, the magical in question was proven innocent?"

"Well, the Suppressor is only applied after a sentence is laid out," Krieger replied. "It's not impossible to remove it; it's just tedious. You see, it's a very small object, about the size of a fingernail. It's implanted in a bone and, as the tissue regenerates, it's difficult to detect. It often doesn't show up on X-rays. I would recommend starting there. But then there is the question of how to remove it without harming you, physically and magically. It's tamper-proof and requires a certain surgical skill to extract it without triggering its tamper-proof mechanisms. Dempsey thought of everything when he devised it, I'm afraid."

"What if I push myself? In training, I mean, and with my Esprit? Wouldn't I ever be able to break it?" I asked.

"I strongly advise against that, Miss Merlin. It may hurt you in ways beyond repair," Krieger warned. "Remember, Dempsey created it to suppress exceptional but criminal magicals. Imagine what would've happened if any of them had been able to just bypass it with sheer willpower. It wouldn't end well for you."

I felt like a deflated balloon. Krieger didn't enjoy seeing me like that. I could feel his angst and frustration. He wanted to help me. In addition, he was insanely curious. Much like me, I was sure he wanted to see the exact limits of my Chaos powers.

"Hiram put it there for a reason," Krieger added. "It was meant to protect you from discovery. I must say, your powers, or at least some of them, still managed to slip through. The Dempsey Suppressor is designed to be much more powerful. Frankly, it shouldn't even have let all four of your Elemental abilities out! Even after your first Reading, you were puzzling to most, simply because you're a full Elemental, an Empath, and a Telekinetic. I can't help but wonder if there's more lying beneath that limitation..."

"Shocked" didn't begin to describe my current state. Stunned? More or less the same thing. Baffled? Absolutely. Resigned? Still—hell, no. A thousand times, no.

"So, what you're saying is that... even with the Suppressor on, my powers still slipped through," I concluded.

"Exactly. I will look into a detection and extraction procedure, Miss Merlin, as I myself am personally intrigued," Krieger said, grinning.

I chuckled. "Yeah, I can feel that. Thank you, Doctor. At least I know now."

"I'm pleased I could give you some good news. Even though we often refer to Mediocrity as being just a label, it does have an impact on our lives as magicals. Nobody really wants to be a Mediocre, after all. In your case, it's even preposterous!" Krieger replied. "Give me some time to research the Dempsey Suppressor properly, and I'll advise you on the next steps once I know what to do. In the meantime, I will report this to Alton. I'm sure he'll be interested in hearing these results."

"Yeah, I'll bet. In fact, I think he'll be pleased. He did say there was more to me than met the eye," I said, then remembered Garrett's advice from the previous night. "Doctor Krieger, I wanted to ask you something, and I think it's related to this. Light and Darkness—I've read about a magical's affiliation to one or the other, but I don't understand exactly how that works, or what it means."

Krieger paused, his pale blue eyes fixed on mine. His lips curled into a devious little smile. "I guessed you would ask, at some point. Adley never mentioned it in the report she wrote after your first

Reading. It struck me as odd, but, thinking of you as a Mediocre, I wasn't sure it mattered much. Now, however, it's different. Allow me to explain."

He rushed to his desk and fumbled through one of the drawers, then came back with an old book, flipping through its pages until he found what he was looking for.

"Light and Darkness are primordial Children of Chaos. It's not a matter of good and evil here, because that isn't how we quantify Light and Darkness," he continued, and handed me the book. He showed me an illustration depicting two dragons flying around each other, one black, the other white. "It is true that many magicals connected to Darkness end up committing terrible crimes, but it's always been my belief that it is more a question of character than of Chaos. Light and Darkness amplify a magical's abilities differently. It would be difficult for me to explain right now, but I will leave this book with you for reference."

"How does this connection work?" I asked, holding on to the book.

"You're born with it. We all are. I, for example, belong to Darkness. My abilities are intense and can be extremely destructive," Krieger said.

"But you're such a sweetheart," I replied, smiling.

"Don't let the good versus bad prejudice cloud your judgment," he shot back. "I told you, that's not how we view Light and Darkness. Light-affiliated magicals experience a different kind of intensity in their powers. They're more inclined toward Telekinesis and Herculean abilities, for example, as well as Air and Water Elementals. Darkness is better connected to Shapeshifting, Empathy, Earth and Fire, Necromancy, and other death-related powers. Perhaps that's where the stigma comes from. Like I said, that book will give you more insight on both."

"I thought Elementals were all drawn to Light."

"It's not a rule," he replied. "Most are, but many aren't," he added, smiling. "Like I said, there's no set value for Darkness and Light.

You can still find a Necromancer who's on the Light side. Extremely rare, but still, it proves it's possible."

"Okay. So, what am I connected to?" I asked.

"That's the million-dollar question," Krieger said. "Your connection right now is inconclusive at best. I would need to remove the Dempsey Suppressor to know exactly where you fall on the spectrum. Given your combined abilities, it's difficult to even guess right now. You might as well know that Raffe Levi, Alton Waterhouse, Tatyana Vasilisa, and Garrett Kyteler are connected to Darkness. Your other friends are part of Light."

That did come as a surprise, but, based on Krieger's explanations, it made sense. After all, Tatyana and Alton had death-related abilities, for example. Alton's notes from my parents' file became even more intriguing.

"I'm told that my mother was Darkness and that my father was Light," I replied.

"Which will make your full power even more interesting, once we take that thing out of you and figure out which connection you inherited," Krieger murmured.

Looking back, my father's wish to have me grow up like a normal human felt like a double-edged blade. On the one hand, he'd probably wanted to protect me by keeping me hidden. On the other hand, however, it seriously impaired my development as a magical.

I let out a heavy sigh before giving Krieger a faint nod. "Thank you for everything, Doctor. And for the book."

"Don't let the Suppressor's existence weigh down on you," Krieger said.

"I won't. But I am curious about a few things and have questions. I think Adley will have the answers to them. I'm wondering if she did notice the Suppressor during my first Reading and chose to hide it from me. I don't know, maybe I'm reaching."

"Not really. In the magical world, nothing is absolute. Given your Empath ability, you may sense deception in her if you ask the right questions," Krieger replied. "If you'd like, I can join you. I have some inquiries of my own where her work is concerned, anyway."

I smiled, touched by his kind nature and slightly amused by his inquisitiveness. Krieger was nothing like what the rumors said. He sure did inspire dread and chills, and that German accent didn't help, but the guy was amazing.

"I'd like that, thank you," I said.

"Besides, after everything that happened, I don't think you should be left alone with Adley."

He had a point there. And it was going to work in my favor if I had another pair of eyes in the room with me. If Wade was right in his suspicion that Adley may be able to deceive my Empathy, Krieger could, perhaps, spot that. He didn't strike me as the kind of guy who could be easily fooled.

Krieger and I agreed to meet later to speak to Adley, after which I left the infirmary with a positive attitude. I wasn't a Mediocre, and I was looking forward to rubbing that in Wade's face. But I was being suppressed… and that needed fixing, as soon as possible.

SIXTEEN

Tatyana

I'd spent most of the previous evening by Dylan's side in the infirmary. Krieger's nurses were wonderful and kind, allowing me to stay there well past visiting hours. Dylan slept for most of the time, only waking up for a few minutes now and then. He'd mumble something, then doze off again. That beastly hex had drained the life out of him, and it was going to take a while for him to make a full recovery.

That morning, I felt as though it was the start of a fresh, new day. The optimism was more than I usually dealt with prior to coffee, but I welcomed it.

After all, I'd been feeling so guilty about what happened to Dylan.

And I hadn't found out anything more about Will or how he'd died. Astrid's search through Smartie didn't return any useful results. Alton figured it was probably because Will's family wasn't registered with the coven. There had been no record of a William living at that address in the electronic database. So that was a dead-end for the time being, and since it had probably happened a long time ago, long enough for Will to lose track of time altogether, I assumed it wasn't in any way related to our issue with the Ryder twins.

In the end, I had to focus on any information or facts that were recent and fresh. Once a trail went cold, it seemed nearly impossible to find anything.

I slipped out of a hot shower, feeling rejuvenated and energized. If someone were to make me run around a football field in that instant, I would've darted off willingly. I wrapped a towel around my body and removed the shower cap, letting my long blonde hair loose.

I wiped the steam from the bathroom mirror to look at myself, then froze. I was nowhere to be found in the mirror. Oberon Marx was my reflection.

He was watching me. He *was* me.

Dammit, he never left!

"What the hell?!" I croaked, feeling my blood boil.

Oberon stilled, surprised by my reaction. "Oh, crap, you can see me."

"The mirrors never lie, Oberon! You should've known better than to stow away in my body!"

"Okay. Okay. Take it easy, Tatyana, I don't mean any harm." Oberon tried to calm me down, but fury was blazing through me like a firestorm. In my mind, I was already trying to remember an expulsion chant. For some reason, those memories were fuzzy.

Scratch that. It's not just some reason. It's him! He's messing with my head!

"I'm not messing with your head, Tatyana, I swear!" Oberon continued, having read my mind.

I gasped. "Crap."

He smirked. "I can hear your thoughts, sweetheart. Sorry."

I took a deep breath, trying to regain my composure and find a solution to this problem. With Oberon still in my body, I wasn't really myself anymore. It was only a matter of time before he'd try to take over completely. They all tried that. I should've paid more attention to my mother's teachings as a kid. She'd warned me about this, but I was too absorbed in talking to dead people at the time. The Kolduny were a rare and strict magical typology. There weren't that many books about us.

And why the hell couldn't I remember any of the expulsion spells? Oberon was definitely messing around in my noggin. I didn't like it. I had to figure out a way to get him out without him knowing it—*challenge of the century.*

"What do you want?" I asked. "Why are you still here?"

"I swear I have zero intentions of taking over your body. It's not why I'm here, I promise," Oberon replied. "If it were, you'd be gone by now, trust me."

"Okay. That still doesn't answer my question."

I gripped the edge of the sink with both hands, trying to analyze my situation and surroundings as best as I could, knowing that Oberon was tuned in to my thoughts. I had to be careful.

"Listen, Tatyana, you touched me in ways I didn't think possible," he said, wearing a pained expression. "I've been drifting around this place for so long, I was becoming cynical and jaded. But you brought me back to life. The lengths you were willing to go to in order to save your friend... That's hardcore, girl. I like that." He chuckled, then turned serious all of a sudden. "You've got trouble in this coven, and I want to help you."

"What are you talking about?" I asked.

"There's darkness lurking around here. I can't quite put my finger on it, and the other spirits whisper to each other," he replied. "It's hard to get something concrete out of them, but they all say the same thing, on a very annoying loop. A storm is coming. A storm is coming. A storm is coming. I've been hearing that line since Harley Merlin first set foot inside the San Diego Coven."

My stomach churned. "And you think you can help me?" I murmured, frowning.

It agitated me to no longer see my own reflection in the mirror, because it reminded me of how easy it was to lose control.

"I've been quiet in here," Oberon said. "I'm being gentle and not interfering in anything you do. I'll keep doing that, I promise. But I need you to let me ride along, until the trouble—the so-called storm—passes. You'll need me, Tatyana. You'll need my strength, my Herculean abilities, especially now that Dylan is indisposed."

"Wait, so you want to stay in me for a little while longer? Have you lost your damn mind?" I hissed.

"I can help you!"

I glared at him. "You've gone nuts. I guess that's what happens when you wander through the veil for so long, without moving on, huh?"

"It's not that!" Oberon snapped, then inhaled deeply in order to keep himself leveled. Ironically, I could feel his frustration as if it were mine. I wondered if that was how Empathy felt for Harley. "Tatyana, I like you. You're a good girl with a strong connection to Darkness. You're a Kolduny, for heaven's sake! You're a rare gem among the magicals, but you don't have my strength, and you don't know the people I know... in the spirit world, that is."

That captured my interest, and I paused for a moment before muttering, "Go on."

"Let me stay with you for a little while longer, at least until you catch the Ryder twins. I think they have something to do with this impending storm. I can feel it in my gut," he said.

"You don't have a gut anymore. You're piggybacking on mine," I fired back.

He grinned. "You know what I mean. Tatyana, you may be able to contact the spirit world and call out to them, but you know they don't always cooperate. I can help you with that. I know everyone in this coven, darling. And I can put you in touch with some dead folk who knew the Ryder twins."

I thought about it for a while, well aware that Oberon could hear my thought process. He could separate himself from that and give me some privacy, but, at that moment, it was in his best interests to listen. He was trying to convince me to let him stay.

"Can you reach out to them soon?" I asked.

He smiled. "Yes. It will take some time, though. Maybe a day or two. They're holed up somewhere in the veil. I'll have to put the word out for their wispy butts to find me. But I guarantee you they will come, and they will cooperate with you, because of me. I swear. All you have to do is let me stay here for a little while longer. That's all."

A minute passed in grueling silence as I measured the pros and cons. I had to maintain control of the situation. I'd never had a spirit stay with me for so long, but I had enough confidence in my mental strength. I couldn't expel him on my own, but Santana had been trained for situations like this. She could take me down, tie me up, and use an ancient Roman exorcism to drive Oberon out, if needed. Until then, I could take this ride and maybe get to the Ryder twins sooner rather than later.

"You'll stay out of my mind," I said.

He nodded, visibly excited. "Absolutely. You'll have your privacy, at all times. I'll just be here, in the background, enjoying the senses of touch, smell, hearing, and taste again... Ahhh! I can't wait to feel coffee on my tongue!" He chuckled, then switched back to his serious mode. He was making it hard for me to be angry at him. Even in death, Oberon Marx could be quite charming. "And I'll lend you my strength, should you need it."

"I call the shots, at all times. Do we have an agreement?"

"Yes. Absolutely. You're in charge, Tatyana."

"Okay... You can stay. Just don't make me regret this," I replied.

I wasn't comfortable with this decision, but Oberon did have a point. If the Ryder twins were planning something big and bad, I needed to do my part and gather as much intel as possible. By whatever means necessary.

"You won't regret it. I promise," Oberon said, beaming like the morning sun. "I'll reach out to the spirits today. I'll find your Ryder links and bring them to you."

I nodded once. "Let's keep this between us, though. I'll avoid mirrors, so my crew doesn't spot you."

"I get it. I'll be discreet," he replied.

Spirits had tried to take over my body before. It never ended well for them—or for me, either. They always drained the energy out of me, knocking me out for hours on end. Oberon felt different, though. He fueled me. It was a fascinating type of symbiosis, one I was interested in studying further, now that I had that chance.

I also knew Santana and Dylan would be the first to object.

But if I could do anything to help catch the Ryder twins and stop them from poisoning the minds of other magicals, I was ready to do it. Even if it meant bending my Kolduny ethics.

SEVENTEEN

Harley

After the Reading, I made my way to the banquet hall. It was breakfast time, and I was dying for a cup of hot coffee. The lack of sleep from the previous night was callously reminding me that I needed a lot of caffeine to get through the day.

However, the knowledge that I wasn't in fact a Mediocre put a huge grin on my face. Of course, the magicals I passed by along the way didn't know that and probably thought I'd lost my marbles, but it didn't matter. *I'm not a Mediocre. Suck it, haters!*

But something else was on my mind, too—besides the Dempsey Suppressor and the risks of its extraction via surgery. I'd used the dreamcatcher last night, and I'd gotten a better look at Isadora Merlin inside one of my earliest memories. I had a clear picture of her in my head. The long, undulating black hair, the sky-blue eyes that mirrored mine and my father's, the stern look on her face, and the mild furrow of her slim eyebrows... I wondered whether she was still alive, or whether Katherine Shipton or some other vicious magical had gotten to her

Alton didn't know much about Isadora, but the one thing he could tell me with absolute certainty was that she was hated by a lot of criminal witches and warlocks. It turned out, my Merlin auntie had put away a lot of baddies in Purgatory, back in the day.

I couldn't help but grin as I walked into the banquet hall, eager to share the news of my faux Mediocrity with the rest of my crew. I came to a sudden halt when I found Santana, Tatyana, Astrid, Raffe, and Wade at the same side of a table with Garrett. Poe and the others on his old team were on the opposite end, scowling at my people. That sight was confusing, to say the least, and I doubted that Wade and Garrett had somehow gotten past their differences over the course of one night.

Nevertheless, my head felt heavy, so I loaded up on coffee first, then went to our side of the table, giving both Wade and Garrett a questioning look. No one on the Rag Team seemed particularly happy that Garrett was there. He was sporting a smug grin, complete with his signature dimples.

"What's up, fellas?" I asked, my voice stuck on a higher pitch than usual.

I glanced around the table. Astrid was confused. Santana was irritated. Raffe, as always, was an absolute mess for me to read, and Tatyana was on edge. There was something slightly different about her, but I couldn't tell what, exactly, since Garrett was an obvious disruptor for everyone's emotions. Wade was nearing the boiling point, while Garrett... well, was Garrett. Unreadable but clearly pleased.

"Is that mocha?" he asked, nodding at my mug.

I shook my head. "Nah, latte. I'm having plenty of these babies today, so I'm thinning them out with milk," I replied. "So, what brings you to our end of the table, Garrett?"

Wade sighed, unable to look at me and, instead, resigned to staring at his coffee. "Garrett is joining our team," he said. "Alton assigned him while Dylan is recovering."

"Ah." My reply was flat. I had mixed feelings about this. I'd seen Garrett in action during the gargoyle bonanza, but I hadn't had the chance to work with him. I knew he was a highly skilled magical, so, to that credit, he seemed like a good addition to the Rag Team. At the same time, I was worried about friction. Garrett was the kind of guy who spoke his mind and loved it when that pissed people off. He was what I commonly referred to as a "social sadist." Since the post-Finch shift in his behavior, he was actually nice to me, despite his occasionally abrasive comebacks, but I couldn't say the same for his dynamic with the others. I took a sip from my coffee and gave Garrett a brief nod. "Well, that explains the sour faces on everyone this morning."

"Hey, orders are orders," Garrett said with a casual shrug.

"We've agreed to take Garrett with us," Tatyana added, "to preserve yesterday's split. You, Wade, Raffe, and Santana can do your thing in peace. I can handle Garrett."

He chuckled. "Don't worry, Tatyana. I'll be on my best behavior."

"It's not your behavior I'm worried about. It's that rotten mind of yours. It bypasses your mouth, and it gets on my nerves. Lucky for you, I'm well equipped to smack you around if needed," Tatyana said. Her eyes glimmered with what felt like excitement. From what I could tell, she would've liked for Garrett to challenge her, as if she was itching for a fight. That wasn't like her.

I figured she'd had a rough night, with Dylan still recovering. Maybe lashing out was her way of coping with what had happened, especially since I knew she'd blamed herself for the whole Kenneth Willow incident.

"I'm sure Garrett won't do anything to get on your bad side," Wade interjected before Garrett could open his mouth and object to her sharp warning. "He's a good magical and a professional. He's grown since the Finch incident."

Both Garrett and I were surprised to hear Wade talk like that. Deep down, I sensed relief. Wade wasn't happy with Garrett on our crew, but he certainly was fine with passing him over to Tatyana and Astrid. He was pleased to not have to spend the day in his presence.

Making the best of a bad situation, I guess.

"How did your Reading go?" Wade asked me.

All eyes were on me now. It was time for the not-so-grand reveal. I put on a confident smile. "My dad put a Dempsey Suppressor in me when I was a baby," I said.

They were all stunned. They apparently knew what the device was and what it did. A few seconds passed before Wade put two and two together, his eyes wide with surprise and his heart filled with... joy. *This is unexpected.*

"It makes sense," he replied. "You're an Empath, a Telekinetic, and a full Elemental. Alton was right. There was definitely something off about you being a Mediocre."

"Is that why you kept hammering the prospect of Mediocrity in my head?" I replied with a raised eyebrow, prompting Garrett to chuckle. I scowled at him, too. "You were no better, remember?"

As expected, my comeback was enough to wipe the grin from his face.

"I was trying to be realistic! I was working with what we were given from the first Reading. I just didn't want you to get your hopes up and then be disappointed," Wade muttered, though I sensed regret oozing out of him, thick and heavy.

"It's cool. Krieger said the regular Reading wouldn't have spotted the Suppressor anyway," I replied.

Astrid jumped up and hugged me. "I knew it!" She giggled. "I called it!"

"That she did, that she totally did," Santana chimed in, smiling.

They were all happy for me. It filled me with light and hope, thankful to have people like them around. I would've gone to the end of the world for them, simply because of how supportive they'd been.

"So, Krieger found the Suppressor, huh?" Raffe asked.

"Nope. He knows it's present, but he needs to do a full body scan, X-rays and stuff. Plus, there are risks in removing it because of how it was designed," I explained. "He's looking into it, though. I guess we'll cross that bridge when we get there. The interesting part is that it was supposed to fully suppress my abilities."

"Obviously, it didn't," Santana murmured.

"Which Krieger says is amazing," I added. "He thinks it's because—"

"There's so much power in you that it couldn't be held back properly with a Dempsey Suppressor," Wade replied, in genuine awe of me.

I smirked, relishing the ripples of pride swelling my chest. "Yup," I said, then let out a heavy sigh. "But it's kind of useless if it's not set free. So, technically speaking, I'm not a Mediocre, but, in practicality, I kind of am. For now."

"Hey. At least you know the truth!" Santana said encouragingly.

A phone beeped. Tatyana checked hers. "Okay, we'll need to get ready soon. My first alarm just went off."

I still had something to do before delving into day two of our magical operations.

"You guys go ahead and get ready. I need to talk to Krieger about something else," I said. "I'll meet you by the dragon fountain in an hour?"

They all nodded, and I left them behind as I made my way out of the banquet hall. I could feel Wade's eyes on me. One quick glance over my shoulder confirmed it: he was watching me. The emotions coming off him were different. Warm and curious...

I texted Krieger. It was time to talk to Adley.

EIGHTEEN

Harley

As soon as I set foot in the basement, O'Halloran's voice boomed through the main underground hallway. I was surprised to hear him, given that he was supposed to still be in recovery. I advanced through the wide corridor, chills running down my spine.

This wasn't a dungeon, but it didn't exactly inspire fuzzy feelings, either. The walls, the ceiling, and the floor were made of cool, gray concrete, with sharp white overhead lights. Several corridors connected to this main one. As I passed by some of them, I noticed the metal doors, all kept under lock and key and covered in charmed etchings. The magic used to keep criminals in was similar to that in the Bestiary. Those who broke the coven laws were treated like monsters.

Down here, the coven kept the witches and warlocks whose crimes demanded sentences of up to five years. Everyone else was shipped off to Purgatory. Judging by how this place looked, I didn't even dare imagine what Purgatory would be like.

The deeper I ventured, the louder O'Halloran's voice got, until I found him in a corridor to my right, yelling at two security magicals. He'd returned to his black uniform and was leaning onto a cane for support. There were some bruises still healing on his face, as well.

"Every four hours!" he barked. "You're supposed to tour every damn hallway, every four hours! Not five hours! Not six! Not four hours and four minutes because you needed to finish your baloney sandwich! Four hours!"

The security magicals were quaking in their boots. They both stilled when they saw me.

"What's the matter, you ninnies? You look like you've seen a ghost, and, last time I checked, we only have one Kolduny on the premises!" O'Halloran growled. He was in a bad mood, but then again, it was in his nature to be perpetually grumpy—that much I'd learned from Wade's descriptions of his numerous training sessions and security seminars. When O'Halloran yelled at you, he was just slightly irritated. Most of us had gotten used to the half-Irish powder keg, but the newer security magicals had yet to wrap their heads around his moods.

O'Halloran turned around to follow their gazes and found me standing at the end of the corridor. He lit up like a Christmas tree.

"Merlin! You little bundle of raw Chaos!" he exclaimed, clearly happy to see me. O'Halloran was one of the magicals I couldn't read, but his face usually did the work for me. "Where have you been hiding?"

"Uh, nowhere, sir," I replied, giving him a weary smile. "Working and learning, sir. I thought you weren't due to come out of the infirmary for at least another week—"

"Hah! Is my presence here inconvenient to ya, Merlin?" O'Halloran asked, pursing his lips. "Should I have stayed in bed long enough for you to sneak around the basement prison? Huh?"

It was always hard to tell whether he was joking or whether he was serious, because he always sounded like he was seconds away from beating somebody up. His tone was always clipped or harsh, even when he was jesting—his humor was too subtle, at best, making it hard for some of us to catch on. I chuckled nervously, putting my hands behind my back and adopting a pious posture.

"No, sir, not at all. I'm happy to see you're out and about!" I replied. "I just didn't expect to see you out so soon, that's all."

He scowled at me for a moment while the two security magicals held their breaths, probably also wondering whether he was serious or not. O'Halloran had a way of keeping people on edge. I thought he secretly liked it. Maybe a little too much.

He then burst into laughter and motioned for me to get closer. "I'm kidding, Merlin! Get over here! I haven't seen you in a while."

That was the security magicals' cue to loosen up a little bit, since O'Halloran was laughing—a rare sight. I sheepishly walked over and found myself trapped in a bear hug as he put his arms around me and held me tight. The security magicals were stunned. There was some fear in them, and not all of it because of O'Halloran and his disciplinary fire. Some of it was because of me... because of my last name. They knew I'd had nothing to do with what my dad had done, but, still, there was a certain degree of reserve.

"I never got to thank you for saving my life," O'Halloran said, gently pushing me away. The hug was over, and he switched back to his formal self.

"No need to thank me, sir. I was just doing what's right," I replied, giving him a polite nod.

"Well, not everybody jumps in the line of fire like you did. You've got grit. I appreciate that," he insisted. He looked back at the guards. "What the hell are you two still doing here? Do your rounds!"

They nodded and rushed out into the main hallway.

"Remember, four hours!" O'Halloran shouted after them.

They vanished behind the corner. I kind of felt sorry for them, having O'Halloran as their superior, but at the same time, I knew the SDC needed a firm hand to help it run seamlessly, especially with all the eyes that were on us—mainly because of the Bestiary, but also due to the return of Katherine Shipton.

"So, what are you doing here, Merlin?" O'Halloran asked, his voice low and calm, a complete 180-degree switch from two seconds ago. There was genuine concern in his eyes. "You shouldn't be down here."

"Sir, I have full clearance now," I replied.

"I know that! But still. You know who's down here. The toll it took on you must've been terrible," he muttered.

He was referring to Adley de la Barthe. I was touched by his somewhat fatherly concern. It was a funny thing, really. I'd spent my whole life as a foster kid, stuck in the homes of some terrible people prior to the Smiths, and dreaming about finding my own family. Now, the coven was trying to fill that void. It had given me more than one "dad." After Alton and Tobe, O'Halloran seemed to be just as worried about my wellbeing, and I had to admit it was sweet.

I smiled. "I know, sir. I'm here to talk to Adley."

"Why in the blazes would you want to do *that?*"

"She might have answers to some of my questions," I replied with a shrug.

Just then, Krieger joined us, and I felt a pinch of relief. With the good doctor by my side, O'Halloran had no chance of trying to sway me from my mission.

"O'Halloran!" Krieger exclaimed, slightly amused. "I thought my nurses were sturdy enough to keep you down if you tried to escape!"

"Eh, I'm fine, Krieger," O'Halloran retorted, rolling his eyes. "Just a little sore, but I'm fine. I couldn't take another minute in that damn bed," he added, and scowled at him. "You're not here to take me back, are ya? Because I'm not going down without a fight."

Krieger laughed. "No, no, relax. I'm here to see Adley with Miss Merlin here," he said, giving me a quick sideways glance.

O'Halloran sighed, his brows furrowed as he looked at us.

"I'll take you to her cell," he grumbled, sounding defeated.

I understood his concern, and it was much appreciated, but my feelings were meaningless if I couldn't get some useful information out of Adley. With the possibility of the Ryder twins being connected to Katherine Shipton, Adley and Finch were my only viable leads.

We followed him down the corridor, until we stopped in front of door number thirteen. Not that I was superstitious, but I couldn't help but smirk at the sight of that number and compare it to Adley's predicament.

"Thank you, sir," I said to O'Halloran.

He gave me a brief nod. "Just don't let her fool you. Ever since I found out how she protected Finch, I've not been able to look at her the same way. And don't even get me started on Finch himself. My favorite kid in the whole damn coven." He sighed, shaking his head, clearly disappointed.

"Don't let it get you down, O'Halloran," Krieger said. "You survived, and you'll make sure nothing like that happens again."

"You're damn right," O'Halloran replied, and unlocked door number thirteen. "I'll be outside if you need me."

We went in to find Adley sitting in a chair, reading a book. Her cell was small and contained the basics: a bed, a table, a couple of chairs, a trash can, and a tiny adjoining bathroom. Because she was a nonviolent criminal, she had some amenities included, judging by the pitcher of iced tea and plate of cookies on the table.

Adley had lost weight, almost resembling a ghost in her black prison garb. She looked up and froze at the sight of me. Her hair had grown a bit, covering the upper arch of her ears. Dark rings had settled under her eyes, and her skin was pale.

"Harley," she murmured, but didn't move. "Doctor Krieger. What… What are you doing here?"

The door closed behind us with a clang. O'Halloran was just outside, quiet and patiently waiting. Krieger gave Adley a soft smile.

"Hi, Adley," he said, "We're here to talk to you about a few things, if you don't mind."

She blinked several times, shame and grief hitting me from all angles—all hers. She closed the book and turned in her chair to face us.

"Please, have a seat," she replied, pointing at the bed and spare chair.

I didn't feel like sitting down, but Krieger didn't refuse the offer and plopped himself in the chair. I stood, arms crossed, frowning, trying to get a full read on her emotions.

"Do you get any sunlight at all?" I asked.

She nodded, wearing a resigned smile. "Once a day. Security rounds up the prisoners every morning for an hour. There's an open space specially designed for us. It's still part of the interdimensional pocket, but the walls are transparent, enough for us to get our fix of vitamin D."

I'd already had enough of the small talk. "Adley, we haven't spoken since they took you away, the day I woke up," I said. "I need to ask you something."

Adley looked at me, then at Krieger, and exhaled deeply. "Sure, Harley. I'll tell the truth, the whole truth, and nothing but the truth."

"Why did you do it?" I asked. "What happened, exactly? I only got the summary from Wade and Alton, but I need to hear it from you."

"I was stupid, Harley, that's what happened. I met Finch back in Los Angeles. I fell in love. I thought he loved me, too. I didn't care about the age difference or the fact that there were so many things about him that I didn't know. I went in blind, and now there's blood on my hands."

"So, you knew Finch before you came to SDC," I said. She nodded again. "And you did his Reading shortly after he transferred here."

"Yes. It was standard procedure. I didn't even know he was a Shapeshifter until I did his Reading," she explained. "I knew the stigma surrounding that ability, and I understood why he didn't want people to know. I found it odd that he didn't want Alton to know, either, but I was stupidly blind and head over heels in love with him. Whatever he wanted, I did it. For that, I will always be sorry."

"You lied for him, basically. You never registered his Shapeshifter ability," I said. "Didn't he do a Reading in the LA Coven, too?"

Adley shook her head. "No. I discovered him as a magical in Los Angeles, living with Agnes Anker, whom he said was his grand-mother. I had no idea about his connection to Katherine Shipton. I swear."

"Okay, so let me get this straight. You met in LA, when he was discovered as a magical, and hooked up, right?"

Krieger chuckled in the background. The man was proper in the way he talked to people. My loose tongue cracked him up, it seemed.

Adley sighed once more. "We met in LA, *before* he was discovered as a magical. He didn't want to go in and get registered at the time."

"You kept him hidden."

"Yes. But we both knew we couldn't keep that up for much longer, so I begged him to come in on his own. He didn't want to. He said he hated the LA Coven, that he didn't trust the magicals there. Some stories were coming out in the magical community back then about corruption in the coven. Finch knew some people there, though he never revealed himself as a magical to them either. He pretended to be human."

I stared at her. "This is incredible. You knew what a deceiver he was, and that didn't raise any red flags? Seriously?"

"As I said, I was stupid!" she replied. "I didn't want him to stay rogue, though. So, I suggested we move to San Diego. He agreed, and we left LA. I came to the coven first, as the physician. Finch followed shortly afterward."

"And you failed to disclose crucial information about him to a coven that had just taken you in," I pressed.

"That is correct. And there isn't a day I don't hate myself for it. I withheld his Shapeshifter ability. His Telekinesis was known, as was his Earth ability," Adley explained. "We kept our relationship a secret because, well, we were both new here. I didn't want people to talk about us. Finch didn't want us to go public, either. Actually, he was quite adamant about it," she added, frowning slightly. "That should've been a warning sign."

"Hey, you were blindly in love, remember?" I sighed, my stomach churning from her mixed bag of guilt and regret. "Were there any signs that Finch wasn't exactly forthcoming about who he was?"

"Yeah, there were tiny alarm signals here and there," Adley said. "I didn't always know where he went or what he did. He didn't like it when I asked questions. He'd flip out if I so much as looked at his phone screen. But he was sweet and kind in private, so I let most of that slide."

I remembered the medication I'd seen Finch take during our only training session, and I wondered if that played any part in the image he'd built for the coven.

"He took pills. Do you know what they were or what they did?" I asked.

"Oh, they definitely had a role in all this," Adley replied with an energetic nod. "He didn't tell me what they were, but he took three every day. I stole one when he wasn't looking and had it tested. A very potent antipsychotic."

I went back to the last image I had of Finch, in charmed cuffs, shortly before he was taken away. "I think it makes sense to assume that the Finch we saw in chains was the real version of him, not the pill-popped one," I said.

"I had no idea what was hiding underneath," Adley continued. "Once he was captured, they took all his possessions away, the pills included. They're in evidence lockup if you need them for anything. The prescribing doctor's name will be on the bottle. O'Halloran can give you access."

"Thank you for that, Adley," Krieger chimed in. "It might be a good idea to talk to his psychiatrist back in LA... Oh, but then there's the confidentiality issue."

"It would be unethical, but—" Adley paused and laughed lightly. "I'm the last person to talk ethics here."

A moment passed in silence, before Krieger spoke. "You know, Adley, I did Harley's second Reading today."

That got her full attention. "Oh. What were the results?"

"I went deep, this time. She's not a Mediocre, for starters. She was fitted with a Dempsey Suppressor as an infant," Krieger said.

Adley gasped, genuinely delighted from what I sensed. She gave me a broad smile, her eyes twinkling with excitement. "I'm glad to hear that, Harley! I knew a second Reading would shed more insight into what you are. I'm just sorry I didn't get to be the one to deliver such news, but... I have crimes to pay for. I deserve my time here."

"Oh, and Adley, I've taken over your research, as you know," Krieger added, trying to prevent her from slumping into a sad bubble. "Fantastic work you've done, so far. I have a few questions, though, if you don't mind. There are some notes that don't make much sense to me. Perhaps you can shed some light."

"Of course, Doctor. I'm here and happy to assist with whatever you need," she replied, smiling. "I was never an enemy of the coven, and I will continue to help however I can, even from my little cell." She then looked at me. "Will you go see Finch anytime soon?"

I'd thought about it, sure, but I hadn't decided yet. "I want to, yes," I said. "Probably soon, but I'm not sure when."

"Well, when you do go see him, can you please tell him I love him?" she asked. "I just want him to know that."

My heart ached with sadness and longing—all Adley's. Even after what had happened, she still loved him. *Unbelievable.*

"Why, though?" I asked. "He lied to your face, for years. He didn't even give a damn about you while you both testified in front of the California Mage Council. Why would you want me to tell him that?"

Adley smiled, wiping a solitary tear from her eye.

"You wouldn't understand. I was with Finch for more than two years, Harley. I know he didn't fake all aspects of our relationship. He couldn't have," she said, her voice shaky. "I know there's a part of him that loves me back. I know it. Finch's mind was poisoned by his mother."

"That doesn't change what he did, Adley," I said.

"No, of course it doesn't! But you all need to understand something. I *know* Finch. He's a fundamentally good person. I never would've stayed with him otherwise. I might have been blinded by love, but even I have my limits. In his day-to-day behavior, Finch was wonderful. He had lapses and dark times, which I'm sure were connected to his mother, but other than that, I'm telling you, he's a good soul. He was radicalized by Katherine. I'm willing to bet my life on it!"

Krieger hummed slowly, wearing a pensive expression. "You think he could be swayed back to a socially adjusted, non-criminal individual."

"Yes, yes, I do!" Adley replied.

"He killed people, Adley. All he has to look forward to is Purgatory for life," I said.

She truly believed what she was telling us. Whether it was true or not, however, remained to be seen. Though, I didn't exclude the possibility that Finch had been manipulated by his mother. That, in and of itself, made me wonder whether she could have done the same to my father...

"True. But that doesn't mean you can't get him to help you," Adley replied, smiling. "You see, there's a soft side of him that you can reach. Just tell him I love him. He needs to know that he is still loved, Harley. I don't know if Katherine has any way of reaching him, but I do know that love can be a powerful light in the darkness."

"I'll tell him," I conceded. "I don't think it'll do much, but I'll tell him in return for your help today."

"Thank you, Harley." Adley sighed, clearly relieved and almost serene.

"I need to go now," I said and gave Krieger a polite nod. "I'll let you talk to Adley about your work. I'm due to meet with Wade and the others."

"Be careful out there," Krieger replied.

I waved them both goodbye before knocking on the door. O'Halloran let me out with a raised eyebrow.

"Are you okay, Merlin?" he asked.

"Yes, sir!"

I wasn't. My heart was heavy. My soul was riddled with emotions that weren't mine. My mind was loaded with billions of thoughts and worst-case scenarios. I wasn't okay at all. But I was determined to push through and bring the Ryder twins and Katherine Shipton to an end. I'd had enough of this nonsense.

"Good. I'll see you in training tomorrow, then!" O'Halloran said, grinning.

"Wait… What do you mean?"

"Well, Nomura says you need a trainer for your Esprit. I'm here to oblige, Red. Six am, sharp and early in Training Hall C. Don't be late!" he barked with his usual grumpy snap.

I chuckled. "Yes, sir!"

Sure, I had a Suppressor holding me back. But I could still learn to efficiently control my powers and get the most out of them, given the circumstances. An Esprit amplified what my Chaos could give. Until Krieger could get that thing out of me, I had my Esprit to rely on. I was training to cast magic without it, too, but I'd already made my soul connection to the object. I knew that, if push came to shove, and even without much exercise, my Esprit could still come through for me.

NINETEEN

Harley

The Lee family was fairly easy to handle, even though the human parents had to deal with the news that their twelve-year-old adopted son, Min-Ho, was a magical. He'd only just begun to manifest his Herculean and Earth abilities. His mom and dad had suspected that he was different, given how ridiculously fast and strong he was for a little boy.

At first, they were taken aback, giving Min-Ho a bit of a scare. As a foster kid, he'd already been moved through several homes and was likely hoping that this might be his forever family. Wade let me do most of the talking with his parents. In the end, they were proud and considered themselves blessed to have gotten such an incredible child.

There were, of course, serious concerns regarding the Lee family. We found a Ryder twins card in the hallway, but, just like with the Cranstons, neither Min-Ho nor his parents had ever spoken to anyone named Emily and Emmett Ryder, or anyone claiming to be from the San Diego Coven. They only had the occasional visit from Social Services, but that was standard practice, due to the adoption laws in California.

Santana placed charms in every room of the house and left one in the family car for good measure. Wade got the parents to agree to bring Min-Ho to the coven every day, moving him from the human school to our custom-tailored courses and training for young magicals.

We left them in good spirits but warned them to stay away from anyone they couldn't verify as actual members of the San Diego Coven, and Wade left them his card in case of emergency.

As we drove to the Hamms', the next family on our list, I had a more positive vibe. I felt as though we were off to a good start to the day. I'd learned that I wasn't a Mediocre, and I'd also spoken to Adley. The Lees seemed safe, for the time being, and other charms from the previous families we'd dealt with hadn't gone off either.

"Are you crazy?" Wade blurted as he pulled the Jeep up the Hamms' driveway.

I'd just told him I wanted to talk to Finch, since my conversation with Adley had given me potential leads about Katherine Shipton to follow up on.

"I'm perfectly sane, thank you," I replied. "I don't get why it's a big deal! I need to talk to him. I need to find out more about Katherine Shipton, and he's the only one who can tell us."

"Don't you think they've tried already?" Wade said, getting out of the car.

Santana and Raffe were quiet, but I could feel their concern and amusement. Wade and I had a knack for entertaining them with our back-and-forths.

"Maybe he'll talk to me. We're family." I chuckled, but Wade didn't find it funny. "It's worth a shot!"

"Harley, Purgatory is a dark and dreary hellhole. They have ways to make people talk in that place, and trust me, none of them involve asking nicely. You're not going. It would be useless," Wade insisted.

Raffe cleared his throat. "She does make a point. She could play the family card," he murmured.

Wade gave him an outraged look. "Et tu, Brute?!"

"Well, if what Adley said is true, and there *is* a part of him that's not entirely evil, a blood tie might work," Raffe replied with an innocent shrug.

"I'm confident I can at least try to reason with him. I'll bet it's lonely in that cell," I added. "Wade, seriously, use your investigative brain. Finch is a viable lead. We could try and turn him against Katherine. If the Ryders are working with her, and if we take them down, it'll give me something to show Finch that, you know, we're not to be messed with. That he's on the losing side. Think about it!"

Wade sighed, then shook his head. "We'll talk about it later. Come on, we've still got work to do," he muttered.

We reached the front door. Wade knocked twice.

Anna Hamm opened, and my heart instantly broke. She'd been crying, her eyes puffy and her mascara smeared. Fatigue came off her in waves, and she was wearing a stained sweatshirt. The poor woman was a broken mess, filled with anguish, grief, and despair. It tore me apart on the inside.

"Mrs. Hamm, what happened?" Wade asked, frowning.

She wiped her nose with a crumpled tissue, staring at Wade in confusion. "Who are you? Are you FBI?"

I felt Wade's elbow nudge me, instantly kicking me into lie-your-ass-off mode. Based on how quickly we searched through our jacket pockets for the right fake IDs, we were all on the same page. We were no longer introducing ourselves as Social Services workers for the Hamms. We were whipping out the FBI personas.

Wade was the first to flash his badge. We carried four types of ID in our jackets, at all times—Homeland Security, FBI, Social Services, and the local PD.

"Special Agent Johnson," Wade said. "We were told you're having some trouble. Mind if we come in?"

"No, please... please, do," Anna said, then stepped to the side.

We went in, and I immediately caught the frayed emotions of the father, Frank Hamm, who was in the living room. He, too, had been crying and was genuinely distraught. I saw the photos on the mantelpiece—the Hamms with Marjorie Phillips, a seventeen-year-old they'd adopted a year back. I skimmed through their file to get as much information as possible before handing the folder over to Wade.

We had to be quick in our answers, so as not to give the Hamms any impression that we didn't know what we were doing. Professionalism was key here, even when we were lying through our teeth.

"Thank you for coming," Anna said as she motioned for us to step into the living room, where she joined us. "Police sent you over, right?"

"They told us to come, yes, but they didn't give us details," Wade replied. "Would you mind walking us through what happened from beginning to end?"

Anna took several deep breaths and picked up a photo album from the bookshelf. She showed it to Wade. Frank sat down, his hands trembling. They were both worried sick. Something terrible had happened here.

"That's Marjorie Phillips," Anna said, pointing at one of the photos. "She's an only child. Her father disappeared before she was born, and her mother killed herself when Marjorie was five. She's been in the foster system ever since."

"She's a good girl," Frank added, his voice breaking. "She wouldn't… She wouldn't have…"

"We took her in about a year ago," Anna continued, flipping through the photo album pages for Wade to see them as a family. I stood next to him, catching glimpses of Marjorie, a curly redhead with bright green eyes and a splash of freckles. "She warmed up to us, albeit gradually. It took a while to get her out of her shell, I suppose."

"Let me guess, the foster system wasn't easy on her," I replied, giving her a sympathetic smile.

Anna nodded. "She had trouble with some of the previous families, but she never said why. I wasn't blind, though. I saw the scars. I saw how she flinched whenever Frank got close... She'd been through some terrible things, and Frank and I made it our mission to show Marjorie that life didn't have to be that way for her."

I looked at Frank, whose eyes were tearing up again. "So, what happened, Mrs. Hamm?" I asked.

"A couple of nights ago she went missing," Anna said. "She was supposed to be home at six, but she never came back from school. Her phone is off. I left her dozens of texts and voicemails. We put up missing posters, we've alerted the police. They said they were going to hand the case over to the FBI because they didn't have enough resources in the city for a wide radius search."

"Marjorie is missing," I breathed the dreadful conclusion. I glanced at Santana and Raffe.

Santana had brought her duffel bag, filled with small leather charms. "Mrs. Hamm, do you mind if my colleague and I have a look through the house, including Marjorie's room?"

"Yeah, sure," Anna replied, and shifted her focus back to Wade and me, while Santana and Raffe disappeared upstairs. "She wouldn't have left on her own."

"The cops said she might've run away. That's nonsense," Frank said, shaking his head.

"You don't think there's any possibility of that?" Wade asked.

"Absolutely not!" Anna blurted. "Just last week she was telling us about how happy and relieved she was to be living with us. She was safe here. She had nowhere else to go."

One of the photos drew my attention. It showed Marjorie on the beach wearing a dark green hoodie, her red curls fluffed up by the breeze. She was laughing. Her eyes twinkled in the sunset. I gently pulled the photo out of the album and inhaled sharply when my fingers touched it.

Fear... Blood-freezing dread... So much emotional pain...

I didn't understand how it was possible for me to get a feel for someone from a photo like that, but I was certain that these were all

Marjorie's feelings. The horror was real. The sheer terror cut through me like a knife. She'd felt so sorry to leave the Hamms behind.

Marjorie had, indeed, run away, but she hadn't made that choice easily. Something had driven her out of this safe haven.

I decided to follow my Empath instinct and this weird little glitch with the photograph. "Mrs. Hamm, do you know if Marjorie had any enemies? Anyone she didn't get along with, maybe?"

Anna thought about it for a moment, then shook her head. "She had a few friends but kept mostly to herself. She's an artist, you see. She likes being alone. When she paints, it's just her and the canvas, you know? She didn't stir any trouble, nothing like that, no."

"So, there were no threats made by anyone toward her, directly or indirectly," Wade replied.

Anna shook her head again. "No, definitely not."

"Do you remember anything out of the ordinary that happened in the past week?" I asked. "Anything strange? Anything at all?"

Frank and Anna looked at each other, then back at me.

"Last Sunday we were having dinner, and she was telling us how happy she was," Frank said. "That's when we both knew that Marjorie felt safe here. It was like a 'Mission Accomplished!' kind of moment for us."

"Monday was fine. Frank took her to the art supply shop. Gosh, she was beaming when they came back," Anna added, smiling. "Frank got her pastel chalk, and she was eager to try it out. Then, Tuesday, all okay, she got home on time, had a school friend over for homework help. She was in bed by midnight."

"Then, Wednesday we had a Social Services visit after school," Frank murmured.

That rang an alarm bell in my head. "Social Services?"

"Yes. Part of the first two years after adoption. They come by every month to check on us, make sure we're okay, that Marjorie is fitting in. Stuff like that," Anna explained.

"Okay, and how did the visit go?" Wade asked.

We were both concerned. We'd already seen a similar pattern. I looked around, noticing a marble bowl on the mantelpiece next to the framed photos. Anna's brow furrowed as she and Frank exchanged glances once more. They were both realizing something they hadn't noticed before.

"The people were very nice. Two men in their late forties... Decent type, nice suits, soft voices. They gave us their card—it's in that bowl over there," Anna said, pointing at the marble piece I'd been eyeing already. "They were twins, which I found interesting."

My stomach dropped as I approached the mantelpiece and saw the business card sticking out from between several knickknacks.

"What were their names?" Wade pressed.

"John and Steven Ryder," Anna said.

I picked the card up and showed it to Wade. The Ryder twins had been here. We were both chilled to the bone over this. What was really confusing to me was their choice of first names, which seemed to vary from one family to the next, along with their age and appearance, and now, even gender. Was this deliberate, just to mess with us?

"What did they do and say?" Wade asked. "I need you to remember very carefully, Mrs. Hamm. It's important that we get as many details as possible."

"Well, they asked the usual questions. We go through this with Social Services every month, so there wasn't anything out of the ordinary there." Anna sighed, getting frustrated.

Frank, on the other hand, was on to something. "Remember they wanted to talk to Marjorie in private?"

"Yeah, but they do that every month, honey," Anna replied.

"Something was different this time," Frank insisted, his brow furrowed. "After they talked, and Marjorie came back with them in the kitchen, she seemed... different. We were supposed to sit down for dinner once they were gone, but Marge said she wasn't hungry anymore and went to her room."

Wade and I looked at each other. They must've said something to her. What if we were looking at another Kenneth Willow scenario here? My stomach shrank into an uncomfortable little ball as I thought of the implications.

"What about the following days?" I asked.

"Oh, God. Frank, you're right," Anna croaked. "She was different after that. Thursday came, and Marjorie barely ate anything for breakfast. She wasn't too chatty in the evening, but she blamed it on a headache."

"Then Friday... She didn't come back from school. No one saw her leave school, either," Frank continued.

"Did she go to classes?" Wade replied.

"Yeah. All of them. Her teachers confirmed. Police checked CCTV, too. It's like she vanished into thin air. She was last seen in the hallway with the rest of the kids as they left the school. But there was no sign of her outside," Anna explained.

"And you haven't heard from her since," Wade concluded.

"Nothing. Her phone is off, so they can't trace it," Anna said, rubbing her face in frustration.

A sense of urgency took over, my heart skipping beats like a dog at an obstacle race track.

"Mrs. Hamm, can you describe more what the Ryders looked like, if you remember?" I asked. Wade took out a small notepad and a pen.

"Um. You could tell they were twins. Identical features. Round faces, blue eyes, light blond hair. Both about 5'9". Gray suits, white shirts. Nothing out of the ordinary. Why? Do you think they had something to do with our Marge's disappearance?" Anna asked.

"No, no. Just gathering details, like I said. Everything helps at this point," Wade answered quickly. Given their human status, I understood that there was no point in giving them any magical-related information at this point in time.

Still surprised by the photograph's effect on my Empathic senses, I decided to explore this new avenue. "Mrs. Hamm, I'll be right back. I need to have a look at your daughter's room." I left the living room and rushed upstairs.

Raffe was just coming down.

"Anything?" I whispered.

He nodded. "Yeah. I'll brief you all outside. Don't want the Hamms hearing this," he said, then went downstairs and joined Wade and Marjorie's parents.

I found Santana in Marjorie's room, stuffing one of the charm bags under her bed. She got up, then exhaled sharply. "I had my Orishas check the place out. Something weird happened here, Harley," she murmured.

"Define weird, because the Ryders were here. This time, however, they interacted with both the human parents and the magical kid on her own," I replied.

Santana stilled, her eyes wide. "Crap. Like with Kenneth Willow's family."

I nodded. "They came on Wednesday evening. By Friday afternoon, Marjorie was missing," I said. "Something tells me she ran away, but not to join the Ryders," I added, showing her the picture I'd brought up with me. "The weirdest thing happened. I don't know how else to explain it, but I can feel Marjorie's emotions just by touching this photo."

Santana blinked several times. "That's not weird. Some good Empaths do that."

"Oh. I didn't remember reading that anywhere."

"It's rare. It's in some footnote, somewhere in Ickes's manuals," Santana replied. "So, what did you pick up?"

"Dread, Santana. Fear like nothing I've sensed before. Well, except maybe the time I had gargoyles trying to eat me."

"You think she ran to get away from the Ryders?" Santana asked.

I moved around the room, trying to get a feel for the place. It was oozing similar emotions to the photograph. Marjorie was afraid—not just for her life, but for the Hamms', too.

"I'm almost positive, but obviously I won't know for sure until we find her and talk to her," I said. "What did your Orishas pick up?"

Santana smirked. "Pretty much the same as you. Some were Empaths when they were alive, and they still have the gift, I guess. Something scared Marjorie so badly that she had to get out."

I nodded, taking a moment to recall the differences between Santana's and Tatyana's abilities as I moved to the window. Santana's Orishas were former spirits of magicals that had transcended to a higher level, maintaining their glowing, shapeless forms. She didn't talk to them, since the exchange of information was done on a different level, well beyond our comprehension. She simply knew what they picked up, and she'd spent years forming a permanent relationship with these entities. Tatyana, on the other hand, was a mere communicator with spirits, magical or human. The more powerful ones were able to possess her, lending her their abilities. But her interactions were always passing, never as permanent or as deep as Santana's connection to her Orishas.

I liked them both, because they offered different insights and assistance. I stopped by the window, running my fingers over a curtain bow.

Movement in the backyard caught my eye. I froze, unsure of what I was seeing. Someone was hiding behind a sturdy palm tree, curiously watching me as I stood by the window. I narrowed my eyes and stifled a yelp when I recognized him: Jacob! The Smiths' new foster kid.

"You okay?" Santana asked.

"Uh, y-yes," I replied, giving her a quick glance. "Yeah, I just..." I shifted my focus back to the garden.

Jacob was gone.

"I... I thought I saw something," I said.

Where did he go?

Or did I just imagine it?

I remained staring out the window for another long moment,

but when Jacob didn't appear again, I heaved a sigh and turned away from the window.

"Anyway, something nefarious definitely went down here," I murmured.

The vision of Jacob nagged me, and I decided to stop by the Smiths' place again today. Whether I'd imagined it or not, it didn't hurt to check in on the Smiths and see what he was up to. I could easily play the part of the concerned foster sibling—which I technically was, anyway. My instinct was telling me something... though I wasn't sure what.

We left the Hamms with the assurance that we'd do everything in our power to find Marjorie. Wade gave them his card, and as soon as we were outside, he called the coven.

"Send a complete cleanup crew to the Hamms' place. They're human parents, and the kid has gone missing," he said. "Yes, wipe their memories, too. It's in their best interests at this point. I'll send you some details about the girl. The Ryder twins are involved... Yeah, put out an APB on her. Marjorie Phillips. Aha. Cool, thank you."

After he hung up, we stopped by the Jeep to catch up.

"So, remember how the djinn picks up on the energy of something that happened in a place?" Raffe asked, looking at Wade. "Any kind of tragedy or difficult, painful decision. Anything that stirred grief and suffering, in general."

"Uh-huh," Wade replied, as Raffe had his full attention.

I had no clue what they were talking about. "What djinn?" I asked.

Raffe smiled. "I'll explain at some point, I promise. This whole Ryder twins issue is more important and demands our full attention," he said. I understood then that the djinn had something to do with his magical abilities, and I figured it was better not to pursue this now. He was right. We had bigger fish to fry. "Something bad happened in that house. Something made Marjorie leave."

"And it wasn't an easy decision," I replied, corroborating his and Santana's findings. "We're all picking up on the same thing here, albeit differently. I'm getting mine directly from a photo of her. The feelings are so dark, so intense… It's mind-boggling."

"You're reading from a picture now?" Wade asked, raising an eyebrow. He was quite impressed.

I shrugged. "Yeah… I don't know why it's happening with Marjorie, but it doesn't matter. Point is, she was scared out of her mind, Wade."

"The Ryders probably freaked her out," Santana replied.

"Another thing bothers me," I said. "The Ryders' description. It doesn't match the photo we have, or what the other parents said."

Wade gave me an appreciative nod. "You're right. The descriptions don't match. The names are different from one family to another, too. These aren't different people. These are different personas altogether."

"Oh, crap," Santana gasped.

"Shapeshifters," Raffe concluded.

Wade agreed. Shivers ran through me, making me tremble. I had flashbacks of Finch shifting into Clara Fairmont, the bubblegum blonde witch that Wade had briefly dated. I let out a frustrated groan.

"Not again," I grumbled.

"It makes sense, if you think about it," Wade said. "Different people, similar scenarios. I wouldn't be surprised. I'll bet they're both Shapeshifters."

"It wasn't in their file," Santana replied.

Wade shrugged. "This wouldn't be the first or the last time that magicals would go to great lengths to conceal their Shapeshifting abilities after a Reading, and most covens accommodate that request. You know how our people tend to frown upon Shapeshifters in general. It's a terrible stigma to have, and centuries of progress haven't changed that mindset. People still don't trust them."

"No offense, but with the likes of Finch and the Ryders, I'm not surprised." I sighed, crossing my arms and leaning against the Jeep.

"The Ryders are doing things a little differently, though. It's like they're teasing us, leaving enough room for us to connect the dots and realize they're around here somewhere, prowling," Santana said. "It's like they want us to know it's them, and that they're Shapeshifters. At least, that's how I see it. Either way, Shapeshifters are always such a pain."

"Some are difficult to detect, too," Wade explained. "A Reading can miss the ability, if it's carried out by a less capable physician, though that's extremely rare. I don't know why, exactly, but Krieger can better explain that part. Point is, Shapeshifters aren't all that common, and most of them manage to keep their ability a secret. Some, as clearly demonstrated by Finch and the Ryders so far, do bad things. We have to find them."

"Oh, yeah. It'll be a breeze to find two people who can basically turn into anyone." I chuckled bitterly.

Raffe grinned. "There may be something about them that would work in our favor," he said. "Shifting is a very painful and complex process—the first time around, when there's a new persona to... put on. If they're shifting into personas they've done before, it's not as bad. Therefore, it would make sense that they use a limited number of identities they've morphed into before."

Santana narrowed her eyes at him, as if processing the information. "So, we'd need to keep an eye on the descriptions that the parents give us, to spot a repeat identity."

"Exactly. Like I said, it hurts like hell to shift into someone new, but once the magical's body memorizes that identity, it gets easier. It makes sense for them to use two, maybe three personas at most, for whatever it is they're trying to do," Raffe replied. "On top of their real appearance, that is."

"I'll have Astrid put all the descriptions into the system and widen the search for them, then," Wade said, swiping through his phone. "The one thing we know for sure is that they scared Marjorie into leaving, though I doubt that was their intention. I think she didn't want to put her parents in any danger, figuring she was better off running away."

"That's why you want the cleanup team to wipe the Hamms' memories," I mumbled, putting two and two together.

"Yeah. If anything goes wrong with Marjorie, at least they won't suffer over her loss. I know you might think it's inhumane or whatever, but—"

"No. I agree. Given the circumstances, it's for the best," I said to Wade. "But hold on, I get deleting the parents' memories, but what about everybody else that Marjorie knew since the adoption?"

Raffe chuckled. "The cleanup crew is very good at what they do, don't worry."

I was officially curious.

Santana sucked in a breath and grabbed her side, hissing from pain. It burned through me, too, but it wasn't as bad as it was for her.

"What's wrong?" Wade asked.

"Ah…" Santana struggled to stand up straight for a moment. Once she regained her composure, she gave us an alarmed look. "The Cranstons. Something set off their charms. Something happened."

An icy wave hit me hard as I realized the horrible truth. Our worst-case scenarios were starting to come true.

TWENTY

Harley

W ade drove like the devil, darting down the streets and taking sharp turns, slipping between lanes and cars, as we rushed to the Cranstons' place. As soon as the Jeep screeched to a halt outside, I knew the worst had happened.

The front door was open, and I wasn't getting any emotions from inside the house.

The silence was almost unbearable.

Little Micah...

We jumped out of the car and raced inside. My heart stopped for a moment, dread clutching my throat. The hallway side table was knocked over. Papers and shoes were scattered across the floor. Jackets and hats, too. The wall mirror was down, broken into hundreds of shards.

"Weren't there supposed to be alarm charms and traps in place in here?" I whispered.

"Yes. I don't think they worked as intended," Wade replied.

His rings lit up bright orange, ready to hit in case of an attack. He moved forward, carefully stepping over the items on the floor.

This was definitely a crime scene, and we needed to touch it as little as possible, for the purpose of a proper investigation.

Wade cursed under his breath when he saw the living room. Santana, Raffe, and I reached him. We all froze.

Horror cut my breath off. I saw Susan and Larry lying on the floor, in the middle of the living room. They were both dead, staring at the ceiling with eyes wide open—lifeless and glassy. Their throats had been slit. Blood had pooled around their heads. Their skin was paler than usual, but rigor mortis had yet to properly set in, judging by the color of their lips.

"Oh, God," I gasped.

Wade went in and checked the bodies. He whispered a spell as he moved his hand over Susan and Larry. His rings lit up white as he took a deep breath and closed his eyes for a moment.

"They've been dead for ten, fifteen minutes, tops," he said. "They bled out."

"Micah!" I shouted, praying to Chaos itself to hear him or see him alive. "Micah! Can you hear me? It's Harley! MICAH!"

Santana squeezed my shoulder. "He's not here, querida," she murmured, wearing a pained look on her face. "Neither is the Orisha I left with him."

I broke into a cold sweat as I looked around the room. There had been a violent fight here. The coffee table was knocked over. Most of the books from the shelves were on the floor. Coffee had been spilled on the carpet, the cups smashed into pieces. The framed photographs were down, the glass broken and smoke swirling from beneath.

"What... What the hell?" I croaked, pointing at one of the images.

The photograph showed Susan and Larry, holding a little boy between them—Micah, only his face had been burned out. The others were the same. Everywhere I looked, Micah's face had been taken out with fire.

Santana came by my side. "That's not good," she said. "That's a very ugly and dark spell."

"What is it?" I asked.

"Obliviscaris in Perpetuum," Wade breathed as he joined us. "It's a forbidden curse. It rips a person out of everything. Photos, clothes, memories… anything that Micah has touched or left a trace on." He pointed at various black spots in the room. "Every strand of hair or fragment of skin he's left behind… it's all burned out of existence."

"Why… Why would they do that?" I replied, trying to wrap my head around the purpose of such a heinous act.

"They don't want us to use a tracer spell to find him," Raffe concluded. "The Ryders took him. I know it in my bones."

"They don't want us to—" I paused, then took a deep breath, trying to keep myself calm. My palms were itching. My blood was boiling. "What do we do?"

"I'll check outside," Raffe said.

He left us there, with the lifeless bodies of Susan and Larry Cranston, who had adopted little Micah, hoping to give him the best family possible. The cruelty of what the Ryders had done was beyond monstrous.

"My Orisha is gone," Santana repeated, frowning. "That's not normal. I can't feel her anymore. I didn't feel anything earlier, either. Whatever magic the twins are using, it overrode all my charms…" The color drained from her face. "I think they *killed* my Orisha!"

Wade was stunned. I was even more confused.

"Santana, that's some incredibly dark and evil magic the Ryders are conjuring," Wade said. "That's worth a life sentence in Purgatory."

"They killed my Orisha!" Santana replied, tearing up. "She would've fought them. She never would've allowed them to take the kid! They killed her!"

I felt her pain, and it was more than I could take, on top of my own.

"Santana, check the boy's room, please," Wade said, trying to keep her focused. "Take photos, imprints, anything you can. I'll handle this room and call a cleanup crew."

She nodded slowly and went upstairs. I had to get out of the room, so I went around the ground floor to check the rest of the place out. I hadn't spotted them at first, but there were charcoal smudges all over the place, even in the hallway.

The kitchen was a mess. The fight had spread throughout the house, from what I could tell. There were broken dishes and pots everywhere, food splattered over the floor—mac and cheese, pieces of bread, mashed potatoes… They were preparing Sunday lunch when the attack happened.

It was vicious. It took me a while to reconstruct the entire scene, but I managed to get all the clues together. Outside, Raffe was looking around, checking every corner of the backyard. We briefly looked at each other, and I could feel the confusing mix of grief, sadness, and excitement coming from him.

I went back into the living room, measuring my breaths as I carefully walked along the edges of the carpet. "The door wasn't broken, and there was no sign of magical tampering on it," I said.

"They likely knew them," Wade replied.

"Assuming the Ryders *are* Shapeshifters, they must've somehow adopted the personas of people that the Cranstons were familiar with, maybe even Social Services. They came in, then all hell broke loose. The parents tried to fight them off. From what I saw in the kitchen, my guess is that Micah made it all the way there."

"Susan and Larry went down fast," Wade said. "There are barely any defensive wounds. I'm guessing by this time they'd already disabled all the charms and traps."

"Which means they were left with apprehending Micah—"

"Who didn't go down easy. I guess he employed all his abilities against them," Wade continued my line of reasoning.

"Which, again, explains the mess in the kitchen."

Santana came down, tears streaming down her cheeks. It took her a while to say something.

"The bedroom is black. Everything was burned to a crisp," she managed, her voice shaky. "But it was controlled, part of the spell."

"They wanted us to find all of this. Otherwise, they would've just burned the whole place down for good measure," Raffe added, coming back in. "They wanted us to find the bodies, the burned spots, everything."

"But why?" I asked hoarsely. "To mess with us?"

Every single thing we'd discovered about the Ryders pointed them out as extreme psychopaths, the most vicious magicals I'd encountered so far, for sure. They made Finch look like a Boy Scout. He didn't get his hands dirty—he let the gargoyles do the dirty work for him. The Ryders got up close and personal.

I resisted the urge to puke, though I could feel my coffee and half a bagel struggling to come back up. A few deeper breaths in, and I got it under control, but I couldn't shake the chills that had settled in my bones.

"To make us aware of what they can do. To make us feel helpless," Wade replied. "They want us to understand that they can stop us from tracing the people they take. They want us to see the damage they can do."

"They want us to be afraid of them," Santana murmured.

"Well, screw that!" I snapped. I didn't let Finch get to me. I had no intention of letting these bastards break my morale, either. This entire scene made me rage with the fire of exacting revenge, but not fear. No, the Ryders made me furious, not scared. "We're going to find them, and we're going to put them in Purgatory. And I hope, I really hope they put up a fight, because then I can just light them up and watch them burn!" I shouted.

The air felt heavy as Wade, Santana, and Raffe stared at me, speechless and befuddled. I thought about what I'd just said, realizing it may have come across as extreme. My cheeks burned.

"Okay, scratch the last part," I muttered.

"No, no, leave it in. I'm with you there," Santana replied. "They killed one of my Orishas. They're not getting away with this."

At least we were on the same page, as I was getting a similar vibe from Raffe and Wade—Raffe's was particularly interesting, since, despite his calm demeanor, there was a thirst for blood bubbling beneath the surface. It was a tad creepy, but I was in no position to judge.

I'd just expressed interest in burning two magicals alive.

Susan and Larry Cranston didn't deserve this. I was determined to get justice for them, by any means possible. Most importantly, I had to save Micah. He was an innocent child. All he ever wanted was a home and a family, and the Ryders had taken that away from him.

As a foster kid myself, I took this personally.

Wade called a cleanup crew to the Cranstons' place and put out another ABP on Micah. The fixers were going to make it look like a home invasion gone wrong, torching parts of the place and turning the sprinkler system on. I didn't want to know the rest of the details, as I was still wrestling with my undigested coffee and bagel.

We couldn't stop doing our jobs. We had to keep our emotions in check and go through the rest of the list. The other families were okay, though. The Ryders had left cards there, as well, and in one case with magical parents, they'd pretended to be from the San Diego Coven, trying to convince a couple to send their kid over.

I tried to understand why they'd gone to such lengths to get parents to send their children to the coven, until a possible answer hit me. In addition to the fact that the Ryders didn't want to risk conflict with magical parents or early exposure by killing them and taking the kids, they might also want them to essentially give up on their children. They might want the chicks out of the nest, so they could snatch them. So the parents would feel miserable for letting them go and even blame the coven for their disappearance. That would be devious, indeed… But they didn't succeed, and I wound up walking out of the last house on our list with a half-smile on my face.

I breathed a sigh of relief as we reached the Jeep.

My heart hurt, but I had to keep going. Santana rigged all the homes with additional and more potent charms, hoping they might at least alert us in case the Ryders showed up. Wade called Alton, demanding additional security details on each family. The Ryders were bound to strike again, though we weren't sure when. Fortunately, Alton was totally on board with that.

"We should round up all the families we still have and bring them back to the coven," I said out loud while Wade was still on the line with Alton. "We shouldn't leave them out here where the Ryder twins can get them!"

Alton said something to Wade, but I couldn't hear it. Once he hung up, however, I felt his anger boiling through me.

"We can't. All we can do is get security magicals to watch over them until further notice," Wade said.

"Why not?!" I asked, my voice getting louder.

"Because the California Mage Council wants us to see this through! Because they ordered us to keep the families where they are and wait for the Ryders to strike again. They want them caught," Wade snapped.

"What if the families *want* to come to the coven for protection?" I asked.

He shook his head. "We'll assure them that it's not necessary."

"But that's insane!" I croaked. "They'll be sitting ducks…"

"They've got charms and traps set up. There are security magicals on their way out to each of the families on our list," Wade said. "Alton wouldn't tell me more, but these are the orders, and we are to follow them. Period!"

On our way back to the coven, we didn't speak much. There wasn't much to say, really. What happened with the Cranstons felt like a phenomenal failure. The more time that passed, the worse I felt. I'd insisted that Micah stay with his parents. And now, his parents were dead, and Micah was missing.

I looked at Wade. He was livid, but he held it all in beneath a straight face. Whenever his eyes found mine, rage blared through him and echoed in me. That just made me feel even more responsible. I didn't know what to say. If I could go back and undo yesterday's decisions, Micah would've been safe, with us, in the coven. *Susan and Larry would still be alive.*

And I hated that we couldn't even round up the rest of the families and take them to safety. But there was nothing I could do about that now.

"Can you drop me off at St. Clair's?" I asked, my voice barely audible.

"Why?" Wade asked, his tone clipped.

It felt like a punch in the gut. He was so angry with me.

"I need to do something," I replied.

"Harley, given what we're dealing with right now, a little more transparency would be appreciated," he replied.

God, I feel so horrible.

"I just need to be alone," I conceded, tears streaming down my cheeks. I caught a glimpse of Santana and Raffe in the rearview mirror. They were just as broken as I was, but they weren't experiencing the crippling guilt that was building up inside me. No, that cancerous darkness was all mine and mine alone to bear. And I deserved it. "I just need to be alone. I'll take a cab back."

The Jeep came to a rough halt, a couple blocks before St. Clair's. Wade gripped the steering wheel, his knuckles white. Again, he stared ahead, not looking at me.

"Thanks," I murmured. "I won't be long."

"Whatever," he replied coldly.

The frustration and pain were too much to handle. I got out and slammed the car door. Santana and Raffe watched me as the Jeep roared back into traffic. A few seconds later, I was all by myself in the middle of a busy sidewalk on a Sunday afternoon.

The sun was out. The weather was perfect.

And I felt like crap.

TWENTY-ONE

Harley

I stood there, in the middle of the street, unable to move or think for a while.

Tears rolled down my cheeks as I went back over everything that had happened. Hindsight was always great, but I didn't have the ability or the luxury to turn back time. I wondered if any magical could do that. I probably would've heard about it.

I could only go forward from this point. However, I needed to clear my head first. Most importantly, I needed to be around people who weren't involved in any of this. I often thought of the Smiths' place as a refuge, and this certainly felt like the right time to pay them another visit.

Besides, I needed to see what Jacob was up to, and confirm whether I had, in fact, spotted him earlier at the Hamms' house.

I stopped by St. Clair's and picked up some sweet and savory pastries in a small gift basket, then made my way to the Smiths'. I composed myself as I walked up the narrow pathway leading to the front door. I did my best to make sure that my expression reflected the weather, not my emotions.

The door opened, and Mrs. Smith greeted me with a warm smile.

"Sweetie! What a joy to see you again so soon!" she exclaimed, before she noticed the pastry basket and chuckled. "Do you intend to bribe me for anything?"

"Hah, no… I just had the rest of the day off, and I wanted to spend it with people I love," I replied, smiling.

"Oh, honey," she murmured. She took the basket from my hand and used one arm to hug me. I sank my face in her soft hair, welcoming the scent of freesia. *Still using the same fabric softener.*

We went inside, to find Mr. Smith in the living room, flipping channels on the TV.

"Harley!" he said, beaming at me. "You're making our weekend even better!"

"Hey," I replied, and went over to hug him, awkwardly, bending downward over the sofa. "How's your Sunday turning out, so far?"

"Fantastic! I get to watch the game, the missus gets some yummy treats, from what I can see," he said, grinning, "and Jacob's out in the backyard, fumbling with a project for school."

"Ah. I was hoping I could talk to him," I said.

I followed Mrs. Smith into the kitchen and helped her get the pastries out of the basket and fairly redistributed across several plates. Jacob was outside. I could see him through the wide kitchen windows. He was trying to build some kind of device, kneeling under a massive umbrella, with lemonade and half-eaten sandwiches next to him on a small rattan coffee table. He didn't seem to know what he was doing, barely able to clamp down on a couple of wires, but he was definitely enjoying it—I could feel it in my tummy.

"You've come by to spend some time with Jacob, huh?" Mrs. Smith asked me, smiling.

I nodded. "I see he's busy, though."

"Stick around. He needs all the help he can get, and there's not a single mechanical engineer in the Smith household to assist him."

She giggled. "You might be able to save him. And, since you're here, do you want to have dinner with us?"

"I'd love that," I replied, unable to stop myself from smiling.

"I'm making lasagna," she added with a devilish grin.

Mrs. Smith handed me one of the pastry plates and nodded at Jacob. "Well, why don't you go out there and give him a hand? You've got your car, now. I'll bet you understand what he's doing over there more than us."

My car. I missed Daisy like crazy. I hadn't yet decided what I was going to do with her. Murray the dirtbag gargoyle had crushed her a month ago, and I was still recovering from the heartache. Daisy was a heap of mangled metal at this point, held in storage, but I couldn't bring myself to take her to the salvage yard. I didn't have the courage to buy another car, either. It would've felt like a betrayal to Daisy.

In the meantime, Wade or Santana hauled me around if I needed it. Cabs were okay, too.

I sighed, brushing aside the sadness of Daisy's "passing away," and shifted my focus back to Mrs. Smith.

"You don't like leaving him out there on his own? Turning into a helicopter mom, now?" I forced a laugh.

"No, not at all. I'm just trying to get to know Jacob a little better, and he doesn't talk to me much. Maybe he'll open up to you. I don't know, I'm just positive there are things he isn't telling us, and maybe you can get more out of him than we can."

I gave her a warm smile and took the plate out into the backyard. Jacob turned his head when he heard the sliding door open. He struck me as nervous. I was making him nervous.

"Hey, Jake, brought you some goodies," I said. "Mind if I join you?"

"Sure, have a seat," Jacob replied, keeping his focus on the small device in front of him.

I did just that, crossing my legs and settling the plate next to the sandwiches and lemonade.

"St. Clair's?" he asked, eyeing the pastries for a moment.

"You betcha!" I replied, grinning, then pointed at the device. "What are you doing there?"

"Oh. It's an automatic pet feeder," Jacob said.

"Are you sure?" I asked sarcastically.

I figured he was halfway through with it or something, because to me it looked like a box with some circuits and gadgets on the inside. I doubted Mrs. Smith had actually thought that I could help the kid better than them—it was most likely just an excuse to get me out here with him.

I could at least pretend to help while I asked Jacob some questions, including whether he'd been near the Hamms' place or not.

Jacob looked at me, raising an eyebrow and making me laugh. "I'm kidding, dude," I said, then pointed at the device again. "Need me to help?"

"Nah. But you can keep me company, if you want," he replied, his voice low. "Just don't tell Mrs. Smith about my cursing. This damn thing's getting on my nerves."

I chuckled. "When is it due?"

He sighed. "Tomorrow. I always leave the important stuff until the last minute."

"Meh. It's cool. You'll figure it out. And someone's dog will be grateful to you in the end," I said.

Despite his seemingly jovial attitude, Jacob was *definitely* on edge. There was a mixture of fear and guilt burning through me, and it made me think that I had, indeed, seen him at the Hamms' house. This irked me.

"That's cool! So, what do you do for a living again? I think Mrs. Smith told me, but I forgot," Jacob asked.

There was something odd here. A pattern I'd been picking up on, lately. My Empathy varied from one person to another. The magicals, in general, were a tad more reserved in their emotions—except the few I couldn't feel at all. I'd yet to figure that one out. But the humans were so raw, so intense in their feelings, that sometimes

I thought a magical detector wouldn't even be needed, if I were to really fine-tune this ability of mine. I kept the idea to myself but did use it to make an assessment of Jacob. I could feel him, but not as vibrant as the Smiths. Maybe he was a magical.

"For a living? I'm working for Homeland Security," I replied.

Jacob was quiet, his concern bubbling beneath the surface as he continued to fiddle with his pet feeder thingy.

"How are you coming along here, with the Smiths?" I asked, wearing a soft smile.

Jacob shrugged. "I'm good. Honestly, the Smiths are awesome. They're kind and sweet and always looking after me. I hope I get to pay them in kind, someday."

I paused, wetting my lips and considering my next question, while I eyed him closely. Going back to my previous reasoning, the Smiths hadn't shown up on Alton's list, and it certainly wasn't automatic for every foster kid to be a magical. Magicals were still rare— perhaps one for every thousand humans or more. But my gut was telling me that Jacob was special, in a Chaos kind of way.

"They changed my life for the better," I said. "I doubt I would've been here today had it not been for them. Have you met Ryann yet?"

He nodded. "Uh-huh. She's really cool. I think she wants to become president one day or something."

For the second time in the past ten minutes, I was laughing. After everything that I'd witnessed today, I needed this flicker of innocence in my life. But time wasn't on my side. In a moment of "Screw this!", I took a gamble. I'd feel better once I blurted it out.

"You know your way around magic, don't you?"

My question stunned him. He stared at me for a few seconds, gripping his screwdriver with unnecessary force. His knuckles were white, and beads of sweat blossomed on his temples.

"What... What do you mean?" he asked, barely breathing.

Panic was rumbling through me like an icy wave. Oh, I'd hit a nerve, for sure.

"I'm just looking at this pet feeder. It looks like the stuff of magic," I said, deciding to drag him along for a suspenseful ride. Not that I was a sadist, but I did find his emotional discomfort somewhat amusing. It was best to shock him now, so I could later ease him into the fact that I was a magical, too.

"It's not. It's just science. Mechanics. Basic principles of physics," Jacob murmured, then kept on tinkering.

I glanced around, wondering if there was any chance that the Ryders could have been here, if he was in fact a magical. I'd already checked the entrance hall and the living room on my way in. There was no sign of the Ryders' business card, and it seemed safe to assume that they hadn't discovered Jacob yet. Reason and logic dictated that I address this with Jacob, just to be sure. Plus, after what had happened with the Cranstons, I had to do a better job of protecting people—especially the Smiths.

"Pour me a glass of lemonade, please," I said, keeping my tone soft.

Jacob put the screwdriver down, then grabbed the pitcher and filled a glass with chunks of ice and fresh lemonade. Mrs. Smith had dropped some mint leaves in there. For décor, she'd always say, but they definitely gave it an extra kick of deliciousness.

I used my Telekinesis to nudge the glass off the table. As soon as it tumbled, Jacob's hand twitched. Before his fingers could reach the glass, it was back on the edge of the table. He looked at me, and his heart stopped beating altogether. I'd caught him on reflex alone. I hadn't even known he was Telekinetic, but it seemed like a good test to run, just in case. Lucky for me, it had worked. Jacob was a magical. No doubt about it.

"Thanks, buddy," I said, and took a long sip from the glass in question.

"You're welcome," he whispered, practically quaking in his boots. The poor guy was caught red-handed, reflexively performing magic, and he was probably waiting for me to say something. My cool demeanor, however, kept throwing him for a loop.

"You didn't tell me you were a magical," I added, setting my gaze on him.

Jacob was clearly surprised about the conversation's sudden turn, but not exactly shocked. Deep down, I was beginning to sense that he did, in fact, know what I was. *But how?*

"I don't know what you're talking about," Jacob mumbled, staring at me. This was an act. I could smell the deceit from a mile away. It would've been cute and downright endearing, had I not spotted him earlier.

It made me angry, but I knew I couldn't blow a fuse right then and there. The Ryders' effect on me wasn't his fault. This kid needed patience from me, more than anything.

"Let's not play this game, Jake," I said. "You're a magical, and something tells me you know I'm one, too."

He let a deep sigh roll out. His head dropped, shame swallowing us both whole.

"I… I didn't know how to talk to you about it," he said.

I scoffed. "Nice to see I'm still right, at least once in a while."

He didn't say anything, but the guilt ate away at him. I rose to my feet and crossed my arms.

"It's not the kind of thing you just pop into a conversation with a complete stranger," he replied finally.

"So I did see you a few hours ago, in the Hamms' backyard."

His gaze shot up, finding mine. "It's not what you think."

"Then explain it to me, Jake, because I've got a lot on my plate right now," I shot back. "You were following me."

"No. I was just in the neighborhood, I swear!" Jacob replied. "I'd gone out for a walk, I had my music on… I don't know anything about the Hamms or whatever. I just saw you go into that house, that's all."

I wasn't buying it. Not after the day's horrible events. Susan and Larry's lifeless expressions were forever etched into my retinas. The smell of blood refused to leave my nose. Worry gnawed at my stomach as I thought of little Micah. I certainly didn't want the same thing to happen to Jacob.

But I also knew how tough of a nut to crack a foster kid could be. We didn't trust people easily. It was going to take some time to get him on my side. But I didn't want to leave him in a potentially risky situation, where he couldn't come to me if he felt like he was in danger. If Katherine's goons did come around, I needed him to trust me and ask for my help.

I didn't think the Ryders had found him. They would've left the card. They would've wanted me, specifically, to know that they'd come by. I didn't want him to be another Kenneth Willow, and there was something about his emotions that made me feel confident about my assessment. I couldn't be 100 percent sure that Jacob hadn't met the Ryders, but my instincts rarely failed me.

"Jake, I didn't know you were a magical until a few minutes ago," I said, then blew out. "But you knew about me. I think that warrants some explaining on your part."

He blinked several times. There it was again. The guilt, the fear of discovery.

"We need to be able to trust each other, dude," I added. "There aren't that many of us, to begin with. Especially not in the foster system. We have to stick together. I've got your back for life, but you have to let me in."

"I figured it out," he whispered. Relief washed over me—all his. He hated keeping secrets, it seemed.

"How?" I asked.

"I saw your bracelet. Didn't work with your pantsuit. I know how an Esprit works."

"Don't give me that crap," I muttered, gritting my teeth. "I can barely spot someone like that, and I've been a magical longer than you. There's something you're not telling me, Jake. I can feel it."

"How do you know?" he challenged me.

"I'm an Empath. I can read you like an open book."

He stilled. His heart shrank with sheer horror. He was headed straight for a panic attack. My pulse was racing. His breathing became staggered and heavy.

"I can't read your thoughts, relax," I continued, trying to reassure him. "I can feel what you feel, that's all. If you're sad or hungry or... feeling happy or guilty... stuff like that. It takes a lot more work for me to figure out exactly what your emotions relate to. Chill, Jake."

He seemed to relax. I couldn't blame him for being fearful. Nobody liked having their mind read, after all. It was the worst kind of privacy violation.

"Like I said, I know you're lying to me," I added, eager to steer the conversation back to my point of interest. "How did you know I'm a magical? Don't give me the Esprit crap. That's flimsy. I should know, I've tried it."

Jacob sighed, his gaze dropping to the grassy ground. "I can... I can sense you."

"You can sense me," I murmured, unsure of what that meant.

"I can feel other magicals," he said. "It's one of my abilities."

Holy crap!

This was huge. Krieger would've had a field day testing him. But was such an ability even possible? If so, how? What combination of magical bloodlines could lead to such a development? I found myself in awe of Jacob, stunned by his confession.

Then I realized the implications.

Jacob, if discovered, could lose his freedom, his livelihood... his everything. The Ryders and the likes of Katherine Shipton would've loved their own living, breathing magical detector. The same went for the coven, too. That made everything a million times more difficult for me. He'd just found a home with the Smiths, and I had no idea where he'd been before.

"You can feel magicals?" I asked, my voice barely audible.

He nodded once. "My skin tingles."

"What, like a Spidey sense? You've got to be kidding me!" I gasped.

Jacob shrugged. "Kind of? I don't know. It's difficult to describe."

It didn't really matter how he could do it. What mattered was that he could. It made him more valuable than gold. I could think of plenty of magicals who would've done anything to get Jacob on their team. Covens with enough influence and money could capture him, maybe even take him by force, since he wasn't registered.

That was the downside of being a rogue magical, and not a Neutral. The former meant he was off the books, anyone's for the taking, basically. As a Neutral, he was registered with a coven. Frankly, with such an ability, I doubted they would allow him to remain Neutral.

I could almost hear Alton's heart explode once I told him about Jacob.

But did I want to tell anyone about him? Wasn't he, perhaps, safer under the radar, able to steer clear of magicals? At the same time, I didn't want a Cranstons repeat, either.

"Does anyone else know this?" I asked. Jacob shook his head. "Okay. Let's keep it that way for now, until we figure out what's going on in San Diego."

He sighed. "I was going to say the same thing. I'm not sure I want myself out in the open."

I frowned. "Are you scared of something?"

Fear did trickle through me, but not with enough intensity to trigger a serious alarm. It was more angst than fear, in fact.

He shook his head again. "Just cautious."

I was inclined to believe him, but not completely. There was always a catch, somewhere. A hidden page. A well-kept secret. In my experience, people like Jacob and me were never fully honest with those who claimed to want to protect us—not in the beginning, anyway.

TWENTY-TWO

Tatyana

W e had quite a doozy on our hands.
Nine-year-old Andrew Prescott had gone missing yesterday afternoon. His biological parents had just moved to San Diego about a month earlier and had yet to register with the coven. We got as much information out of them as possible, then rigged their house with charms. If the Ryders, whose card we'd found there, were going to come back, we'd be notified.

Astrid spoke to Alton and got him to put a pair of eyes on the house, just in case. By the time we were done debriefing the Prescotts, the worst news came from Wade's team. Micah Cranston was missing, and his human parents were dead. It broke my heart, but I couldn't let it get to me.

Oberon was nestled inside me and, to my surprise, kept me focused on the task at hand.

Garrett fit in quite easily on our team. He maintained a professional demeanor and a calm approach. That, too, helped.

We drove up to the Devereaux mansion next, all three of us quiet as the Cranstons' death sank in. The Devereaux couple were rich, owners of a gorgeous hacienda-type property up in Tierrasanta. It was part of a seemingly safe, gated community, with distant views of the Mission Trails Regional Parks at the back.

The house itself was huge, built on three levels, with sumptuous arches and sprawling gardens. Magnolia trees trembled in the late spring breeze, their pink petals drifting away.

As soon as we reached the massive iron gate, we knew there was something wrong. There was a police car outside by the main steps, its red-and-blue lights on.

A terrible thing happened here, Tatyana... Oberon's voice echoed in my head.

"That can't be good," Garrett muttered, frowning as he eyed the cop car. The front door was wide open. He fumbled through his jacket pocket and pulled out his fake FBI badge. "Let's use these for good measure. We have Marjorie Phillips missing, too, so plenty of reasons to stop by the Devereauxes' if their kid's gone."

I nodded and took out my fake FBI badge. Astrid rang the intercom. We listened to it ring twice, before someone picked up, their voice crackling through the speaker.

"Who is it?" the man asked.

"FBI, sir. We're here to talk about Louella," Garrett replied.

"What if the cops are there for something else? What if the kid isn't missing?" Astrid whispered.

Garrett smirked. "After everything that's happened since yesterday, do you really think this isn't what happened here?"

The gate buzzed and slid open. We made our way to the entrance on foot, carefully analyzing our surroundings. There was definitely a bad vibe here, but I couldn't exactly put my finger on it.

The spirits are restless, Oberon said. *They saw something.*

Hold your horses, I thought my reply to him. I had to pay more attention this time around, and make sure that Astrid and Garrett didn't hear me accidentally talking out loud with my ghostly passenger. *Let's talk to the Devereauxes first.*

As soon as we reached the front door, however, I knew that all those bad feelings I'd been having about this place were justified. A side table had been knocked over. Stuff was thrown across the floor.

Sirens wailed in the distance, just as we made it into the living room, where we were greeted by two police officers in uniform and two dead bodies. It didn't take a scientist to guess who the dead couple were. Ted and Lucinda Devereaux were quite well known around San Diego, their faces plastered on several local tabloids. They came from a wealthy oil family from the Midwest and had moved here about five years ago. I remembered the notes on their profile, from Alton's list.

Their throats were slit, and there were black smudges all over the place.

"Obliviscaris in Perpetuum," Garrett muttered, his brow furrowed and his jaw clenched.

Both cops were pale, their eyes wide as they stared at the bodies. The Devereauxes were pale, too, their eyes glassy and their lips purple. They'd been dead for at least five, maybe six hours, judging by their looks and the dried-up blood on the wooden floor.

"How'd you know to come here?" one of the cops asked. I spotted his nametag: Bowman. His colleague was Fraser. "We haven't even called this in yet."

"How'd *you* get here, then, if this wasn't called in?" Garrett replied, flashing his FBI badge.

Bowman narrowed his eyes at it, before he sighed and shook his head slowly. "An alarm went off on the property. It's linked to our station."

"When did that happen?" Garrett asked.

"About twenty minutes ago. Dispatch tried to reach out to the Devereauxes over the phone, but there was no answer, so they sent us here," Bowman explained. "So, what's the FBI doing here?"

"The kid's missing," Garrett said.

Personally, I thought this was a gamble. The cops could've known about this. Judging by the surprised looks on their faces, they didn't.

"Again, how'd you know?" Bowman asked, visibly concerned.

"The Devereauxes called us last night," Garrett replied, absolutely winging it. "What can you tell us about the crime scene?"

Bowman glanced around, visibly disturbed by the bloody sight. Astrid wasn't looking great, either, as she slowly moved back and slipped out of the living room altogether.

"No sign of breaking and entering. The door was open, the locks intact," Bowman explained. "The alarm went off twenty minutes ago, but these two have been dead for longer than that. My guess is maybe the maid came in, saw the couple, freaked out, and ran off before punching in the security code."

"No CCTV then?" I asked.

Fraser shook his head. "No murder weapon either. The kid's not here. If she was missing since yesterday, then that's a whole other case."

"That's ours. This isn't the first child to go missing this week. We have a couple others from Friday and today, actually," Garrett replied. It was a good strategy. We had to give them some information in order to get them to more easily relinquish theirs.

"Oh, yeah. The Phillips kid, right? Gone missing on Friday if I remember correctly," Bowman said. "Two of our colleagues in Missing Persons were on that. You took over?"

Garrett took a deep breath, resting his hands on his hips. He practically towered over the two middle-aged cops. "Yeah. It became an FBI matter since more than one child has gone missing, and your PD is understaffed for this."

"Who's the other kid?" Bowman asked.

"Have you checked the rest of the house? Any sign of Louella Devereaux?" Garrett replied, bluntly changing the subject.

Bowman evidently noticed the shift but didn't pursue it. Instead, he pursed his lips. "Nothing. From what we know, they adopted her six months ago. Raucous little thing, had some run-ins with the law before that. Sixteen and perpetually angry, covered in tattoos. We'll pull her file up for more details, but I specifically remember busting her once for a misdemeanor. She was hanging with the wrong crowd."

"Do you think she might've done this to them?" Fraser murmured, unable to take his eyes off the dead father.

"I'm not excluding the possibility," Bowman said. "But frankly, I doubt it. The moment she got into the Devereauxes' place, she stayed out of trouble. I didn't see her in the back alleys of El Cajon anymore, either."

"Maybe something happened to her," Garrett suggested. "Looks like there was quite the struggle here. What if some old nasty friends of hers followed her up here and did this, huh? She's been missing since yesterday. Maybe someone took her first, then came in and killed the parents."

I knew where this was going. Garrett was planting early suggestions.

Astrid came back in, swiping on her tablet screen and frowning. "Says here Louella might be a Telepath, based on the eyewitness reports. Some people said she knew too much about them, that she used that information to get favors. You know, better seat in the cafeteria, discount on a blouse, minor stuff like that. She unknowingly tried it on a couple of Neutrals, too, who followed her around for a couple of days and observed her behavior and interactions with people. It's how she was brought to our attention, in the end."

That got Bowman and Fraser's attention. Their eyebrows shot up. Garrett cleared his throat, prompting Astrid to look up.

"Seriously?" Garrett muttered.

"What? I thought you were flashing them," she retorted.

"What are you people talking about?" Bowman asked.

Garrett walked up to them and slowly raised his left hand, his Esprit watch glistening blue. The cops stilled, their eyes twinkling yellow for a split second. "You never met us. We were never here. You'll stand here in silence until you hear a honk outside. After that, you'll resume your investigation. Louella is missing. Something must've happened to her. You'll put an APB out on her."

The cops stood there, idle and absent-looking, as we left the house. I found the Ryder twins' card on the floor in the hallway. I picked it up and handed it to Garrett.

"They'll be in there for a while," Garrett said, looking at the card. "Hm… This does have their stench all over it."

"This is just like the Cranstons," Astrid replied.

"Despite what you said to the cops, we have no idea what happened to Louella." I sighed. "Could she have run away, or did the Ryders take her?"

"We won't know for sure until we canvass the area," Garrett said.

Tatyana, there are spirits here. They saw what happened, Oberon chimed in, startling me.

"Hold on," I murmured. "Let me check with the spirits."

Garrett and Astrid waited patiently at the bottom of the stairs, while I remained at the top, closing my eyes.

"You'd better come through for me, Oberon," I whispered.

As the darkness settled around me, I noticed the spirits drifting around—most of them in the yard, though there were a couple standing right next to Garrett and Astrid, motionless and semi-transparent.

There, in the yard, Oberon said. *They know something.*

I made my way down the stairs and stepped onto the green space, where dozens of hydrangeas and rosebushes blossomed in rich shades of pink, lilac, and red. Four spirits stood in the middle, in the shade of a massive magnolia tree. They didn't look from this era, but rather from the early 1900s. Three of them were Latinas, and the fourth was African American—she caught my eye.

With or without Oberon's guidance, as a Kolduny I was able to spot spirits that could help me. I could see it in her eyes. The African-American girl had seen something.

"There's a ghost inside you," she said, her voice barely a whisper.

"I know. He's helping me," I replied, giving her a soft smile. "What are you all doing here?"

They looked at each other, then over my shoulder at the other two spirits, next to Garrett and Astrid. The African-American girl sighed. "We died together. There was a fire here in 1912. Well, those two back there, by the stairs, died sometime in the fifties. A party went horribly wrong."

"I'm sorry," I said. "But why are you all still around? You should've moved on."

"We don't know about the two starlets, but *we* couldn't," one of the Latinas replied. "The young lady of the house at the time, Estrella, was only five. We had to look after her."

"Then she had children. We wanted to protect them, too," the African-American girl added. "Then the Devereaux clan bought the mansion and kicked them out. For some reason, we were stuck here. We couldn't follow Estrella's family."

"That's all very nice, but what did you see?" Oberon cut in, his voice louder and clearer than before. Suddenly, I felt tired and heavy, as if Oberon was draining the life out of me.

"Get back inside," I said. "You're wearing me out! This isn't part of the deal, Oberon!"

I heard him grumble something, before I felt the enormous pressure leave my shoulders. I could breathe again.

"Something horrible happened here," the African-American girl said. "Two people... with strange powers... They came up to the door very early this morning. I think it was three, maybe four o'clock. The Devereauxes let them in, because they said something had happened to Louella. The Devereauxes were already worried. They hadn't seen her since Saturday morning."

"Then they talked for a while about Louella," one of the Latinas added. "The strangers wanted to know where she could've gone."

"They didn't know where Louella was?" I asked. The spirits shook their heads simultaneously. "Which means they probably tried to catch her outside the Devereaux property, maybe somewhere in town. They came here knowing she wouldn't have come back home, and inserted themselves onto the property."

"They killed them," the African-American girl said, her lower lip trembling. "They slit their throats and trashed the place, then dropped a card on the floor and left, laughing. They were laughing!"

"What did they look like?" I asked.

"The girl had short black hair and brown eyes. The boy had long black hair and brown eyes. They were related, undoubtedly. Perhaps siblings," she said. "They looked alike. They were vicious. So vicious."

"When is the last time you saw Louella?" I replied.

The African-American girl exchanged glances with the others, and frowned at me. "Early morning on Saturday. She left the house in a hurry, but I don't know why. I wasn't inside at the time. Her mother came out, shouting her name and asking her to come back, but Louella wouldn't listen. She kept going, until she vanished up the road. None of us could follow."

"I suppose you're all tied to the property, that's why," I said. "Thank you all. Thank you."

I left them beneath the magnolia tree and headed back to Garrett and Astrid, the darkness dissipating around me as I returned to the living plane.

You should ask those other two standing behind your friends, Oberon suggested.

I stopped in front of Astrid and Garrett, then closed my eyes again. Two young girls in midcentury garb were chatting behind them, giggling and giving me sideways glances.

"Did you two see anything?" I asked them.

They both shook their heads. One of them was a redhead, the other a luscious brunette. Their skirts and ruffled tops reminded me of movies from Hollywood's Golden Age. They must've worked in the business. They had the theatrical gestures and demeanor of Californian starlets.

"I think you did," I said, smirking.

"We're not interested in talking to you," the redhead replied. "You're bland."

"That hunk you've got in you, though... He can chat us up if he wants to." The brunette grinned, revealing two rows of pearly white teeth.

I pinched the bridge of my nose, sighing with frustration. "Do you have anything to share about what happened last night, or do you just want me to hook you up with another ghost? Because he can't take you girls out on a date, if that's what you're hoping for."

"We know that!" the brunette snapped, then pouted. "But it's been a long time since we've met someone as dashing as your... friend. We just want him to talk to us, and we'll tell you what we saw."

"You're not yanking my chain here?" I asked, raising an eyebrow.

They both seemed insulted, their nostrils flaring angrily. At this point, I had a choice. Leave them be, or let Oberon talk through my body. That meant revealing him to Garrett and Astrid. Information was crucial at this point. I didn't feel like I had much of a choice.

"Take over for a minute," I said to Oberon.

His glee tickled my throat, shortly before I felt crushed under the weight of a pickup truck. That was how intense it was when a ghost took control of my body. It wore me out.

"Hey, ladies." Oberon chuckled, and my lips stretched into a sly grin. I could only imagine what Astrid and Garrett were thinking in that moment. I couldn't hear or see them in the veil, but I had lost my ability to rein in my voice, as well as control over my body.

"Hi, handsome," the brunette replied with a seductive wink.

"Aren't you a sight for sore eyes!" the redhead exclaimed, clapping with excitement.

I was having a hard time not only consciously supporting the full weight of Oberon's spirit, but also struggling not to roll my eyes at them.

"Glad to know I'm making two gorgeous creatures such as yourselves happy," Oberon said, turning his charm up to eleven. "How about you tell me what you saw last night? My spirit talking friend and I would really appreciate it."

"Oh, so that's why you're in her! I never tried possessing someone before!" the brunette murmured.

Oberon sensed my alarm and chuckled nervously. "Well, don't, toots. It's not for amateurs. This is a powerful conduit I'm riding, not your run-of-the-mill type of human. Now, come on, tell me what you saw. Louella's life is at stake."

"Ugh. That dramatic little brat," the redhead groaned. "She got so lucky to get her scrawny ass adopted into the Devereaux family, and she still threw fits. 'I wanna go there! I wanna do that! Why won't you let me see my old friends?' Boo-friggin'-hoo! Girl didn't know how good she had it until last night!"

"Wait, she was here?" Oberon replied.

They both nodded. "She was at the gates," the brunette said. "The other ghosts... you know, the maids and whatever... they were inside with the Devereauxes. Front seats to the gruesome murder!" she added with sinister laughter.

"But Louella was out here. She's a weird one, you know? She can see through walls. She can hear from miles away," the redhead added. "Something is wrong with her."

"Anyway, we think Louella was coming back home, when she heard her parents getting slaughtered in there," the brunette said, nodding at the house, then pointing at the gate. "She stood there for a minute or two, then ran off crying."

I understood then that Louella had some special abilities, indeed. Some I'd never heard of before—not without the use of a spell, anyway. Maybe she'd learned magic from somewhere. We couldn't know for sure until we found her.

"Anything else, ladies?" Oberon asked, detecting my raw nerves as they stretched to new limits. He knew how much his full presence weighed on me.

"The killers came out, cackling like devils," the redhead replied, "and walked out through the front gate. They said, and I quote, 'Katie's going to hang our asses out to dry if we don't catch the little mouse,'" she added, mimicking a nasal tone.

"Thank you." Oberon sighed. "Your assistance was incredible. And, might I add, you two look fantastic, given that you're, you know... dead."

They both fawned over him, fluttering their eyelashes and almost melting before us. I felt Oberon slip into the backseat of my consciousness. I could breathe again.

Leaving the spirit world behind, I opened my eyes to a very troubled Astrid and a highly amused Garrett. Astrid put her phone out, its screen dark, long enough for her to spot Oberon's reflection in the glass. She gasped, then took several steps back.

"It's okay," I said, trying to keep her from freaking out. She'd seen me possessed before. "I've got him under control. He's helping me."

"You let a ghost ride you? Seriously?" Garrett chuckled. "I heard about the last time you were taken over, Tatyana. You still haven't learned your lesson?"

"I told you, I've got him under control!" I insisted. "I have full command over my body at all times!"

That was a white lie, of course. Only minutes earlier, Oberon had completely taken over with the first group of spirits before I snapped at him. But I didn't need to admit that. Oberon had been incredibly helpful just now. I had to give him credit.

"Tatyana, seriously, this is messed up," Astrid said. "You *know* you're not fully developed, so you can't withstand a possession without the spirit eventually taking over."

"Astrid, don't worry about it. I mean it. I'm fine. We agreed to work together, Oberon and me. And he definitely helped!" I replied. "I just found out that Louella left the house early yesterday morning after an argument with the parents. Something happened during the day. Late last night, at around three or four, the Ryders came in."

Now I had their full attention, the issue of Oberon and me slipping somewhere in the background. I gave them all the details I'd gathered from the spirits, including the last time they'd seen Louella, specifically during her parents' murder.

Garrett and Astrid were silent for a while.

"The description you have of the Ryders," Astrid murmured, flipping through her Smartie tablet files. "I've heard it before. Yup, here it is. They're Shapeshifters, all right, just like Wade said. And they're recycling identities. This wasn't the first time they used these personas."

"It hurts less to recycle identities," Garrett said.

"One thing I could never wrap my head around is how do they get all the physical details right? They can't possibly do it with just a photo," I chimed in, further steering the conversation away from Oberon.

Garrett's shoulders dropped. "They need to touch the person they're copying. Or something that carries their DNA, like a hair or a nail or something."

"Wow, that's creepy," Astrid replied, then frowned at him. "Wait, how'd you know that? It's not in any of the manuals. It's not common knowledge, for sure."

"It isn't," I muttered, eyeing him suspiciously. "I've never heard of that before. As a matter of fact, from what I remember, non-Shapeshifter magicals are unable to fully explain the transformation process."

"It's because we keep it to ourselves. Usually, anyway. I feel like I can trust you two," Garrett said.

"Holy crap!" Astrid gasped. "You're a Shapeshifter!"

"And you're a human, and Tatyana here has a ghost riding her," Garrett fired back, irritated. "Nobody's perfect!"

"Does anyone in the coven know?" I asked, slightly on edge.

"Alton, Wade, and Adley. That's it. Well, and now you two. I'd appreciate it if we kept it at that. The stigma is still real and present," he said. "I'm not comfortable with more people knowing about this, but I am aware that my ability can give you some insight into how the Ryders operate. And that's what matters right now."

Astrid stood in silence, processing the discovery. Then she

looked at me. "You need to tell Wade about what you're doing with the ghost. Wait, whose ghost is in you?"

"Oberon Marx," I said.

"Oh. He helped you with Dylan, right?"

I nodded. "I'll tell Wade, but not yet. I don't want him expelling Oberon."

"But—"

"You know that's exactly what Wade will do, the moment he hears I've got a ghost in me!" I cut her off, my tone clipped.

"For good reason, too!" she said.

"It's not the same, Astrid. I'm conscious, and I have a grip on things. Please. Just bear with me. We need all the help we can get. I mean, look at this mess," I said, pointing at the Devereaux mansion. I wasn't entirely honest, and Oberon probably had something to do with it, but he'd proven himself useful. I wasn't ready to let go of him. "Bodies are dropping, magical kids are going *poof*. And Katherine Shipton might be involved. This is not a good time to play by the rules."

"Tatyana does have a point," Garrett said. "Special circumstances call for extreme measures. You know that. It's why you were brought back to life three times, right? Special circumstances?"

Astrid nodded slowly. I remembered her previous, tragic deaths. As a Necromancer, Alton was able to bring her back, though each time it threw him straight into a Purge, given the intensity of the entire process. But he had to bring her back. Astrid was a human, and she'd died while helping us magicals. He had the coven authority to do that.

"I'll put all the data we gathered from here through Smartie and send it out to Wade and the others. I'll leave Oberon out of this for now," she said, and I breathed a sigh of relief. "But the moment I smell something fishy, Tatyana, I'm telling Wade. Okay?"

"Okay. Thanks," I replied, smiling.

"I'll put all the descriptions we have of the Ryders into the system, too. We're clearly looking for different people, imperson-ated by the same magicals."

We left the Devereaux property and got back in the car. As soon as the engine roared to life, Garrett pressed the horn a couple of times, enough for the idle cops inside the mansion to snap out of their hypnotic state and resume their investigative work.

"We'll send a cleanup crew out here today," he said, driving off.

My heart felt heavy. I didn't like how Oberon had been able to take the wheel earlier, but he had definitely helped us back there. I was split between letting him stay and expelling him.

Trust me, Tatyana, Oberon whispered in the back of my head. *I won't cross you again. It was pure reflex back there, completely uninten-tional. You have full control, I promise.*

Given our circumstances, I didn't have much of a choice. There was still so much we didn't know, and considering what we'd seen from the Ryders so far, we had to be ready for the worst.

TWENTY-THREE

Harley

"Have you ever gotten a visit from two people with the last name Ryder? Or any... I don't know, wonky social workers, maybe?" I asked Jacob, mentally crossing my fingers for a no.

"No. Just the usual social workers I've known for years. They come around once a month to check up on me, but they're good people," Jacob replied.

I nodded slowly, breathing a sigh of relief at the same time. At least he was safe, for the time being, still undetected. Maybe that's why the Ryders hadn't found him. Yet. Besides, since Jacob was a part of *my* foster family, they would've definitely left a clue or something behind, just to mess with me and the coven, based on their behavioral pattern.

"So, you knew what I was from the moment we met," I said to Jacob as we played another round of cards in the garden. The sun had already set, and we'd been at it for a few hours. Dinner was going to be served soon. I could already smell the lasagna that Mrs. Smith was cooking in the oven.

"Yeah... I just... I don't want anyone to know I can do this kind of stuff," he replied. "The Smiths are so nice. I don't want to lose them."

"You know what you are, then. You know about Chaos, the coven, all of us."

We'd kept the conversation away from him for a while, as I told him my life story, from the very beginning that I could remember—foster care, and up to the present, describing my trials and tribulations, as well as my own experiences with the coven, Finch, and Katherine Shipton.

He nodded again. "I learned from the witches and warlocks I came across. Most of them rogues in small California towns. This is my first stable home in San Diego."

"What happened to your previous foster family?" I asked. "I heard there was a death involved."

He sighed, lowering his head. "I wasn't in full control of my abilities. My foster mom came in at the wrong time and... she died."

His grief and guilt tore me apart. I gave him a gentle shoulder squeeze, in an attempt to comfort him. I wanted more details, but he didn't seem ready to give them.

"And you've got a grip on your magic now?" I asked.

"It's better than before, I guess."

"And you never thought of coming to the coven? Dude, they could give you a safe home. They could teach you stuff."

Jacob shrugged. "I don't know. I haven't heard great things about the San Diego Coven. It's why there are a lot of rogues in this city."

Given his ability to sense them, Jacob could spot the ones that the coven had been unable to identify yet. Maybe he was better off with the coven, after all. He could help us reach out to unidentified magicals, so other hostiles wouldn't reel them in first. The one thing I knew for sure was that having too many rogue magicals on the loose didn't bode well for us, not even if they were on their best behavior.

We had to keep track of who came, who left, and who stayed,

especially with the likes of Katherine Shipton and the Ryder twins in town.

"You should think about it," I said.

"Don't tell on me, please!" he replied, slightly alarmed. He was afraid, but I still wasn't sure of what, exactly. The kind of crippling urgency bursting through him couldn't possibly all be related to the coven. There had to be something else... something deeper inside him. "I don't want the coven to know about my ability to sense magicals. I haven't told anyone about it. I've kept it to myself even with other rogues, I promise! I know what my power can do in the wrong hands. It's why I'm okay with just staying here, in the Smiths' care."

"So, you keep your abilities under control, huh?" I asked, my voice low.

He nodded. "I got some tips from several rogues," he said. "I keep my head down, I don't hurt anyone, I don't look for trouble, and I go to school. I swear."

"Okay, I believe you," I replied, smiling softly. "The secret about controlling your powers is to focus on what you want from them. Determination, Jake. You tell them what to do, not the other way around. They're a part of you. You're not a part of them. If you set your mind on that, you'll always have a better grip."

"Thanks," he murmured, returning a faint smile.

I breathed out, partially relieved for having had this conversation, but something still weighed on me.

I knew I had unfinished business back at the coven. Today's events were coming back to haunt me. Not just the guilt over what had happened to the Cranstons, but also the heartache stemming from Wade's anger. He had every reason to be mad at me. After all, I'd been the one to push for Micah to stay with his human foster parents. Those alarms and traps we'd set hadn't prevented the Ryders from killing them. Neither had Santana's Orisha. I had my own demons to wrestle now.

I rose to my feet and let out a long sigh. It was time to go back and face the music. "Listen, Jake, I have to go, but I'll be in touch. Here's my number," I said, giving him one of my cards. "Call me if you need anything, if you get into any kind of trouble... whatever. Just call me, okay?"

"Yeah, thanks," he mumbled.

"I won't tell the coven about you, but I need you to watch your-self and take care of Mr. and Mrs. Smith, too, okay? They're human. They don't know any better. And stay away from the Ryder twins, if, by any rotten chance, they come around."

"The Ryder twins," he repeated after me, his voice faded.

My stomach hurt. It wasn't hunger. It was stress, along with the dread of losing another life today. "They're bad people, Jake. I think they're working with Katherine Shipton."

"Oh, your aunt."

I groaned, rolling my eyes. "Yeah, crappy family. Not my fault," I replied. "Either way, if they come around... If anyone magical comes around, claiming to be from the coven or the Mage Council or whatever, you call me immediately. No matter what. Your life depends on it. And so do the Smiths'."

He nodded again.

"Thank you, Harley," he said. "I'm glad you're here."

"I'm not sure that's such a good thing, given what's been happening lately," I murmured, sighing. "Be good, Jake. Keep your nose clean."

He smiled, and I gave him a forced one back, as he resumed work on his pet feeder. I then went back inside, a weight still keeping my shoulders down. Mrs. Smith was just about to pull the lasagna out of the oven.

"I have to skip dinner, I'm afraid," I said to her. "I'm sorry."

"Oh, sweetie, that's a shame!" she replied. "It's going to be deli-cious. I added fresh parsley from the garden."

"I have to meet some friends tonight, and I completely forgot. Next time, I promise!"

She moved around the counter island and pulled me in for a

hug. "That's okay, Harley. I'm glad you're coming by more often, and thank you for spending time with Jacob."

"It's my pleasure," I breathed, tears stinging my eyes as I reveled in her warmth. "For what it's worth, Jacob's a good kid. He keeps his head down. But if there's ever anything wrong or if you're worried about him, please call me immediately. Okay?"

She smiled and nodded, then kissed my temple.

"I'll see you soon, honey," she said.

Once I left the Smiths' house, my heart sank further. As soon as I detached myself from their loving and jovial presence, reality came crashing down on me completely. My phone beeped. I checked the message. It was from Astrid, and it made me want to die right then and there. Two other magicals were missing, and another couple of foster parents had been murdered, just like the Cranstons.

Whatever the Ryder twins were up to, it was escalating, and I was afraid we couldn't keep up.

I headed to the nearest bus stop, a couple of blocks away. It was on a street corner, dimly lit and empty. There were barely any souls outside after dark. This was mostly a residential area. Anything that wasn't directly connected to the main boulevard looked practically abandoned after nine p.m. I loved this place at night, and I'd often gone on walks throughout the neighborhood before I moved out.

I reached the bus stop and checked the schedule. The next ride was coming in fifteen minutes. I had time to kill, so I decided to text Wade, just to see if his mood had improved.

On my way back. Need anything? HM. I always signed my texts like he did, just to mess with him.

But his reply was swift and sharp, and it hurt me deeply.

No. I briefed Alton. We'll talk in the morning. WC

Even his signature wasn't enough to lift my spirits.

I sensed a foreign feeling creep into my consciousness, and I lowered my phone, wondering where it was coming from. Concern…

mixed with affection. Intriguing and confusing, to say the least. I stepped away from the bus stop shelter and moved toward the street corner, glancing around. There wasn't anyone out here. Streetlights flickered on along the sides of the street as nightfall finally settled.

Then I caught movement to my right. I turned my head and spotted two figures slowly moving toward me, from the other end of the alley leading to the main bus route. But there weren't any emotions coming from *them*.

That set off my alarms instantly.

Male and female.

They were dressed in black, wearing hoodies beneath their leather jackets. Something glistened in their right hands. I noticed the Esprits before I could see their faces. The alley was dimly lit.

My instincts kicked in.

I had a feeling I knew who they were. And it spelled massive trouble for me.

The moment I could see their cold grins, however, I knew for sure. These were the Ryder twins—wearing two of their known faces, with deep blue eyes and pale blond hair. The vicious glow in their eyes was what truly gave them away. They knew who I was. The fact that I couldn't sense their emotions was further cause for alarm. It was also setting up a strange pattern, but I didn't have time to think about that anymore.

"Merlin," the girl said, her voice coarse like sandpaper and her tone clipped as she and the brother kept walking toward me, seemingly calm and relaxed. "I was wondering when we'd get a moment alone."

"I take it you're Emily and Emmett Ryder," I murmured, preparing myself for the worst. My eyes darted about, checking every single escape route and potential weapon I could use against them.

"Our reputation precedes us," Emmett replied, grinning.

"No, but you keep leaving your cards everywhere. It's a little desperate, if you ask me. It's like you're begging for attention," I said, my blood boiling. I was finally coming face-to-face with two of the most vicious magicals I'd ever dealt with.

Flashbacks of Susan and Larry's lifeless bodies rattled my brain, setting my skin on fire. I was itching for a fight. Judging by their sneers, so were they.

"Well, we had to get your attention," Emily remarked.

"Oh, you have more than that," I answered, taking an attack stance.

Emily laughed, her Esprit bracelet lighting up orange. "You really think you can take us on, noob?"

"Why don't you try me, you monster!" I shouted, fury blazing through my every nerve.

She threw a fast fireball at me.

I ducked. It missed me by an inch, tops, and I smelled burnt hair. I patted the top of my head and checked my ponytail, just in case. *All good. I think.*

Emmett used Telekinesis on me before I could react. The invisible force gripped me by the throat and threw me to one side.

I pushed a Telekinetic pulse out from my hand, just before Emmett's force could slam me into the bus stop. The counter-punch of my Telekinesis helped break the hold he had on me, and I dropped on the ground, then shot back up and released a flurry of fireballs.

Emmett did his best to dodge them, but one nipped him in the shoulder. The flames burst bright and orange, before he dropped and rolled to put them out. Emily, however, revealed herself to be a Herculean like Dylan, as she darted left and right with lightning speed, then rammed into me.

The tackle knocked the air out of my lungs and I was thrown backward. I landed painfully, with Emily straddling me. She tried to punch me, but the sudden jolt of energy flowing through me kick-started my adrenaline. I served her an uppercut before she could hit me, then grabbed her by the throat with a Telekinetic grip and threw her to the side.

Emmett muttered a spell.

Knowing I only had a split second till whatever hex he'd cast would hit me, I leapt up and ran toward the other side of the street, trying to put some distance between myself and the twins. Emily got back on her feet, grunting and cursing under her breath. She threw a massive ball of fire.

I used my Elemental ability and slapped the fire hydrant next to me to summon its water. Thankfully, laws required that one of these babies be mounted every five hundred feet along the road. It moaned and trembled before a thick water jet broke out and shot upward. Keeping my focus, I spread the water out in a fan just as the blaze was about to swallow me whole. The fire sizzled and died out.

Emmett's Telekinetic grip took hold of me again. I was nowhere near strong or capable enough to handle both of them at the same time. Once more, I was hurled into the air like a rag doll. I summoned the winds to break my fall, but it didn't do much as Emily slammed into me. I cried out in pain, every inch of my body aching.

I rolled away, the asphalt scratching my face and hands as I tried to stop and regain control of the situation. I wound up lying on my belly, taking deep breaths and quickly assessing my physical state. Nothing felt exactly broken, but something told me I was going to be hurting even more in the morning, when the adrenaline was gone.

"Man, I was told I'd have to bring my A game with you," Emmett sneered. "From the looks of you, Merlin, that fancy bloodline of yours isn't worth much these days."

I groaned, trying to push myself back up. "I don't know much about my bloodline, but I do know a pompous jerk when I see one!" I hissed, then focused my Esprit on his head.

The Telekinetic punch was so concentrated and powerful that it knocked him back, blood spraying out of his nose. He hadn't seen that coming, and neither had Emily, who stared at me in shock.

I didn't give her a chance to hit back. I channeled all my anger into a second Telekinetic punch—it smacked her hard in the chest. I heard her grunt as she was flipped backward by the force.

They were both down. This was my chance to get out of here.

My knees were weak, and I felt bruised all over, but I had to move. I growled as I staggered to my feet and hurried away.

Ten yards later, Emmett's Telekinetic grip had me by the ankles. All of a sudden, I was back down, flat on my face, getting dragged back to hell itself.

A massive bubble of blue energy shot out around us. I gasped at the sight of it. It was a time-lapse spell. My heart skipped a beat as I glanced over my shoulder, hoping to see Wade, but there was no one there.

Either way, good call, I guess. Can't have humans watching us battle it out.

The Ryders were shocked, though, looking up and scowling at the time lapse. It was enough for me to realize that they hadn't been the ones to cast it.

"What the—" Emmett tried to speak, but he was suddenly lifted and rammed into the blue energy ceiling with enough force to make him yelp in agony. He landed with a painful thud, spitting blood.

A shadow darted to my right. Emily's eyes moved fast as she tried to spot the assailant. Whoever this was, they were incredibly swift. Another Telekinetic pulse came out—even more powerful than the one that had broken Emmett. It hit Emily hard, throwing her head to the side.

She collapsed, moaning.

Before I could even think of my next step, I was pulled back up on my feet and turned around. My so-called savior was clad in a black hood. I couldn't see the face, but a feeling of urgency seared through me.

"Hold on, this is going to hurt," the stranger said with a feminine voice.

A woman.

She put an arm around my waist and pulled me close, holding me firmly as she put her other hand out, the ring on her finger lighting up bright green.

I lost my breath as I watched the air tremble and rip open like a gash, revealing the kind of pitch blackness that sent shivers down my spine.

"No! Stop them!" I heard Emmett cry out.

I didn't get a chance to do anything, as the stranger pulled me into the strange blackness. I may have screamed. I wasn't sure at that point, as the very fabric of the universe warped and warbled into a billion colors. It only lasted for a second, before I found myself falling.

We both landed on the grass, from a significant height.

It was painful enough for me to employ some of my ear-burning curse words, in a litany that could make the devil himself gasp with shock. I looked up and saw the gash in the air disappear as the stranger got back on her feet with a soft grunt. Only... I wasn't in the Smiths' neighborhood anymore.

"What in the ever-living—" I stopped myself by covering my mouth, and sat up, taking in my surroundings.

We were in Waterfront Park.

"Sorry for the rough ride," the stranger said. Her voice sounded awfully familiar.

"What... What just happened?!" I croaked.

"You've never been through a wormhole before, huh?" she replied.

A what, now?

Her tone was amused, but her emotions revealed a sense of endearment. Whoever she was, she meant well. I could feel it in my bones, along with the brutal beating I'd just gotten from the Ryders.

"Who are you?" I asked, still panting. "I mean, don't get me wrong, thanks a bunch for saving my ass back there, but... who are you?"

She took her hood off, and my stomach dropped. I forgot how to breathe altogether as I recognized the witch standing before me.

The long black hair had streaks of white in it, but it was hers, all right. I'd seen it cascade down her shoulders like that, more than once. The sky looked at me through her eyes. And a piece of me was embedded in her smile. I knew that face.

Isadora Merlin.

TWENTY-FOUR

Harley

F or a moment, I thought I was stuck in a dream, and I wasn't
sure which kind.

Isadora Merlin, my father's sister, was standing before me,
clearly very much alive. The years had been kind to her. Fine lines
accentuated her expressions, but her bright blue eyes were brimming with youth—the kind that the soul carried throughout
the years.

I sat there for a long moment, controlling my breathing to ease
the pain of a bruised rib. But my heart was pounding. I'd been
carrying an image of her in the back of my head for days, now, a
snippet of her I'd seen in a distant memory that had reemerged in
my dreams.

"You look like you've seen a ghost," she said, smiling.

"Am I not looking at one right now?" I breathed, my eyes wide
and my mind stunned.

She offered me her hand. I gripped it and, in an instant, felt a
flurry of emotions rush through me, much like a spring that had
just broken through a rock wall. There was concern and affection,

warmth and… the sheer joy of seeing me. I gasped, overwhelmed by the sensations.

"Your Empathy must be intense," she replied. "Then again, I do wear my heart on my sleeve."

"How are you here? How did you find me? Where have you been?" I bombarded her with just some of the questions I had.

She chuckled, then helped me up. I groaned from the rib pain but managed to stand on my own. The adrenaline was still pumping through my limbs, but I was pretty sure I was going to suffer a lot more later. I'd been slammed left and right back there, after all.

"How are you feeling?" she asked, frowning as she measured me from head to toe.

"I'll live. What was… Seriously, what did I just go through?"

"A wormhole. It's one of my abilities. Extremely rare and highly sought after by the darker elements of our magical society. I'm one of two who can open such portals," she explained. "There's a membrane that permeates everything, the same in which we build our covens. I am able to cut open these little holes and slip through them. Space is relative to me."

"So… We just traveled through a wormhole."

"More like tumbled," she replied, her lips stretching into a smirk. There was so much of her that reminded me of my father, I could almost feel my heart tearing. "Harley, there isn't much time. You need to jump in the first cab and head straight for the coven. You are much safer there."

"Yeah… No. Not until you tell me what the hell is going on," I shot back. "Have you been following me?"

She sighed. "I've been watching you for a while," she said. "I'm sorry I didn't come to you sooner, but I'm a wanted magical, Harley, and not by the covens. Dark forces are at work, and they're after my Portal ability. I'm extremely valuable to certain people, and my portals could lead to many unnecessary deaths if I let them take me, which is why I've been under the radar and presumed dead."

I nodded slowly. I supposed I could understand the reasoning behind her decision to vanish. It didn't make me feel any better, but I could see how a magical like her could be used by the likes of the Ryder twins—or, worse, Katherine Shipton.

"How long have you been tailing me?" I asked.

"Since you came to the coven. The moment you were discovered I had eyes on you. I have friends there and in many other places… quiet, discreet people who know how to send me a message when my attention is required," she explained. "I've kept my distance for your own safety. We can't be together in the same place at once for too long, Harley. My very presence puts you in even more danger. You've got your plate full enough as it is."

"Those were the Ryder twins back there. Do you know them?" I asked.

She nodded. "I've seen them before. They've never met me. They've been looking for me, but I'm old and seasoned enough to steer clear of them. They were after you, Harley. Katherine is like a cat, now, playing with her food. You're her dinner."

Anger and grief blazed through me. Some of it was mine, but Isadora shared my feelings. We'd both lost family because of that witch. But then it hit me: Isadora just confirmed the connection we'd been suspecting already.

"So, the Ryder twins are working with Katherine Shipton," I concluded.

"Yes. She's the one who stopped them from showing up at their new covens. She recruited them," Isadora said. "She's planning something, and the Ryders have a role in it. So do the young magicals that were abducted. Some joined her willingly."

"Kenneth Willow," I murmured.

"That's right. She's gathering an army of rogue or undiscovered magicals. She's reaching out to the new ones who have just moved to San Diego, as well. She's trying to get the Neutrals on her side, too. And the Ryders are just some of her recruiters. She's got spies infiltrating most covens, including yours. Eyes and ears everywhere. I've been trying to find out who's working for her, but they're all very good at covering their tracks," she replied.

"They've been leaving cards for us," I said.

"I know. They're a message to you, specifically, Harley. They want you to know what they're doing. They want you to know you can't stop them. It's psychological warfare. They're trying to get into your head and destroy your morale. They're doing it because they're afraid of you. Katherine wants you to suffer. She wants you dead. Not because you mean much to her—no one was ever worth much in her life. You're a problem she needs to get out of the way."

"But *why*? I don't even know where she is!"

"It doesn't matter. You're smart and inquisitive. You're determined and ambitious. And, Harley, the power inside you... it scares her."

I scoffed. "I'm suppressed."

"I know, Harley. I'm the one who helped your father with the Dempsey Suppressor."

My blood ran cold. "Wait, what? You were in on that?! Why'd you let him do that?!"

She sighed. "We had no choice at the time, Harley. You were like a little nuclear reactor, incredibly easy to detect. Your abilities were already manifesting. We had to do whatever we could to keep you safe and hidden. Katherine was on the loose, your father was a wanted man... You weren't going to live if you were found at the time. I'm sorry," she replied, then put her hands on my shoulders. "I promise, I'll come find you, and we'll talk about everything. I will answer all your questions in due time. Right now, you need to go. The Ryders will be getting out of that time lapse in a few minutes, and they'll be looking for you. The one thing they've been unable to do is get close enough to kill you. Tonight, they almost succeeded."

I thought about it for a moment, trying to wrap my head around this new and troubling development.

"When will I see you again?" I asked, afraid to let her go.

"I'm not sure, Harley. There's something I need to take care of, first. People to see. Some things to put in place," she said.

"Did you know about Jacob and the Smiths?"

"I did, yes. Jacob is extremely rare and valuable, as well. He's got the street smarts he needs to keep a low profile. The Ryders don't know about him. They want *you*. You're their next target."

"How do you know all this?" I replied.

"I've been trailing this whole operation for years, now, Harley. As best as I could, anyway. I don't have all the facts yet. I knew it was only a matter of time before Katherine would resurface again. Finch was just the beginning," she explained. "She'll be testing you, poking and prodding until she gets a chance to kill you. So, please, I may not have been around for most of your life, and I will never forgive myself for having had to keep my distance, but... Please, just listen to me on this. Go back to the coven and watch your back."

My throat tightened. "What about Jacob? I'm afraid to leave him with the Smiths, especially after the Cranstons."

"I'll keep an eye on him," she said, giving me a reassuring smile. "You keep doing your job and helping the coven. You've got a good team working with you. I think you're all more than capable of taking the Ryders down. But don't do it alone. Don't go anywhere alone, either. It's for the best."

"I... I don't know what to say," I breathed.

A taxi pulled over just fifty yards away, on one of the roads that outlined Waterfront Park. The driver honked twice. Isadora exhaled, seeming to recognize the guy behind the wheel.

"That's your ride, Harley. Go," she said.

I frowned. "Huh? You already called me a cab?"

"He's one of my go-to guys," she replied. "His name is Dicky, and he's very efficient. He'll give you his card, if you need to use his services in the future."

"Wait, is he human or magical?" I asked.

"Human."

"And he knows about us?" I croaked, making her laugh.

"Relax, Harley. He's good. Don't worry about it. Just go, honey, please."

I glanced over my shoulder, checking the car. The engine was on, and the driver was gazing straight ahead, patiently waiting.

"What really happened to my mom and dad?" I asked Isadora, my voice shaky. "I need to know."

"Don't believe everything you've read in the newspapers," Isadora replied bluntly. "I can't tell you much right now, but I can point you in the right direction. There's a curse, an ancient spell called Sál Vinna. Look it up. You'll understand more once you read about it. Now, go!"

She stepped back, then put her hand out. Her ring lit up green once more as she opened another portal—this time, the slit was longer and vertical. I had a feeling the quality of the wormhole depended on how much time she had to open one. Back by the bus stop, she'd only had a second to work with, before the Ryder twins came after us.

"I'll see you soon, I promise," she said, and vanished into the wormhole.

The air rippled as the portal dissipated, leaving me all by myself on the edge of Waterfront Park.

The taxi honked again.

It was time to go.

TWENTY-FIVE

Harley

Dicky was surprisingly quiet. I figured it must've been one of the reasons Isadora kept him around. After everything I'd witnessed, I found it difficult to think any human could really deal with the magical world. Sure, some of the foster parents we'd met were aware that their kids were special, but that didn't mean they were anywhere near ready to accept the existence of an entire secret society. Hell, the Cranstons had just been killed because they were raising a magical son.

Yet as Dicky drove his cab down the streets of San Diego, he felt calm and serene. He wasn't terrified of me. He seemed wary, at most—probably his survival instinct still adjusting to our existence, but his head was properly screwed on his shoulders.

"So, you've known Isadora for a long time?" I asked, my voice dry and raspy.

As I slumped in the backseat, I understood just how sore I was going to be in the morning. It reminded me of the gargoyle incident, the pain disturbingly similar—like being hit by a bus, repeatedly.

A thousand thoughts were shooting through my mind, and I

figured I could strike up a conversation with Dicky to find out more about this other aunt of mine. There was so much I didn't know, and so many mysteries she could clear up if only I had more time with her.

"Uh-huh," Dicky replied, keeping his eyes on the road.

He was in his mid-forties, with a receding hairline and rebellious brown curls at the back. He smelled of Old Spice—which was better than the olfactory disaster that was his cab. Someone had recently eaten Indian in the back.

"And, um, you know about magicals, from what she told me," I said, hoping I'd get him to say more.

"Uh-huh."

A moment passed in awkward silence.

"You're not going to tell me anything about what you've seen or heard about Isadora, are you?" I asked.

"Nope."

"All right…" I muttered, sinking farther into the backseat.

I knew a zipped mouth when I saw one, and I wasn't good at drawing blood from stone. Dicky was clearly under instructions: *don't tell the girl anything, just drive her to the coven.*

By the time we reached Fleet Science Center, nightfall stretched its starry sky over the city in deep shades of indigo. There were barely any souls out—a couple of late-night joggers doing their usual routes around the museum, and the nighttime security guards.

"How much do I owe you?" I asked Dicky, who waved me away.

"It's paid for. Don't worry about it, kiddo."

There was an affectionate familiarity in his voice. As if we'd met before… or better yet, as if he knew me. "Have we met?" I asked, narrowing my eyes as I tried to get a better look through the passenger window.

"Go on, go in," he said. "It's not safe out here."

"You don't seem scared," I remarked.

"I'm not the one being hunted by Shapeshifters, tootsie-roll. Have a good evening!"

He drove off, leaving me outside the Center with a baffled expression.

"What in the world is happening?" I breathed, as if hoping the universe would answer.

Nothing made sense when taken apart. However, when I put it all together, there seemed to be a narrative I hadn't thought about before. Of course, without a confirmation that the Ryders and Katherine Shipton were, indeed, connected, I wouldn't have been able to generate a clear picture of what was going on.

After failing to sabotage the Bestiary with Finch's help, Katherine was looking for new ways to screw with us. We'd captured Finch before he released the heavyweight monsters. We'd only had a swarm of gargoyles to deal with, which, in hindsight, seemed easier than, say, any of the Gorgon sisters, Leviathan, or Echidna. The Bestiary was riddled with ill-intended creatures of raw Chaos, and some had been loose for long enough to become the stuff of human legends. Some, like Quetzalcoatl, had been worshiped as gods. Others, like the changelings, had scared the daylights out of the Middle Ages.

But we'd gotten that under control. The Bestiary was safe, and Finch was in Purgatory.

Katherine had recruited the Ryders to help her as well, and they struck me as much more evil and vicious than Finch. Heck, the Ryders made Finch sound like an angry teenager. They'd been circling around the rogue magicals in the city, grooming the parents or the kids... or both, in some cases, so they could get them out of their homes.

They'd left cards for us to see, to taunt us.

Then, they'd killed the human parents and stolen the kids. Some, like Kenneth Willow, had joined them willingly. Others, like Marjorie Phillips, had run away from them. Either way, they seemed central to Katherine's plot. She was planning something against the covens, and she needed these kids for some reason.

It hit me then that maybe we had overlooked something about the children's abilities. There had to be a method to this madness. A reason for Katherine to want specific young magicals. She definitely got her intel from inside our coven, and that further confirmed that we still had a spy in our midst.

Jacob, for the time being, was safe. *But for how long?*

The Ryders had tailed me extremely close to the Smiths' place. What were the odds that they'd find them next and use them to get at me? I couldn't bear the thought of losing them or Jacob, so I decided to talk to Alton and Wade about all this. They needed to know.

My stomach churned as I thought of Wade. I wondered whether he hated me, and whether he would ever forgive me for my insistence on keeping the magical kids with their parents. I was mad at myself, but, in retrospect, I knew there wasn't much else I could've done to prevent the tragedy. I had a feeling that the Ryder twins would've found a way to get to the kids even if we'd brought them to the coven.

Looking at the whole picture, the pattern of a well-designed plan came fully to light in my mind. Katherine had calculated everything, down to the last detail—including our movements, coven protocols, and reactions. They knew what we were going to do and when. That mattered for counterintelligence operations, which was our next step. We had to stop the leaks from endangering other kids.

A twig broke as I walked toward the staff entrance of Fleet Science Center, prompting me to shoot a glance to my left.

Standing by the water fountain in Balboa Park was Jacob, wearing a concerned look on his face. I gasped, understanding that my evening had not yet run out of surprises.

"Jake, what... what are you doing here?" I whispered, checking our surroundings to make sure nobody saw us.

He motioned for me to follow him, then darted off behind a line of trees on the edge of the park.

"You've got to be kidding me." I cursed under my breath and ran after him.

He waited for me beneath a sturdy oak tree, one of the park's newest additions, an import from a nearby nature reserve and part of the mayor's initiative to "green up this city." Jacob was nervous, and he was giving me the jitters.

"Are you okay?" he asked me, genuinely concerned.

While it warmed my heart to see and feel him worried about me, there were still some gaps he needed to fill. I gave him a brief nod. "I'm fine," I said. "Why do you ask? And what are you doing here?"

"I saw what happened," he replied, his voice low.

A couple of seconds passed before I registered that particular morsel of information. "Wait. What? You were out by the bus stop?" I asked, and he nodded, guilt adding a reddish pink to his cheeks. "You were following me, weren't you? You were following me at the Hamms' place, too. What's up with you? Seriously!"

He sighed. "I just wanted to see what you were doing... what you're like," he mumbled. "I'm good at hiding my tracks, in general, so I can just look at people without them knowing I'm watching."

"Like a professional stalker." I scoffed.

"Sort of." He chuckled nervously. "I'm sorry. I was... I don't know, I had a bad feeling when I saw you leave earlier. I just wanted to make sure you got home safe."

I couldn't help but laugh. "And here I am, worrying about *your* safety and wellbeing," I said. Then I frowned. "So, you saw the Ryder twins attack me."

The color drained from his face. Dread clutched my throat—all his. "Those were the Ryders," he gasped. It was my turn to nod as I carefully analyzed his reaction. "I'd heard about them, but I've never met them."

"What? You made it seem like you'd never heard of them before!" I snapped.

Jacob shrugged. "It takes a while for me to trust people. I decide what information I give, and whether it's a risk for me. Right now, I'm taking a chance on you, Harley."

I stared at him for a long moment, not sure whether to stay angry or accept his reply as a compliment. Finally, I breathed out and muttered, "Thank you, I guess. Better late than never. So, about the Ryders. What have you heard?" I pressed.

"The other unregistered rogues are terrified of the twins. Some are considering joining the coven just to get away from them."

"What about you?" I asked, making a mental note of his relationship with unidentified magicals. It could come in handy later if I persuaded him to join our coven. A boy with his knowledge was valuable and could be used to do good—provided he was in the right hands. But I couldn't bring myself to tell Alton or Wade about him, because I knew that once word got out about Jacob, the SDC might not be able to keep him. Strings could be pulled, and I didn't want Jacob to be taken away from me. Or the Smiths, for that matter. He deserved a home and a family, dammit.

"I'm keeping a low profile, I told you," he replied.

Well, it wasn't too low of a profile, in my opinion. Isadora knew what he was. That, too, could help us later, where Jacob's protection was concerned.

"Jake, you saw what happened. You know what the twins are capable—"

"Which is why I didn't come out to help you," he cut me off, hurting deeply. "I'm so sorry for that. I wanted to help you, I did, but I couldn't let them see me and… well, they're way too powerful for me."

I let out a heavy sigh. "I get it. You did the right thing. It's better they don't know you, trust me. Is that why you came all the way here? Because you wanted to—what, apologize for not getting involved in my encounter with the Ryder twins? Do the Smiths know you're out? Did you take a bus here?"

He shook his head. "I snuck out the window and hailed a cab."

"Hold on, that doesn't make sense. How'd you know to come here?" I asked. "I basically vanished into thin air back at the bus stop."

Jacob pressed his lips in a thin line. "Isadora has a message for you," he said.

My knees were ready to give out. Yet another piece of the puzzle was falling on top of me, and I had no idea where to place it in this enormous mess. I ran a hand through my hair, taking a deep breath and exhaling slowly in an attempt to keep my cool.

"You know Isadora Merlin," I said in a low tone.

"I didn't know you were acquainted," Jacob replied with a shrug.

"We have the same last name. You knew that. I told you tonight! Didn't the thought occur to you? How many Merlins can there be, in this day and age, in the same city at the same time?!" I snapped. "Jeez, kid. Come on, you've got to be more open with me here!"

"She helped me keep my head down, okay?" Jacob said, visibly frustrated. "She taught me how to keep certain abilities under control. I owe her a lot. She's part of the reason why I've been off the coven's radar for so long, Harley. I only realized you were connected when you told me about your family and what happened to them. But I also promised Isadora I'd keep my mouth shut about her."

"You were just sticking to your promise," I replied with a sigh, and resisted rolling my eyes. "Okay. I get it. So what did Isadora say? She could've told me earlier, but heck, we're here now, so, shoot!"

"She wants you to keep me a secret," he said. "You have spies in the coven. The moment I'm out, identified, and registered, I'm fair game, and not just for Katherine Shipton. My abilities make me very… desired, I guess."

"You're better than a mountain of gold, yeah," I retorted. "I know. Ugh."

"She gave me a charm," he added, holding up a small silver

medallion. "The moment I'm in trouble, I can let her know. You've seen how quick she can get from A to B."

I snorted. "Yeah. Got my first-hand experience of the wormhole, sure."

"Point is, she's got her eyes on me," he continued. "She needs you to focus on catching the Ryders before they take other kids. She says they're key to preventing Katherine Shipton from doing something terrible. Though, she hasn't said what that is, exactly."

"Ah, good to know she's just as cryptic with you." I shook my head in frustration. "Fine, I'll keep my mouth shut about you, Jake, but the moment I get so much as a whiff that you're not safe, I'm hauling your ass to the coven. Is that clear?"

Jacob looked somewhat baffled. "Why do you care so much about what happens to me? Is it because of this Shipton lady?"

My throat closed. Tears were threatening to rise. "I know what it's like to wander aimlessly through the foster system," I said, taking a deep breath. "I know what it's like to be alone and not know if things are ever going to get better, especially with those abilities. You don't fit in anywhere, you can't trust anybody, and... I lived through all that, okay, Jake? I lived through all that, and more. Finding the coven was incredibly confusing at first, but it gave me a sense of purpose and direction I'd never thought possible. I just want you to have a better shot at tackling this whole magical thing than me. As much as I love the Smiths, I'm just worried they're not enough for you. I would've given anything to find the coven sooner, now that I think about it. So, yeah, Jake, I care. I want you to be safe and happy. That's all."

I sensed him immediately warm up on the inside, a pang in my heart signaling that I'd definitely flipped a switch inside this young warlock. My statement had struck a chord, and I was glad for it.

"So keep your head down, going forward," I added, trying to think of a reasonable way to get the coven to help us without exposing Jacob. That was the real challenge.

"You should be careful, too," Jacob muttered. "If there are spies in the coven, they'll have their eyes on you. Whatever this whole thing is about, it's a problem for you, too."

"Tell me about it." I chuckled nervously, then gripped his shoulder. "Go home, Jake. Keep that pendant on you at all times, and put my number on speed dial. Be good, and we'll get through this. Most importantly, don't talk to strangers."

"Sure, *Mom*," he responded with a childish pout, making me smile.

"Think of me as the annoying older sister, Jake. I promise to be that kind of pain in your ass. Now, go!"

I watched him walk out of the park and head for the main road back into town. He stayed in the shadows, light on his feet. My heart thudded as everything began to sink in. Too many things were happening at once, and I still couldn't get Susan and Larry's dead faces out of my head.

Despite the handful of answers I'd gotten, along with the incredible surprise of Isadora still being alive, I had even more questions and very few people whom I could trust to ask. Going over what had happened throughout the day, I managed to identify the first item on my to-do list—that spell Isadora had told me to research.

It was about my father.

TWENTY-SIX

Harley

I headed straight for the Forbidden Section, before anything else, positive I'd find something about Sál Vinna in one of those journals and spell boxes. All the secret, sensitive, and powerful stuff was in there, and I doubted Isadora would've made me research a hair growth spell or something equally harmless. My incident with the Ryders could wait a couple of minutes before I brought it to Wade and Alton. Hell, my bruises could wait, too! My father's life and demise had taken center stage since Isadora's tip, and I had little control over that. I needed to find out.

This had to be some of the heavyweight stuff that magicals went to jail for, and it had to do with Hiram Merlin. I was determined to get that out of the way quickly so I could move on and gather the courage to seek out Wade. I needed to talk to him. Or maybe just listen to him yell "I told you so!" in my face, over and over, until he got it out of his system. I just couldn't bear the thought of angry silence between us. It didn't feel natural.

As soon as I touched the doorknob, preparing to whisper the opening spell, Wade's voice made me freeze

"You're back," he announced, standing in the middle of the hallway a few yards away from me.

I hadn't seen or heard him, nor had I felt his emotions. Either he was getting better at concealing himself around me, or I was too focused on the spell to even notice him. His deep green eyes were dark, his expression firm, and his jaw snapped shut. I could cut a pineapple with those cheekbones.

He was still wearing his dark gray suit, though he'd lost the tie and released a couple of buttons on his white shirt. Despite his stern appearance, he seemed weary. I didn't want him to be angry—he didn't want that, either. I could feel it in the pit of my stomach. He just wanted to talk, and I was terrible at apologizing. My heart fluttered nervously as I tried to think of a decent answer. Nothing seemed right, though.

"Yeah. It's been a long day," I replied, almost whispering. "I'm... I'm sorry I bailed on you earlier."

He blinked twice, then glanced to his side. "You didn't bail. I was perfectly capable of taking care of the rest. You weren't needed."

"Yeah, well, still. I'm sorry, okay?"

My hands were shaking. He noticed, and a painful sensation settled in my chest.

"What are you sorry about, exactly?" he asked. "I told you, you didn't bail. The job was practically done, and I briefed Alton on everything."

"I'm... I'm sorry for insisting that Micah stay with his parents. I'm sorry for thinking a couple of charms, traps, and an Orisha could stop the Ryders from hurting the Cranstons. I'm sorry I let my past as a foster kid get in the way of my rational thinking. It got Micah's parents killed. I'm... I'm just sorry," I gasped, tears clouding my vision.

Wade didn't say anything for a while, but the grief and discomfort were absolutely there, burning inside him. I just couldn't make out the rest of his emotional makeup. Maybe I couldn't focus because I was being eaten alive by guilt.

"We all agreed to it," he finally said, snapping me out of my misery. "I had no right to be mad at you alone for this. We all agreed it was a good idea, to smoke the Ryders out. Alton said yes. We all share the blame in what happened to the Cranstons and the Devereauxes."

I lost my breath for a second. "The Devereauxes?" I croaked, remembering their name from Alton's list. "You mean Ted and Lucinda Devereaux. Louella was the suspected magical... They're dead, too?"

"Yes. The Ryders hit them too. They killed the parents, but from what Tatyana gathered at the crime scene, they didn't get Louella. She ran away," Wade replied. "They might've caught up with her, but we don't know for sure."

"Oh, no." I choked back a sob, covering my mouth with my hand.

The bodies kept piling up, and I didn't know how to cope with that. I wasn't sure I'd ever get used to the concept of people being murdered. Wade came closer, his brow furrowed with concern.

"We were too late to talk to them. Don't blame yourself," he said, his voice lower than usual and peculiarly soothing. "The Ryders clearly have a plan, and we're one step behind them."

"It's still... so horrible," I breathed.

"What happened to you? You look like a mess," he said, clearly concerned.

Where could I even start to explain everything that had happened to me after he'd left me at St. Clair's? I offered a weak smile, but somehow, the words had trouble coming out. And he didn't insist, as if he'd guessed my ragged state of mind.

In fact, for a moment, I thought his arms would reach out and wrap around me. I wouldn't have said no to his embrace. Really, I needed to feel his warmth. I couldn't help but remember the time he'd taken me in his arms, lifting me from the infirmary bed and gently settling me in the wheelchair, shortly after I'd woken up from my gargoyle bonanza. My pulse raced as the air seemed to thicken between us.

We were separated by only a few inches, but Wade didn't seem like he was going to do anything to curb my longing for his embrace. He was conflicted, and I couldn't spend any time trying to figure him out. I had too much to deal with already.

"Bit of a long story," I finally said. "I'm okay, though. Nothing broken."

"Not sure I'm satisfied by that answer," he replied, but let it pass. He cleared his throat and nodded at the Forbidden Section's doors. "What were you doing here?"

"Um. There's a spell I wanted to look up. I'm pretty sure it's in there," I replied.

"What spell?"

"Sál Vinna," I said.

He frowned. "It doesn't sound familiar. But you don't need to waste your time in there trying to find it. Text it to Astrid. She recently connected Smartie to the coven's physical archive. She can fish the spell out for you. Smartie can't be hacked, and only she has access to it, so that took care of our previous archive fears."

"Oh. Thanks," I murmured, and quickly proceeded to type a message for her. A second after I hit send, I looked at Wade. "Wouldn't Alton know it if I told him about it?"

Wade shrugged. "I'm not sure. He's not a walking encyclopedia. You could try, but it's a little late to knock on his door now. You should get some sleep, too," he said.

The clarity I'd lacked earlier about what I'd gone through this evening had finally come back to me. I had Astrid on the spell, so I could focus on the Ryder twins.

"I have to knock on his door anyway. I need to talk to you and Alton," I said. "Now."

"Did something happen?" he asked, cocking his head to one side.

I breathed a sigh of relief, finally accepting that Wade hadn't been angry at me, specifically. He'd been furious with all of us, including himself, regarding the Cranstons—and, as he'd just revealed, the Devereauxes. We hadn't been on the ball with the young magicals, and the Ryders had practically stolen the game from under our noses.

"I met the Ryder twins," I said.

Dread hit him like a cold wave.

He nodded once, then gripped my wrist and escorted me to Alton's office. It was close to nine p.m., and it wasn't a surprise that Alton was still there, skimming through a pile of old books.

"Wade, Harley, what are you two doing here?" he asked, raising his eyebrows.

We reached his desk and sat in the two guest armchairs in front of it.

"Tell him," Wade said to me.

I took a deep breath, carefully going through the string of weird events in my head, to make sure I didn't bring up Jacob. If Isadora was right and there was a spy in our ranks, I had to be careful. At this point, I wasn't worried about Alton or Wade being the moles—I trusted them with my life. But for all I knew, someone else could be eavesdropping. The coven wasn't safe. For the time being, I decided to keep Jacob to myself, just until I could find out more about what was going on.

"After I separated from Wade, I took some time out to get my crap together." I sighed. "I suppose you've been told about every-thing that happened today with the Cranstons and the others?"

Alton leaned back into his chair, curiosity blooming in his eyes. "I've made sure we have eyes on each of the families on that list," he replied. "What's wrong, Harley? You seem—" He paused and narrowed his eyes at me. "Are those scratches?"

I touched my face and cringed as soon as I found the small cuts on my temple, previously concealed by my hair. Wade's hand shot out and caught my chin, forcing me to look at him. He frowned as he brushed the hair aside and discovered the scratches.

"You got hurt," Wade murmured. His touch made my skin tingle. *Focus, Harley.*

"It's nothing serious. A couple of painkillers will take care of most of it. I'll sleep the rest off." I pulled myself back and shifted my focus to Alton. "So, as I was saying, after I was left on my own, I took some time to just mull things over. I was about five or six blocks away from St. Clair's Café, at the bus stop, ready to come back here. The Ryder twins either found me or followed me there. We... We had words."

Alton's forehead smoothed. I shook the shivers away and relaxed in the armchair. My ribs were still sore, the pain pulsating through my chest.

"They attacked you," Alton whispered.

"And then some!" I chuckled nervously. "They're vicious, Alton. Literal killing machines. Emily's a Herculean with Telekinesis, and Emmett has Fire. That's on top of their Shapeshifting. Oh, and they're pretty good with what I assume were deadly curses. I dodged a few bullets back there."

"But you escaped," Wade replied. "How?"

"Thanks for the vote of confidence and for assuming they kicked my ass," I shot back, slightly irritated. "Granted, that assumption would be correct. They beat me six ways from Sunday and were seconds away from killing me, when I had some... unexpected help."

I took another breath, waiting for the pain in my ribs to subside. My hunched position wasn't helping, so I slowly shifted my weight, leaning to my right. I closed my eyes for a moment, thankful to breathe properly again.

"Well? What happened?" Alton blurted, clearly on the edge of his seat.

"Isadora Merlin happened," I replied. "She showed up out of nowhere, opened up a wormhole, and transported me to Water-front Park."

Both Alton and Wade were stunned.

Alton was the first to speak, his eyes wide with shock. "Isadora's alive."

"Oh, yeah," I said.

"And she's a Portal Opener?" Wade added, staring at me in sheer disbelief.

"Ahem," I said, nodding. "One of two in existence, according to her."

"Two?! They were supposed to be extinct. We thought the ability died with her," Alton replied.

"You *assumed* she was dead." I sighed. "She's not. And she saved my life back there."

"Did she tell you anything? Where has she been this whole time?" Wade asked.

I raised a hand to stop them both from asking the same questions I'd already tried to ask Isadora. My head was about to explode.

"She didn't say much. But she did emphasize how dangerous it was for her to be around me. She's wanted by some pretty dark magicals, apparently. Including Katherine Shipton, who, by the way, is definitely working with the Ryder twins. She's orchestrating this whole thing with the magical kids, and she's toying with us," I said. "She's doing it on purpose. Having the Cranstons and the Devereauxes killed, stealing some of the kids and recruiting the others. She's planning something big and bad, Child of Chaos stuff, but Isadora doesn't know what, exactly. She's looking into it."

"You let her go?!" Wade said, mildly annoyed.

I rolled my eyes at him. "Seriously, Crowley? I just got my ass handed to me by the Ryders. Do you really think I had any strength or skill to take on a seasoned witch who can *open friggin' portals in the fabric of space?*" I snapped, raising my voice.

Wade went silent but didn't take his eyes off me.

"Fair enough," Alton cut in. "What else did she say?"

"She said I shouldn't believe everything I've read in the newspaper archives about my father, then gave me a spell to research. Sál Vinna," I replied.

Hope sprouted somewhere in the depths of my soul, and, for a split second, I could've sworn it wasn't just my feeling. Something told me that both Wade and Alton were hoping that there would be more to Hiram and Hester Merlin's story than what they already knew.

"I asked Astrid to find me some information about it," I added.

"Good. Let me know what you uncover," Alton replied. "It sounds Icelandic in origin. And the Northerners are not known for their light and positive spell-work. In the meantime, I'll double security on the families on our list. If Katherine is behind all this, we must expect the worst."

"Okay… Listen, there's one thing that's been bugging me," I said, worried about the magical kids we could still bring back here for protection. "Don't you think we should bring the families and the kids in and keep them safe here? I mean, haven't we learned anything from the Cranstons?"

Alton pinched the bridge of his nose. "I want to, believe me. But like I said to Wade earlier, I have direct orders from the Mage Council now to keep them where they are and look out for the Ryders," he said. "I had to confer with them on the matter after we learned about what happened with Kenneth. Humans nearly died because of magic. Special protocols require that I inform the Mage Council about it. They were adamant that we leave the families where they are and do our best to secure them remotely. They want the Ryder twins caught at all costs."

"And they want you to keep the kids and their parents in the crossfire, even after all that's happened? Seriously?" I asked, still alarmed by their reasoning.

"It's the best way to catch the Ryders, especially since they're clearly circling in. They won't dare come after the coven again. We've strengthened security here," Alton said. "Listen, I don't like it either. But this wasn't my call, and we can't disobey them. If anyone else gets hurt, that blood is on their hands."

"Ugh! The Mage Council *sucks*!" I groaned with frustration, but then tried to blow out a calming breath. There was clearly no point ramming my head against this issue any longer. "Okay. So, we can't do anything about the families. What next, then?"

"We have APBs out on the missing kids," Wade said. "We'll monitor the police comms and scan the city's CCTV resources as well. We keep an eye on the families and the remaining magicals. And we dig deeper into the Ryders and Katherine Shipton. That's all we can do at this point."

"Well, that and look into Isadora Merlin. A Portal Opener is an absolute gamechanger for us!" Alton replied. "She could be of incredible help. Can you reach out to her, Harley?"

I shook my head. "No. She'll find me when she deems it safe enough. She's very cautious, Alton."

"When she does get in touch, let me know, okay?" Alton said.

The request made me nervous. "I will, but… what are you thinking?"

"I need to talk to her myself, Harley. No matter what," he replied bluntly.

Whether it had anything to do with my parents or not, I couldn't tell for sure. But doubt was definitely creeping up on Alton. He was worried about something. Unfortunately, I wasn't a Telepath. To my surprise, I didn't even know such an ability existed until this mission.

I found it irritating how I wasn't told a lot of pretty important things, despite the training and magical courses. I was picking things up as I went, and I didn't like that. It felt as though I was being kept in the dark on purpose.

TWENTY-SEVEN

Tatyana

There wasn't much for us to be happy about after the grim discoveries we'd made throughout the day. But when the infirmary called to tell us that Dylan was awake, smiles bloomed on all our faces.

Santana, Raffe, Astrid, and I went to check on him in the evening after the nurses and Krieger cleared him for visits. He was pale and sluggish, but he was recovering nicely from the beastly curse. The moment he saw me come in, however, Dylan's brows drew into a dark frown and he looked away.

"You shouldn't be near me," he mumbled.

"Oh, don't give me that crap!" I said, smiling. I was determined not to let him be consumed by guilt. "You're functional again. That's what matters."

"I almost killed you!" Dylan insisted, shifting his gaze back to me.

A brief yet awkward silence followed as Raffe, Astrid, and Santana exchanged glances.

"Dude, it happens to the best of us," Astrid said, "You were just the one to take the hit this time around. That's all."

"I'm sorry," Dylan murmured, his eyes fixed on me.

I gave him a soft smile, my heart tingling with relief. Dylan was going to be okay. He was strong and resilient, and the coven wouldn't have been the same without him.

We'd both come to San Diego around the same time. Though, we were both so different. I came with hefty magical baggage, while Dylan had been plucked out of the human world, after having slipped through the cracks of the foster system. I was a relatively seasoned witch, while Dylan was still coming into his own as a warlock. I was frosty and kept most people at arm's length. Dylan, despite his shyness, was warm and kind and open with everyone who crossed his path. He was like daylight, and I was the darkness of the night. Still, it was this exact contrast that made us work.

We got along better than most. And we never really had to say much for one to understand how the other felt.

Which was why, despite his frowny face and pouted lips, I knew that, deep down, Dylan was just happy to see me. I moved closer to his side, while the others settled at the foot of his bed. There were dark rings under his eyes. IV tubes went into his arms—next to us, bags of fluids and vitamins quietly dripped into his veins, building him back up, one milliliter at a time.

"You have nothing to apologize for, Dylan," I whispered. "There was nothing you could've done to beat that curse. You were incredibly strong, enough to hear me, just before I gave you the cure. I know you did your best."

"I could've killed you," he replied. He sounded like he was in a lot of emotional pain—perhaps more than the physical exertion provoked by the curse itself, and it hurt me inside, too. "I was out of control."

"That was the purpose of the curse, Dylan. To make you lose control," I said. "Enough with the self-flagellation, already!"

He chuckled, then grimaced from the physical discomfort.

"How are you feeling?" Raffe asked, keeping his arms crossed.

Dylan grinned. "I think I'm doing better than *you*!"

Indeed, Raffe wasn't looking his best, but he was extremely good at keeping his darker nature hidden. He had his own demons to deal with, and, sometimes, it spilled out into the physical plane. Raffe's eyes were almost black, sheltered beneath black brows. The difference between a "Good Day Raffe" and a "Bad Day Raffe" wasn't easily noticeable, though. Those of us who spent more time with him were able to tell.

"Do you need us to help you with anything?" Raffe replied, brushing Dylan's observation away. "Anything at all?"

"I'm good, thanks," Dylan muttered. "Just sore and embarrassed, really."

"Nothing to be embarrassed about," I reiterated. "That was heavy-duty dark magic that Kenneth Willow used on you."

He sighed. "Any news on the jerk? Have you tracked him down yet?"

I shook my head. "Nothing. He's in the wind."

"I've got his photo and physical description in the system, statewide," Astrid replied. "We'll know if he pops up anywhere on the grid. Until then, we just keep our eyes open. There isn't much else we can do."

"Man, I can't believe I got my ass kicked like that by a seventeen-year-old," Dylan grumbled, rubbing his face with his palms.

"You're nineteen yourself. It's not like the age gap really makes a difference," Astrid said, slightly amused.

"Normally, I'd agree with you, but I'm a Herculean. We're supposed to be more agile. You know, fast enough to not give anyone the opportunity to take us down with a curse. Especially not a kid," Dylan said, pursing his lips.

I covered his hand with mine, squeezing gently. He looked up at me, his gaze softening on my face. "Kenneth had a morbid ace up his sleeve. Dark curses don't care how strong or fast you are, Dylan."

He nodded, and my pulse quickened. Then, out of nowhere and in no way commanded by my brain, my hand pulled back. My stomach hurt with frustration, and a familiar, yet uncomfortable weight settled on my shoulders. Every muscle in my body hurt, my joints bucking under the pressure.

That was Oberon's doing. For some reason, he didn't like me touching Dylan, and it irritated me to the point where I mentally pummeled him, throwing a flurry of Russian curse words at him. His chuckle echoed in my ears, while Dylan stared at me, frowning.

Sorry, Taty... I forgot you were behind the wheel, Oberon said.

Well, that wasn't something the likes of Oberon could easily forget, and it was extremely annoying to experience—since the deal had been for me to always be in control. I had to keep my guard up, it seemed. At the first sign of relaxation or weakness, a spirit could slip into the front seat and bump me to the back. I couldn't let that happen.

"Are you okay?" Dylan asked me, his voice low.

"Yes. All good. Don't worry about me. Focus on yourself," I replied, feeling the fake smile stretching my lips.

"Yeah, we need you back, buddy," Astrid interjected. She gave me a warning look, then groaned and moved her focus back to Dylan. "We've got Garrett until you get better."

"Ugh! No! Why?" Dylan whined.

"Well, he's very good at what he does," I replied. "And he's familiar with our cases. I'll take Garrett over Poe or Mont-Noir any time!"

"Wouldn't you rather have me back, instead?" Dylan quipped.

"Absolutely!" I laughed. "Which is why you need to eat your veggies, listen to Krieger, and get yourself back in shape as soon as possible. Garrett may be good, but he's still quite insufferable."

Santana scoffed, crossing her arms. "Yeah, tell me about it."

"Hey, you don't have to work with him. Consider yourself lucky," Astrid replied, grinning.

"Fair enough. I only dated him for a few weeks. Ew..." Santana grumbled.

Astrid's phone beeped. "Oh, got a little bit of research work from

Harley," she said. Her eyes nearly popped out of their orbits as she read through the rest of the message. "Holy crap, she had a run-in with the Ryder twins!"

Shivers ran down my spine, and dread gripped me as flashbacks of the Devereaux crime scene came back to haunt me. The Ryders were absolutely horrible magicals—the kind that even the worst of my ancient Vasilis family looked down on. My great-great-grand-parents were historically recognized villains in their own right, responsible for the deaths of many, and even they would've disap-proved of the Ryders' dirty methods.

"And she lived to tell the tale," Raffe breathed. "I think our little Merlin is not done surprising us."

"Wait till they get that Dempsey Suppressor off her!" Santana said.

"Alton is sending an updated report shortly," Astrid went on. "I've put the spell Harley sent me through the system, but it'll take a while before I get some results back. In the meantime, we should all get some rest."

We all nodded in agreement. I gave Dylan a weak smile. I wanted to tell him, Raffe, Santana, and the rest of our team about Oberon's presence, but I knew they would overreact. On one hand, I appreciated their concern, since they only wanted what was best for me. However, as a Kolduny, I had to improve my ability to hold a spirit inside me and keep it under control. That only came with practice, and Oberon was the perfect exercise. Plus, he'd promised to help me. He knew I'd kick him to the curb if he didn't come through.

I had Slavic blood running through my veins. I didn't respond well to waffling. My skin tingled—a silent nod from Oberon, telling me he'd gotten my message.

No waffling. I promise, he whispered in the back of my head.

Then deliver. You promised you'd put me in touch with spirits who know more about the Ryders, I replied in my mind.

I'm having a little trouble finding them, but I will. I swear, he said.

I instinctively rolled my eyes in response, prompting Dylan to narrow his eyes at me.

"Something wrong?" he asked.

I shook my head. "All good. In fact, everything is much better now that you're awake," I said, smiling.

I would tell him after my work with Oberon was done. Until then, however, I had to juggle the outside world and the balance I was trying to maintain on the inside. Carrying a spirit within me did take its toll on my energy.

TWENTY-EIGHT

Tatyana

W e left Dylan to rest and went our separate ways for the rest of the night.

The next couple of days passed in bone-crushing tension. We kept an eye on the other magical families we'd discovered in San Diego. There were charms in place and security magicals tailing each kid, twenty-four hours a day.

There was no sign of the Ryder twins, though. After their attack on Harley, they seemed to have simply vanished. We knew, however, that it was only a matter of time before they'd pop up again. Their job wasn't done. There were still innocent magical kids out there, and, if Harley was right, they were all a part of Katherine Shipton's plan.

Of course, we didn't know what that plan was, or when she or her minions would strike again. There was no sign of Kenneth Willow or Marjorie Phillips. Micah Cranston was still missing, too, and the magical community of San Diego was on a general high alert. We were lucky to have additional security forces from the Los Angeles Coven, by order of the California Mage Council. They'd been sent over shortly after the gargoyle incident, and there were plenty of them to also help us keep track of the magical kids who had yet to move into the coven.

We didn't like having them out there in the open, but we knew we wouldn't get a better chance to catch the Ryders without them.

Dylan was close to making a full recovery. I had a feeling he'd be out of the infirmary by morning. Astrid was busy monitoring all channels for any sign of the Ryders or the missing kids, while also waiting for her Smartie system to return some information on Sál Vinna, the Icelandic spell Harley had mentioned.

On top of it all, we were checking the archives and old CCTV footage from the San Diego area, looking for images of Isadora Merlin. Alton had asked us to look into her and find out where she'd been and what she'd been up to. Needless to say, that was an incredibly difficult task, since Isadora seemed to be quite the expert at hiding her tracks.

Much like Katherine Shipton.

On Wednesday night, I was still languishing in one of the archive rooms, looking through a pile of journals and newspaper clippings, trying to find something on the Ryder twins and Katherine Shipton. But something was off. Entire pages were missing from some of the notebooks. Certain articles had been torn from their slots.

"This isn't right," I murmured, flipping through a fifth journal.

I was the last one in the hall, except the nighttime clerk, of course, who was huddled at her small desk all the way on the other side. I had enough privacy to talk to Oberon without anyone thinking I'd lost my mind.

Somebody didn't want you to dig up information on these people, obviously, Oberon said, his voice echoing in my head.

"That would mean we've got Katherine's people inside the coven," I replied, frowning. "Or maybe Finch cleaned these pages out during his two-year tenure here."

By that logic, Finch knows the Ryder twins. Oberon sighed.

"He's untouchable while he's in Purgatory. They won't let anyone near him."

What are you looking for in particular?

I exhaled, pulled my hair into a loose bun, using one of the bands I always carried around my wrist, and proceeded to check online maps, using the few snippets of information I'd gathered so far.

"Possible hideouts, for the most part," I murmured. "They've got to have some kind of base of operations in town. Without a Portal Opener, they're dependent on the usual modes of transportation, and, based on how quickly they get from one part of the city to another, they must be somewhere in San Diego."

Ah... Finally! Oberon exclaimed. *Close your eyes, darling. There is someone here to see you!*

I looked around, checking to see if anyone else had come into the hall. Fortunately, it was still just me—well, *us*—and the clerk, who was gradually dozing off in her seat. I closed my eyes, welcoming the darkness of the veil as it unraveled around me.

"Did you find who you were looking for?" I asked Oberon.

"And then some!" he replied, his voice becoming clearer and sharper as I descended into the spirit plane.

I looked down and noticed Oberon's spiritual form visible over mine, like an iridescent glaze of sorts. I hadn't paid attention to myself back at the Devereaux mansion, but I could definitely see how those spirits had been able to spot him.

"This is still weird," I said.

"Well, I don't want you to feel suffocated, darling," Oberon replied, and I could feel him smiling. Needless to say, this partial separation between us, even though we were still occupying the same space, made me feel less anxious about his presence in me.

Above us, dozens of wisps hovered around the room—spirits of magicals that had died in this interdimensional pocket, warlocks and witches whose lives had either come to a natural end or had been cut short. No matter how many times I saw them, it always felt eerie to watch.

One of them approached us. The closer it got, the better I could see it.

It was a girl. Medium height, slender, with long brown hair and hazy blue eyes... semi-transparent, like the others, but somewhat more colorful, as if her spirit was stronger. She wore a pair of jeans and a white flannel shirt. There was a large bloodstain on her chest. I figured it was her cause of death.

"What are *you* doing here?" the girl asked, scowling at me.

"Do I know you?" I asked her, confused.

"I'm not talking to you. I'm talking to the arrogant dweeb you've got inside you!" she retorted. I'd already forgotten that spirits could see Oberon riding along in my meatsuit. "What are you doing here, Oberon? I thought I told you years ago that this hall was off limits!"

"Helen, please don't be such a grouch!" Oberon replied, chuckling. "You can't let a bad date define the rest of our relationship, darling. We could be looking at an eternity together."

Oh, these two clearly had history, and it made me blush. This was getting awkward, fast.

"I'd rather burn in hell forever," Helen snapped.

"Then move on, sweet cheeks," Oberon retorted.

"Hey, guys... still here," I said, raising a hand. I smiled at Helen. "I'm Tatyana. And sorry you have to deal with Oberon. Though I'm not sure what happened between the two of you—"

"I'll tell you what happened!" Helen hissed. "Oberon thinks that no means yes. I had to kick him in the nuts, twice, to make him understand that, in fact, no means no."

I couldn't help but roll my eyes. Ironically, Oberon's embarrassment was burning through me, pumping more heat into my face.

"Okay, I'm sorry," I replied. "But Oberon is helping me. It's important. Lives are at stake, Helen."

She raised an eyebrow. "So, that's how you called out to me, Oberon? By hitching a ride inside a Ghost-Whisperer?"

"A Kolduny," I muttered.

"Same thing. Different name," Helen said, crossing her arms.

"Helen, please. You know I've kept my distance like you asked. It took me forever to find you again, and trust me, it doesn't give me any pleasure to have to reach out to you. But we do need your help," Oberon said.

Helen stared at me for a long moment, then let out a sigh of defeat. "Fine. What do you want?"

"You knew the Ryder twins, didn't you?" Oberon asked. "I know you mentioned them a couple of times, since... you know, since you've been around."

I found myself intrigued by how even dead people tiptoed around their condition. Death was never an easy word to work with, it seemed.

"Yeah, I knew them back in the Houston Coven, before I moved here," Helen replied. Only then did I finally identify her accent—that Texan drawl that spoke of hot summers and spicy barbecues.

"You were in the same coven," I said. "What can you tell me about them?"

Helen put on a sad smile. "They were decent kids, you know? Thoroughly misunderstood, from the beginning. They wanted to be good, but the other magicals didn't like them much," she explained. "Some looked down on foster kids in general. They were picked on a lot. I was one of the few who knew about their Shapeshifting abilities. I caught them changing into two of our preceptors at the time. They begged me not to tell anyone. I'm not the kind of girl to gossip, so I kept my mouth shut."

"What happened in Houston then? What got them kicked out?" I asked.

"They crossed a line," she said. "To be honest, those bullies had it coming. They'd been tormenting Emily and beating the daylights out of Emmett on a weekly basis. The twins just had enough one day. They snapped. They shifted and infiltrated the bullies' group and set them up with a very dangerous curse. They nearly killed three magicals."

"Whoa," I breathed.

"Like I said, those guys did deserve some punishment, but what the twins delivered was far too extreme. Besides, the curse they used was forbidden," Helen replied. "There was an investigation, and a couple of weeks later the Ryders left town. I never saw them again."

What Helen had just told me wasn't crucial information, but it did shed some light on what might've triggered the Ryders to descend into such brutal darkness. I was well aware that some people were just born with a predilection for violence and evil, but there had to be turning points—switches one could flip at various points in their lives. The Ryder twins were victims of their circumstances, all right, but the choices that followed were theirs and theirs alone.

"Did you ever see them in San Diego?" I asked.

Helen shook her head. "If I did, I wouldn't have recognized them. By the time I moved here, they'd already gone AWOL after their third strike in Albuquerque. They would've shifted to stay under the radar. It's one of the reasons why magicals are wary of Shapeshifters. Most of them don't mean any harm, but not knowing who they really are or who they can turn into… that doesn't sit well with anyone. And the Ryders did plenty of damage before falling off the edge of the Earth, if you know what I mean. They certainly didn't help diminish the stigma."

A second spirit came closer, a middle-aged man with salt-and-pepper hair and brown eyes, stocky and still wearing his bathrobe. He'd died in it. Poor thing. He stopped by my side, staring at a fixed point in the darkness, specifically where my laptop was in the living plane.

"What's up, Martin?" Helen asked the spirit.

"I overheard you and couldn't help but step in…" Martin replied. He bent down to get a better look at my laptop's screen, then remarked, "If *that's* where you're looking for the Ryders, you're wasting your time."

"Huh? You know Emily and Emmett?" I asked.

"I sure do," Martin grumbled. "I gave them shelter before I moved to the coven. I'd only been in San Diego for a month at the time."

"Oh, wow," I gasped, exhilarated by the prospect of a new lead. "What happened?"

"Nothing much," he replied. "They were quiet and mostly out of the house. Didn't give me much trouble. They begged me not to tell anyone that they were in town. They creeped me out, though. Honestly, they could be really scary sometimes. Given that I'd opened my door to them, I didn't want to risk it, so I kept my mouth shut. After I got registered with the coven, I snuck back into my own house while they were out, packed a bag, and skedaddled out of there. I was safer here!"

"When was that?" I asked.

"About three years ago, give or take. I don't keep track of time in death. It's useless."

"And what happened to your house?" I replied.

"Oh, I sold it," he said. "I called the cops first and told them I had squatters in there. It was enough to send the Ryders away. Afterward, I got in touch with a realtor and got rid of the place. It wasn't safe anymore."

This sounded more like the Ryders I knew. I took a deep breath, trying to imagine them as they shared a house with Martin. I got goosebumps.

"You were saying something about locations, I think?" I asked, drawing his focus back to my laptop and the notes I had up on the screen.

He nodded, chuckling. "They won't be using an interdimensional pocket, sweetheart. That takes Bestiary energy. The managing coven would be immediately notified if they did. They'd need approval from the California Mage Council for that."

"So what should I be looking for?"

"Warehouses. Abandoned properties. That kind of stuff," Martin replied. "Judging by the location of all your new magicals and crime scenes, I'm thinking they'd be holed up somewhere in Chula Vista, close to the water and the freeway. Easy access into the city and close enough to the ocean for an escape route. Based on the rumors that have been circulating through the spirit world, those kids have built quite the criminal operation. I should know, I was a prosecutor for the San Diego Coven for twenty years," he added.

I gave Martin a grateful smile, my pulse quickening as new opportunities emerged in my mind regarding the Ryders' potential location. "You're a genius, Martin. Thank you."

He laughed. "Yes. Gone too soon, I'm afraid!"

"How did you both die, if you don't mind me asking?" I looked at him, then at Helen.

Martin sighed. "Heart attack. I was just getting ready for a bath."

"As evidenced by my shirt, I got stabbed," Helen said.

"I'm sorry, for the both of you," I replied. "Do you know who did it, Helen?"

"Oh, yeah," she said, scowling at me. "Absolutely. It was—"

Everything vanished, all of a sudden. I was back in the living plane. The darkness and the spirits were gone. My laptop was right in front of me, and Oberon's spiritual weight was crushing me again. I panted from the effort as I pushed back and took a deep breath, but I managed to overpower him.

"What the hell, Oberon?!" I croaked. Beads of sweat trickled down my face.

We got everything we needed from those two, don't worry, Oberon said, once again echoing in the back of my head. *Now I think you need to tell your computer whiz kid about Chula Vista.*

My chest tightened as I worried that he'd cut me out of the spirit plane on purpose.

"What didn't you want me to find out?" I asked, gritting my teeth. Anger bubbled up in my throat. "I'm not stupid, Oberon!"

A few seconds ticked by in heavy silence. I thoroughly disliked it.

"I can always go back and look for Helen," I said.

I'm to blame for what happened to her, Oberon said quietly. The bitterness in his distant voice was obvious. He felt guilty. *Helen and I got off on the wrong foot. Bad date, like I said. But after that, we patched things up. I introduced her to some of my friends. You know, she was new in the coven, needed to form some social bonds and stuff. One of them... Well, one of them killed her in a fit of rage. I didn't know he had all that darkness inside him. I actively encouraged her to go out with him, to stay with him, even when she told me that she felt there was something off about him. We found her in her room a few days later with a knife in her chest. I never forgave myself for that. And neither did Helen.*

The candor was refreshing. Though, truth be told, I wasn't sure if that was completely my own reaction, or if he was messing with my emotions. Either way, there wasn't much I could do for the time being. I figured I'd have him around to help me deal with the Ryder twins, then eject his lying ass with a little help from my favorite Santeria witch. I slowly relaxed, allowing him to settle in my head again. His voice became a little clearer.

I just didn't want you to know what a failure I was, as a man and as a friend, he added. *I'm sorry.*

"It's fine, Oberon. Just stop hijacking my body. It's not just uncomfortable, it's scary. Stop doing that, okay? You pulled my hand away from Dylan the other day, too. You have to hold back. This isn't what we agreed on."

You're right. Forgive me, Tatyana.

For a dead guy, he sure had his charm. It didn't work on me, but I could see others falling for it. There was no point in a conflict with the ghost that had hijacked my body, just yet. "If you keep taking over like that, you'll give us away to Santana or Raffe. Those two won't hesitate to tell Wade and Alton about our agreement, and that will buy you a one-way exorcism back to the spirit world. I'm trying to watch out for the both of us here."

I appreciate that, Oberon said.

I could feel him watching as I wrote an email to Astrid, asking her to look into the Chula Vista area for any warehouses or abandoned properties, based on Martin's assessments. My gut told me that we were one step closer to finding and bagging the Ryders before they could do any more damage. Too many people had suffered already.

The more time passed, despite Oberon's outbursts, the more I knew I needed his strength. After Harley's account of her encounter with the Ryders, it became clear that I required a spirit's power to face off with those two. Luckily, I already had a Herculean nesting within.

My heart felt heavy, though. The same intuition that pointed me toward the Ryders was also warning me about Oberon. Something was off about the way he'd tried to take over. I didn't like that.

I reacted foolishly with Dylan, Oberon said, reading my mind. *It's been so long since I've felt anyone's touch, Tatyana. And, right now, I'm feeling every fiber of your body. I can't begin to describe what that's like. I got jealous. Forgive me.*

He was tugging at my heartstrings with that statement, making my cheeks flush.

"It's okay," I muttered, clicking the send button.

Let's get you some fresh air, Oberon whispered. *It's gorgeous out there by the dragon fountain, at this hour.*

I couldn't shake the uneasiness of his presence, but the end, to me, justified the means. I took a deep breath, then let it out slowly. A walk sounded nice.

TWENTY-NINE

Harley

While Astrid was busy digging up that Icelandic spell and looking for any sign of the missing magical kids or the Ryders, I had a small task to cross off my list. There wasn't much else I could do, since Jacob refused to put me in touch with Isadora, and I couldn't find any other useful information on Katherine Shipton in the archives. Nothing I'd come across would help me smoke the witch out.

Dinner with the brooding studs was as awkward as I'd expected it to be.

Wade, Garrett, and I sat in silence at one of the tables at Carluccio's. I'd ordered the ricotta cannelloni, Garrett had opted for pizza and fries, and Wade had gone the extra mile of pretentiousness and went for the arugula salad with parmesan shavings. Most of the food was just getting poked and pushed around our plates as we all tried to restart the conversation.

Our previous attempt had died off when the plates were first brought to the table. Though, the eerie silence had more to do with Wade's rebuttal of Garrett's contributions to our current investigation than the food's arrival. In his opinion, Garrett was "a whole lot of talk and little to no action."

"The pasta's good," I mumbled.

They both looked at me as if I'd just farted.

Maybe this was a bad idea, after all.

"Salad's not half bad, either," Wade conceded. His angst made my stomach clench, my appetite dwindling with each minute that went by.

Garrett chuckled. "Didn't peg you for a salad type of guy."

"We're both different people now," Wade retorted. "Well, I am, anyway. You're *always* different people."

I got confused, fast, as I realized that I was sitting on a gunpowder keg with these two, and that Wade had just lit the fuse. The *boom* was coming.

"What... Um, what are you talking about?" I asked, my voice barely audible.

"You're still hung up on that, huh?" Garrett said to Wade, virtually ignoring me. "Here I am, trying to reestablish a communication channel, and you're stuck in the past. Really, Crowley? After all these years?"

Oh, I was definitely missing some crucial pieces of information here.

"It's not something you easily forget," Wade replied, glowering at Garrett.

"Well, you haven't made it easy," Garrett answered.

I had a front seat view of their dashing profiles—each of them handsome and gorgeous in his own way. Wade's features were dark and sharp, highlighted by his sea-green eyes, the black curls on top of his head, and the smooth blade of his nose. In contrast, Garrett's short dark hair, azure eyes, and devastatingly cute dimples offered me another type of beautiful, the kind that was accustomed to breaking hearts.

Yet both of them were incredibly dysfunctional, perfectly evidenced by their fraught friendship. Something had definitely happened between them—that much I knew. I had a feeling I was about to find out what, exactly, and I was on the edge of my seat.

No way I'm finishing my cannelloni.

"You two need to bring me up to speed here if I'm to mediate anything," I interjected. "You promised."

Garrett gave me a brief sideways glance, then smiled. It irritated Wade. It was such a shame that I couldn't feel Garrett's emotions, too. I was willing to bet they spoke volumes.

"As you probably know, Wade and I go way back," Garrett said. "We were best friends at one point. Our parents are still close. Our dads are on the Texas Mage Council, after all. We were *tight*."

"Yeah, I'm aware of that," I replied. "So, who screwed things up?"

Wade and Garrett stared at each other, until Garrett laughed lightly, shaking his head. "That would be me." He chuckled and nodded at Wade. "Go on. We had an agreement not to talk about it, but I'm dying to tell her what got you all riled up. But you should do it. I want to hear your version of events."

I groaned with frustration as another minute passed. Wade's anger and shame were bubbling beneath the surface, poking me right in the head.

"Oh, come on," I grumbled.

"Seven years ago," Wade said, not taking his eyes off a slightly amused Garrett. "You should've told me..."

"I kind of did," Garrett replied, stifling his laughter.

"Garrett is a Shapeshifter," Wade said in a low tone, his jaw locked. I found myself staring at Garrett in pure disbelief. "I suppose you didn't know that," he added, and I shook my head, unable to look away. "Yeah. Shapeshifters tend to be secretive about it. I told you about that."

I nodded. "Who else knows?"

"Just Wade, our closest family members, my previous coven director, and Alton," Garrett replied. "Well, Astrid and Tatyana recently found out. I told them. Oh, and the other Shapeshifters in our coven. Alton introduced me to them, though I kind of knew about most of them. We can sense one another sometimes. It's a bit hard to explain. Not that many people know, let's leave it at that."

"We were best friends, and Garrett didn't think I deserved to know the proper way," Wade continued. "You know the proper way, right? Where you sit your best friend down, and you tell them you're a Shapeshifter. No. Garrett decided to shift into Melanie Williams..."

Garrett covered his mouth, struggling not to laugh out loud. He looked like a boy who'd just put a whoopee cushion on the teacher's chair and was waiting for the poor guy to sit down.

"Melanie was his crush," he said, grinning at Wade. "He was thirteen, and Melanie was sixteen. She was tutoring him in Alchemy and Magical Chemistry. Once a week, every Sunday evening."

Wade exhaled sharply, doing a remarkable job of keeping his cool. He was boiling inside. I was going to hear a teakettle whistle, soon enough.

"One Sunday evening, Melanie came over as usual," Wade took over. "I'd been working up the courage to ask her out for ice cream. She showed up in a beautiful summer dress. I'll never forget it. It had an orchid pattern on one side. Her strawberry-blonde hair was loose and perfectly straight. And she kept smiling at me. It took me an hour to finally pop the question. To my shock, she said yes, then gave me a peck on the lips," he added, then frowned at me. "Just so you know, this information is strictly between the three of us. Tell no one, or I will skin you alive."

I held my breath, my eyes nearly jumping out.

"Okay," I managed.

"It was my first kiss," Wade said. That was such an endearing thing for him to say, but I braced myself for the reveal. Deep down, I kind of already suspected what was coming, so I focused on keeping a straight face instead. "It meant the world to me. Remember, I was thirteen, and girls weren't really my field of expertise at the time."

"When were they ever?" Garrett croaked, before pressing his lips into a thin line. He was terrible at concealing his amusement.

"Shut up," Wade snapped, then shifted his focus back to me. "Thing is, that wasn't Melanie who kissed me. I found out the hard way when, one minute later, she shifted into Garrett. He was laughing like an idiot, and I felt—"

A chortle escaped my throat. I instantly covered my mouth with both hands. I felt terrible for him. It must've been a horrendously jarring experience. But, at the same time, being on the outside and looking in, I had to admit—it was hilarious.

Wade's icy glare made me swallow my laughter altogether.

"Come on, buddy. Tell her everything," Garrett prompted.

Wade's glare remained on me for another handful of seconds, before he swallowed hard and continued, "I had a bad reaction when I understood that Garrett was a Shapeshifter. I admit that I said things I wasn't proud of, though he certainly could have found a better way of breaking the news to me." His eyes snapped back to Garrett. "Regardless, it drove a wedge between us, and we've picked on each other repeatedly ever since."

"Basically, he never missed an opportunity to fry me like Southern chicken, and I kept shifting into his girlfriends," Garrett said. "We were both kids at the time, but we managed to carry the flame well into adulthood, as you can see. Crowley's ego is the size of the damn Bestiary, and I'm not one to say sorry more than once. So, there you have it, Merlin. The scoop."

A minute went by in awkward silence. I tried to measure Wade and Garrett against each other. Garrett had screwed up with the Melanie Shapeshifting thing. Wade had said some hurtful things. Then they just kept going after each other, until it became their second nature to sort of hate each other. I guessed I could see that happening.

I sighed. *Boys.*

"Well, I... I'm sorry that happened to you, Wade," I murmured. His eyes still felt like they were drilling holes into my skull. "But you are both responsible for this mess you two are in, friendship-wise," I added, looking at Garrett.

"I said I was sorry! But *he* never apologized for the bigoted things he said to me," Garrett replied.

"I was angry and humiliated!" Wade spat. "I needed time to cool off, but you didn't give it to me. Instead, you just kept shifting into even more people I liked! I felt I could never trust you again."

I guessed I understood where he was coming from, and all of a sudden, this wasn't as funny as I'd initially perceived it. I had to put myself in the shoes of a thirteen-year-old boy to get that. Then, a different thought wandered into my consciousness and got stuck in the middle of my mental corkboard of facts and musings about the Ryders.

"Plus, I was hurt that I had told you everything about myself, even things I didn't tell my parents," Wade added. "And there you were, keeping a massive secret like that. We'd promised each other to never keep secrets. You knew for more than two years at the time that you were a Shapeshifter, yet you chose to keep it from me. Not only that, but you decided to reveal it through a, might I add, very cruel prank. And saying sorry meant nothing when you kept impersonating the girls I was dating."

Garrett chuckled softly. I felt the urge to smack him—that was mostly Wade, but I had an itch of my own, too.

"And you two seriously never talked about this?" I asked.

"I guess we were too busy being angry at one another," Garrett muttered, crossing his arms.

"What the hell did you expect?" Wade asked. "You messed with my head in ways that would send normal kids straight into therapy!"

"But you were never a normal kid. I thought you could take it. Besides, how many times did I have to draw my eyebrows on with a damn pencil because you burnt them off, you vengeful jackass?"

"I was your friend, Garrett. Your *friend*. I deserved better," Wade said.

I lost my focus for a moment, as the thought I'd just had was coming back with a vengeance, sending a wave of alarm through my body.

"Hold on," I cut in. "Pause the bromance for a second. Garrett, you're a Shapeshifter."

"Stating the obvious," he replied.

I looked at Wade. "I can't feel him. Just like I couldn't feel Finch. Who's also a Shapeshifter," I said. "Riddle me this. Is O'Halloran a Shapeshifter, too?"

Wade straightened his back. He could clearly see where I was going with this. He nodded, and I broke into a cold sweat. "Very few people in the coven know, but yes. He's a Shapeshifter."

"I can't feel him, either," I breathed, the realization smacking me over the back of my head. "Preceptor Bellmore?"

"Yup," Garrett said. Wade seemed equally shocked by this revelation. Garrett smirked. "You didn't know, huh, Crowley? Well, it doesn't surprise me. We tend to keep a tight ship. We even have a support group," he added, then looked at me. "I told you. There's a stigma. This general consensus that we can't be trusted. The likes of Emily and Emmett Ryder aren't helping. Ever since it became public knowledge the other day, it's gotten even tougher for us. Bad rep's a doozy."

"Imogene Whitehall… I can't feel her, either," I said.

"That, I don't know, but I'd be inclined to say yes, since there's clearly a pattern here," Garrett replied.

"You can't feel Shapeshifters as an Empath," Wade concluded. "That's… interesting, to say the least."

"You can detect us, when others can't," Garrett added, his eyes widening as it sank in. "Oh, damn."

"Yeah," I murmured, taking it all in.

For some reason, my instincts tugged my mind back to Jacob in that moment. Given his abilities, the Ryders would've stopped at nothing to get to him. I figured I could check up on him a bit more often, just to make sure he was okay. After all, those Shapeshifters could literally be anyone.

"We both blew this, didn't we?" Wade asked Garrett. "Our friendship, I mean."

"I guess. Never thought I'd say it out loud," Garrett replied.

"Yeah, me neither," Wade mumbled.

They kept talking, somewhere in the background of my consciousness, probably addressing the Shapeshifter thing, but I was busy texting Jacob.

He didn't text back, so I tried calling instead. Five rings later, it went to voicemail. I called again. Five rings. Voicemail. It didn't feel right.

My instinct was now telling me to go check on him, and I never ignored it. I was incredibly uneasy about him and the Smiths in general, with the Ryders prowling.

What if they're already there, watching somewhere? Waiting to snatch him? They kill human parents. The Smiths are sitting ducks.

My stomach churned, and I rose to my feet, surprising both Wade and Garrett.

"Sorry, I have to go," I said.

"What's wrong?" Wade asked, visibly concerned.

"Nothing. I think. There's something I need to check," I replied, then put my hands on his and Garrett's shoulders. "You two need to get over this animosity between you. Sure, Garrett withheld some-thing important from you and chose the wrong way to tell you about it, then went and did it again and again, like the idiot that he clearly is," I added, scowling at him, then shifted my focus back to Wade. "But you clearly didn't give him a chance to properly explain his poor choice of prank, either. You said unforgivable things, and you never apologized. Instead, you indulged his grudge and made it worse, until your friendship was clinically dead. You were both dumb and proud kids. But you're grownups now. So start acting like it. The past is the past, and you can't change it. Let it go, already."

I left them there, gawking at me, and hurried out of the restaurant. That was all the time and energy I was going to put into a broken friendship.

I had work to do.

My Empath ability allowed me to detect Shapeshifters. That was incredibly important, because it could help me identify the Ryders, too, going forward.

First and foremost, however, I needed to make sure Jacob was okay. I couldn't let anything happen to my Smiths, and I certainly couldn't let those Shapeshifting bastards take Jacob away from us.

As I rushed out the door, I barely even heard Wade's rushed reminder that I wasn't advised to go anywhere on my own, thanks to my brush with the Ryder twins. I couldn't let him or anyone else from the coven find out about Jacob.

And I didn't need a babysitter. Not when I knew that Isadora Merlin had an eye on me.

THIRTY

Harley

Dicky was a godsend for me, and I owed Isadora a bottle of something good for bringing him into my life. I had his card, and ten minutes after making the call, Dicky showed up outside Fleet Science Center.

"Hey, Dicky," I said, as I climbed into the backseat.

He watched me in the rearview mirror and gave me a friendly nod. "Where to, Miss Merlin?"

"Forty-ninth and Heller, please."

"Ah, Jake's new place," Dicky replied.

Of course he knew Jacob, since they were both tied to Isadora somehow. There was still a lot I didn't know about her and her connections, but I had to admit, I was a little more at ease knowing there were eyes on Jacob at all times—or, so I hoped.

Dicky was an excellent driver, too. I wished I had his reflexes behind the wheel as we darted through the city and made our way to the Smiths' place.

I tried calling Jacob again, but still no damn answer, just that automatic voicemail.

The lights were out when we got there. Everybody was probably asleep already, since it was past ten p.m. and they all had an early start in the morning. I probably shouldn't have been surprised they didn't pick up the phone.

The neighborhood was equally quiet and dark, which was one of my favorite aspects of living in the area. I was a bit of an old soul, and my eyes got droopy by eleven p.m. I'd certainly enjoyed the tranquility during my last two years as a ward of the state.

I was still wound up tight, though, worried that something might've happened to Jacob and the Smiths—or that something was about to happen. The Ryders were out here, on the loose and pretending to be other people. The potential danger was all too close to home.

Dicky pulled up outside the Smiths' house and turned the engine off.

"You know, I checked on him this morning. Everything was okay," he said calmly, just as I opened the car door. It didn't mean Jacob was okay *now*.

I waited for a second before replying, genuinely befuddled by the man. "Out of curiosity, how are you so cool and totally not freaked out about us?" I asked.

Dicky chuckled. "I get where you're coming from, but you should know... Not everybody would flip out if they found out about the existence of magicals. Sure, there would be an adjustment period. Some extremists here and there. But the people, Miss Merlin, the people are inherently good and understanding. It's the government you want to be afraid of."

"Fair enough. How'd *you* get involved, then?" I asked. Dicky was chattier than the night before—perhaps he was warming up to me— and I wanted to take advantage of it.

"Isadora was in trouble. I helped her. I begged her not to wipe my memories. I proved myself useful. We've been working together ever since," Dicky replied. "I love driving, I've got no kids to worry about, and I want to help her. It's a no-brainer for me."

"How long have you been helping her?"

"I lost track. Maybe twenty years."

I nodded, then got out of the car. "I'll be back in a few minutes."

"Take your time. I'm here."

I couldn't help but smile as I snuck around the house. It was good to know that there were people like Dicky out there, who did the job and didn't ask questions. Most importantly, it made me feel as though I wasn't really alone in the world—granted, I had the coven, but I lacked the family connection to them. Isadora's reemergence, along with Dicky, an impressively chill human, somehow made everything better. I had a hard time explaining why, even to myself. It just felt right.

During my two years at the Smiths', I'd learned to expertly climb in and out of my first-floor bedroom. I used to go out a lot, at night, to try and better understand my abilities. I needed a more secluded green space to do that, where I didn't have to explain why an oak tree had suddenly popped out of nowhere, for example. I didn't have full control over my Earth Elemental ability then, and frankly, I was still getting the hang of it now.

I climbed the rugged masonry siding of the house, pulled myself up, and made my way across the slanted slate roof, careful not to make any sound. Jacob's room (previously mine), was dark and seemingly quiet. I moved closer to the window and peered inside.

I could see him sleeping, sprawled across the double bed. His emotions were soft and fluid, like everyone's while in a dream state. I got a sense of longing and fear, but also happiness and relief. The mixture was something I, too, had experienced at his age. It came with the territory as a foster kid. Heck, I still felt that way sometimes. The life spent hauling a black bag from one home to another tended to leave a mark on us. We never outran that kind of loneliness, no matter how good the foster family was. We'd always feel unwanted, mainly because our own parents couldn't or didn't want to raise us.

Pleased and incredibly relieved to see that he was okay, I sent him another text, reminding him of our six p.m. meeting the next day. We'd agreed to hang out and hash a few things out about where he came from and what he knew about Isadora. Or, at least, what he could tell me about her. I was dying to find out more about this aunt, since the other one had turned out to be a raging psychopath.

I saw the phone light up on his bedside table, but he didn't react. He was going to wake up to it in the morning, along with the previous text, six missed calls, and two voicemails.

My fear subsided, at least temporarily, as I'd seen he was okay with my own eyes. The fact that I could feel his emotions was also downright soothing, given what I'd just learned back at the restaurant.

I climbed off the roof and checked the backyard. It didn't take long for me to find the protective charms. Isadora had most likely left them. She'd hidden one in every potted plant, and she'd painted small symbols on the corners of the house, too. I went around the property and checked the decorative ferns by the front door. She'd left tiny leather pouches in there as well.

I slipped back in Dicky's cab and asked him to take me back to the coven.

The ride back was quiet. Not because I didn't have more questions for him. I totally did. But I was too busy racking my brains and trying to remember everyone whose emotions I'd been unable to sense. The conclusion was the same. They all had to be Shapeshifters. There was just no other reasonable explanation.

Jacob could sense magicals, but he wouldn't have been able to tell me what kind of magicals they were. This was as close as I was going to get to a "natural" magical detection method—at least until Krieger finished his prototype, based on Adley's research.

Dicky dropped me off in the parking lot outside Fleet Science Center and drove off into the night. I watched the red taillights shrink in the distance, lost in the late-night traffic leading back into the city—a river of twinkling crimson eyes.

As soon as I turned around to go in, I yelped and leapt back a couple of yards, startled by the tall, dark figure standing between two cars. It took me a second to realize it was Wade.

"Whoa! Are you trying to give me a heart attack?!" I snapped, catching my ragged breath.

My heart had nearly jumped out through my throat. Wade didn't say anything, keeping his hands behind his back. Only then did I notice that one of the cars he was standing between was his Jeep, the other covered by a black tarp.

"I was waiting for you to come back," Wade finally replied.

"You could've texted," I said.

"Where's the fun in that, when I get to scare the daylights out of you?" he retorted, slightly amused. My heart was still thumping—but this time, it was because of Wade. He was nervous... excited, even.

"Ah. So, you are a sadist. Just like I've been saying," I retorted.

He gave me a half-smile, then let out a deep sigh. "I wanted to thank you for tonight," he said. "It was eye-opening, to say the least."

"Don't mention it," I replied. "It's not like I did much. Someone just had to sit you and Garrett down for an hour."

"Well, you were the first to see past his... difficult nature. Others usually tend to walk away when Garrett lets his inner jerk out."

"Which is every five minutes. Yup. I get it." I chuckled.

"Point is, thank you. I mean it, Harley," he said. "You made an effort, and you helped me see things from the outside. Garrett and I aren't exactly on speaking terms yet, but I think we're getting there. At least we got the bulk of our discord out of the way."

"About that. I'm sorry," I replied. "I get that what he did was terrible. It's actually kind of funny, but—" I giggled, then stopped myself when I noticed his sullen expression. "Terrible. Just a terrible gesture, on his part," I said, putting on a serious face, even though I was laughing on the inside. "It's in the past, though. He said he was sorry. It's time to move on."

"I agree."

Silence fell between us for a while. He was working up the courage to say something else, I could feel it. A minute went by as I waited patiently, until my gaze settled absently on the covered car. As soon as he saw me looking at it, he was plugged back in.

"I wanted to... um, I wanted to do something special," he said. "As a... Well, as a 'Welcome to the San Diego Coven' kind of... gift."

I raised an eyebrow at him.

He lowered his head, then pulled the cover off the car in one, swift move.

I squealed with joy as soon as I saw her. My Daisy. *My Daisy!* My beloved '67 Ford Mustang was whole again. She'd been given a full makeover, painted in a luscious, shimmering black with sterling detail work. There was no sign of Murray's fiendish aggression anywhere. My baby looked brand new!

My eyes were filled with tears as I covered my mouth and kept staring at Daisy.

"You were so broken up about this car, I figured it would make you happy to be able to drive it again," Wade added. Warmth filled me up, and I wasn't sure if that was me or him. "I found a good mechanic. We had to do a lot of digging online to find some of the parts, but..." He tossed me the keys, complete with a small porcelain globe keychain. "We found them all. Your car is fully functional again."

"Holy moly," I croaked, staring at the keys, then back at Daisy. I walked around her a couple of times, running my fingers against her smooth lines. "Your mechanic did an incredible job."

"He's actually a specialist in vintage cars. Anything before the seventies is his area of expertise," Wade replied.

I dashed forward and threw myself in his arms. I held him tight, resting my head on his shoulder. Wade responded, and I felt his embrace tighten around my waist. His heart was on a rampage, as was mine. Touching him like this had an incredible effect on me.

"Thank you, Wade. I... I don't know what... or how to repay you," I said.

"You don't have to. You deserve it."

His voice was low and smooth, like balm for my rickety little soul.

A twinkle caught my eye as I relished the feel of him against me. My Esprit had lit up—each of the gemstones sparkling in a way that made me smile. I couldn't help but wonder if that was just my sheer happiness, manifesting through raw Chaos. It certainly felt like that. After all, the Esprit was supposed to be an extension of my soul, and my soul was way up there, thrilled and brimming with joy.

"Thank you," I whispered again.

Feeling Wade without touching him suddenly felt bland. I could get used to letting him hold me like this. My senses were on fire, each sensation amplified. I had a hard time letting go.

I moved to gently pull myself back, but he firmly kept me in place, making my heart skip a beat. My breath left me, lost in his embrace. He didn't want to let go...

"I'm hoping this will make you stay," Wade said, his lips danger-ously close to my ear. His breath brushed against it, making my skin tingle all over.

"Stay?" I asked.

"With us, here, in the San Diego Coven."

"Pledge my allegiance, you mean," I replied.

He pulled his head back to look me in the eyes. That was such a dangerous thing for him to do, since I instantly melted inside those deep green pools.

"The coven needs you, Harley. It's not so much about your abili-ties as it is about your character and strength. We could use people like you in the long run," he said.

"Well, once we get this Suppressor off, surely my abilities will count, too," I replied, grinning.

Wade frowned, then gently let go. For a moment, I felt cold. Oh, how quickly I'd adjusted to his embrace.

"Are you sure that's a good idea?" he asked. "It might put your life in danger. That thing was made to stay there. Forever."

I shook my head. "I can't live a life of Mediocrity when I have so much potential bubbling beneath the surface," I said. "I'd rather risk it and get it out of me than settle with limits. I can't even consider that."

He nodded, processing my response. Adrenaline was still pumping through me, the result of his touch. The effect that Wade had on me was undeniable at this point. But what really got me curious was the effect that I had on *him*. How much of what I was feeling was mine, and how much was *his*?

"Do you want to get behind the wheel?" he asked, his lips stretching into a satisfied smirk.

He was clearly content with himself—and for good reason. Despite our head-butting and his sometimes-insufferable attitude, Wade meant well. He'd made that much clear with Daisy, though it came as quite a surprise after he'd told me to get over her, that she was just a pile of metal. An object of no significance.

Well, it turned out he did, in fact, understand what Daisy meant to me.

I nodded enthusiastically, then got in the driver's seat. I breathed in deeply. The scent of leather and pine flooded my brain. I looked at him standing by the car door and let out a devilish cackle. With a trembling hand, I put the keys in the ignition and twisted them.

"She's alive!" I exclaimed, sounding like Dr. Frankenstein, as Daisy's engine roared to life. "Good grief, I missed your purrs, baby! Momma loves the sound of your voice! Yes, she does!" I addressed Daisy as if she were a golden retriever—such a good girl.

Wade chuckled, rejoicing at the sight of me as I wiggled in my seat.

"This is amazing," I said to him. "Thank you, Wade. I will never forget this."

"Oh, I don't plan on letting you forget," he replied with a smile.

His phone rang. He checked the screen, his brow furrowed. "Santana," he muttered, then answered the call. "Yeah... *What?!*"

The color drained from his face as he hung up and looked at me.

"What?" I asked.

"We're needed in the dragon garden. Something's wrong with Tatyana," he said.

He rushed inside the center through the service door. I quickly took my keys out and locked my beloved Daisy, then ran in after him. I cared about my teammates, and the thought of any of them getting hurt made me feel worse than my car getting smashed by a gargoyle.

In hindsight, Wade did have a point. The car could be replaced. One of us, however... never.

THIRTY-ONE

Harley

"I don't get why everyone is so fussed about this," Tatyana said, her voice emerging from the garden inside the coven.

Wade and I arrived just in time to find her standing by the dragon fountain, keeping her distance from Santana, Raffe, and Astrid, who looked on edge. They were all worried and scared for Tatyana, but none of them dared to approach her.

"What's going on here?" Wade asked.

Santana exhaled. "I told you! She's possessed!"

Astrid was frantically looking for something on her Smartie tablet, flipping through folders and files with shaky fingers, while Raffe kept his dark blue-gray eyes on Tatyana. She looked fine to me, until I got a whiff of her emotions. Most of them were doubled in intensity, and not in a way that felt natural. I could feel two people in her body, for sure.

"Oh, damn," I said. "She's right. There's someone in there."

"How did that happen?" Wade replied, equally outraged and confused as he glared at Tatyana. "I thought we talked about this! You know what happens when you let a spirit in for too long!"

"I've got this under control!" Tatyana fired back. "Oberon is helping me, okay? You guys are blowing this out of proportion. Take a chill pill!"

"Yeah, no!" Santana snapped. "Not taking a chill pill! Not after the last time you got your skinny ass overthrown by a spirit! You almost killed Preceptor Redmont, remember?!"

"Ooooh, that bad, huh?" I asked, pursing my lips.

"Yup!" Wade said, his Esprit rings lighting up white. He was getting ready to intervene. "Tatyana is a phenomenal Kolduny, or, better said, Ghost-Whisperer, but she's yet to learn to fully control her body while a foreign spirit is in there. That takes time and practice, and it needs to be done in a controlled environment. *Not behind our backs!*" he added, raising his voice at the end.

"She used Oberon Marx's spirit to save Dylan during the Kenneth Willow incident," Santana replied. "But the wonder jock is still hitching a ride, and I'm not sure Tatyana had much of a say in it. Right now, I'm not even sure that's Tatyana we're talking to."

"Of course it's me," Tatyana exclaimed, laughing nervously. I couldn't feel her usual cool and curiosity. There was anger and longing—the toxic kind that burned holes through my stomach. This all felt different.

I put my hand out, the white pearl on my Esprit lighting up like a miniature star. I'd recently learned that if I aimed my Esprit at someone, while focusing on my Empathy, I could dig deeper and get an even better read on a person. I hadn't used it often because my instinct was good enough on its own for most circumstances, and it took a toll on my energy—but right now it was worth it, and I was able to instantly identify two independent strands of emotions.

One was strained and fearful, desperate to get back to the surface. The other was furious and missing someone... I could almost see her face before me. Long, flowing hair. Wild green eyes. A smile that made my heart flutter. I gasped, realizing that I'd tapped into a string of emotions that carried powerful images with them. That was something I'd never seen or experienced before. It scared and enticed me, all at once. It also confirmed a most dreadful fact.

"Tatyana's not in control anymore," I said.

Wade noticed my Esprit and the look on my face and frowned. "You can feel Oberon?"

"Oh, yeah. Absolutely. He's behind the wheel," I replied.

"Tatyana, you have to push him out!" Santana shouted. "Push the bastard out! He's controlling you!"

Tatyana smirked, crossing her arms. "You're way too loud, you know that?" she replied dryly. "I told you to chill out. I've got this under control."

"Oberon Marx. You don't belong here," Wade hissed. "Leave now or you'll regret it."

"What part of 'I've got this under control' didn't you understand?" Tatyana spat.

"I have a hard time believing that," Raffe said. Rage was boiling inside him, tainted with malice and a thirst for blood… violence. At that point, I wasn't sure whether I should be more scared of him than of a possessed Tatyana. "Unless you're speaking as Oberon, in which case, yes, you have control. Over a body that's not yours. Release her!"

"Don't you have anything better to do than butt into my business?" Tatyana asked, her Esprit bracelet twinkling blue.

"That's it. I'm pulling your ghostly ass out of there!" Santana said, darting toward her.

Tatyana smirked, then used her Telekinesis to swat Santana away like a fly. She gripped Raffe by his throat, trying to suffocate him. Wade cursed under his breath and launched a fireball at her— he didn't aim to hurt her. The purpose was to distract her.

It worked. Tatyana let go of Raffe, dodged the blaze, and jumped back a couple of steps. She grinned, her eyes glimmering yellow. That wasn't a good sign, since it probably meant that the spirit was sinking his teeth into her flesh, determined to never let go.

I took a step forward, ready to use my Telekinesis on her, but Wade motioned for me to stand back.

"Hold on," he said. "Don't. There's a mighty Herculean in there. Force clearly isn't an option here. It'll take more than a tackle to stop him."

"We can't just let him—"

"Just listen to me, for once, and wait!" Wade cut me off.

"Well, at least you kids aren't as stupid as I thought," Tatyana announced, her voice doubled—both female and male, as if she and Oberon were speaking at the same time. It was freaky, to say the least.

"Let go of her, Oberon," Wade warned. "You know there's a soul in there already. And you know what happens when you possess someone in the long term, right?"

"It doesn't matter!" Tatyana-Oberon snarled. "I have a body now, and I'll use it to do what I have to do. Once I get my own body back, this one can burn for all I care!"

Santana managed to get up, panting and holding her side. "You're *loco* if you think I'm going to let you destroy my friend!"

She charged Tatyana—this time, however, her Orishas came out to help. A dozen bluish wisps of raw energy swirled around Santana, before dissolving into her body and lighting her up from the inside. Glowing and seething with anger, Santana rammed into Tatyana.

Tatyana grabbed Santana by the throat, delivered a series of crippling punches into her ribcage, and tossed her aside. Santana rolled on the ground, limp. Raffe leapt to his feet and let out a bloodcurdling roar. I'd never heard or seen him like this. Judging by the looks on Astrid's and Wade's faces, however, they had, and it seemed to spell serious trouble for all of us.

"Raffe, stand down!" Wade commanded.

Raffe shot him a glance over the shoulder. Only then did I spot the change—the fiery red in his eyes, as if volcanoes were erupting in there. Raffe bared his teeth, seemingly feral and raring to tear into Tatyana. He panted, his chest swelling with every breath. The malice and viciousness I'd sensed coming out of him earlier was now blaring at full volume, as if his otherwise calm and composed nature had been literally trampled, making way for... the beast.

"Raffe! I said stand down!" Wade raised his voice.

"Raffe, don't... You'll kill her," Santana croaked, propping herself up on one side. Blood was trickling from the corner of her mouth.

The sight of her seemed to be enough to make Raffe's inner storm subside. Tatyana-Oberon grinned, watching as Raffe exhaled heavily, before rushing to help Santana.

"You're in over your heads," Tatyana-Oberon said. Then she darted toward Wade, but his instincts were fast, and he managed to beat her back with a bright blaze. She stilled several feet away from him and carefully eyed each of us, probably looking for the weakest spot. Santana was off limits, it seemed, since Tatyana-Oberon gave Raffe a nervous grin. She preferred not to cross him.

"And you're about to get your ass thrown back into the veil!" Astrid shouted. She looked at Wade. "Use the Krinkman-Sadler exorcism. This area is secured for that."

"What's that?" I asked, moving slowly to the side as I looked for attack angles. I wanted to have a shot of my own at taking Tatyana down, immobilizing her without hurting her.

A split second later, Wade released another fireball at Tatyana-Oberon. She dodged it, but it exploded just above her—a nifty trick I'd seen him use before. It forced her down on her belly, coughing and wheezing from the sudden burst of heat she'd inhaled. It hurt me to see her like this, but we had to stall her as much as possible until we figured out what to do.

"I had to double check the coven's blueprints to make sure," Astrid said. "The Krinkman-Sadler exorcism is a difficult thing to do since it requires a ton of Dark energy. There are parts of the coven where the walls are imbued with Light energy, and parts where it's Dark. This garden is Dark, and Wade will need some of that to perform the exorcism."

"I'm confused. Are we talking about Darkness and Light? As in the Children of Chaos? The kind of energy that's supposed to run through us, naturally?" I asked.

"Well, you're behind on your theory, it seems," Tatyana-Oberon sneered at me, then got up and stepped forward, assuming an attack stance. The spirit was taunting me, banking on anticipation to make me nervous and cripple my concentration. *How the hell am I the weak spot?*

"Yes. I'm not Dark by nature, I'm Light," Wade explained. "So, I need extra Darkness energy to perform the Krinkman-Sadler exorcism."

He threw out a trio of exploding fireballs this time, forcing Tatyana-Oberon to drop and roll in order to avoid another throat-burn.

"Which is a Dark ritual," Astrid added. "Raffe's Dark, but his is not the kind of energy you want to let out for this, trust me."

"Why not?" I replied.

"I'll explain another time! Just stand your ground and keep your eyes on Tatyana!" Wade said. "We need to find a way to restrain her. My fire won't stall her forever."

Tatyana-Oberon laughed. "Good luck with that." She raised her hands and pushed out a Telekinetic barrier so powerful it felt like a tidal wave, throwing us all backward. I wound up rolling over the garden path stones, then lying on my back, the air knocked out of my lungs.

Wade grunted as he tried to get himself back up, but Tatyana-Oberon wasn't done. Her Telekinesis was amplified by that of the spirit, making it twice as powerful and potentially deadly. She sent out another pulse that pushed us all back down. It felt as though she had her boot pressed against the back of my head, stuffing my face against a patch of hard ground and grass.

I cursed under my breath, struggling to release myself.

"Lordy, you kids are stupidly easy to overpower," Tatyana-Oberon said in a double voice.

"Tatyana..." Dylan's voice emerged from the other side of the garden.

I managed to look ahead, spotting Dylan as he staggered toward us. He was wearing his infirmary garb—the open-back gown. Had I not been under the pressure of a ghost's Telekinesis, I probably would've thrown out a backdraft joke at Dylan's expense.

He saw us, then frowned, setting his sights on Tatyana-Oberon, since she was the only one standing.

Surprisingly, she stilled at the sight of him.

"What are you doing here?" she asked, her voice barely audible.

Tatyana's emotions flared through me. She was trying to reach out to him from the depths of her consciousness, where Oberon had stashed her.

"Astrid left me one of her tablets, to patch into CCTV and check out the place if I'm bored with streaming movies," Dylan said, frowning. "What's going on with you?"

"She's possessed," Santana groaned.

Dylan's shoulders dropped. His concern and fear rammed into me. But it was quickly drowned out by determination. Dylan wasn't one to wallow in the dark stuff.

"Why would you let that happen?" Dylan asked Tatyana, his voice husky.

"I was trying to help. I needed Oberon's strength and power," Tatyana said, having somehow caught the mic for a second. "But he's not letting me back in—" She paused, then returned to her creepy double voice. "Now, now! Where were we? Ah, yes. Kill you all, then go be with my beloved Katherine."

"Tatyana?" Dylan breathed, visibly confused.

"Wait, *Katherine*?!" I yelled in alarm.

"I need her. I have to be with her," Tatyana Oberon replied. She grinned and raised a hand toward Dylan, while she kept the other focused on us.

"Katherine *Shipton*?!" I gasped.

She glowered at me, then smiled. "Ever since I heard she was back, I've been looking for a way to find her."

As I absorbed the shock, I realized that it sort of made sense. Everything bad that happened in the coven was always somehow related to friggin' Katherine Shipton.

"You met her," I said, stalling. Now I needed to focus on giving Dylan a window to take her down.

"Met her?" Tatyana-Oberon laughed. "I was with her. I loved her! I *still* love her. Hell, my love for her is what killed me."

"What happened?" I asked.

"That's none of your concern," Tatyana-Oberon replied, the grief oozing out of the hijacking spirit. The bitterness and guilt, the pain and the longing… It felt like poison, tainting my blood."

That was Dylan's shot, and he took it. "You're not taking her away from me!" Dylan shouted, sprinting forward and tackling her like the pro footballer that he was. They both landed with a thud and viciously wrestled, rolling and tumbling through the grass.

Punches were thrown. Some missed, some nailed the ribs and the sides.

Tatyana-Oberon swerved around and caught Dylan in a choke-hold. Now free of her insanely powerful Telekinesis, I was able to use my own. I launched a targeted pulse, hitting her right in the forehead. It threw her head back, and she loosened her hold on Dylan, who then took control of the situation.

Wade reached them just as Dylan straddled Tatyana, forcing her hands behind her back. Even with Oberon's spirit strengthening her, she couldn't do much from that position.

"Let me go, you son of a—"

"Tatyana!" Dylan shouted, cutting her off. "Throw him out! Come back to me, please! Throw the bastard out!"

"I'm sorry, Tatyana's not available at the moment." Tatyana-

Oberon chortled. "Please try again la—" She stilled, her yellowish eyes wide with shock. "No... No, no, no!"

She went into a seizure, shaking uncontrollably. Dylan held her down, and Wade checked her vitals. We all gathered around, watching helplessly as Tatyana fought Oberon for control of her body.

"Come on, Tatyana, you can do it," I whispered.

"Kick his ass, chica!" Santana snapped.

"Please, Tatyana. Please, fight him. Come back to us... To me," Dylan breathed, tearing up as he kept a tight grip on her.

Tatyana roared from what felt like incredibly intense emotional pain. I clutched my chest, shocked by how horrible it felt for her. Wade gave me a concerned glance. I nodded reassuringly in return. I didn't want anyone to get distracted by my Empathy. Tatyana's wellbeing mattered the most. Even as I dropped to one knee, subdued by the pain, I held on to that conviction.

"Come on, Tatyana! Do it!" I cried out, tears streaming down my cheeks, as every muscle in my body seemed to tear from my bones.

Tatyana screamed, the veins in her temples throbbing as she delivered a final push and sucked in a breath. A wisp of white smoke puffed out of her body and dissipated. I could almost hear Oberon's wails as he vanished into the invisible veil of the spirit world.

I pointed my Esprit hand at her, the pearl lighting up white again. I could feel her—ashamed, exhausted, and angry. "She's back," I said, sitting down with a heavy breath.

Dylan got off Tatyana and helped her up into a sitting position. She was covered in a sheet of sweat, panting and sobbing at the same time. Dylan put his arms around her and pressed his lips against her temple.

"It's okay," he whispered. "You did it. It's okay... It's over."

"No, not yet," Tatyana choked out. She reached into her boot and retrieved a small pocket knife. She flipped it open and hissed from the pain as she carved a small rune symbol into her left forearm. I was the only one shocked by what I was watching, it seemed.

"What the hell?!" I blurted.

"It's a banishing sigil. It keeps the last spirit to have entered the body from ever coming back," Wade explained, then took out a handkerchief—because that's the kind of guy he was, all suited up and always carrying a monogramed handkerchief around—and handed it to Tatyana, who tied it around her bleeding forearm.

"Thanks, Wade," she sighed, then gave us all an apologetic smile. "I'm so, so sorry."

"Hey, it's okay. What matters is that you're safe now," Santana replied. "It could've been a lot worse."

"Hold on, you literally carve runes into your skin to stop the likes of Oberon from possessing you again?" I asked, still wrapping my head around that unpleasant little nugget.

Tatyana nodded, then lifted her shirt to show me five other scars on her left hip—five other runes, for five other spirits that had taken over her body and refused to let go. I'd known she had a history with rogue spirits, but I hadn't known the details or the repercussions.

"It's not my first rodeo," she said. "I was stupid this time. Given what the Ryders are doing, I thought I could use someone like Oberon..."

Her voice trailed off as she passed out.

"I'm taking her to the infirmary," Dylan said, immediately scooping her up in his arms and racing toward the building.

Santana, Raffe, and Astrid followed. They all needed some light medical attention. Judging by the scratches and bruises on my arms, I could've used a couple of Band-Aids too. I was already partially purple here and there from the beating I'd gotten from the evil twins—a few additional grazes were practically nothing.

I now understood why Tatyana's ability was so dangerous. It could easily kill anyone around her, not to mention Tatyana herself. What was Oberon thinking? He'd sounded so obsessed, so desperate to get to Katherine Shipton. He didn't care who he hurt or what he had to do. He would've stopped at nothing to find his way back to her.

It scared me to think of the kind of power that Katherine Shipton could have on a man, to cause him to frantically search for her, even in death.

THIRTY-TWO

Tatyana

M y head hurt as if it had been split in half like a watermelon. My eyes peeled open, instantly squinting to filter the blast of white light. It took me a couple of seconds to figure out that I was in the infirmary.

My mouth and throat were dry. I licked my lips, then looked down. I was in bed, still in my clothes. And Dylan was sleeping next to me, half of him in a chair and the other half leaning into my bed, his head resting against my hip.

I raised my arm slowly and saw the rune I'd carved into my skin. A heaviness weighed down on my shoulders as I realized that I hadn't dreamed any of it. At some point, Oberon had taken over my body, without me even realizing. He'd probably noticed I could sense his spiritual pressure when he got behind the wheel and figured out a way to trick me.

I didn't even realize he'd hijacked me until I saw myself casting Telekinetic attacks against my friends out by the dragon fountain. Shame set my face on fire. I couldn't be in here for another second. I needed to crawl into a dark space somewhere and wait the embarrassment out.

Dylan felt me stir and put his arm out, pinning me down.

"You're not going anywhere," he grumbled, then raised his head to look at me.

Our eyes met, and I couldn't stop the tears from flowing. He gave me a soft smile but didn't say anything for a while. I felt so bad, so foolish… I would've loved it if the earth could've just opened up and swallowed me whole to spare me the misery. I'd been duped by a ghost.

"Don't feel bad about it," Dylan said, as if reading my mind. "You did what you thought was best. Besides, this wasn't my first ghostly adventure. Remember?"

How could I forget? Dylan had barely marked his first week in the coven when the spirit of a former criminal warlock had hijacked me and nearly killed Preceptor Redmont. Apparently, the scholar of International Magical Cultures had made some enemies down in the basement prison some time ago, after testifying against several murderous rogues—including the one who'd snuck into my body.

Sometimes, if I wasn't careful, I couldn't even see a spirit coming. They'd wait around, quiet and patient, until they felt a temporary weakness in my spiritual defenses. It was going to take a lot more time and practice for me to be able to keep all the spirits at bay, as well as to control them while they were riding my meatsuit.

Dylan had joined Santana, Raffe, and Wade in taking me down and helping me exorcise the malevolent spirit. He'd actually found it… fascinating. That wasn't a word I'd heard before, when describing a Kolduny's ability to let spirits in.

"I was so stupid," I said. "I believed Oberon. I thought he really wanted to help. I figured all he was getting out of this was the opportunity to feel everything again inside a body. What an idiot I was."

Dylan squeezed my hand gently. The tingling sensation of his touch spread through my whole arm, then traveled all the way to my heart, where it settled and emitted a series of heatwaves. I definitely had feelings for Dylan, and I didn't know what to do with them. I was a liability to anyone who got too close to me, as evidenced by the Oberon incident. I'd hurt my friends. I would've hurt Dylan, too, if I hadn't found the strength to return to the surface.

I got away easy this time, but what about the next? I could never forgive myself if something happened to Dylan. He'd come quite late into the magical world. I didn't want to ruin the experience for him, or worse, kill him. I just… I couldn't.

"Don't be so hard on yourself," Astrid said as she came in, accompanied by Harley, Wade, Santana, and Raffe. They were all pretty roughed up, but nothing that couldn't be fixed with some ice or concealer. Again, guilt gnawed at my stomach. "Oberon played you like a fiddle, but I figured out why and what happened to him," she added, taking out her Smartie tablet as she came around to my right side of the bed.

"What do you mean?" I asked, confused. "I heard him talking about Katherine Shipton, but I don't know anything about that. He locked me out completely when he took over. I couldn't even sense his intentions anymore."

"I've done some research. Put two and two together. Plus, the 'homework' that Harley gave me the other day came in super handy," she replied.

"Wait," I said, frowning. "How long have I been out?"

"Oh, about ten hours," Harley answered, grinning. "They're serving breakfast downstairs. How are you feeling?"

"Like crap," I breathed.

She chuckled. "Figures. You'll be okay, though. Krieger checked your vitals and everything. Your body is fine. I guess it's just your ego that's bruised."

"And my ribs," Santana muttered.

"I'm so sorry—"

"*Chica*, enough! Don't worry about it!" Santana stopped me, then nodded at Astrid. "Go on, genius. Tell her what you found out!"

Astrid smirked and handed me the tablet so I could see the files she'd pulled up. A mixture of documents and images were scattered across the screen—crime scene photos, autopsy snapshots, and investigative reports. I recognized Oberon in some of the images. Specifically, his dead body.

"So, here's what I got so far, and I didn't realize I had it until I read Oberon Marx's autopsy report," Astrid said. "The Icelandic spell that Harley wanted me to research, Sál Vinna... it's very old, extremely dark and evil. Obviously forbidden. We don't even have any references about it in the coven. I had to go into the nationwide database and dig really, *really* deep. It's a powerful, perverted mental control spell. It feels so natural, but so strong that the victim won't know he's under it until it's too late, and he's lost control."

"Is that what happened to Oberon?" I asked, trying to make a connection.

"Sál Vinna implants the thought of someone so deep in your mind that it feels like you've always thought about that person," Astrid replied. "It is stronger than any form of hypnosis or mind control, and it's very dangerous because it's known to be unbreakable and incurable. Once you get it, that's it. You're done. So, that's the curse. Now, as you can see, I pulled up everything we had on Oberon. He died here in the coven. Fatal head trauma, but the circumstances of his death weren't clear. I only know that it was ruled an accident. He bled out."

"He said that his love for Katherine Shipton killed him," I said, even as I remembered his bloody shirt.

Astrid nodded, before pointing at another file on the tablet, complete with grainy footage of a woman with red hair. Harley crossed her arms, visibly angered and concerned.

"I gave Smartie all of Katherine Shipton's details, including a last official photo of her. I had the system search through the CCTV archives and pulled this little gem up," Astrid continued. "She wasn't affiliated with the coven or registered here, but she matches Katherine Shipton's facial features—otherwise Smartie wouldn't have pointed her out. Thing is, this footage is from a period of three months preceding Oberon's death. So, naturally I figured that, based on what Oberon told us, Katherine Shipton was definitely here at some point, and had something to do with his death. It seemed pretty obvious."

She tapped on the tablet screen again and zoomed in on an autopsy photo of Oberon Marx. I was looking at a blackish purple puncture wound behind his ear, surrounded by a small rune symbol of Celtic origin, burned into his skin.

"Then this came up and I had a connect-the-dots moment!" Astrid went on. "The Sál Vinna works as a liquid spell. A mixture is concocted, then injected into the victim—hypodermic needles are the bomb. But it needs to be sealed into the victim's body, so the rune is added to keep it tight and evil. From there on, it's good riddance for the poor fella. And this is proof that Oberon Marx was under the Sál Vinna. The mortician at the time didn't spot it because he already had cause of death. His skull had been crushed on the other side. Whether Oberon fell or Katherine bashed his head in, though, we don't know. Results were inconclusive."

I held my breath for a moment, following Astrid's line of reasoning, then looked up at Harley. "Why did you want Astrid to look into Sál Vinna?" I asked her.

"Isadora told me about it. She said not to believe everything I read about my dad, and to look into that spell," she replied, her voice uneven.

We were both thinking the same thing at that point. I could see it on her face. "You think your father was under the influence of Sál Vinna when he... did what he did?"

"We're considering the possibility, yes," Wade said.

"We definitely think that Oberon was cursed with Sál Vinna by Katherine and got himself killed with it. He couldn't move on as a spirit, and he took the curse with him," Astrid continued. "From the moment you let him in, he had a plan to get back to Katherine. His spirit is still obsessed with her."

"The point is," Dylan said, "this wasn't your fault, Tatyana.

Oberon knew exactly what he was doing. He wasn't going to leave your body even if you told him no. He was going to fight you for it. Nothing was going to stand between him and Katherine."

"Though, he probably had no idea where to even begin looking for her," Santana said.

"And even if he were to find her, chances are that Katherine would've chopped his head off. Well, your head. Sorry," Harley replied. "You dodged a bullet with that guy."

"We do appreciate the fact that you saw this as an opportunity to help our team," Wade said to me, then squeezed my shoulder. "You had good intentions."

"Shoddy execution." I scoffed.

"All Oberon's fault." Harley sighed. She looked at Wade. "If my father was under Sál Vinna, too, that might explain a few things, including Finch's account of my father getting back together with Katherine, then killing my mom and the other magicals."

"There should be mortuary records available," Astrid said. "Photos, for sure. They wouldn't have had to do an autopsy on Hiram Merlin, since they knew exactly what killed him—they did."

"Would they be in the New York Coven?" Harley asked.

Wade nodded. "Probably. But not available to the magical public."

"Let me check," Astrid said. She took the tablet back and did her magic through the inter-coven electronic database. She pouted as the results came back. "There are no electronic copies. Which is kind of weird."

"How'd you get access?" Wade asked, clearly surprised.

Astrid gave him a playful smirk. "I've got higher clearance than you, it seems," she replied, chuckling.

"So, what, there are only hard copies?" Harley cut back in.

Astrid nodded. "The covens were supposed to have digitized everything over the past ten years," she said. "Including all the data they had from judgments, executions, investigations, autopsies, and so on. This is a bit odd, if you ask me."

"I may have to make my way up to New York to check the archives myself," Harley concluded. "I'm sure Alton will sign off on that. I have to find out whether my father was under Sál Vinna. If he was, then he was definitely innocent. Like he said…"

Santana cried out in pain, dropping to her knees. Bright blue-and-green Orishas shot out from inside her, chaotically darting through the infirmary.

"What the… What's happening?" Harley gasped.

Raffe helped Santana up. She was trembling from head to toe. I froze. I knew exactly what all this meant.

"The charms," Santana panted. "They all went off at the same time. Every single one I put in. Something happened to the kids… the families… something bad."

Harley turned white as a sheet of paper. "The Ryder twins made their move."

THIRTY-THREE

Harley

Nothing could keep Tatyana in bed at that point. We all rushed into Astrid's computer room, a place I rarely visited but always found myself in awe of. An entire wall was covered by giant screens, connected to the central AI node, which, in turn, was powered by a dozen processing units.

Astrid connected her tablet to the node directly through a slim cable and proceeded to pull up the information she'd gathered so far, as well as live CCTV footage from different parts of the city. Wade got on the phone with the magical security command center and had them dispatch more people to each of the houses we'd been to.

Santana was breathing heavily and sweating, her Orishas nervously buzzing around the room, while Dylan held Tatyana close, with one arm snaked around her waist.

"They're sending people to each magical location," Wade said, once he got off the phone. "I told them to expect the worst."

"We can't cover them all ourselves," Santana replied. "We can't do anything there, now. We need to find the Ryders. If the kids are gone, we know they'll be with them."

"The Ryders wouldn't be able to pull off a mass kidnapping by themselves, though. They must have some help," Raffe said, frowning.

"Where can we start looking for them?" I asked, fear clutching and crushing my heart. "Where could they possibly be hiding?"

Tatyana gasped. "Oh. I think I know," she said. "I was looking into something in the archives last night, just before Oberon kicked me out. I met a guy, a spirit, who'd once helped the Ryders out some years back. He regretted that because they ended up squatting in his house. Anyway, he said that based on what I was looking for and what he knew about the Ryders, they'd likely be shacked up in a warehouse or abandoned property."

"Yeah, they wouldn't open up a rogue interdimensional pocket," Wade agreed. "That requires Bestiary energy, and we'd be immediately notified."

"Exactly. So, he suggested we look into the Chula Vista area," Tatyana replied. "It's got easy access to both the highway and the ocean, and it has good links into the city and the neighborhoods where our magical watchlist resides."

Astrid nodded as she typed the data into the system. After a few minutes of searching, she pulled up three possible locations: two warehouses and an abandoned residential property, all within reasonable distance of the freeway.

"This is what Smartie came up with," she said. "I added Chula Vista into the parameters we've already gathered, starting with the gargoyle incidents and everyone involved."

"Okay, so, how do these three places fit in?" I asked, frowning as I stared at the screen.

Astrid opened the detail files for each property, then exhaled as she pointed at a warehouse on the water's edge. "That right there. I think that's it."

"What makes you say tha—oh…" I mumbled, noticing the detail lines.

My blood ran cold.

"Look who rented it for the past couple of years paid up in advance," Astrid said.

"Finch Anker," I read out loud. "Holy. Crap."

A minute passed in dreadful silence as we all made the connection. We already knew the Ryders worked with Katherine Shipton, but we weren't sure of the extent of her network, barring what Isadora had told me about her spies being everywhere. Seeing Finch pop up again further enforced my original assessments: they were all connected, and they all had different plans to carry out, independent of each other. I hadn't voiced this before, nor was I ready to do it now. Everything we had was still circumstantial.

I had a feeling the contents of that warehouse might shed some light—not to mention the Ryders, whom I was dying to take down in shackles.

"Okay. Let's gear up, then," Wade said. "Security is looking into the magicals and their families. We need to get these bastards."

Twenty minutes later, I had Garrett, Dylan, and Tatyana in my Daisy, driving fast behind Wade's Jeep. Santana, Astrid, and Raffe were with him.

"Thanks for taking me along for the ride," Garrett said from the passenger seat.

Blood rushed through my veins with enough force to power an entire city. The adrenaline had me plugged in, my gaze darting all over the place as I tried to focus exclusively on the road. My stomach was churning, a thousand thoughts booming through my head at once.

"We need the extra pair of magical hands," I replied, gripping the wheel to the point where my knuckles turned white.

"Harley, what about Isadora?" Tatyana asked me. I'd already told them about her in the morning. "Do you have any way of getting in touch with her?"

I shook my head. "I tried. She'll be the one to reach out to me, and I don't know what the hell she's doing right now," I said. "I wouldn't count on her if I were you. There's still so much about her that we don't know."

"But she did help you," Garrett chimed in. "I doubt she's a baddie in this picture."

"I didn't say she's bad. I just don't think she's reliable. She should've come to me by now," I replied. "She's on the run, anyway. Everybody wants her for what she can do, for what she knows."

"Ugh, right. Portal Opener." Tatyana sighed. "That's a tough act to follow."

"Maybe something happened to her," Dylan said.

We reached Chula Vista, the sun rising over the ocean and a multitude of storage facilities lining that portion of the shore. Wade sped up, prompting me to slam the accelerator to keep up. We both stopped with a spine-tingling screech outside the warehouse in question.

I took a moment to quickly glance around. It looked abandoned —one large unit with black walls and a metallic roof, flanked by other similar boxes. There weren't any cars around, or any sign of people in the area. The place looked downright deserted. Behind it, a narrow, overgrown road connected the storage facility to the main access route we'd come down from. A wavy strip of wilderness and sand stretched beyond it, leading to the ocean.

We climbed out of the car, reuniting with Wade and the others. The look on his face told me he didn't have good news from the security units he'd sent out.

"Four parents dead, three in critical condition. All the kids missing," he said, his voice low.

It felt like a punch in the gut. "They took them," I replied, swallowing back tears. "What about the eyes we had on them?"

"All dead," Wade said.

I had to take a deep breath to stop the crippling fear from taking over. We were dealing with coldblooded magical killers. The lives of twelve innocent children were now at risk, including Micah, Min-

Ho, Marjorie, Mina, Samson, Louella, and the others. Then again, we didn't know whether any of them, besides Kenneth Willow, had willingly joined forces with the Ryders. They were recruiting, after all.

"Okay. How do we do this?" I asked, trying to stay focused on the mission.

"Astrid, stay back here," Wade replied. "Be ready to call for back-up," he added, putting on his Bluetooth earpiece. "The rest of us will circle the warehouse, check for signs of life, then go in through the front door. We're already here. If they're inside, they know we're coming at this point. Stay on your toes."

We all nodded and split up into two groups. Wade took me, Santana, and Raffe, while Garrett took Tatyana and Dylan. We headed for the east side, and Garrett handled the west. We moved quietly along the walls, listening carefully for any kind of movement or voices, but we didn't hear anything. There was nothing but silence.

My stomach was tied up in knots, the anticipation causing beads of sweat to trickle down my temples. We met back in front of the storage unit and exchanged curious glances.

"A little too quiet for my taste," Garrett whispered.

Wade gave him a brief nod. Something was definitely better between these two. Mainly, I wasn't getting bad vibes from Wade anymore.

Raffe looked at the extremely wide and tall metal roll-up door, then crouched and checked its lock. Garrett joined him, taking out a slim leather pouch. He produced a steel rod with bent ends, which he used to pick the lock.

I raised an eyebrow. "Really, Garrett?"

"What? I'm keeping my career options open, in case this warlock thing doesn't pan out," he shot back with a devilish grin, then took the lock off and got up.

Raffe pulled the door up, leaving a two-and-a-half-yard height of space for us to walk through.

It was dark inside. Wade found the light switch to his right and pressed it.

As soon as the overhead neon strips flickered on, I knew we'd come upon a treasure trove of disturbing yet crucial information. There were dozens of wooden crates and storage boxes, each with an individual lock. We spread out to check everything. In the middle was a large table, with piles of books and manuscripts, rogue sheets of paper, and notepads with frantic scribbles. One quick look, and I realized I was looking at spells and curse alterations.

"They're using stolen magic," Wade said, his brow furrowed as he checked the papers. "They got some of these from our coven. I'm guessing the rest came from other covens. They're modifying and adjusting their recipes and chants."

"And they have plenty of supplies to go with them," Santana said, watching as Garrett picked the lock on one of the crates and revealed its contents. It was filled with bottles and jars, strange powders and herbs. The smell alone was enough to make me quiver. "This is all Dark stuff. Like, evil. The predecessor of evil, actually."

"What do you mean?" I asked.

"At first glance? This is ancient mojo," Garrett explained. "Think two to three thousand years back. It's the kind of stuff that should've been lost in the annals of history. Egyptian, Greek, Celtic… dealer's choice. It's raw and difficult to work with."

"Which would explain these alterations," Wade concluded, pointing at the notes. "They're refurbishing the classics."

"Guys. Look at this," Dylan said, stopping by the eastern wall.

We all joined him, to find a giant corkboard mounted on it. Red string and colored pins had been used to connect various locations and notes. There were printed photos all over it. I held my breath as I recognized all the kids we'd been looking for. Micah Cranston, Marjorie Phillips, Mina Travis, Min-Ho Lee, Samson Prescott, Kenneth Willow, and a few others. Their snapshots were all marked. There was a tick next to Micah, Mina, Min-Ho, Samson, and four more kids under the age of twelve. Marjorie's head was circled in red. Louella Devereaux was crossed out, as were her parents.

Then, I noticed the other photos—*all* the parents. Half of them were crossed out, like the Devereauxes. I was paralyzed by the conclusion. "They crossed out the dead people... The ones they killed," I whispered.

Kenneth Willow and three other teenagers were separated from the cluster, with little hearts drawn in red around their faces. I assumed that was psycho Emily Ryder's way of pointing out that they'd gotten these kids on their side. It made me sick to my stomach.

"Look here." Tatyana pointed at several Post-It notes. "These are all details of their abilities."

"Who's this?" Raffe asked, narrowing his eyes at another photo mounted on the other side of the board. There were several red strings connected to it.

I moved over to get a better look, and instantly froze. I recognized the light brown skin, the deep-set eyes, and crow-black hair, and around it all was a very angry circle. Crippling fear took over.

They know about Jacob.

THIRTY-FOUR

Harley

I was unable to think. My brain was frozen, each synapse glitching with dread like nothing I'd ever experienced before. I'd been scared out of my mind in the past, but not like this. I'd let Isadora and her cabbie/little helper Dicky keep an eye on Jacob. I'd been comfortable with that idea, thinking that the Ryders didn't know about him.

But they did.

They were just saving the best for last. Based on how they'd marked all the other people, it did seem like they'd yet to catch him. But that hardly made me feel any better.

I couldn't keep this to myself anymore. I had to tell Wade and the others. However, I'd been hiding this from them for a while, now. *Gah, they're going to be so, so mad.*

"Are you okay?" Wade asked me, noticing my expression.

I couldn't take my eyes off Jacob's photo, partially because I was about to tell Wade about him, and I was fearful of looking him in the eyes as I did it.

"Um, no," I said, my voice breaking

"Call a support unit over here," Garrett told Santana, somewhere in the background of my unraveling horror picture show. "We need all this bagged up and taken back to the coven."

She did as asked, moving away from the corkboard to make the phone call.

"What's wrong?" Wade pressed. I could feel his eyes on me. My skin burned.

"There's something I didn't tell you," I said.

The silence that followed confirmed what I'd been fearful of. Wade was about to get really, *really* mad.

"Harley. What's going on? Do you know him?" Wade asked, pointing a finger at Jacob. "If we're to compare what we know with the markings on this board, they've yet to catch him."

"His name is Jacob. Jacob Morales," I said. "He's sixteen. A foster kid and a magical, like me."

"How do you know him?" Raffe asked. "He's not on our list."

"He wouldn't be. He's kept to himself, stayed under the radar, learned a few tricks to control his abilities along the way," I explained. "He's afraid of discovery… of the covens."

"That doesn't answer Raffe's question," Wade said sharply. "How do *you* know him?"

"The Smiths took him in a few weeks back. *My* Smiths." I sighed.

"And you didn't tell us. You didn't notify the coven, Alton… anyone," Wade concluded.

I shook my head slowly. "He begged me not to. Isadora asked me to keep him hidden—"

"Isadora freaking Merlin?! You're taking orders from her now?" Wade exploded. "What the hell were you thinking, Harley?!"

"I didn't see a Ryders card in the house! Isadora has been keeping an eye on him. She rigged the house with charms and stuff! The Ryders were targeting the people on our list!" I replied, raising my voice. "Isadora said there were spies in the coven. That I couldn't bring Jacob in because it was too dangerous for him!"

"Why? All the kids would've been safer in the coven! Whatever charms Isadora rigged your house with are worthless; we've seen that already!" Wade shouted. "Had we brought them all in, none of them would be missing! Their parents would still be alive! And we'll all have that cross to bear, forever. What makes Jacob so special that you couldn't tell the coven about him? That you couldn't even tell *me* about him?"

A second went by as I chose my words carefully. "He can feel other magicals," I finally said. "He's a living, breathing magical detector."

Everyone was stunned, their jaws dropping and their eyes growing wider. Shock crashed into me as they all wrapped their heads around this revelation. It didn't take long for Tatyana to figure out why I'd kept Jacob hidden.

"He'd be an invaluable asset," she said. "The covens would be fighting each other to get their hands on him. The rogues, too. Oh, not to mention Katherine Shipton and… the Ryders."

"I didn't know they had their sights set on Jacob," I replied, nodding at the photo. "If I'd known, I would've dragged his ass into the coven myself, whether he liked it or not. That would've been the lesser evil, all things considered. I thought no one knew about him, and that he could go on like that, at least for a little while. At least until we caught the Ryders and Katherine Shipton. I… I was wrong."

Wade scoffed. He was fuming. "You were more than wrong. You put his life in danger. The Smiths', too!"

"I know!" I cried out, tearing up. "Now, I know."

With trembling hands, I took my phone number and speed-dialed Jacob.

"What are you doing?" Wade asked.

"Trying to call him," I whispered. "No answer…"

Despair was taking over, cutting off my breath and making my entire body shake. Tatyana put a hand on my back in an attempt to make me feel better. It didn't do much, but it did keep me focused long enough for me to try calling the Smiths next. Still, no one was picking up.

"It's just voicemail," I said, looking at Wade. "They're not answering my calls. They always answer my calls."

"I don't get something," Garrett said. "If the Ryders knew about Jacob, why didn't they leave a card? They must've known about your connection to the Smiths. They wouldn't have passed on the opportunity to taunt you... and us."

"I don't think they knew *where* to find him," I said.

"But they did," Wade replied, pulling the photo from its pin and showing it to me. "Look at the background."

He was right. That photo had been taken outside the Smiths' house. I recognized the brickwork, the porch lighting. *Oh God.*

"Now I'm confused," I breathed.

"If they knew and kept it from us, they probably meant business," Garrett suggested. "At least, that's how I'm seeing it. Maybe they wanted to make sure they got to him without your interference."

Yet another horrible thought crossed my mind as I took a step back and looked at the entire board again. "Or, maybe they somehow knew we were coming. Maybe they knew I was only going to see this here, too late for me to do anything. If we're here, they'll have sent their underlings over there."

I heard a swoosh. My head snapped to the right, and I saw the flash of enormous fireballs.

"Watch out!" I yelled, dropping to the ground.

The whole crew ducked the attack.

Four young magicals stood in the wide doorway, their Esprits lit up and vicious grins slitting their faces. I recognized them all from the photos on the corkboard—Kenneth Willow, Anna Phelps, Evie Ramirez, and David Brooks. All magicals, all ticked as willing participants.

Behind them, Astrid was on the ground. For their sake, I hoped she was just knocked out. My heart shrank painfully in my chest as I shot back to my feet.

"Fancy running into all of *you* here." Kenneth sneered. "I'm kidding. We knew you were going to pay us a visit. This place is rigged to the ground."

"Where are they?" I asked, gritting my teeth.

"I was wondering how long it would take you to find this place, though. We've been waiting for you for what feels like forever now," he replied, the pin on his bow twinkling red. "Where's who?"

"You've picked the wrong moment to play dumb," Garrett said, taking a step forward. I had to admit, I appreciated his bravery and rational thinking. Despite his thorns, Garrett was a valuable magical.

"Oh, you're looking for the kids!" Kenneth chuckled. "Sorry, can't help you. But they're being well looked after, don't worry."

"Let me guess, Emily and Emmett Ryder have them," I said.

Kenneth grinned, then gave me a wink. "Bingo!"

"Where's Jacob?" I asked. It felt like a long shot, but I had to try.

"The wonder kid? Why? You want him? You're a little too late for that, cupcake, since you're here, instead of watching over him. He's being dealt with," Kenneth answered.

Garrett took another step forward, then gave Wade a brief nod over the shoulder. Wade took a deep breath and shifted his weight onto his left leg. He was about to attack.

"I've got a hot date tonight with a gorgeous pair of Puerto Rican twins. I don't want to be late for that, so why don't you just cut to the chase? What do you want?" Garrett asked.

"The Diaz sisters?" Santana replied, raising an eyebrow.

This was a deliberate exchange. It slightly confused the four hostiles. Garrett smiled at Santana.

"Yup. You have no idea how hard I worked to get them both to say yes," he said. "There's no way in hell I'm letting four psycho brats ruin this for me."

He didn't wait for a response, and just darted forward. His Esprit watch glistened a pale shade of blue, as the ocean rumbled by the shore—loud enough for all of us to hear it. Garrett rammed into Kenneth and took him down. At the same time, thick and flexible columns of ocean water shot through the storage unit, extending like endless arms directly from the shore. Each crashed into the other three magicals. It was incredible to watch, given their arched stretch and the amount of water and raw force that each carried with it.

That was all we needed to get on the offensive. Santana released her Orishas and tackled Anna. The little sprites smacked her with high speed and precision, hard enough to daze her and prevent her from casting any spells.

Wade and Raffe ganged up on Evie, who had a serious Fire game going. She was quick in her releases, but both Wade and Raffe were too fast and seasoned to let themselves get torched by fireballs. Wade shot out a Telekinetic barrier that hit Evie right in the solar plexus, knocking the air out of her lungs. She fell backward, and Raffe pinned a special charm into her hand. It threw out a string of pure energy, which then tied itself around her wrists.

The coven called it an Atomic Cuff, not only because of its composition, but also because of its properties. Any attempt to tamper with that string of pure energy would cause an explosion and potentially blow off Evie's hands. She stilled and cursed under her breath, realizing there wasn't much she could do at that point. She was done for.

Tatyana and I set our sights on David Brooks, the fourth evil minion recruit. He wasn't older than seventeen, and he was tall and wiry. His Esprit, a silver bracelet, shone white as he put his hand out to launch a Telekinetic attack.

I used my own Telekinesis to put out a shield, leaving room for Tatyana to dash to our right, then circle around and come at him. David turned around to stop her—that was my shot to take him down. Using my mental lasso technique, I focused on the back of his neck. My hand moved as I launched the "rope," caught him, then jerked it back. It pulled him down, and he fell backward.

Just as Tatyana was about to pin the Atomic Cuff on him, he kicked her in the stomach. He whispered a curse and threw out a bright red pulse. It hit both Tatyana and me with its short-range radius, and it felt like hot knives piercing my skin. I gasped from the pain, rolling on the ground in a desperate attempt to stop it from burning me alive—at least, that's how it felt, since I couldn't see any flames.

I reached a hand out, the sapphire on my Esprit lighting up blue. The ocean rumbled, not far away, and, a couple of seconds later, I managed to draw enough water out to splash all over me. By the time I got back up, David had vanished.

Tatyana was on the ground, writhing in agony. Whatever curse that was, it could be counteracted with water. I pulled another stream of water from the ocean and used it to hose Tatyana down.

She instantly relaxed, smiling as the water cooled her down.

"That's the Ardenti Pellis curse," she breathed. I helped her up. "How'd you know to stop it? I'm screwed without a Water ability like yours."

"I didn't know. My skin was on fire, and I thought water would stop it," I replied.

She chuckled. "Smart girl."

We both heard Garrett cry out in pain. Kenneth had just taken him down with what looked like Telekinesis. Garrett was on his back, and Kenneth was chanting something that filled Tatyana with dread—it nearly froze the blood in my veins.

"Oh, no," Tatyana murmured. "The beastly curse again. Son of a—"

I sent out a Telekinetic pulse of my own, enough to knock him to the side and interrupt his chanting. Garrett scrambled backward, desperate to get away from him. Tatyana ran toward Kenneth, taking out another Atomic Cuff to immobilize him before he could do any more damage.

Kenneth sprang to his feet, then laughed as he moved back. His grin faded when he saw Anna get immobilized by Wade and Raffe. Two down, and only Kenneth left in the storage unit. I stepped toward him, my fingers wiggling as I produced two fireballs with both hands.

He saw me, then snorted. "Good luck finding your Indian boy."

I threw both fireballs at once, with such rage and energy that they continued to swell as they hurled toward him. "He's Native American, you tool!" I grunted.

Kenneth put a Telekinetic shield out, blocking my hits—however, the blow was powerful enough to push him back by a couple of feet. I kept firing, pummeling him and his shield. Kenneth bared his teeth at me like a furious animal.

"*Hera, dóse mou tin anása sou,*" he barked, then bit into his palm and pressed it against the invisible shield he'd been holding up against my fire attacks.

The moment his blood touched the shield, a powerful energy pulse was released—much stronger than the flash of red that had made my skin feel like it was burning. It knocked everybody back like the shockwave of a controlled explosion.

I wound up tumbling across the ground, thrown backward like a test dummy.

Once I came to a scratchy halt, I looked up. Kenneth had vanished.

"Ugh, he used Hera's Breath, a Greek attack spell. I hate Greek magic!" Tatyana groaned.

Evie and Anna were down, bound with the Atomic Cuffs. Wade and Raffe were the first to get up and run out, searching for Kenneth and David, but, judging by the frustration oozing out of them as they came back, both were long gone.

Tatyana helped me up, while Santana and Garrett shook the scuffle bruises off and proceeded to pull Evie and Anna up. Dylan was already by Astrid's side—she was starting to come to. My relief was short-lived, though.

"They might have Jacob already," I said.

"Then we'll have to find them and get him back," Wade replied, his brow furrowed.

Therein lay the challenge, the source of my increasing despair. Where was Jacob? Were the Smiths okay? Where did we even begin to look for the kids?

THIRTY-FIVE

Harley

W ith our Bluetooth earpieces on and connected to our internal comms network, we jumped back in our cars, leaving the newly arrived team of security magicals to take care of Anna and Evie and to collect all the evidence we'd gathered from inside the storage facility.

I drove behind Wade's Jeep as he took sharp turns, left and right through the city, making our way toward the Smiths' house. Something was wrong over there. I could feel it in my bones. I didn't say anything for a while, instead listening to Garrett, Santana, and Raffe as they talked to Wade, Tatyana, Dylan, and Astrid about these new developments.

"We're going to the Smiths' place first," Wade replied through the earpiece. "If there's nothing there, we'll have to lean on Evie and Anna."

"Thinking of employing unorthodox interrogation methods?" Garrett chuckled.

"Whatever it takes," Wade replied.

I blinked several times to stop my tears from flowing. I felt horrible, on top of the physical pain. A few more tumbles like the one in the storage unit, and I was going to finally break some ribs.

"Harley, we'll find him," Santana said, noticing my angst. "Don't worry. We'll get Jacob back."

"Don't make promises you can't keep," Wade retorted.

That felt like a punch in the gut. "You know what, Wade? I'm sorry, okay?" I snapped. "I'm sorry I didn't tell you or anyone else about Jacob. I am! But I'm not going to apologize for what made me keep quiet! I believed Isadora when she said there are spies in the coven. Finch was a prime example, and we all know he couldn't be the only one. After all, how did the Ryders know to chase down *our* magical kids, from *our* list? They got that information from inside the coven, for sure. So, yeah, I was wrong to not tell you about it, but, come on. Look at the state of our so-called society! We're busy gathering points and following the rules, while Katherine Shipton gets Tweedledee and Tweedledum to do her dirty work for her, kidnapping magicals they can't recruit and killing their parents!"

"You didn't trust me, Harley!" Wade shot back. "You should've at least trusted me!"

"I made a mistake, okay? I trusted Isadora. She's family. That means something to me," I replied. "And you know what? I'm starting to think she was right. If I'd brought Jacob in, he would've been fair game for a lot of people. Given his abilities, Alton would never let him go. Jacob would never get a chance at a normal life, if he wants one, not even as a Neutral. They'd keep him on lockdown simply because of how many rogues like Katherine & co. would kill to get their claws on him!"

I took a deep breath, then exhaled slowly as I gathered my thoughts.

"This entire mission has been difficult, from the very beginning. We chose to leave the kids with their families, thinking the alarm charms would help. The Ryders were one step ahead of us on that— they probably had inside help for that, too. Our collective choices have led to the deaths of innocent people. But in hindsight, now that we have clear evidence of spies in our coven, do you really think any of the new magicals would be 100 percent safe with us?" I added.

A minute passed in awkward silence.

"You know, she has a point, Wade," Santana said. "Someone's been helping the Ryders from inside. They supplied them with the list and details for each of those kids. They gave them forbidden spells and curses. Some of the stuff in the storage unit is some pretty hardcore magic, from *our* archives. If we brought Jacob in, he would've been a sitting duck for whoever's working with the Ryders. It wouldn't take much to make someone disappear. I mean, come on, let's face it, even with additional security and whatever, nothing's really impenetrable in our world. Magicals always find a way in. Or out."

"We would've at least kept the boy in a secure location," Wade replied. "I would've had him stay with Tobe, for example. Who in their right mind would so much as try to do something to the Beast Master, huh?"

"Finch pretended to be Tobe and got him arrested for a couple of hours," I pointed out. "Enough for him to set all the gargoyles loose at once."

"That's a completely different thing, and you know it! I'm not—"

"Enough!" Garrett shouted, cutting Wade off. "Enough with the bickering, okay? Jeez! First of all, you're both right. Harley should've told you, Wade, but, at the same time, she was wise to keep her trap shut, since I don't think you would've kept it to yourself. I know you better than you think. You would've told Alton eventually. Having a natural magical detector in our possession is like having the power of a dang god. I'm well aware of how important Jacob is. Now, let that go, already. This isn't the first time any of us made poor choices, nor the last!" He paused and threw me a sideways grin. "Harley, don't take Wade's words to heart. If he's this angry and hung up on the issue, it's because he likes you and you hurt his feelings."

"Wait, what? Garrett, shut the—"

Garrett chuckled as he interrupted Wade again. "Give it a rest, Crowley. You're mad because you care."

"I agree with Garrett on this one," Santana chimed in from the backseat. "He gets intense when he's emotionally invested."

Even so, it still hurt me deeply. I couldn't stand the thought of Wade being angry with me, though I knew I'd brought it on myself. I was already going through sheer emotional torture as I prayed to find Jacob at the Smiths' place, alive and in one piece. Feeling Wade's wrath and disappointment on top of that was too much.

I decided, then and there, to put all those thoughts aside, choosing to focus exclusively on Jacob and the Ryders. I was ready to haul those twins to hell if they so much as touched a hair on the kid's or the Smiths' heads.

Good people didn't deserve to get dragged into this mess.

THIRTY-SIX

Tatyana

I was in the front passenger seat, with a full view of a grumpy Wade.

If not for the dreadful situation at hand, I would've found this situation amusing. We all knew he had a soft spot for Harley, and that her choice to withhold knowledge of Jacob from the coven had hit him hard. However, I also agreed with Garrett—which was quite astonishing, considering that, up until a few days ago, I would've rather chewed glass than work with him.

Wade turned his Bluetooth earpiece off, prompting us to do the same. We were just a couple of blocks away from the Smiths' place now, and the tension was high, keeping my pulse racing.

"You know Harley had good intentions, right?" I asked him.

He exhaled sharply. "It doesn't excuse her actions."

Astrid reached out from the backseat and smacked him on the shoulder.

"Wade Crowley!" she said, sounding like a very angry mom. "After everything we've all been through, and especially Harley, you choose to be a jerk! Enough with the drama, already! Either tone it down or ask the girl out on a date. This is getting ridiculous."

"What the hell are you talking about?" Wade asked, visibly annoyed.

"Puh-lease! You know damn well what I'm talking about," Astrid replied, leaning back into her seat.

"You're wrong," Wade insisted. "This isn't about me lashing out due to some… unresolved feelings or whatever. This is about trust. Which she broke. I trusted her. She made a mistake, and she needs to stew in it, at least for a little while."

"Oh. So, it's not enough that she's got this horrible family history to deal with, along with these missing kids. You want to pile on this crap and make it worse. Got it," Astrid said. "I thought you were more mature than this."

"She needs to understand that there are consequences to her actions," Wade replied, gritting his teeth.

"Harley is already going through hell right now, not knowing what happened to Jacob and her foster parents—if they're even okay!" Astrid said, holding her ground. "Wade, I get why this whole thing about Jacob upset you, but you have to move past it, and quickly. We don't have time for grudges. Not now. Not with everything that's on the line here."

Dylan cleared his throat. "You should also try to understand Harley's point of view. I totally get why she'd be reluctant to bring Jacob in. The entire magical world would pounce on the poor boy."

"As for your feelings regarding Harley, pardon me, but the jury is still out on that one," I chimed in, stifling a smirk.

Wade sighed, shaking his head in disbelief. "Why are you all ganging up on me?"

Astrid giggled. "You deserve it. Now, let the attitude go, and be a good friend to the Merlin girl if you want her to stay."

Our fleeting moment was already over as we pulled up outside the Smiths' house. Something was definitely off, starting with the exterior aspect of the property. Runes had been spray-painted across the brick walls, and the front door was open.

As we tumbled out of the car, the silence pouring out of the house was downright deafening. I dry-swallowed, hoping to get rid of the lump in my throat. Wade motioned for us to turn our Bluetooth pieces back on.

"This isn't good," Astrid whispered.

"Stay in the car," Wade replied. "You're banged up enough as it is. Call for any available magical security units, too. See who's closest to our location."

Astrid nodded, then unlocked the screen on her tablet and got back inside the Jeep, while Wade, Dylan, and I moved closer to each other, unable to take our eyes off the Smiths' house. Harley's Mustang reached us, and she pulled up behind Wade's Jeep.

Something was awfully wrong with this picture, and, judging by the look on Harley's face, she knew it, too.

THIRTY-SEVEN

Harley

F ear curled up in the pit of my stomach, scratching at my insides.

We regrouped just outside the Smiths' house, all of us confused by the symbols painted on its exterior walls. The open door wasn't a good sign, either.

"What are those runes?" Tatyana asked. "I don't recognize any of them."

"Me neither," Wade said, frowning.

Garrett breathed out. "They can't be good." Then he looked at me. "Unless your Auntie Isadora painted them? I'm guessing she's much more versed in magic than we are, given her years of experience."

I shook my head. "I doubt it. She had small runes painted in the corners. These… These give me a bad vibe."

I checked my phone. No messages. No missed calls. I tried calling Jacob again. Still no answer.

"Chances are there may be hostiles inside," Wade said. "We should learn from what we've seen so far. It could be a trap."

"Okay, so, how do we do this? We have to get Jacob and the Smiths to safety," I answered.

He looked at me, and I was instantly filled with his fear and determination—equal quantities, rippling through me like a bad fever. We were all scared, but we had to keep moving. If dark forces were at work here, we had to stop them. There was no other choice.

"You and I go through the back," Wade said. "The rest of the team takes the front. If anyone's waiting in there and they're not friendly, it'll be up to you and me to take them down. Can I count on you, Harley?"

I smirked. "You know damn well that's a yes."

"Good," he replied, the corner of his mouth twitching. I figured that was our way of making peace. It gave me a sense of direction. "Earpieces on."

We split up. Garrett led Santana, Raffe, Tatyana, and Dylan in through the front door, while Wade and I snuck through the back. The large spray-painted symbols weren't the only new additions to the Smiths' house. The backyard was riddled with animal bones, positioned in the shape of a symbol—a circle surrounding a triangle, with a small green fire burning in the middle.

"That's weird. What's that?" I asked, keeping my voice down.

"It's a Gaelic Battery," he replied, then walked toward it. "Astrid, whoever you've got coming from security, tell them to be on high alert. Hostiles have been draining energy from nearby residents using a Gaelic Battery."

"Roger that," Astrid replied, her voice audible in our open channel.

"What does it do?" I whispered.

Wade kicked some of the bones away with his shoes. The green fire in the middle began to shrink, releasing white sparks. "It hijacks the energy produced by humans within a three-mile radius," he whispered. "Whoever is around it gets tapped into. Magicals can use their energy to increase the power of their spells," he added, then stomped the fire out completely.

Suddenly, I felt like I could breathe a little easier. "Did the battery tap into us, too?"

"For a couple of minutes, yes," he replied. "Garrett? What's it looking like in there?"

There was no answer from Garrett. Wade took a deep breath, his Esprit rings glowing white.

He mumbled a spell under his breath, closing his eyes in the process. A bright blue pulse shot out of him, flitting through the air. The sound reminded me of a swarm of birds flying at once. I instantly recognized the magic at work here—a time lapse. It spread outward and settled in the shape of a giant globe that swallowed the entire property. But it didn't last. It crackled and flashed white before it vanished into thin air.

"What the..." I said.

"It's not working," Wade concluded. "I can't put out a time lapse. I think it may have something to do with those symbols," he said, nodding at the house. "Garrett? Santana? Anyone?"

Still, no one replied. That made me feel uneasy. But I couldn't stay out here for another second. If something was going down inside, I had to be there. Wade seemed to read my mind. He joined me as we slipped through the kitchen's back door. Thankfully, the sliding mechanism was quiet. I was careful to close the door behind me. If any hostile thought of escaping, I certainly wasn't going to make it easy on them.

Everything looked fine in the kitchen. Nothing out of place. No sign of struggle. But the air felt thick and heavy. Fear rumbled through me... It wasn't mine, though.

I looked at Wade, and he brought his index finger up to his lips. We were going to do this quietly. We made our way through the narrow hallway leading into the living room on the right and the den on the left, which the Smiths had recently converted into a game and reading room.

I saw Garrett and the others slowly advancing through the front corridor. We were all going to meet in the middle, where the two double archways awaited, on both sides. As parts of the living room came into view, my heart skipped a beat. I moved to get there faster, but Wade put his arm out and held me back. I gave him a questioning glance, to which he responded with a sullen glare. His nerves were stretched to their limits, but I could feel his anticipation. He'd noticed something that drove him to keep me from going farther.

We both heard the muffled gasps. Just as Garrett and the others stopped in front of the living room, I craned my neck and froze, identifying the sources of the noise. Mr. and Mrs. Smith were tied up in a couple of armchairs, facing the archway entrance. They didn't look injured, externally. But they were terrified. Their feelings suddenly exploded through me, dread crystallizing in my veins.

"What the—" Garrett was the first to react to the sight of the Smiths in their chairs. He and Tatyana rushed to release them, when a familiar voice cut through from the den.

"Don't move, Shifty," a male said.

Everybody froze, then slowly turned their heads to look behind them. Wade shifted us both to the right wall of the corridor. We had enough of a view from that angle to see... Emily and Emmett, the latter holding a long knife up to Jacob's throat.

Horror crippled me almost entirely as I tried to make sense of what I was seeing.

"Let me guess," Tatyana said, then pointed at the girl first. "You're Emily." She shifted her gaze and index finger to the guy next. "And you're Emmett. Together, you're the infamous Ryder twins."

Emmett grinned. "I love hearing that. I guess our marketing game is on point."

"Don't kid yourself. Those crappy business cards were an absolute waste of paper," Santana replied. One by one, a dozen bright green Orishas shot out of her.

"Ah, ah, ah!" Emily warned her, pressing the blade against Jacob's throat. "Don't do something stupid, unless you want me to redecorate this den in fresh red."

The fear I'd been sensing earlier was Jacob's and the Smiths', but it had already morphed into paralyzing dread—the kind that shut an entire system down. Mrs. Smith was crying, tears streaming down her cheeks. Mr. Smith was trying to say something, but the tape on his mouth turned his words into muffled noises. My heart broke to see them like this, and the horror they were experiencing almost paralyzed me. Despair smashed into me repeatedly, like debilitating waves that cut my breath off.

I got them in this mess. I'm getting them out.

Garrett gave us a discreet sideways glance. It was his way of telling us to stay back. Wade's scenario had come true, and I had to learn to trust his judgment better.

"What are you two scabs doing here?" Garrett asked the twins.

"Isn't it obvious? We were planning a surprise party for you all!" Emily giggled.

"Yeah, bad idea. Security magicals are on their way as we speak," Santana replied, her Orishas orbiting nervously around her. I could almost feel their frustration. We would've loved nothing more than to tear into the Ryders, right then and there. But they'd prepared their playing field—a little too well, in fact.

Emmett chuckled. "We know. But you're still screwed. We rigged this entire place to blow up into tiny little pieces. The moment you went past those lovely runes outside, you triggered the whole spell. If anyone else sets foot through the door, poof!"

"That's a bit suicidal," Santana said.

Emily shrugged. "You continue to underestimate us."

A couple of seconds went by as I thought about possible courses of action. With the Smiths' and Jacob's lives hanging in the balance, there wasn't much we could do. The Ryders had us right where they wanted us.

"I take it your real goal was to get the kid," Garrett said, nodding at a perplexed and terrified Jacob.

"Obviously!" Emily exclaimed. "Jakey here is a gamechanger for what we've got planned!"

"Why? What makes him so special?" Garrett asked.

Emmett laughed. "Oh, man, you people really suck at your jobs, you know that? Don't tell me you're not aware of Jake's abilities!"

"Enlighten me," Garrett said, remarkably calm, despite the twinkle in his Esprit wristwatch.

"Nah. I'm not wasting my time with a coven drone," Emmett replied. "Get me Harley. She's the one I want to talk to."

"Emmett, honey, someone broke the battery out back," Emily said. I assumed she'd finally sensed the dimming in her power levels.

Emmett narrowed his eyes at Garrett. "You found our little gadget already?"

"Mm-hm," Garrett replied with a smirk. He had no idea what Emmett was talking about, but he played along nonetheless.

"That's cool. We've got enough to turn you all to dust, anyway," Emmett said. "This day will go down in history, I tell ya!"

"Oh, yeah. Katie's going to be so proud of us!" Emily chimed in like the little psychopath that she was. "We really brought our A game to this crappy town!"

Referring to the queen of evil as "Katie" sounded odd and down-right mismatched, and definitely too cute for the monster that Katherine Shipton really was. But, then again, none of her followers seemed anywhere near the "normal" bar, so I pushed the thought aside.

Garrett groaned, rolling his eyes. "Ugh. Don't tell me you're shilling for Katherine Shipton. That's just pathetic."

"Why? She's only the most powerful Dark witch of the century. Soon, she'll become a Child of Chaos," Emmett spat. "She'll command Chaos itself. She'll decide who deserves the power, and she'll reward those loyal to her. We'd be idiots not to join her, given what she's got planned for you and your stupid, bureaucratic night-mares posing as covens!"

"What has she got planned, exactly?" Tatyana replied. "Get two more suckers to kill innocent people, since Finch got caught?"

Emmett laughed again. His guffaw gave me actual goosebumps. "Again with the idiotic assumptions. Shut your trap, Tatyana, and get me Harley. I've got a message for her," he spat. "Harley! I know you're here, honey! You're too weak to stay away from an obvious trap! Come on! Join us!"

Wade gripped my wrist, shaking his head at me.

"Okay, let's up the stakes a little bit," Emily said. She raised her voice, calling out to me. "Harley, if you don't get your ass in here in the next ten seconds, I'm going to fillet Mrs. Smith like a fish! Your choice, sweetheart."

I pulled my hand away from Wade and motioned for him to stay back, then advanced through the hallway slowly enough for the Ryders to see me coming. They both grinned, eyeing me like I was their Sunday dinner.

"There you are!" Emmett exclaimed. "Harley Merlin. The rising star of the San Diego Coven. The lost child of America's most powerful magical bloodlines. The kid with the grit!"

He and Emily suddenly shifted before my very eyes, their bones cracking and skin rippling as they turned into Mr. and Mrs. Smith —the real ones were still gagged and terrified in their chairs. It was a punch in the gut, but I didn't want to show them that, so I forced myself to keep a straight face. Laughing, Emmett and Emily reverted to their original forms. This was miles beyond creepy.

"I'm sorry, is this supposed to be psychological torture, or are you trying to kiss my ass?" I asked, putting my hands up. I briefly glanced at the Smiths, who were stunned to see me here, unable to understand anything that was going on. I mouthed an "I'm sorry," at them, then shifted my focus back to the Ryders and Jacob. "Hey, Jake. Sorry I'm a little late."

"Uh, it's okay," Jacob said, his voice trembling.

"Yeah, we've been waiting for you!" Emily cut in.

"I take it the whole storage unit scene was set up to keep us busy while you slathered your filthy magic all over the Smiths' house and took them hostage?" I asked, my tone clipped. "You must've somehow had us followed to time this so well."

"You're not as dumb as I thought you were," Emily replied dryly. I didn't need to feel her to know that she and her brother absolutely hated my guts. It was written on their fake faces. "But you're almost half-right. We didn't have to follow you anywhere. We knew it would only be a matter of time before you found the warehouse, so we had our loyal apprentices rig the daylights out of it. Once we knew you were there, we could come here and set up this fabulous ensemble."

"How about you tell us what's with this whole Child of Chaos crap, instead of droning on and on like two wannabe megalomaniacs? What's the deal with the kids? Is Katherine building an army?" I asked, then smirked. "Or a kindergarten?"

Emmett sighed. "You'd love to know more, wouldn't you? Sorry, toots, you don't tell us what to do. You don't make the rules. We do!"

"Okay. Cool. So, what now? I'm here," I replied. "At least let the Smiths go. They've got nothing to do with this."

Emily laughed. She was making it very hard for me not to hurl a heavy object at her. "Harley! The Smiths have *everything* to do with this!" she said. "Who do you think made sure that they took Jakey here in?!"

Oh, no...

"You knew Jake was here from the very beginning," I murmured, the whole picture looking a lot clearer. I broke into a cold sweat. Jacob had no idea. He was so confused, the poor thing.

"Yes!" Emily said. "We made sure Jakey came here after we found him in the foster system, because we needed him out here for *you* to find him next. Katie thought of it. Personally, I loved the idea. Emmett wasn't entirely on board at first, but when he saw you fawning over this new little brother, even he had to agree that Katie is a damn genius."

"Katherine wanted me to meet Jacob here, for you to then take him away," I concluded, the full extent of Katherine Shipton's viciousness slowly dawning on me.

Emily nodded enthusiastically. "And we got the Smiths as a bonus!"

"No, they have nothing to do with this! They didn't... They don't know anything!" I shot back.

"Like we care about that," Emmett said. "Honey, this is all about you. Well, granted, it's also about this precious little kid here, but it's mostly about you and how you're about to watch the people you love die... in agony," he added, then looked at his sister. "Care to do the honors?"

"Absolutely," Emily replied with a grin.

She pushed Jacob to the side as Emmett took her place in keeping him still with a knife against his throat. She then used her blade to carve a Chinese symbol into the palm of her hand, whispering a spell in Mandarin.

"What are you doing?" I asked, my voice hoarse.

"Oh, you'll love this part." Emmett snickered.

"Crap," Garrett muttered.

"Crap, what?" I asked, shooting him a glance over my shoulder.

"Death by a Thousand Cuts," he said, his eyes bugging. "She's casting Death by a Thousand Cuts."

It didn't take long for me to remember the curse. I'd read about it during International Magical Cultures classes. It was a horrid thing to put someone through. I moved to stop Emily, but Emmett threateningly cleared his throat, reminding me that he still had Jacob.

Emily finished the incantation and slapped the carved palm against her chest. A red pulse shot out of her, before vanishing into thin air. Silence settled for about a second, until Mrs. Smith's muffled scream made my blood curdle.

One by one, deep cuts were showing on her legs, the blood seeping through the beige fabric of her pants. This was a literal disaster unfolding, as the ancient Chinese curse was extremely literal. The victim suffered a thousand cuts, bleeding out in the end. Time was running out for Mrs. Smith, and I felt excruciatingly helpless.

THIRTY-EIGHT

Harley

E very thirty seconds brought with them a new cut, the curse working its way up to Mrs. Smith's knees. She struggled against her restraints, her screams muffled by the gag. I had to do something. I couldn't let this go on.

"What do you want?!" I shouted at the Ryders.

"Take off your Esprit and toss it to the side," Emily commanded.

That wasn't a good idea. I'd grown accustomed to using my powers with it. It had become a part of me, and without it, I didn't have the same strength and precision.

"Do it *now*, or I'll have the hubby join in on the fun!" Emily added, gritting her teeth.

The last thing I wanted was for the same to happen to Mr. Smith. He was already crying out against his gag, tearing up as he watched his wife suffer. I took my Esprit off and tossed it on the floor. My brain was working fast, looking for ways out of this mess.

"What do you want?" I asked again.

"Why, for you to suffer, of course!" Emily answered. "We've been at this for a long time, pumpkin. It's good to see it all finally come to fruition!"

"A new age is coming, Harley Merlin," Emmett hissed. "Katie will ascend as a Child of Chaos. She'll lead us into the future if we help her, and here we are, doing just that!"

"Again with that bucket of crazy," I snapped. "You've been impersonating social workers and coven representatives, recruiting young blood—and when that didn't work as well as you'd hoped, you started kidnapping them and killing their parents. Some of the kids, like Marjorie Phillips, ran off before you could get your claws on them, huh?"

Emily and Emmett didn't say anything, but they both looked annoyed. I figured it was my chance to rile them up some more. Wade was still in the house, looking for a smart entry angle. I just had to play my cards right and take these two monsters down. The Ryders were worse than any of the creatures held in the Bestiary. At least those were mindless creatures of pure, toxic Chaos. Most couldn't control what they were. Emily and Emmett, on the other hand, were perfectly aware of what they were doing. To me, that was unforgivable.

"Let me guess. Your boss, Katherine Shipton, has had you do her dirty work for quite some time, right? You, Finch, and who knows what other suckers she got to," I continued. "But, you see, you underestimated the San Diego Coven, and, most importantly, you underestimated me. We caught some of your kids. They'll rat you all out sooner or later. The coven knows we're here. They know you're here, too," I said, pointing at my earpiece.

Emily sneered. "I told you. Anyone sets foot in here, and you're all blown to bits."

"You won't be able to hold them off forever. You know that, right? By the way, where's Katherine? Why isn't she here, huh?" I asked, then chuckled. "You're cannon fodder, you dweebs. Whatever she wants to get out of this whole thing, she failed. And you're the ones taking the fall for it."

"And that is where you're wrong. Katie has new recruits now.

She's spreading the word and setting the stage, Harley. We all have our part to play," Emily retorted.

"Besides, we already have what we came for," Emmett said, nodding at Jacob, then at the Smiths. "We've got this little tyke here, and your beloved foster parents—again, Katie's idea, by the way. The downside is that we couldn't get to Jakey ourselves, once he joined the Smiths."

"Why not? You're Shapeshifters. You could be anyone you want," I fired back.

Emmett scoffed. "He's a Sensate, you idiot! Besides, you kept popping up like a persistent zit by the time Katie gave us the green light to go after him."

I glanced back at Mrs. Smith, the pain suddenly unbearable. It burned through me, almost melting my skin off. Her agonized expression sent chills down my spine as the cuts grew increasingly worse. We had to stop this. Now.

"Why not just compel him? Why all the elaborate theatrics?" Garrett asked, pretending to play along.

Emmett groaned. "It turns out Jakey here is immune to every mind control spell possible. It's in his genes. Chaos designed him to be the perfect tool. We needed him to get emotionally attached to someone so he could lower his guard."

"Then along came Harley Merlin, with her ethics and feels and all that garbage. And it worked," Emily said, grinning.

"What does Katherine plan to do with him?" I asked, my blood boiling.

Emmett nudged Jacob. "Show her, Jakey. Show her why you're so precious."

Jacob sighed, then slowly put his hand out to the side, his eyes fixed on mine.

"Careful, though!" Emily warned him. "Don't do anything stupid!"

Jacob began to tremble. The air moaned and rippled by his hand, before a bright blue gash tore through the very fabric of our reality. I was breathless.

"You're a Portal Opener, too," I gasped.

How the heck did he have so many rare abilities? What was so special about him?

I wasn't going to get answers to those questions anytime soon. Saving him and Mrs. Smith was a priority, and I had to figure out a way to get to them before it was too late.

"This boy is truly precious!" Emily exclaimed, while Jacob closed the wormhole, his hands shaking. "The moment he started talking to magical rogues, we had a line on him. Took us a while to find him, though. The little scab sure knows how to hide!"

"And all these machinations so you could grab him and hurt me," I concluded, then looked at Jacob, the obvious idea hitting me. "How well can you control your wormholes?" I asked him.

Jacob's brow furrowed. "I'm still getting the hang of the destinations, but there are a few places I've been to, repeatedly." Somewhere in the back of his head, I hoped the same idea was shaping up.

Though the Ryder twins weren't going to make it that easy.

"You're not going anywhere anymore unless we tell you to," Emily retorted, narrowing her eyes at me. "Katie wants you to feel loss and guilt, helplessness and despair. We're here to make sure that happens."

"*Katie* underestimates me," I spat, my fists balled at my sides. "Besides, she's nineteen years too late to *this* party," I added, pointing a thumb at myself. "Jake, remember that brief talk we had last Sunday, about control and determination?" I asked. Jacob nodded quickly. "I need you to apply what I said to everything you do. It's universally true."

"What is this? Pep talk crap hour?" Emily snorted.

Just then, Wade emerged from the wall between the bathroom and the den. The Ryders had warded the outer walls, but they hadn't thought to do the same to the interior. Then again, they didn't know exactly what Wade was capable of, where magic spells were concerned. In this case, I, too, was astonished.

Emily and Emmett didn't see or hear him come in behind them. I nodded at Jacob. He was quick to understand what he had to do, and he discreetly wiggled his fingers and opened up another wormhole this time behind the Ryders and Wade. They didn't even know what was coming.

"The Death by a Thousand Cuts curse starts with a hex bag," Garrett hissed behind me. "Take these bastards away, and we'll handle things here. Mrs. Smith has a few minutes before the cuts get closer to deadly."

"Please hurry!" I gasped, trying so hard not to tear up from the Smiths' emotions, and Mrs. Smith's increasingly desperate screams.

The Ryders seemed confused. "What? No one's going anywhere —" Emmett said, but got cut off when Wade slipped an arm around his neck and jerked him backward.

I dashed forward and tackled Emily. We fell through the wormhole. I heard Jacob cry out. I landed on top of Emily, on a patch of grass. She punched me in the ribs and pushed me aside.

I quickly glanced around and recognized our new location. Waterfront Park.

Then a punch rammed into the back of my head, and everything went white.

THIRTY-NINE

Tatyana

"Find the hex bags!" Garrett shouted, anxiously looking around the living room.

The curse was still cutting away at Mrs. Smith, moving past her knees now. Her pants were drenched in blood. Dylan, Santana, and I turned the entire room upside down, tossing pillows away from the sofas, checking every nook and cranny in search of two small leather pouches.

Garrett whispered a spell in Mrs. Smith's ear, making her pass out. He gave Mr. Smith an apologetic smile as he untied him. "Sorry, sir, I had to do something to ease her pain until we break the curse," he told him.

"What the hell is happening here? Who are you people? What... What's happening to my wife?!" Mr. Smith stammered as soon as Garrett took the gag off.

Garrett pressed two fingers against his forehead, knocking him out as well. "Not a good time to explain all this," he replied, settling Mr. Smith on the floor.

"I can't find the damn things anywhere!" Santana gasped, then rushed into the den.

Dylan made his way into the kitchen. I could hear dishes and pots being moved, the clanking noises adding to my anxiety. Every second that went by brought more deep flesh cuts to Mrs. Smith's legs. Garrett grabbed one of the woolen throws from the sofa and ripped it into several pieces, using them to apply pressure on her calf wounds.

"If we don't find those hex bags soon, she's going to bleed out," Garrett said to me.

"Santana! Anything?" I called out.

"Dammit! No!" she shouted as she came out of the den. She raced up the stairs. Based on the noises coming from above, she was tossing and trashing everything, in a frantic search for the hex bags.

My heart was pumping, worried sick, not only about Mrs. Smith, but also about Harley, Wade, and Jacob. They had two raging psychopaths to deal with.

Santana came back downstairs, cursing in Spanish.

She plopped herself down in the middle of the living room, crossing her legs. "I couldn't find anything. My Orishas can give it a try."

She closed her eyes, took three deep breaths, and exhaled. Green sprite lights came out of her. I counted twelve as they shot out and buzzed through the room. They quickly spread out, swooshing anxiously and bursting through the walls.

If anything of Chaotic origin could find an expertly hidden hex bag, it was an Orisha. With twelve of them, I hoped that we stood a chance.

I settled by Mrs. Smith's side, joining Garrett in tending to her wounds, as more opened along her hips and across her stomach. Blood was beginning to pool beneath her, drenching the carpet. I swallowed back tears as I desperately thought of other ways to stop her from dying. I had to dig deep into my arsenal of dark magic to stop the curse from killing her.

I uttered a string of old Russian spells to slow everything down in Mrs. Smith. It bought her a handful of precious seconds, but we needed to find those hex bags.

FORTY

Harley

It took me a couple of seconds to regain my eyesight.

The image before me became disturbingly clear when I saw Emily tackling Jacob, shoving his head into the ground. Wade shot to his feet and pushed out a time-lapse bubble with a fifty-yard radius, the air glimmering blue all around us.

Emmett took him on, using a combination of Telekinesis and physical attacks, but Wade stood his ground, employing his own exquisite skills. Wade's military-type training was obvious, compared to Emmett's raw and inconsequential moves. My warlock launched fireballs in quick succession, following up on each round with a Telekinetic pulse. Still, Emmett was ferocious and fast, pushing Wade into some spine-tingling brushes with death.

I, on the other hand, felt only half-functional without my Esprit. But I had to try something. I ran toward Emily, who was still straddling Jacob. She put her hand out and launched fireballs at me. I dodged them all like an athlete, suddenly aware of how much Nomura's Esprit-less training had actually helped me.

She tried to hold on to Jacob and stop him from getting away through another wormhole. Unfettered by her attacks, I used my Telekinesis to grab her by the throat, then tackled her. We quickly became a mass of two bodies, squirming and wrestling each other, and I delivered punches wherever I could.

She wasn't easy to take down, though. I'd seen what she and her brother were capable of, back by the bus stop. But it wasn't just my life hanging in the balance anymore. I pummeled her in the ribs, then slapped the ground around us, prompting it to shiver and crack. The earth opened up and began to swallow her.

"*Ex Parte Titan!*" Emily chanted, and rammed her fist into my chest.

The blow was so hard, it threw me backward. The air left my lungs as I landed on the soft ground, ten yards away from her. My limbs were made of jelly, but my consciousness refused to let go. I had too many people to save, including myself.

"There's... no way... in hell... I'm letting Katherine freakin' Shipton take me down," I groaned, rolling on one side in an attempt to catch my breath. My whole torso was throbbing, and it felt like Emily had finally broken something in me.

She stalked toward me. I caught a glimpse of Wade delivering a devastating blaze to Emmett, who ducked and whispered a curse. Whatever it was, it had an immediate effect on Wade, gripping him like paralysis and forcing him down on one knee.

My pulse was racing as I suddenly found myself in a vulnerable position. Not just about to get killed by Emily Ryder, but also about to watch the single most important man in my life get destroyed... I couldn't envision such an ending. My brain did not compute.

So, as Emily towered over me and took another knife out, grinning with the anticipation of slitting my throat, like she'd done to the Cranstons and the Devereauxes, I took a deep breath. It hurt like a thousand knives being driven through me all at once, but I had to do this. I instantly relaxed, and I put my arms out, my fingertips tingling. The winds were coming. They'd answered my call.

It had been impossible to maneuver my Air ability without an

Esprit. The few times I'd succeeded, I was holding on for dear life. This was my Hail Mary, it seemed.

"Time to go bye-bye, Merlin bitch!" she said, baring her teeth at me like an animal. Emily raised the knife in the air, then came down fast and hard.

Just before the tip of the blade reached my chest, a powerful gust of air knocked her to the side. The impact was so powerful that I heard her bones break, just before she was thrown on the ground and rolled to a stop. Lying on her belly, Emily Ryder's left leg and arm were bent at unnatural angles. She screamed in agony.

It wasn't over yet. I rushed to her side and tore a piece of my shirt off, which I stuffed in her mouth. I was in a lot of pain, barely able to even sit up straight, but I'd managed to take one of the psycho-bundle twins down.

"Can't have you casting curses and crap," I grumbled, then produced my own set of Atomic Cuffs from my back pocket. "This is going to hurt, and I am so not sorry about that."

I pulled her broken arm down. The bone cracked. She howled until she passed out, while I put the cuffs on, relishing the sight of the bright energy string surrounding her wrists.

"Yeah, I don't know any anesthesia spells or whatever," I added, my tone flat and anything but sympathetic. I knew she couldn't hear me anymore, but it felt good to say this stuff out loud. "You'll just have to suffer. Hopefully forever."

I then looked up. Wade had finally taken down Emmett, who was lying in the grass, blood trickling from the corner of his mouth. His face was pretty roughed up, his eyes swollen and quickly turning purple—and Wade didn't look much better, but at least he had control. Wade was on top of him, fumbling through his pockets for a pair of Atomic Cuffs.

Jacob had managed to get back up in a sitting position. He let out a tired groan and glanced around, before breathing a sigh of relief at the sight of Emily on the ground. He then looked to his side, where Wade and Emmett were.

Dread punched a hole through my very soul, quickly followed by Jacob's scream.

"Watch out!"

I followed his horrified gaze and saw Emmett's lips moving, just as Wade put the first cuff on. An invisible pulse pushed Wade back. Emmett managed to get up, something glimmering in his hand. A blade.

Oh, no.

"Wade!" I cried out, snapping my hand out.

I shot a Telekinetic pulse, but I was a split second too late. Emmett threw the knife into Wade's back, just as my pulse smacked him right in the head.

"WADE!" I screamed, struggling to get back up.

But my knees were weak. I couldn't stand for long. I dropped back down, limp.

Wade stilled, the knife in his back. He stared at me for a couple of seconds. A look of shock was imprinted on his face, breaking my heart into tiny, painful little shards that slashed everything through me.

"Wade!" I gasped, tears glazing my eyes.

Emmett stood up, snarling and cursing, and tried to finish the job.

"No! You've done enough!" Jacob shouted and put his hands out. He roared from the strain he put on himself as he opened up a wormhole right in the middle of Emmett's stomach.

I froze, unable to look away.

The wormhole's edges glowed bright red, but inside there was nothing but darkness. Emmett was stunned, his eyes bulging. The small portal then vanished, leaving behind a gaping hole, a few inches in diameter. I could see the rest of Waterfront Park through it. Emmett collapsed, the life dimming from his perplexed face. He gave his last breath in the grass.

Jacob sobbed, lowering his head. He brought a trembling hand up, then pulled a small medallion from beneath his shirt and bit into it. His grief and guilt were almost too much to handle.

"Jake, don't move. Stay there," I said, my voice weak and shaky.

I managed to get up again, this time a little more confident about my legs, and staggered over to Wade. I fell to my knees and helped him turn onto one side. He groaned from the pain.

"Wade," I croaked. "Hold on, okay? We're going to get you patched up."

"Ugh. I doubt it. But thanks for trying..." he replied, panting.

I took my jacket off and bundled it against his wound, making sure the knife stayed in. Even so, blood was pouring out at an alarming speed. I applied additional pressure, making him gasp. "I'm so sorry," I whispered.

"What the hell are you sorry for?" Wade shot back, turning his head to look at me. He looked worryingly pale already.

"I-I haven't learned any healing spells," I said, my lower lip trembling.

"I'm pretty sure you and the kid just saved my life," he replied, struggling to keep his breathing measured and failing miserably. "If I were you, I'd take that as a win."

"We'll get you the help you need, I promise," I said, caressing the side of his face. Golden warmth filled me as our eyes met.

A moment went by in silence.

"I doubt he hit any vital organs; otherwise, I'd be dead already. You should really brush up on your anatomy knowledge, Merlin," he retorted, his tone clipped.

I breathed a sigh of relief, internally thrilled to see him still alive, kicking and just as obnoxious as before. I had a feeling that he was the kind of guy who'd go out flipping everybody off as he gave his last breath. Judging by the fire burning in the pit of my stomach, Wade Crowley had no intention of letting go just yet.

"Bleeding out, yet still an arrogant jerk. Impressive," I muttered. "I left the knife in, so I do know something."

He chuckled, then grimaced from the pain. "Your sassiness might've rubbed off on me."

I laughed despite the tears rolling down my cheeks. "Glad to see I'm an influence, at least."

The air rippled in front of us. A wormhole opened, tall and vertical, its edges glowing green. My eyes immediately snapped to Jacob.

"Is this you?" I asked him.

The boy shook his head, but he didn't seem surprised. He knew who this was.

And so did I.

Isadora Merlin stepped through the portal, her eyes wide as she drank the whole scene in. She gave Wade and me a quick nod, then rushed over to Jacob and helped him up.

"You bit into the charm," she said to him. "I couldn't find you before. The alarms went off, but I couldn't go inside the house. I saw the runes on the walls. I knew they'd rigged the place to explode. And I didn't want to risk teleporting myself in there, either. I knew the Ryders might be waiting for me, prepared to trap me. Two captured Portal Openers would've been worse for everyone."

"I didn't get a chance to call you before we got here," Jacob replied. "The Ryders. They were holding the Smiths hostage, waiting for Harley."

"Oh no, honey, I'm so sorry," Isadora murmured. "I tried to find another way in, but, in the meantime, the house was surrounded by security magicals."

"You're Isadora Merlin," Wade said, staring at her.

"And you're wounded," she replied, coming back to us. "This will stop you from bleeding out, until they get you to the infirmary."

Isadora took a small coin from her pocket; it was encrusted with a variety of symbols on both sides. She pressed it against her lips, whispered a spell into it, and put it in Wade's hand.

"Hold it tight," she added.

He did as asked, closing his fist around it. He then stiffened, looking like a living statue.

"Wade? Wade, are you okay? Wade!" I gasped, suddenly alarmed and terrified of losing him. I had no idea what that coin did, and I had never seen someone paralyzed like this before.

"It's a Time Stopper," Isadora explained. "It'll keep the bleeding in limbo until you take the coin out of his hand. It's the only way he'll survive this."

"He said he didn't think any vital organs were hit," I murmured, looking down at him.

"Yes, well, I've seen enough people get stabbed to know that his pallor is indicative of massive hemorrhaging," Isadora replied, then looked at Jacob. "Are you okay?"

Jacob shook his head slowly. "I had to... I had no other choice."

Isadora frowned at me, confused. "What's he talking about? He's clearly in shock."

I pointed at Emmett's lifeless body. Isadora glanced over her shoulder, noticing him and the gaping hole in his stomach.

"I had to," Jacob repeated, his voice barely audible.

Isadora got up and gripped his shoulders firmly. "Jake. It's okay. You're safe now. It's over, honey."

"It's not over," Jacob replied. He fumbled through his pants pockets and handed me two small leather satchels. I didn't recognize the symbols painted on them, but I already knew what they were. "They had me hold on to them," he went on. "I'm sorry, Harley... I really am..."

"Oh God!" I breathed, forgetting all about Jacob's guilt. "We need to get back to the house!"

Isadora sighed. "Death of a Thousand Cuts," she replied, recognizing the hex bags in my hand. "The Ryders' doing?"

"Yes! *Please*, take us back. Now!"

I was terrified that we were already too late. Garrett had said Mrs. Smith had only had a few minutes as it was. *How long have we been out here?*

Thank God Isadora got a move on. She put her hand out and opened another wormhole to our right.

"Take Wade with you," she ordered. "I'll send word for the coven's security magicals to come pick the Ryders up. I'll take Jacob away."

"Oh, wait. But—"

"You know he's not safe in the coven yet," she cut me off. "He'll be with me. A Portal Opener and a Magical Detector like him will pit magicals against each other. Katherine won't stop until she gets him. I've eluded her for all these years, Harley. Jacob's better off with me. I wanted him to be able to have a normal life, but his abilities are too rare and too precious for him to stay out in the open."

I exhaled, not having the time to argue. "Okay. And when will I see you again?" I asked. "You can't go disappearing on me again. And Alton Waterhouse *really* wants to talk to you!"

"Soon. I promise. And don't worry about Alton. I'll deal with him when the time is right," she replied, then she and Jacob helped me up.

They lifted Wade off the ground as well. I put my arms around him, holding him tight as Isadora used her Telekinesis to pick us both up and toss us through the wormhole. I wasn't sure if she was telling the truth, or if I was ever going to see her again. My instinct told me yes, but the pragmatic side of me wasn't yet convinced. But she did have a point. Jacob was safer with her for now.

In the meantime, however, I still had a life to save.

I landed on my back with a thud, back in the Smiths' living room. Wade was on top of me, horribly heavy and still.

"What the—" Garrett blurted when he saw us.

"Time Stopper. He's got a Time Stopper on him. Get him off me!" I cried out.

Garrett and Tatyana immediately came by my side and pushed Wade off, and I jerked to my feet. Santana's Orishas were shooting across the ceiling, sparkling green as they seemed to notice me—and cuts were working their way up Mrs. Smith's torso, her shirt now also drenched in blood. Her complete silence made me fear the worst had already happened.

My heart in my throat, I tossed the hex bags in the air.

The Orishas darted toward them all at once. The impact caused a small explosion as the contents of the small satchels were obliterated.

FORTY-ONE

Tatyana

I t took me a while to figure out how this all ended.

After Harley finally halted the Death by a Thousand Cuts, Garrett ran into the bathroom and came back with a couple of wet towels, which he used to tend to Mrs. Smith's cuts. She was out cold, as was her husband. But she was still alive, much to Harley's relief.

"Why didn't this place blow up?" I asked, slightly hazy due to the sudden turns and twists of what could've been our demise. "The runes. They were rigged to set this place alight," I added, looking at Harley. "How did you get back here without setting them off?"

Harley sighed, the corner of her mouth twisting. "Emily said this house would blow up if anyone set foot through the door. Pretty sure we came in through a wormhole."

"Wormhole trumps door. Nice loophole!" Santana said, then put her hands out, her twelve Orishas buzzing around her, brimming with energy. "Come on, ladies, you know what to do! Let's take those runes down!"

The Orishas spread out through the walls of the house. A minute later, twenty security magicals spilled in, their Esprits glowing as they joined us on the scene.

Harley was lying on her side next to a frozen Wade. Astrid came in, joining Dylan as they both kneeled before Harley and Wade.

"I heard most of what happened through my earpiece," Astrid said, pointing at her Bluetooth device. "Had we not left the channel on, I wouldn't have known to stop the security magicals from going in."

"Yeah, the Ryders rigged the place up real nice," Garrett replied.

Two nurses entered to check on the wounded. They had Wade lifted by security magicals and carried outside, where the coven ambulance was waiting.

"Is he going to be okay?" Harley asked anxiously.

"He's on a Time Stopper. It pretty much saved his life," one of the nurses replied. "Doctor Krieger will look after him, don't worry."

"What about them?" Harley sighed, looking at Mr. and Mrs. Smith.

The nurse checked them both carefully, frowning as she assessed Mrs. Smith's cuts. "She'll live," she said. "The husband is just knocked out."

Harley nodded slowly. "Can you do me a favor?"

"Sure. What do you need? You don't look so well yourself," the nurse murmured.

"I'll be fine. Can you just… Can you just wipe their memories clean of everything that happened from before they decided to foster Jacob? That's about three or four weeks." Harley exhaled again, cringing from the pain.

I almost felt it too, in the pit of my stomach. I could only imagine what she was going through. She would never have wanted such a solution to be applied to the Smiths, since it went against her general viewpoints of mind control. But this was a tough call, and she had made it.

"We'll do that. We'll do a whole cleanup operation here," Garrett said to her. "Don't worry about it. It'll look like a botched home invasion. We'll have the Smiths unconscious and call the cops as soon as we get rid of every trace of magic in this place, including ourselves."

"Harley, what happened? Where'd you go? Where are the Ryders? Jacob?" I asked her.

She took a few moments to respond. She described the entire series of events that led to her return through a wormhole, along with a paralyzed Wade. Jacob Morales was in the wind, as was Isadora Merlin—but to be honest, I was okay with that. They both seemed too valuable to be held down by any coven, and with Katherine Shipton still out there, I had a feeling they were better off hiding somewhere, as far away from us and Harley as possible.

Emmett Ryder was dead. His sister, Emily, was immobilized and disabled, somewhere in Waterfront Park.

Astrid checked her tablet for recent communications.

"There's a team headed out there as we speak. The time-lapse bubble is still on," she said.

One of the nurses came back to look at Harley's wounds. She'd broken a couple of ribs, and she was covered in cuts and bruises. The Ryders were extremely vicious magicals, but, even without her Esprit, Harley had managed to pull through.

I had a feeling that the Dempsey Suppressor she had inside her wasn't doing its job as well as it should've. It took an impressive amount of Chaos mojo for a magical to survive and even neutralize a hostile as powerful as Emily Ryder.

"The Ryders were one step ahead of us this whole time," Garrett concluded as he picked Harley's Esprit up from the floor and gave it back to her.

She gave him a weak and thankful smile, then put the ring-bracelet back on, its gemstones glistening in different colors as contact was reestablished with Harley's Chaos. There were still a lot of unanswered questions, but one thing was clear to me: there was a vast conspiracy at work here, and it didn't involve just the Ryders and Finch. Katherine had loyalists implanted throughout the magical world, and she was planning something of devastating proportions.

The magical kids on our list were still missing, including Micah Cranston. She probably had them. I wondered if we'd at all hindered her plans by taking out the Ryders and making sure she didn't get her claws on Jacob.

It dawned on me then that I had a duty to help see this through. At all costs.

That included talking to my parents about Katherine Shipton and the Merlins. They weren't just the joint directors of the Moscow Coven. They were part of the same generation as Harley's parents, and they had to know a lot more about what had gone down almost twenty years ago, to set Katherine Shipton on such a destructive path.

Knowing what we knew now, including details about the Icelandic mind control curse, I had to try to get as much information from my parents as possible. We weren't on the best terms, but my options were few to none otherwise.

Looking at Dylan, I found a sliver of inner strength and determination that I'd been missing. I needed it, because my parents really weren't the easiest people to talk to. Personally, I dreaded the idea of reaching out to them.

But with the Rag Team by my side, I felt as though there was nothing that could stand in our way. Not even my cold and extremely complicated family.

FORTY-TWO

Harley

The next couple of days passed in the blink of an eye. I slept through most of my recovery process. Krieger used a combination of Wiccan spells and good ol' medical science to help my ribs fuse and heal faster than the usual three to four weeks of gruesome pain.

The time I was awake, however, I spent mulling over everything that had happened.

Astrid texted me frequently, as the entire team was insanely busy with the cleanup and investigation surrounding the Ryder twins. I knew that Emily was in Purgatory, and that Emmett had been buried—with no ceremony whatsoever.

Jacob and Isadora were also gone. Still, I did get an email from Jacob once a day. Just the general stuff, though, nothing too specific. Lunch in Columbia. Souvenir shopping in Nigeria. Bird watching in Minnesota. That kind of stuff. He had, of course, made sure to send it to my personal email address, to avoid coven monitoring.

I got out of bed on the third day, wondering if Wade was feeling any better. I hadn't seen him since he'd gripped the Time Stopper and turned into a living statue. I knew he'd survived the knife wound, but I was longing to see him again. Life just wasn't the same without him.

The Smiths were recovering from a botched "home invasion," and Ryann was back with them for a while. They were pretty shaken up, after all, and Mrs. Smith had sustained grave injuries. I told Ryann I was out of town with urgent work, but that I was going to see them soon. I was just working up the courage to look them in the eyes, smile, and tell them that everything was going to be okay—while knowing that their memories had been wiped. That they'd had a wonderful young man in their care for a while. That there were dark forces at work, looking to destroy everything that was good and innocent in my life.

I made my way through the coven's ample hallways, my gaze wandering from one dragon statue to another. So fearsome and ferocious... yet just beautifully crafted slabs of stone. They were supposed to inspire a strong and secure coven. But they were nothing but an embellishment. We had traitors in our midst, and they'd played an essential part in what had happened to the magical kids we'd lost.

I was never going to forgive that.

Alton was waiting for me in his office. But he wasn't alone. Wade was sitting in one of the armchairs, sullen and grumpy. Imogene Whitehall of the California Mage Council was standing by the edge of Alton's desk. Astrid, Santana, Tatyana, Dylan, and Garrett were also present.

"Ah, look who made it back into the world!" Alton exclaimed, beaming at me.

I could feel his affection flowing through me and warming me up like a log fire in the middle of a snowy winter. I gave him a soft nod, then looked at Wade. He was guarded, but still, I knew he was happy to see me. A wave of relief crashed into me, and I understood that everyone present wanted me alive and well... and with them.

Technically speaking, there were two people in the room whose emotions I couldn't feel—Garrett and Imogene, both Shapeshifters,

I assumed. It was my clearest takeaway from this entire struggle, especially after my dinner with Wade and Garrett. The only ones whose emotions I couldn't feel seemed to be Shapeshifters. But their expressions told me everything I needed to know. I was quite the sight for sore eyes, and that made me feel good.

"How are you feeling, Harley?" Imogene asked softly.

Santana, Tatyana, and Astrid greeted me with loving hugs. I was still sore from my bruised ribcage, but the fractures had fully healed. I felt as though I'd been run over by a truck, but, by this point, it wasn't my first, nor was it going to be my last, round of injuries. Something else was coming. My instincts were flaring.

Not now. Maybe not tomorrow either. But, at some point in the future, I was going to hear from Katherine Shipton and her minions again. She'd yet to take me down, and I was positive that she was determined to strike over and over until she either got what she wanted or went down in flames. I was rooting for the latter.

"Good to see you, crazy girl," Santana said. "Never seen anyone jump through a wormhole with your confidence."

I smirked. "Well, you know me. Brave and suicidal mean pretty much the same thing in my mind."

"It's good to have you back," Alton said, and motioned for me to take a seat in the spare armchair.

I settled into it, exchanging quick glances with Wade. Liquid sunshine poured through me, and I couldn't help but smile as I shifted my focus back to Alton and Imogene.

"I wanted you all to be here for this briefing," Imogene said. "I've done some digging through other covens, and I've come up with some troubling facts. Unfortunately, our Katherine Shipton nightmare is nowhere near over. I'm glad you all survived your encounter with the Ryder twins, but I'm afraid it doesn't end here."

"Do we know how or when they started working with her, or where the hell they've been this whole time?" Tatyana asked.

"We know that Katherine intercepted them as soon as the Albuquerque Coven ordered them to be separated, but we have yet to find out exactly what they've been doing, or who else is involved," Imogene replied. "Isadora Merlin and Jacob Morales are missing, but we do have magicals out there looking for them. There's an ongoing effort from multiple covens to track down the missing kids, as well. The ones who willingly joined Katherine have gone underground, but I've got some trusted sources in the deepest layers of each American coven. The moment one of them makes a move, I'll know."

My heart broke again as I thought of little Micah and the others like him. They'd been forced out of their family homes and dragged into Katherine's darkness, forced to grow with her poison. My throat burned whenever I tried to imagine what that could be like. Children were innocent. They didn't deserve this.

I exhaled. "Do we know what it is she's planning, exactly? I mean, Finch said she was going to become a Child of Chaos, but how does one even do that? Is there an instruction manual somewhere?"

Where did one so much as *begin* to ascend as a Child of Chaos? It boggled my mind. Children of Chaos were elements of the very universe we inhabited. Darkness, Light, Gaia—mother of the natural elements to which we were connected—Water, Fire, Air, and Earth. Children of Chaos were threads of raw and unlimited power, permeating time, space, and matter itself. How did one even go around finding one?

The road there seemed impossible, if not simply fictional.

"There is certainly no manual," Alton said, looking equally bemused. "She's going to keep trying to recruit magicals, though. We've been looking into Finch's statement, but we've yet to find something credible on the topic of Children of Chaos. Whether she knows something more or she's just plain crazy, she clearly needs powerful magicals for something. At this point, our only hope is that Krieger finishes the magical detector. Without Jacob's Sensate ability, we have no other choice," he added, looking at me.

His doubt sent shivers down my spine. I braced for a rebuttal, since he probably knew I hadn't made much of an effort to stop Isadora from taking Jacob away.

"We'll have to up our game, going forward," he continued, his gaze fixed on my face. But he didn't call me out on the Isadora/Jacob issue. Relief washed over me, and I relaxed in my chair. "The Ryders had inside information from this coven. It means that Isadora's claim is true. We have spies in here, and we must be careful. Which is why, going forward, everything related to Katherine Shipton will be conveyed only to this team here, along with a few other trusted witches and warlocks. Imogene will help us oversee the entire operation and assist us with any resources we may need."

"Katherine definitely has her fingers in more than one pie here," Imogene replied. "She's been leaving trails of bodies across the US for two decades now, and it's taken us a long time to connect her to a number of unfortunate incidents. However, with what you gathered from the Ryders' storage unit, we have a better clue as to how they did what they did, and how we can prevent such a tragedy from happening again. We've got APBs out on everyone who's missing. It's only a matter of time before we find them."

Wade cleared his throat, gazing at Imogene. My heart fluttered, and I knew that was all him. He was still crushing on her! *Ugh.* My eyes rolled, and I pinched the bridge of my nose in an attempt to keep my focus.

"We need to start drilling into Finch and Emily now," he said. "They're viable leads, and I imagine we can work them over hard enough until we get them to talk."

"Good idea," Imogene replied, her lips stretching into a charming smile. No wonder Wade was smitten. Heck, even Dylan and Raffe were swooning over her. Alton, not so much, but then again, Alton was happily married. "However, Emily is quite useless at this point in time. When she isn't sedated, she's crying and screaming after her brother. She didn't take his death well."

"Boo-hoo, cry me a river," I grumbled. "I'd like to talk to Finch, if that's okay with you, Alton. It's time he and I had a chat, anyway."

Alton nodded. "Agreed. But I want you to have Wade with you when you do that," he said. "Just in case he gets out of line. We've tried to have Adley talk to Finch, but he refuses to see her. Perhaps he'll be more open to talking to you. We won't know until we try."

"Then it's settled," I replied, giving Wade a sideways glance. "Ready to get back in the game?"

"I was never out to begin with," he answered, one corner of his mouth curving upward.

"Of course. Nearly bleeding to death was simply the equivalent of five o'clock tea in the magical world, huh?" I said, raising an eyebrow.

Alton laughed. "Good to see you both got your spirits back."

We kind of had. We'd lost people along the way, and we'd nearly gotten ourselves killed, too, but it felt like we still had a lot of work to do. There was still so much that we didn't know, including about my parents. I had questions that needed answering, and that alone was enough to help me power through the grief and hopelessness I'd felt earlier, and to focus on what came next.

Sure, Katherine Shipton had it in for me, and I needed to watch my back, but this was no longer just about me. All our lives were at stake. And I was damned if I was going to let her ruin anyone else's future in this world.

As we moved to leave Alton's office, he motioned for me to stay. Once Imogene and my teammates were out, and the door closed behind them, Alton handed me a small manila file.

"I think it's time for you to start thinking more seriously about the coven and its role in your life, Harley," Alton said, his voice low.

I opened the file and noticed different forms to fill out, each branded with the San Diego Coven's sigil, and his signature at the bottom. "What's all this?" I asked.

"Your choices, Harley. You join the coven, or you register as a Neutral," he replied. "You knew this was coming. Your probation month is over, after all. Frankly, I'd be honored if we could have you here as a member, especially after everything that happened, but I also intend to keep my promise and respect your decision, whatever it may be. Just know that you have a family here. Take as long as you need before you give me an answer. You've earned it. Mind you, by 'as long as you need,' I don't mean another month. We don't have that kind of time, given Katherine's endeavors."

I breathed out, then gave him a brief nod and left the room.

Truth be told, I'd already made my decision. I just needed to tell someone else first. The person who'd brought me here to begin with.

I figured he deserved that courtesy.

FORTY-THREE

Harley

―――――――――

"Ready?" Wade asked me, as we both stood before the six big mirrors in the Assembly Hall.

Aside from extremely rare Portal Openers like Isadora and Jacob, they were the only other magical way for us to get from one place to another without using the basic modes of transportation. Of course, every single travel through the mirror was preapproved and recorded.

In our case, our destination was quite special.

"For what? Purgatory? I doubt anyone is ever ready for Purgatory," I replied.

He moved to stand next to me and took a deep breath as he stared at the mirror in the middle for a while.

"I'm glad you're okay," he said suddenly. "You know that, right?"

"Are you sucking up to me so I say yes to joining the coven?" I asked with a smirk.

He looked at me, and I felt my heart perform athletic somersaults in my chest. I feared it could break my ribs again, all on its own. "No. I'm just glad you're living, breathing, and willing to fight another day, Harley."

My cheeks were on fire as I gave him a sheepish smile. "I know. I was kidding."

"I wasn't," he replied, then shifted his focus back to the mirror. "*Volat in Purgatoris.*"

The reflective glass surface began to ripple. I nodded once and braced myself as I walked right into it. The mirror felt liquid and cold against my skin. I set foot into a different place altogether. Mirror travel was less shocking to my senses than slipping through a wormhole.

When Wade caught up with me, we found ourselves in the reception hall of Purgatory, the prison for our magical world's most dangerous and hardened criminals.

It was huge, stretching out in multiple corridors, with cell doors lining both sides of each passageway on multiple levels, interconnected by stairs and suspended ramps. The reception hall's ceiling was made entirely out of glass, giving us a clear view of Purgatory's cell rows. It was all stark and gray, with black metal and stainless steel bars and architectural details. It was a Brutalist's dream, a recipe for emptiness and depression.

It reminded me of a supermax-type of prison. Only, it was eerily quiet.

One of the security magicals stationed in the hall walked over to greet us. I checked his nametag, noticing his black Kevlar uniform. The guy was dressed for war, equipped with electro-shock batons and his Esprit—a gold pinky ring.

"I'm Officer Mallenberg. Welcome," he said, his tone flat.

"We're here to see Finch Shipton," Wade replied.

"Follow me," Mallenberg said. He turned around and guided us out of the reception hall and through one of the corridors.

White neon bulbs glowed overhead, casting a cold, impersonal light against the cement-gray walls. Each cell door was framed in steel, with a plethora of runes and sigils engraved all over it. Inside, I could see more symbols carved directly into the cell walls. The prisoners had decent living conditions, from what I could see, but they all wore a modified version of the Atomic Cuffs, where the energy crackled around their wrists without holding them together. They had freedom of movement, but they must have known that the moment they tried to tamper with the cuffs, they'd suffer terribly.

There were all kind of magicals in here. Young witches, aging warlocks... even juveniles. They stared at Wade and me as we walked past their cells, but didn't say a word. Their emotions pummeled me—viciousness, simmering anger, resentment, frustration, resignation, sadness, and, in some cases, curiosity.

I focused on Wade's feelings, slightly overwhelmed by the prisoners. This didn't feel like the other crowds I'd learned to deal with, back at the coven. There was something in the air, something about Purgatory that weighed heavily on me. There was so much despair and agony in this place, it was impossible for me to completely block it all out.

Toward the end of the corridor, Purgatory began to feel and look different. There were fewer cells on each side. There weren't any black bars, but solid steel doors with small hatches to open and look through.

"This is the solitary confinement area. Our most dangerous residents are here," Mallenberg said.

We stopped in front of the very last cell, its number spray-painted at the top. Number 230. Mallenberg banged on the metal door.

"Hey, Shipton! You've got a visitor!" Mallenberg shouted.

Wade and I waited for half a minute before we heard Finch reply from inside. "I smell a redhead..."

Mallenberg scoffed, then unlocked the latch with a special key and opened it, giving me a clear view of Finch inside his cell. Nothing had changed about him, with the exception of his yellow prison jumpsuit. His sky-blue eyes were still vivid and burning with chilling hatred. His platinum hair was short, clipped down to a buzzcut. His grin gave me goosebumps.

"Hey, Finch," I said.

Wade kept to the side, staring at the wall behind me. He was quiet and calm, but, inside, a storm was raging. I moved my Empathy focus on Finch—it was empty. Blank. Almost close to soothing for me, like white noise.

Finch rose from his bed and turned so he could face me, leaning his back against the wall. Every square inch of his cell was covered in runes and symbols to stop him from breaking out. Security magicals patrolled the corridors once every ten minutes, as well. There were enough prevention methods at work here that one would've had to be downright stupid or suicidal to try to escape.

"The stench was familiar," Finch replied.

"You knew I was coming. You were notified in advance. Don't try to make yourself appear psychic. It's not a good look on you," I said. "How've you been?"

Finch chuckled. "Peachy, Sis. You?"

"Had a run-in with the Ryder twins."

Oh, that got me his full attention, curiosity glimmering in his eyes.

"I take it they're trouble? I told you, Sis, there's no stopping my mom," he sneered.

"*Were* trouble," I replied dryly.

He stilled, frowning. "Beg your pardon?"

"Were. No longer an issue. Emmett is dead. Emily got herself a private suite here in Purgatory. I doubt you'll meet her at lunchtime, though," I said. "She's going to spend the rest of her life in isolation. Or she might get executed—though I seem to recall reading somewhere that executions are rarer these days than they used to be, am I right?" Before he could respond, I continued firmly. "Either way, until we find Katherine, she's a potential asset. If she decides to be helpful, she might get a life sentence."

Finch exhaled, a vein angrily pumping in his temple. "They should've torn you to shreds. You're a flea compared to what the Ryders can do."

"I suppose you knew them and all about what they were planning to do, long before you had your ass dropped in here, huh?" I asked, offering a smirk to go with it. He didn't say anything, but that, to me, meant yes. It didn't take a genius psychologist to figure Finch out. So I decided to drill, poke, and prod until I got him to open up some more. "I understand you've had no visits or calls whatsoever for the past month," I continued. "You refused to see Adley, the only person who actually cares about you. She told me to tell you that she still loves you, for some reason."

His eyes found mine, and I could've sworn I spotted a flicker of regret where Adley was concerned.

"Anyway, I just wanted to give you some updates about what's going on in the world of the free," I said. "No matter how much scheming and planning you do, Finch, I will still come out victorious. I never drank the poison of Katherine Shipton, who, by the way, clearly doesn't give a damn about you. I thought she would've at least tried to send you a message or something. But no. You're all alone in this cold, dark dump."

"You don't know what you're saying," Finch replied. "And you're certainly not the right person to tell me about what my mother thinks or feels about me. Last time I checked, your daddy was still chasing her, after he murdered your mother," he added with a cold grin.

His skin began to ripple. I heard bones crack. Finch was shifting, but I couldn't figure out into whom or why, until the transformation was complete, and he straightened his back.

"You son of a..." My voice trailed off.

My heart broke in an instant, but I sure as hell wasn't going to give Finch a win. Not today, not after everything I'd been through. Finch had just shifted into my father—just to mess with me. I recognized the rich, black hair... His eyes were like mine and, ironically, still Finch's, too. He looked different from the memories and photos I had of him. He was still wearing the yellow prison jumpsuit, which automatically reminded me of his time in jail, prior to his execution.

"Anything you want to say to the old man?" Finch asked, his voice deeper and smoother, further tearing me apart on the inside. It was Hiram Merlin's voice. It was Hiram Merlin's body he was wearing. But he wasn't Hiram Merlin. He didn't need to obtain my father's DNA to copy him. It was already present in the blood running through his veins. That and a picture seemed to have been enough. He was trying to rile me up, and I found it extremely difficult to keep it together.

"Yeah, actually," I replied, keeping my cool. "I know about Sál Vinna, the Icelandic love curse. Someone close to my father actually told me about it, so we did some research. Turns out it's a powerful spell. Are you familiar with it, Finch? Do you know what it does?"

Hiram-Finch narrowed his eyes at me. "What's your point?"

"I'm positive that it was used on my father, just like it was used on Oberon Marx, and who knows how many other people. It's extremely perverted mind control, the kind you don't even realize you're under until it's too late. Until you do something terrible, like killing your wife, the love of your life, the mother of your child. All because Katherine Shipton didn't like your rejection," I replied, suddenly addressing him as Hiram. It felt therapeutic somehow, as if I was, in fact, talking to my father. "You see, I know the truth, Dad. I know it wasn't really you who did those terrible things, and I will prove it. I will clear your name and let everyone know that you were never a killer. That you were just another victim of Katherine Shipton. I promise you."

A minute passed in heavy silence, until Hiram-Finch finally burst into a mocking cackle.

"You think you're clever, but you're actually delusional," he said. "You really think our dad was that kind of a saint? Hah!"

"Have you ever met him?" I asked.

He shook his head. "He didn't even know I was alive."

"So then why the hate toward him?" I replied, smiling. "Every memory I have of him shows me a man with a good heart and a soft smile, who loved his child more than anything in the world. Had he known about you, Finch, he would've taken you into his home. He would've been your father. He would've loved you like he loved me. You never gave him a chance because it was easier to believe Katherine's lies. I get that. But don't expect me to be as gullible and as easy to manipulate as you."

That was the boiling point for Finch. He shifted back to his original form and lunged at the door, roaring and cursing and punching and kicking as hard as he could. Mallenberg sighed, then closed and locked the latch on his door. Finch's rage echoed through Purgatory. On one hand, I felt sad for him. However, I also knew full well that his circumstances were simply the result of his poor choices.

But I believed every word I'd just said. I was positive that, had my father known about Finch, he wouldn't have stood by. He would never have allowed Katherine to poison his mind like that.

"It's been a while since he's had a fit of rage," Mallenberg said, while Finch continued to snarl and bang his fists against the door. "The prison physician gives him some powerful antipsychotics. You managed to get the beast out again, it seems."

"He deserved some hard, cold truths. Medication can't protect him from that," I answered, then raised my voice for Finch to hear me. "I'll see you again, soon, Big Brother! Like it or not, I'm the only family you've got left."

"Go to hell, Merlin!" Finch punched the door again.

"It will be a while until you figure this part out, Finch," I replied. "But Katherine won't give a crap about you unless you're useful. Right now, you're anything but. Your best chance at any kind of redemption and recovery is if you help me take her and her associates down, before she destroys any more lives."

"You're going to die, Harley! You're going to suffer and die!" Finch barked.

"Keep telling yourself that."

I rolled my eyes and gave Mallenberg a polite nod. He escorted us back toward the reception hall. Wade walked by my side, still silent and curious, while Finch's bellows rippled behind us, fading as we drew farther away from him.

"Do you think you'll make him talk?" Wade finally asked once we were back in front of the reception hall's mirror.

"Eventually," I said. "He didn't know about the Icelandic curse; I could tell from his reaction. He didn't think Katherine would use such magic on her lover, his father... my father. Soon enough, he'll start wondering what else she hasn't told him. Who else she's used the curse on. It's only a matter of time. I'll keep working on him until it happens."

Wade nodded slowly, hands behind his back. I stepped toward the rippling mirror, then glanced over my shoulder to find him watching me.

"By the way, I'm in," I said.

He blinked a couple times. "You're in... what?"

"Is your brain glitching? I'm joining the San Diego Coven," I replied, but didn't wait to see his reaction.

As I strode through the mirror and left him behind, I found myself smiling, filled with sheer excitement and relief—all Wade's. Actually, most of it. Well, more like half. I, too, was glad to have made the decision.

He joined me back in the Assembly Hall and let out an audible sigh.

That was his response. To some, it would've been insufficient. To me, it was more than enough. He wanted me here, and he didn't have to say it out loud. I could feel it in the very center of my soul.

I wanted to be in the San Diego Coven. I really did. It had become my home, the center of my universe.

And it needed me, now more than ever.

Ready for the next part of Harley's story?

Dear Reader,

Thank you for reading Book 2 of Harley's journey. I hope you enjoyed it!

Book 3: **Harley Merlin and the Stolen Magicals**, releases **October 31st, 2018.**

Visit: www.bellaforrest.net for details.

I can't wait to continue Harley's journey with you!

See you on the other side...

Love,

Bella x

P.S. Sign up to my VIP email list and I'll send you a heads up when my next book releases: **www.morebellaforrest.com**

(Your email will be kept 100% private and you can unsubscribe at any time.)

P.P.S. I'd also love to hear from you. Come say hi on Facebook: Facebook.com/BellaForrestAuthor. Or Twitter: @ashadeofvampire

Read more by Bella Forrest

HARLEY MERLIN

Harley Merlin and the Secret Coven (Book 1)

Harley Merlin and the Mystery Twins (Book 2)

Harley Merlin and the Stolen Magicals (Book 3)

THE GENDER GAME

(Action-adventure/romance. Completed series.)

The Gender Game (Book 1)

The Gender Secret (Book 2)

The Gender Lie (Book 3)

The Gender War (Book 4)

The Gender Fall (Book 5)

The Gender Plan (Book 6)

The Gender End (Book 7)

THE GIRL WHO DARED TO THINK

(Action-adventure/romance. Completed series.)

The Girl Who Dared to Think (Book 1)

The Girl Who Dared to Stand (Book 2)

The Girl Who Dared to Descend (Book 3)

The Girl Who Dared to Rise (Book 4)

The Girl Who Dared to Lead (Book 5)

The Girl Who Dared to Endure (Book 6)

The Girl Who Dared to Fight (Book 7)

THE CHILD THIEF

(Action-adventure/romance.)

The Child Thief (Book 1)

Deep Shadows (Book 2)

Thin Lines (Book 3)

Little Lies (Book 4)

HOTBLOODS

(Supernatural romance. Completed series.)

Hotbloods (Book 1)

Coldbloods (Book 2)

Renegades (Book 3)

Venturers (Book 4)

Traitors (Book 5)

Allies (Book 6)

Invaders (Book 7)

Stargazers (Book 8)

A SHADE OF VAMPIRE SERIES

(Supernatural romance)

Series 1: Derek & Sofia's story

A Shade of Vampire (Book 1)

A Shade of Blood (Book 2)

A Castle of Sand (Book 3)

A Shadow of Light (Book 4)

A Blaze of Sun (Book 5)

A Gate of Night (Book 6)

A Break of Day (Book 7)

BEAUTIFUL MONSTER DUOLOGY

(Supernatural romance)

Beautiful Monster 1

Beautiful Monster 2

DETECTIVE ERIN BOND

(Adult thriller/mystery)

Lights, Camera, GONE

Write, Edit, KILL

For an updated list of Bella's books, please visit her website:
www.bellaforrest.net

Join Bella's VIP email list and be the first to know when her next book is
out. Visit: www.morebellaforrest.com